Praise for God

"What a great boo

romance and faith.

Rev. Evelyn Wilson
Carrying Place, ON

Praise for Jennies' previous book, God in My House

"The suspense had me on the edge of my seat! This is an awesome book!"

Rev. Isabel Jewer
Trenton, ON

"It's great to have a fictional title which will appeal to many different people, considering the multiracial components of this story."

Carrie Jeffrey
Michael's Family Books, Pickering, ON

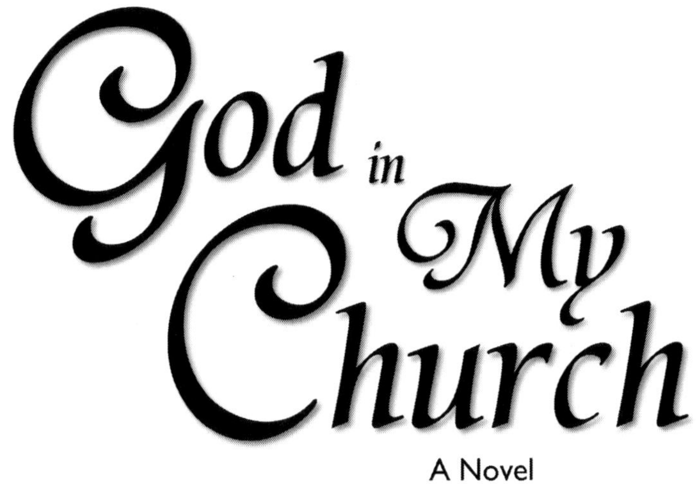

A Novel

Jennies M. Edwards

GOD IN MY CHURCH

ISBN: 978-1-77069-274-9

Printed in Canada

Word Alive Press
131 Cordite Road, Winnipeg, MB R3W 1S1
www.wordalivepress.ca

Library and Archives Canada Cataloguing in Publication

Edwards, Jennies M.
God in my church / Jennies M. Edwards.

ISBN 978-1-77069-274-9

I. Title.

PS8609.D85G63 2011 C813'.6 C2011-902647-3

In loving memory of Katie Wilson who,
even at a young age, left an inspiring legacy of faith.
March 1995 – February 2011

To the Holy Spirit who empowers us.

*"He who has an ear, let him hear what the
Spirit says to the churches."*
Revelations 3:22

Author's Note

As with Georgeton in my first book, *God in My House,* the town of Milward in this book, *God in My Church,* is fictitious; a blending of my husband's names. The names of the main characters in both books are the middle names of my oldest daughter and my son. Note the capitalization of the church rooms in this book, symbolic of the body of Christ in which many parts make the whole.

I would love to hear from you!

Jennies

www.jenniesedwards.com

facepage: godinmyhouse-jenniesedwards

Acknowledgements

I have been very blessed to have had so many willing to help me create this story.

The Lord Jesus Christ, my Everything!

Thanks to Pastors Jerry and Isabel Jewer and my Bethel Church family for your wonderful support... again. I also appreciate the insights into the lives of pastors and missionaries given by Rev. Ernie Klassen, my brother Rev. Wayne Russell, Raynon Rozniak, and Shannon and Bob Rozniak. Major Alister Mackay, I thank you for our frank discussion about the sometimes hidden lives of soldiers. Thomas Streek, you made my construction "problem" more authentic. Lori-Anne McGee, Jordon Teti and Jordan Wilson, thanks for sharing your stories of adoption. I couldn't have fine-tuned everything without your input, Helena Weyer. My constant cheering section, Debbie and Maureen Russell, I appreciate you very much! Thanks to my brother David Russell who promotes my books without being asked.

Katherine Oribine, thanks for the hard work you brought to my manuscript! I think you should envision more of this in your future.

WAP, thanks for what you do and that you do it for His Kingdom!

To my kids, Chantelle, Joshua, Jewelle, Danielle and Gabrielle, you bless me with your love, support and enthusiasm. Thanks for being my sounding boards!

Milton, I couldn't do it without you.... .

About the Author

Jennies Edwards was raised in a Jamaican-Canadian home where her delight in being a "storyteller," in a family of eight children, followed her into adulthood. After working as an RN for six years, she became a full-time homeschooling mom with a passion for God, family and home.

Jennies lives with her husband, Milton, in Carrying Place, Ontario, where she home schools two of her five children and is actively involved in her church and... writes!

Prologue

Jamaica, W.I.

Paul smiled, filled with expectation and... weariness, in the direction of the children as he bumped his way out of the crowded, elementary school room. Warmth filled his chest at the curious, anticipatory expressions on their brown faces; faces like his own, except much younger than his twenty-seven years.

He had just finished a brief meeting with their principal and had assured her that more school supplies, including computers, would be delivered to their school within the next week or so. He was still waiting on Jamaican customs at the Norman Manley International Airport, in Kingston, to clear the Canadian supplies for the school.

He paused in the shadow of the doorway before stepping out onto a paved walkway, bordered by bare ground, into the blazing sunlight. The Jamaican school yard was empty of children now that their lunch break was over, but he could hear the drone of young voices through the "brick-latticed" windows of the L-shaped concrete building. It still amazed him how much, in his own country, Canadian children took for granted when it came to education.

He felt in the pocket of his tan shorts for the keys of his rented vehicle, as he scanned the expanse of dirt before him. A gentle breeze rippled through the surrounding trees, only slightly dispelling the heat. He had started in the direction of his car when he noticed the sudden entrance of another vehicle through the gateway of the school yard. Dust billowed up around the vehicle as it quickly approached him, and he stepped back instinctively.

"Pastor Paul... "

The slight, middle-aged man who hurriedly stepped from the car was his short-term missions contact, and Paul had been expecting him, but not at the school.

"Dan, I thought you were going to meet me down the mountain, at the Church," Paul greeted jokingly. He was told Jamaicans were typically late, not early.

The dust was settling around them, but Daniel was looking decidedly less settled. His brows furrowed his mahogany skin, but it was the desperate look in his dark eyes that sobered Paul.

"We couldn't get you on your cell... we tried... "

Paul stepped closer to the man, a deep foreboding replacing his earlier hopefulness.

"What is it?" Then a dreadful awareness came to him. "Where is my wife?"

Dan's throat worked up and down and he balled one fist in the palm of his other hand. "There was an accident, Pastor Paul." His eyes pooled tears. "Your wife... "

Chapter One

Canada: Three years later

Sounds of the Church Fellowship Hall renovations filtered through the Pastor's Office to Paul.

"There are more than enough people with their hands to the plough, Paul," Samuel, his senior board member, had told him. "You should finish preparing your sermon for tomorrow—you do too much."

Paul sighed deeply and dropped the elastic band he had been fiddling with on the broad, mahogany desk before him. The desk where, two pastors ago, his adoptive father had prepared numerous sermons before he died at age seventy-eight. He had passed away in his sleep unexpectedly four years ago: a year before Paul's wife and unborn child were killed in a tragic car accident; his grieving for his father had been barely finished.

The leather chair squeaked as he leaned back and stretched his head onto the familiar feel of the head rest. His lids closed against the light from the semi-closed blinds at the window to his left, trying to stem the headache he knew was coming on. He felt depressed; he didn't like feeling this way.

Why had he allowed Samuel to influence him like a child told to do his homework? The physical work of the renovations helped him to forget. Just because Samuel had been his dad's best friend, didn't mean he had to take the role of father-figure so seriously.

But Paul knew what Samuel had alluded to often enough: Paul was burying himself in the work of the Kingdom to atone for the deaths of his young wife and unborn child. Deaths he knew he hadn't been responsible for, or guilty of, but his heart beat to a different drum.

What would it take for him to get past it? Only the Almighty knew, and He had his own timing on things. Granted, two weeks ago, he had performed a wedding ceremony and a baby dedication without his own sense of loss threatening an intrusion. Officiating at the funeral of a young husband and father a month before that had been harder on him. But then, funerals were difficult, regardless.

For a moment, Paul fiddled with the wedding band on his finger, then shifted his laptop over and, with his elbows on the desk, rested his forehead on his fingertips and kneaded his temples slowly to ease the discomfort there. A soft rap on the glass door separating his inner sanctum from the Front Office didn't help matters. He looked up to see Hilda Temple, Samuel's sixty-year-old wife, his invaluable church secretary, peeking around the door.

"Another headache, love?" She further opened the door and eased her softly-rounded body into the room, looking at him expectantly.

In spite of the interruption, Paul had to smile. Hilda was one of those people whose very presence emulated comfort and hidden strength, not to mention her cheerful disposition. She certainly balanced Samuel's blunt, practical approach.

"Naw, not too bad, Hilda. I'll be fine." Paul leaned back in his seat, trying, for Hilda's benefit, to appear at ease. Sometimes he appreciated her mothering, but he didn't feel much like being mothered today. He didn't quite know what he felt much like.

Hilda smoothed at her colourfully knitted sweater before resting her hands on his desk.

Her light green eyes had an apologetic look in them. "I hate to do this to you. I know you're doing this because the board," she cleared her throat meaningfully, "and Sam thought it was an excellent idea—"

"The intern," Paul interrupted her.

She sighed in relief. A wide smile lit up her slightly wrinkled face. "So, you have been thinking about it. I'm so glad."

"Well, I didn't have much choice with Sam reminding me at every turn," Paul chuckled.

"Good," she breathed, her bubbly voice dancing. She turned and went back into the Front Office.

"Hilda?" Paul called after her. He stood up to move from behind his desk, but she reappeared.

"He's coming today." Hilda stood before him with hands outstretched, holding some papers.

Paul went to her, his casual leather shoes catching slightly on the carpeted floor. He felt tired.

"Today? What do you mean? I haven't even interviewed him." He was a little befuddled. He knew things were busier than usual at the Church, but surely that's not something he would have forgotten.

Hilda looked concerned. "Paul, don't you remember? You asked Sam to do the interview... and he did."

Paul took hold of the papers, scanning them quickly. The application papers; he remembered briefly going over them with Samuel, and he *had* asked him to handle the interview. He looked down at Hilda, wincing at the concern in her eyes. "You and I *did* talk about him staying at the parsonage with me, but I didn't think he was coming until next month."

Hilda laid short, rounded fingers on his arm and looked up at him directly. "Actually, he *wasn't* coming until next week, but Sam missed an email explaining the change in plans." She paused, then asked, "Paul, are you all right?"

He didn't answer; he just looked down into her wonderfully caring face framed by greying, auburn hair, and he wished he hadn't.

"It's the third anniversary, isn't it?" Hilda held his other arm, and then moved both hands down to rest them against his wrists.

Paul's fingers tightened on the papers still in his hands, he felt his eyes tearing up. He shifted his head to one side, away from her. Hilda's pale skin, contrasted against his, had reminded him of Hannah's hands on his—the wife he would never hold again.

* * *

Hilda's heart was full of compassion for the man before her. He was heads taller than her with a lean build and wiry strength, but she saw him as a young man burdened by more than the demands of pastoring a thriving, mid-sized Church in a growing community. He had been adopted as a baby; a Black man raised in a White man's home. Yes, he had broken ties with the community once to search for his roots—his identity—and had come back richer for it. Now, their community was more multicultural, vibrant and evolving; but for Paul Stephen Rayner, the tragedy of his pregnant wife's death, three years ago, seem to have kept him trapped in a world of relentless activities, commitments and projects.

Hilda reached up and gently moved his face towards her. "Paul, you have recovered, but it's okay to still grieve."

Paul squeezed his eyelids together, then pulled one hand away from her and wiped his eyes impatiently. His dark gaze challenged her. He had such beautiful eyes; his lashes were a woman's envy, but this man was all together masculine. A leader among men, but a man in pain; though, for the most part, he hid it well.

"It's not as bad as you think, Hilda." Paul seemed to struggle momentarily, gathering his control about him. "Time has helped, but I just can't seem to... "

She decided to help him out. "To start anew?"

Deep dimples appeared in his cheeks, as he ran a hand over very tight, black curls cut quite low on his head. "Yes, you're right."

Hilda stepped back a little, letting him go. "Well, Paul, I remember when your father first started as Pastor of this Church. He said, more than anything, he wanted God in the Church." She watched him place the application forms on his desk and lean against it, before she continued:

"I laughed to myself thinking, what else did he expect to find in a Church? But, as time went on, I realized that where you might expect God to manifest isn't always where He does. You have to want Him and make yourself available to Him. You may not notice at first, but then one day you realize God is here—He's *really* here! I think grief is sometimes like that. You can't force it away, but you have to want to move on and do what you can to move on... then one day you'll notice that... you have."

Paul gently touched her shoulders, and it did her heart good to see his eyes clear and his smile reappear. "Thanks, Hilda—don't know what I'd do without you—not just as my secretary either."

She laughed, then glanced meaningfully at the papers on the desk. "Well, as your secretary, I say you better look over that application before the young fellow arrives. He'll be coming by the Church—has his own transportation and everything."

Paul glanced at the desk. “Michael Laroche. Is that last name French, or something?”

Hilda exaggerated a shrug. “I don’t know. Sam hasn’t really told me much about him, except that his parents are missionaries in Haiti. I’ll be leaving soon to see what’s for dinner, then I’ll return. I only came in to see how the renovations were going. I don’t imagine you’ll have anything prepared at the parsonage for him to eat?”

Paul groaned good-naturedly. “I hadn’t really thought about feeding him, Hilda. I just figured our ladies would continue bringing their good stuff over.”

“That’s only once or twice a week, young man, and now there’ll be two of you, so I’d start cooking a little more if I were you. Hopefully, he’s handy in the kitchen. I think it’ll be good for you—maybe put some more meat on that frame of yours.’

“It’s in my genetics, Hilda. Tall and spare, that’s how I come. Nothing I can do about it.”

It came out before she could stop it: “The right woman in your life will fatten—” Her hand went up to her mouth. “Oh, my love, I’m so sorry. I didn’t... ”

Paul gently shushed her. “Hilda, don’t worry about it. It’s okay.”

Chapter Two

The new development seemed to be well on its way, as far as Michaela could see from her vantage point beside one of three gas pumps at Metro's Gas Bar. The latter part of her two-and-a-half hour trip from Toronto into the town—or small city, depending on one's perspective—of Milward had been slow because of the sightseeing she had allowed herself to indulge in, much to the torment of impatient drivers behind her. A couple of times she had pulled over to allow some of them to pass. The place might be old haunts to them; but for her, it was a fresh, interesting project for the next five months.

Now, situated by the self-serve pump, filling the tank of her used Honda and wrinkling her nose at the strong gas fumes, she allowed her gaze to roam. Across two lanes and a fair expanse of grassy shoulder, a huge sign advertised *Milward Seniors Community.* A smaller sign in front had *Falconer's Construction Company* in even bolder letters.

Beyond the signs, an immense construction project seemed to be in the works. Most of the mature trees, not bulldozed over, were surrounded by brown earth and boxed in by unfinished bungalows of the most current styles. It looked like serious business.

Michaela gazed at the fuel reading before returning to her view at what looked like a quiet, yet happening community. The pleasant May weather only served to buoy her positive outlook on the town. She had done a lot of research on Milward before her decision to apply for her final-year internship at Bethel Community Church (BCC). She'd had enough of Bible college—four years. Now, it was time for the real thing.

She had also gleaned a little, from her last campus roommate, about the Pastor there. Her roommate, Matilda Klein—dubbed Tilly—would attend BCC each time she visited her boyfriend's family who used to live in Milward. She'd had nothing but high praises for the passion of the lead pastor and the family atmosphere of the congregation.

"It's kind of cool to see a Black minister pastoring a predominantly White congregation," Tilly had also stated. "Of course, there's a good representative of other races sprinkled in as well."

Michaela had raised her eyebrows at her golden-haired, German friend. "Well, I'm certainly not going because the senior pastor is Black! My parents had past connections with a prominent member there and felt strongly impressed, by the Spirit, I should go there."

Plus, BCC was big on supporting missions! That was her heartbeat! Her parents didn't think so. They thought she wanted to be a missionary because they were. They had admonished her to search carefully for God's plan—His will—for her life. She already knew what His will was; but she would go through the motions of searching, for their sakes.

After gasping at the final dollar value registered on the pump, she reconnected the hose to its port, and then prepared to pay her bill in the store. She was going to have to watch her spending for a while; even trust funds could become obsolete. She really didn't want to give her parents any cause for concern; they had enough on their plate as long-term missionaries in Haiti, especially since the terrible Haitian earthquake.

Driving along once more, Michaela had less opportunity for sightseeing now that she had to watch for street names. She had emailed her time of arrival, but had received no response back from the board member who had done her interview. She hoped her message had been received.

Michaela smiled as she squinted against the afternoon sun, realizing that the street she'd been searching for had evolved from the last—and there was the Church ahead. It was almost as if the street ended at the church driveway, but it actually took a sharp right into a residential area.

She had researched Bethel Community Church (BCC) on the internet, so she recognized it. It seemed bigger in real life. The wide, asphalted driveway turned left away from a large parking lot to her right. The side view of an architecturally dominant steeple faced her and the rest of the building's roofs seemed to rise to try and catch up to it. It was a modern, impressive, brick building, yet it didn't seem overwhelming.

Her eyes were drawn to the large, white Cross atop the steeple.

After parking slightly ahead of the canopied entrance, Michaela gazed through her passenger window at the church's double, glass doors and suddenly felt nervous. She was not a nervous person by nature; but this was to be her home for the next five months, and she was full of anticipation for everything to work out well.

Michaela flipped opened the windshield visor mirror and quickly critiqued her face and hair. She had spent a few weeks in Haiti, with her parents, before starting her internship and hadn't spent much time on her appearance. Wide, dark eyes looked back at her from the smooth, caramel brown backdrop of her skin. Well, at least she had blemish-free skin. She smoothed impatiently at the fluff of black hair that clouded out behind her head in what wasn't exactly a ponytail; that was for straight hair. This was more a captured cloud of woolly hair. She had relaxed, or straightened, her hair once—long ago; but, in the end, preferred her natural look. She closed the mirror's lid and gathered her shoulder bag and a dark brown folder. It was time to go.

* * *

It was two-thirty, Paul noted from his wrist watch. He turned away from the water cooler in the very spacious, commercially carpeted Foyer. He wanted to take one more peek at the activities in the Fellowship Hall. One of the church volunteers overseeing the project was a building contractor, so he knew the project was well supervised, but it was still his responsibility.

Earlier, after his lunch break, Paul had taken a few moments to check on the renovations. He had avoided Samuel's eye the whole time he had been inspecting the room, smiling to himself like an errant school boy. An hour or so had passed since he had left the Hall, and the work would soon be wrapped up.

After he smoothly sailed his paper cup into the waste basket behind the cooler, his journey to the Fellowship Hall was interrupted by a syrupy voice.

"I don't know how many times I've told the custodians not to place that waste basket there. I mean, who wants to see garbage in a church foyer?"

Paul turned to see a tall, willowy form approaching him from the sanctuary doorway. It never ceased to amaze him how Karlene Benedict could move so fluidly, as if walking on smoothly flowing water, but in four-inch heels. Her unusual golden eyes lit up, and she smiled as she ran a hand over the silky flow of long, dark hair running down one side of her chest.

"Well, Karlene, you know as well as I do that it didn't work putting it behind the sign-up tables." He put both hands on his hips. "People ended up always asking for it."

"You'd think it was such a big thing for people to remember," she remarked with a deep sigh, edging closer to him. "Come on, Paul, I'm not the Aesthetic Director for nothing."

"And you do a great job," Paul commented, "but I did warn you not to get too caught up in it. I don't even know any other Church that has one," he said, chuckling.

"Oh, Paul," she pouted, swatting delicately at his arm. "You should be very, very happy to have me. You don't have to worry about Women's Ministries clamouring about how things should be." She splayed long, shapely fingers across her chest. "I put up with all that for you."

Paul braced himself mentally and physically against the need to step back from her. Karlene was close enough to make him uncomfortable, but not enough to be indecent. Her perfume floated to his nostrils, and her pouting, reddened lips set against olive skin kept drawing his attention. This was a routine battle for him with this young woman. She had been the choir director, even before his arrival over two years ago, and was very talented in music and directing, but was only a passable singer.

Not three months after he had assumed the Pastorate at Bethel Community, she had dubbed herself the Church Aesthetic Director. At first, the board—made up of four men and one woman—had been against it, but then decided to have Karlene give it a try. The vote had been four to one. The woman, Ethel Flint, had voted against it.

Under Karlene's direction, the decor of the Church had improved significantly, but the patience of the majority of the congregation had gone in the opposite direction. Of course, the Fellowship Hall renovations had served to improve everyone's mood, even though Karlene was trying to make it seem that it had been her idea all along. Everyone knew differently and seemed to silently resolve to ignore her on the issue.

"Yo—Pastor Paul!"

Paul turned away from Karlene's challenging gaze with relief. Leroy Reynolds was swaggering towards them with his loose-fitted jeans trailing halfway down his backside. His long, black T-shirt served to cover his boxers and part of a large silver chain hanging down one side of his leg.

Paul smile at the youth who just missed matching his own six-two frame by a few inches.

"Hey, how's it going, Leroy?"

Leroy eyed Karlene somewhat belligerently but grinned as he focused on Paul. "Man, all that reno stuff wasn't bad after all. Hey, I learned a few things I could help my mom with."

"No kidding," Paul said, humouring him. He had really grown to like this seventeen-year-old with his cornrows, pierced eyebrow and ear, and attitude. "What did I tell you?" They slapped palms and fisted knuckles, laughing it up.

Karlene cleared her throat. "Well, gentlemen, if you'll excuse me, I have *work* to do." She smiled sweetly at Paul and ignored Leroy before floating away in the direction of the Fellowship Hall, the swirl of her skirt moving in tune with the flow of her hips.

"I—do—not like that girl," Leroy muttered with his lips pursed tightly and dark brows furrowed.

"Now, Leroy—"

"Yeah—I know, Pastor Paul. You, being a pastor and all, gotta like her, but I got my own ideas about her." Suddenly, Leroy's dark eyes widened. "Never seen her before!"

Paul looked towards the front doors; the direction of Leroy's gaze. There was someone pulling at the double doors. It was a young woman.

Chapter Three

She was tall, maybe five-eight, and she handled the inside church doors with an air of strength and purpose. Paul paused, with Leroy, to watch her complete her entrance. Now, she seemed uncertain as she gazed across the distance of the Foyer at them. Paul moved to intercept, but Hilda beat him to it from the Front Office which was closer to the front entrance.

With her back towards Paul and Leroy, Hilda spoke to the young woman in subdued tones. Suddenly Hilda embraced her, laughing out loudly and shaking her head.

Leroy glanced at Paul with raised eyebrows. "You know her?" he questioned.

"No," Paul responded, "but, I'll see what's up?"

"Yeah, I bet you will," Leroy said, grinning widely, then holding his hands up in mock surrender at Paul's frown. "Sorry, dude, I haven't seen a hot, black chick like her under this steep before, just plain Janes and grandmas."

"Steep?"

"Yeah—steeple. I mean, look at her!"

Paul decided to ignore Leroy. He turned and walked towards the women. The young woman glanced at him the same time Hilda turned his way.

"Paul!" Hilda called, reaching for him. "You're not going to believe this, but it's surely a pleasant surprise." She clamped her fingers on his arm, drawing him in to form a little circle.

"There's been a misunderstanding. *This* is Michael Laroche, except she's not a he—she's *Michaela* Laroche."

With Hilda's proclamation, Leroy's snort and the young woman's big, dark brown eyes all clamouring for his attention, it took a moment before the reality of the situation registered in Paul's brain.

* * *

"I'm so sorry, Paul," Samuel Temple's bass voice rumbled for the third time, "I didn't notice the fax had come through with the 'a' missing at the end of her name and that Hilda and the women had decided she was to board with you."

Paul, Hilda, Samuel and two other board members were sequestered in the Pastor's Office for an emergency meeting. Samuel had contrition written all over his broad, slightly flushed face. His blue and white polo shirt was stretched across his generous frame as he sat looking across at Paul.

Paul was feeling very out-of-sorts. He never imagined he'd be working with a female intern. Boarding her with him was obviously out of the question.

"Well, as I see it, we simply have to find her alternative living arrangements," stated Ethel Flint, an elderly woman known for her bluntness.

She was seated between Hilda and Samuel with her bony, well-manicured hands folded on her lap. She was dressed immaculately and her hair and make-up were flawless.

Paul glanced at Ethel from the seat behind his desk. Ethel always seemed to have her nose in everything concerning the Church, but she loved the Lord and seemed to make it her purpose in life to make sure what needed doing for others was done. Her life seemed to exemplify the biblical command to feed the widows and orphans and keep one's self uncorrupted by the world.

"Yes, that is certainly the simple solution," Paul agreed while everything in him was protesting, and he wasn't all together sure why. It wasn't like he had a problem with women in the ministry.

"I think it's absolutely wonderful!" Hilda was the only one who seemed to be truly settled about the mix-up. "I don't believe this Church has ever had a female intern." She peered over Ethel at her husband. "She seems such a dear girl, too."

"I agree with Hilda and Ethel," declared Rashad Hakeem with a slight Hindi accent. He was about Paul's age and was sitting apart from the other three. His olive skin was slightly covered with drywall dust from the renovations. "It's a great opportunity of example for our Church, particularly for our young women."

"You're all right," Paul finally declared. It was time to take the bull by the horn and do the right thing. "It's not your fault, Sam," he said to the older man. "I should have been more involved with this from the beginning."

"No, Paul, I had told you I would handle it," Samuel countered. He straightened his solid frame in his seat, causing Ethel to shift slightly. "I take full responsibility. I knew her parents years ago before they became missionaries. They're incredible people who are doing great work for the Lord among the Haitians. Their daughter was raised many years on the mission field before returning to Canada to live with her mother's sister—who is now deceased—for her high-school years. We need to do right by her. I haven't discussed this with Hilda yet, but I think we should take her in."

Hilda agreed immediately, clapping her hands together. "Sam, dear, that's brilliant! Of course, we'll take her in. We have a spare room and, I'm sure our granddaughter Tristan would love to have the intern board with us."

Before Samuel could respond, Paul placed both hands firmly on his desk. "Are you sure you don't want to think about this some more? It's for five months."

"No," Hilda said, standing and looking over Ethel's head at Samuel. She went over to Paul's desk and leaned over to place her hands on his much bigger ones. "It's settled, dear boy, no more worry, okay?"

Paul had to smile at the genuine sincerity and love in her expression. Hilda was truly a pure heart in a dark world. "Okay," he agreed, then stood up to address the others. "Okay, it's settled. Let's go welcome Miss Michaela Laroche to our fold."

They had all prepared to do just that when a firm knock interrupted them. Karlene opened the door and spoke from the doorway.

"Paul, may I have a word?"

"Can it not wait, Karlene? We have an important matter to attend to," Ethel said, frowning.

"Won't take but a minute," Karlene insisted, her eyes glinting dangerously at the older lady. Karlene's impatience with Ethel was commonplace. Ethel was one of few who stood up to Karlene's forceful personality.

Paul saw what was coming as everyone shifted uncomfortably; most noticeably Samuel, who thought Karlene had too much free reign in the Church. "Ethel, why don't you all just wait in the Conference Room for me," Paul suggested.

Ethel sighed loudly, but kept her poise as she marched ahead of the men. Hilda held back.

"Karlene, be a dear and don't hold him up too long. We're about to welcome the new intern." Hilda smiled meaningfully and left the door ajar before leaving.

Paul read a speculative gleam in Karlene's eyes before she spoke. He remained standing, hoping it wasn't some trivial matter once again. Even so, one thing he had committed to practicing, as a pastor, was to always be willing to listen.

She got straight to the point. "The woman in the Sanctuary—talking to Sarah—is the intern?"

It was asked with such emphasis that Paul was taken aback. Sarah, the Children's Pastor, had arrived just as he and Hilda were becoming acquainted with Michaela Laroche. She had cheerfully taken the intern under her wing while the board met. He guessed that Karlene had either seen or just met Michaela; which still didn't explain her attitude.

Paul decided to tread carefully. "Yes, she is."

Karlene's eyes narrowed slightly, but her voice was softer. "Really? I thought we were getting a male intern."

Paul stepped from behind his desk and pointedly moved towards the doorway. So that's what her beef was. "It turns out not, Karlene." One thing he had perceived about Karlene was her sense of insecurity even though, to the world, she portrayed herself as being very poised and confident. While he felt genuine compassion for her, he realized his need for strict caution in dealing with her. She was the type of woman who drew men like moths to a flame, and that was one burn he didn't want to experience and couldn't afford, in his position.

She reached for him as he moved out the doorway. He felt the warmth of her hand through his sleeve and steeled himself.

"Where will she stay? I thought *she* was supposed to stay with you." She gave a slight laugh at the obvious absurdity of the statement. Yet, her golden gaze begged him to reassure her.

Paul was feeling very uncomfortable. He was realizing more and more that Hilda was right,

Karlene wanted something from him; but whatever it was, he couldn't give her—wouldn't give her.

He gently dislodged her grip as he moved through the Front Office. "I think we can all agree that it wouldn't be appropriate, Karlene. Don't worry, it's taken care of."

She was right behind him as he headed through the Foyer, past the Assistant Pastor's Office and down a wide hall. He paused to face her. "Was there anything else?"

"No, no," she responded. She artfully pulled her long, dark tresses over her shoulder, leaning her head to one side. She didn't even seem to notice another church member who passed them in the hall and nodded at Paul. "I just thought you should know: I could take her in, if you like."

"No need, but thanks for offering." He decided to put the matter to rest. "The Temples have stepped in. Now, I don't want to keep everyone waiting any longer." He smiled, and then continued on to the door on his right. He didn't need to look back to know she was still there in the hall, watching him as he entered the safety of his inner circle.

* * *

Michaela felt at ease sitting on a cushioned seat at the back of the Church Sanctuary. Sarah Hurst reminded her of her friend and former roommate Tilly. They were both very open and easy to get to know. Sarah had told her a little about herself, her husband Brennon, their two-year-old son Conner and the Church.

What she really wanted to know was more about Reverend Paul Stephen Rayner, but it didn't seem appropriate to come right out and ask. After meeting him and realizing the misunderstanding regarding her gender, she had felt very awkward, to say the least. Also, there was something about him that intrigued her immensely, but she was hesitant to put it into words.

"So, your husband, Brennon, has been Assistant Pastor here for... ?"

"About a year and a half—shortly after Paul came. He brought Brennon on staff. They were good friends in Bible college." Sarah swept her shiny, dark brown hair away from her face.

She had pencil-thin eyebrows above heavy-lashed brown eyes and one of the most beautiful smiles Michaela had ever seen. She would hazard a guess that's what had won Brennon Hurst over.

"Will you be here long term?" Michaela asked, her eyes occasionally taking in the beautiful, peaceful Sanctuary. The colour scheme was a warm, comforting blend of pale orange, wine and brown. Tall, narrow windows with tan-coloured vertical blinds covered one wall. It was a large room with a very wide platform to comfortably house various instruments, a row of seats and a tall, transparent pulpit with a wooden cross attached to its front.

"We're not sure how long we'll be here," Sarah answered. "I know Brennon eventually wants a senior pastorate position, but he hasn't been quite ready to assume full responsibility of a congregation, yet. I'm actually on staff as Children's Minister, but I also help Brennon with Youth." She paused momentarily, a wistful expression on her face. "Our son is autistic. We nearly lost him about a year ago due to complications with his heart." She ran a slender hand across the frown lines in her forehead. "It's been difficult."

Michaela touched her shoulder gently. "I'm so sorry. How is your son now?"

She smiled her beautiful smile. "Oh, he's the joy of our lives. He's doing so much better, and my parents have been very supportive. He was born with some respiratory difficulties that seemed to improve as time passed. Just before his first birthday, he relapsed and was diagnosed with a severe heart murmur." She looked away. "Such a tiny body had to undergo surgery." She returned her gaze to Michaela. "The Church had a prayer vigil;

different groups praying so there was prayer around the clock. It's a miracle he's so healthy."

Michaela felt a combination of sorrow and joy for all they had endured. "That's so wonderful. I'm very glad."

A bubble of laughter escaped Sarah. "For a while, it had seemed impossible for me to carry a child to term, but I prayed that God would rescue me from my inabilities, and He did!"

"Wow," Michaela breathed. "You are a living testimony."

"In more ways than one, and our son Conner is a blessed reminder," Sarah pronounced with proud humility. "I had some recurring health problems during my pregnancies which probably accounted for the multiple miscarriages. However, the Lord Jesus worked a miracle in our lives that we'll always be grateful for."

"Oh, Sarah," Michaela reached out to hug her.

"I'm not even sure why I'm sharing all of this with you," Sarah's voice trembled against Michaela's shoulder. "But, I feel like I already know you." She pulled back and looked across at Michaela, blinking rapidly. "There's just something about you."

"Oh my, look at these two, Samuel!" Hilda's voice cut through the moment.

Michaela shifted away from Sarah to look up at some of the people she would be working with for the next five months. She hadn't even heard them enter the Sanctuary. They looked down at her, smiling; even the rigid looking older lady, Ethel. Pastor Paul's dark eyes were searching, questioning. She was not one to fawn over a man's looks, even one with really nice dimples, but she was having a hard time with this one. He spoke to her over the heads of the others:

"Michaela, we're very happy to have you here and have worked out a solution for your room and board." He glanced towards Hilda and then nodded at Samuel. "The Temples have agreed to have you stay with them. We can all vouch that they're a warm, friendly couple who we're sure you'll enjoy staying with."

Standing to her feet, Michaela felt uneasy with so many eyes on her, but she was also starting to sense an early kinship with these people. They obviously wanted her to feel very welcomed.

Sarah stood up and hugged her. "Welcome to the family of Bethel Community. I'm sure you'll love it here."

"Thanks, Sarah," Michaela whispered over her new friend's shoulder as she returned the hug. "I'm sure I will too."

Hilda firmly patted her hand, while Ethel looked on with a pleased smile on her pinched face. The three men stood by smiling.

"Well, perhaps we should take the young lady for a tour, then get her back to the house, Hilda." Samuel's voice was cheerful as he beamed at his wife. "Paul, why don't you come by for supper later—maybe bring Brennon with you?"

Paul glanced at Sarah, a question mark in his expression.

"Oh, I'm sure that'll be okay with Brennon. I'm sure he'll want to meet Michaela before tomorrow," Sarah said enthusiastically.

"And you'll come too, Sarah, and bring little Conner?" Hilda's question was more a statement.

"I'll see how he's doing by then. Speaking of which," Sarah paused and touched Michaela's shoulder lightly, "I really should go relieve Brennon of the little tiger."

Michaela appreciated the warmth of friendship she felt in Sarah's touch. "Thanks, Sarah. Hopefully, I'll see you later and I would love to meet Conner."

As she edged her way around the others, Sarah responded, "That would be great. You all take care of her now."

"Don't you worry," Samuel said with humour, "we'll initiate her in little by little." The other men chuckled at this, while Hilda and Ethel shook their heads.

"Well, I do have to be on my way," Ethel announced, "but I do wish you well here, my dear, and I'm sure you'll do your best to show these men up."

Michaela took the offered hand, surprised at the strong grip from this senior.

"Thank you so much, Ethel. I really appreciate it."

After Ethel's goodbye, Hilda spoke to the men. "Well, I guess you two will have to finish up in the Fellowship Hall," she said, glancing at Samuel and Rashad. "I have to return home due to the increase number of mouths to feed. So, who will give Michaela a tour?"

All eyes turned to Paul, and Michaela found herself suddenly feeling inexplicably overwhelmed.

Chapter Four

Paul stood very still, hands on his hips, in the front hall of the parsonage. The late afternoon, mid-spring air had been exchanged for the scent of Pine Sol. The cleaner had just left, and he usually had a sense of satisfaction that things were good for another two weeks. The cleaner was excellent at her work, and he lived alone—not much mess. Today, he barely noticed the scent.

He had been standing for a while, so he decided he better do something else. He sat on the hall bench. The padded wood squeaked slightly under his weight and his shoes scraped dully along the dark, hardwood floor as he pulled his feet back and rested his elbows on his knees.

Whatever it was would soon come to him; except, it didn't have to come. He already knew what it was. Today was the third anniversary of his wife's death; he had been mourning this morning. So, how was it that one young woman could enter his world the afternoon of the same day and basically drive thoughts of his deceased wife from his mind?

Placing his hands on his thighs, he let his head fall back against the wall and glanced over at the wide mirror on the opposite side. He was too low to see his expression and he wasn't sure he wanted to. He gazed to his right down the hall with its dark brown wainscoting, past the living and dining room entrances on the right, to his home office on the left. He "willed" himself to go there, but couldn't seem to move.

"This is ridiculous," he grumbled, struggling to his feet. "Lord, I'd be curious to know what You're thinking about what I'm thinking right now." He walked down the hall, leaving his briefcase on the floor by the bench. He entered his sanctuary, then checked his phone for messages.

"Hello, honey. Sorry I missed you... " His adoptive mother's voice brought him temporary relief. Her brief getting-caught-up message ended with: "Praying for you and love you." He listened to a few more; including one from Brennon saying he would see him at the Temples' for supper. Paul grimaced at the reminder.

His home office was smaller than the one at the Church, but he liked it much better. It was his private world without transparent doors and people coming and going. Before he came, the board had almost decided to sell the parsonage which was older than the church building, but then decided it was prudent to keep it for the newly hired widower.

Of course, being a widower meant it was easier to have an open-door policy at the parsonage, which he didn't mind. It got lonely at times, even though his church and community commitments kept him fairly busy. He missed being married, but for his protection, he was never alone in the parsonage with any female not old enough to be his mother.

Paul reached for a four-by-ten silver framed picture of his wife on the central shelf of a wall unit bookcase. A picture of his adoptive father was on the shelf above showing a gentle-eyed, grey-haired man with a solid build.

He looked at his wife. He had placed her there at the centre of his books as a reminder of what was really important: people. Things could be replaced, but not people. He knew deep down her picture being there was also like a shrine, his penance that he would remain faithful to her as long as he could. Surely, three years wasn't long enough?

Hannah. Her chin-length, brown hair framed her small, heart shaped face beautifully; a picture of health and beauty. Her eyes sparkled in fun, even as her quiet spirit shone through. He had placed her photo there six months ago after removing it from the bedroom. It had been part of his concession to moving on.

Paul startled at the sound of the doorbell. A deep sigh erupted from him as he replaced the frame before going back out to the hall.

"Hey, Blinder," Paul greeted after opening the front door. "What's up?"

Blinder whose real name was Harry Davis was the same age as Paul. However, he had some cognitive impairment and a limp due to a head injury five years ago. His fishing boat had capsized in strong currents, causing him to hit his head on a rock. Sadly, his life jacket had been left in the bottom of his boat, and he had nearly drowned.

Blinder was standing on the parsonage's wide, polished concrete porch fidgeting nervously with a green cap. His chestnut hair was ill-cut and hung just below the collar of his camouflage jacket. Blinder had great respect for the military.

Paul looked into his grey eyes and smiled. "You want to come in for a while, Blinder?"

"No, Pastor," Blinder responded gravely, his speech slightly slurred. His large nose seemed to take up most of his face, but he smelled clean today. "I just wanted to tell you that Will's been at it again. I-I tried to stop him, Pastor, but he wouldn't listen to me."

Paul glanced around to his left and across the street to see if any neighbours were in sight. The end of the church driveway was to his right. "What do you mean, Blinder?"

"He went to see the m-magic man: the bad magic." Blinder seemed quite distressed.

Will McCree, Samuel and Hilda's son-in-law, was on medical leave from the military for Post Traumatic Stress Disorder (PTSD). He had met with Paul multiple times in the past but had been noticeably reluctant to set up an appointment in the last few months.

"What are you talking about?" Paul questioned, puzzled. He gently directed Blinder to one of two cushioned patio chairs. After they were both seated, Blinder continued.

"The one, w-who tried to get the psych... "

"The psychics?"

"Yes, yes," Blinder agreed enthusiastically, rocking back and forth in his seat. "The man who tried to get them here. Will w-went to see him, even though I told him it was bad."

Now Paul understood Blinder's concern. Recently, many of the Churches had joined in community prayer against a psychic group trying to take root in the community. It had also afforded Paul the opportunity to preach a series of sermons on the reality and dangers of the occult; specifically black magic and Satanism.

Paul knew that Blinder had heard all of the sermons. Blinder was also very protective of Bethel Community's people. Even though Will wasn't a regular attendee, Blinder still considered him "family" because he belonged to the Temples. Plus, Will was always very kind to him.

"H-he helped me with my fear of water," Blinder continued, his full attention on Paul. "He's my friend. I-I don't want anything bad to happen to him."

"Yes, I understand, Blinder," Paul assured him, placing a hand on his shoulder. "How about I give him a call later, or even talk to him face to face? I'll be going to the Temples' later."

Blinder smiled for the first time, his clean-shaven face seemed almost boyish. "Yes, Pastor, I pray for Will all the time, and he likes you."

"Okay," Paul said, smiling back. "If you were coming to eat here tonight, you're more than welcome to come to the Temples' with me. I'm sure they won't mind."

Blinder got up suddenly. His movements were always a little agitated. "No, no, Pastor. I'm h-having supper at the shop. I promised Carmel I would, today." He started moving towards the porch steps, as if Paul would hinder him.

"No problem," Paul assured him, slowly standing up. "I'll see you later."

"Okay, Pastor," Blinder agreed as he limped down the parsonage driveway to the sidewalk.

Paul watched him until he was out of sight. It was good that Leroy's mom had taken such an interest in Blinder. He had been working and living at her blinds and home decor store for the last four years. Interestingly enough, that was how he had ended up being dubbed "Blinder."

As far as Paul knew, Blinder had no family to speak of. He had grown up in the foster care system, and had somehow beaten the odds by leading a productive life as an electrician. That was before the accident.

Blinder's story certainly made Paul more appreciative of his own story of adoption. Even more wonderful was the awesome truth that he and Blinder had both been adopted into God's eternal family.

Paul stretched his arms widely before returning to the house. There were a few things he needed to get caught up on before leaving again. Primarily, he needed to re-visit the information on the new intern. He needed to know a little more about Michaela Laroche.

* * *

"I think it's awesome that we're going to have a girl intern," Tristan McCree said for the third time.

Michaela smiled at the sixteen-year-old's enthusiasm as they made up the bed in one of the spare rooms. Samuel and Hilda's granddaughter had insisted on helping Michaela get the room ready, since Hilda was busy with supper. The cheerful, cherry blonde teen couldn't seem to get over the surprise of having a female intern, and seemed more than willing to participate in Michaela's advent to BCC life.

"And to think, I'm the first youth to know about it," Tristan declared, pausing to giggle as if the idea had just made its full impact on her. She clapped her hands together, then slapped them down on the double-sized bed for a final smoothing of the light-blue duvet. "Voila! Now, we can do your clothes."

Michaela laughed as she sat on the side of the bed closest to the doorway. "Oh, no you don't. Let's not worry about that right now. I'll just live out of my cases for a few days and unpack little by little."

"Are you sure?" Tristan asked innocently, blue eyes wide in a faintly freckled face that slightly resembled Hilda's.

"I'm sure," Michaela assured her. The room had recently had a spring cleaning, so only the bedding and some other minor adjustments had to be made. It was a pleasant room, decorated in soft blue and white, with a wide window looking out into a generous side yard.

The Temples were only five minutes from the Church in a quiet residential area with older homes and mature maple trees lining the sidewalks. It wasn't Haiti's close-knit missionary community, but it most likely would be better than dorm life. If there was one thing Michaela yearned for, it was to have a family twenty-four-seven. After high school, she had returned to Haiti for a year before committing to four years of Bible college. The Temples would do for now, but the sooner she could get back to her own family, the better.

"My mom will be thrilled to meet you!" Tristan chattered. She was sitting cross-legged on the bed. "She doesn't make it out to Church as much as she'd like. Sometimes she's really tired because of her job, but sometimes... " Tristan paused as if she had said too much.

"What does your mom do, Tristan?" Michaela asked after perceiving the girl's sudden discomfort.

Tristan seemed to snap out of it and was all smiles again. "Oh, she's a social worker with the Children's Aid Society here in town. It keeps her pretty busy, but she really likes her job."

Michaela shoved further up the bed to lean against the white, iron headboard. She stretched her socked feet out on the bed, realizing that her journey's weariness was catching up to her. If Hilda didn't have supper ready soon, she might just doze off listening to Tristan ramble on. "How long has your mother worked as a social worker?" she asked, stifling a yawn

"It seems forever—Hello, Michaela." The tired, but pleasantly modulated voice from the doorway was unexpected.

"Oh—hello." Michaela swung her feet to the floor, as a tall woman entered the room.

She had Tristan's hair colouring and was probably in her late thirties.

"I see you've met my very talkative daughter," the woman said, extending a well-manicured hand. "I'm Lucy, Sam and Hilda's daughter."

Michaela walked towards Lucy and grasped her offered hand. She instantly noted an air of burden about this woman. "Hi, Lucy, I'm so glad to meet you, and—actually—Tristan has been very helpful."

Lucy laughed gently and the tiredness in her eyes eased a little. She accepted a brief hug and kiss from Tristan before commenting: "That's great. My mother said she was up here helping you out. She wanted me to let you know supper is in five minutes. I hope you've had enough time."

Michaela smiled in return. "Oh, with Tristan's help, things are perfectly adequate for now. Tomorrow is another day."

"So, did Grandma tell you how they all thought Michaela was—get this Mom—Michael?"

Tristan radiated excitement as she practically stood on tiptoes by her mother's side. She obviously found the whole story of the mix-up quite entertaining.

"Briefly," Lucy said, glancing meaningfully at Michaela, "but we won't get into that now. You come and help your grandma set the table while I go change."

"Aww—Mom," Tristan wailed. "It's such a juicy story though, and I'm the first one of the whole Youth Group to know it. I can't wait to tell—"

"I know, I know, Tristan," Lucy spoke, interrupting her daughter while directing her from the room. "Let Michaela have a moment before joining us for supper." She smiled, shaking her head as they moved into the hallway. "We'll see you downstairs, Michaela."

Michaela smiled back. "Thanks, Lucy. See you in a few minutes."

She left the blue rug she was standing on and stepped onto laminate wood as she went to close the door, thinking she should phone her parents and bring them up to date. She wasn't sure when she would be able to connect again with them tonight.

After a couple of tries on her cell phone, Michaela determined she wouldn't get her parents after all. She sighed; feeling a little disappointed as she set the phone on the white dresser across from the bed. She stared at herself in the dresser mirror. She didn't look as tired as she felt, but perhaps a change from her blouse and slacks would somewhat perk her up.

* * *

Paul let himself into the Temples' house and stood in the wide foyer. He could hear the hustle and bustle of kitchen noise down the hall as the scent of roast beef assailed his nostrils. He hadn't seen the Hursts' car in the

Temples' wide driveway, so he left the door unlocked for them. He gazed warily towards the living room, knowing he was checking for *her* whereabouts, before easing off his shoes.

He started moving towards the kitchen, then stopped in his tracks to focus on movement from the staircase just off the foyer.

Where the staircase changed direction partway up at the landing, he saw long, slender legs encased in dark socks and leggings beneath a dark blue shirt-dress. A slender hand slid along the wooden banister, as the rest of her came into view.

Paul smiled, stubbornly ignoring his discomfort at her sudden appearance. Her dark brown eyes were wide and her softly rounded lips parted.

"You startled me," Michaela accused gently. She continued down and stood observing him, it seemed, warily. "I-it's a very busy house."

He noticed her hair was more loosely bound at the nape of her neck, then fluffed out to her shoulders. The thick kinks of black hair framed her face beautifully. His hands itched to touch the waves, so he looked away towards the kitchen.

"I absolutely apologize—," he remarked causally, returning his gaze to her, feeling anything but casual, "—didn't mean to scare you." She had a particularly direct stare that was going to take some getting used to—five months worth.

"No, it's just me. You'd think I'd be used to it, coming from dorm life." Her gentle laugh was easy and free, and then she sobered. "I really hope I haven't put them out. I'm so sorry for all the mix-up."

"The Temples? No, no." He touched her shoulder gently to reassure her. "Trust me: Sam and Hilda thrive on this sort of thing. I promise you."

"Oh, good," she said, sounding relieved. "I'll take your word for it."

Paul nodded at her comment. He looked towards the kitchen again. Silence reigned for a moment, and then blessed relief came at the sound of the front door opening to let the Hursts in.

After the Hursts' arrival and introductions were made and the table was laid, it seemed like Christmas in the Temples' large, two-storey home with brightly lit rooms; the aroma of roast beef; the sight of creamy scalloped potatoes and carrots, and other assortment of dishes; and the long dining room table filled with people.

Paul noticed how easily the intern was interacting with the others. Michaela seemed to embrace people with her paradoxical personality. On one hand she seemed quite easy-going; on the other, she was instantly intense about certain issues. Presently, the issue was the work of familiar spirits in the Church.

"It's not impossible for demons to manifest in a church service. In some places, it happens commonly." Michaela stated emphatically. The table still carried Hilda's famous apple pie, but the attention was on the new intern who sat between Tristan and Lucy, across from Paul, Brennon, and Sarah.

"Have you seen this often in Haiti?" Brennon asked. He was sitting sideways on his seat so he could watch Conner who was happily playing on the floor. All evening, he had been peppering Michaela with questions, seemingly impressed by her passion for ministry. Sarah sat beside him beaming as if she had found her long lost friend.

Paul was feeling a little troubled. Had they invited a potential powder keg to their Church? Michaela Laroche seemed too confident, too certain, too... he couldn't find the right word.

"It happens all the time. My parents have had to deal with it on a regular basis." Her dark eyes flashed intensely and her hands moved in constant motion with her words. "You see, the people of Haiti often mix Christianity with their cultural spirit beliefs. For some people, it's hard to separate the two which leaves room for ungodly strongholds, even in the Church."

"Yes, I've seen the same on some mission trips," Samuel acknowledged from one end of the table. "I don't imagine it happens here very much." He glanced at Paul, then back at Michaela.

Michaela took a deep breath before responding. "I believe it happens more than we think. We, in Canada, are less believing of the supernatural. It's more easily hidden because we are not as accepting of the manifestations of demons or, for that matter, of the Holy Spirit."

"Whoa—whoa there!" Brennon turned to fully face her across the table, his brows raised over hazel eyes. "*We* don't accept the manifestation of the Holy Spirit?"

"I challenge you that *most* of us don't. We limit Him."

The word finally came to Paul: *inflexible*. For someone who had just graduated from Bible college, she seemed too inflexible. He felt the need to reel her in.

"I think you're making too broad of a judgement statement, Michaela. I agree, in some Churches, the Spirit is limited, but many also allow Him free reign."

"So we think," she responded without batting an eyelid, "but the majority of Canadian Churches don't even begin to know the full working of the Spirit as described in First Corinthians twelve."

They locked gazes.

"We need a revival," she declared, looking away from him.

Hilda chuckled. "Well, Paul, I say we've all been told."

Conner let out a loud scream.

"It's been seconded," Sarah said softly, still smiling.

Paul groaned inwardly. The women were siding with her.

"Pastor Paul?"

Paul focused on Tristan who had been surprisingly quiet during this last leg of adult exchange. "Yes, Tristan."

"What about what you preached on before? You know, about the occult and stuff? Is that what Michaela is talking about?"

He didn't get to answer her. All of their attention suddenly became riveted on loud voices and banging at the front door, followed by the peel of the doorbell.

"Oh, dear God," Hilda cried softly, looking at Lucy.

Lucy and Samuel rose from the table at the same time and rushed out into the hall.

"It must be Will," Hilda added wearily. Paul knew there wasn't much that brought her spirit down, but her son-in-law seem to accomplish that often enough.

* * *

Michaela's unease at what she perceived as Paul's displeasure at her comments changed to surprised curiosity at the unexpected drama unfolding. The noise in the front hall had increased with the opening of the front door. Hilda was clearing the table as if all were well, but she had a worried expression on her face. Tristan had disappeared, Brennon had picked up Conner and was standing behind Sarah's chair, and Paul was moving purposefully towards the commotion.

"It's Will," Sarah explained to her, after Hilda had disappeared into the kitchen. "Lucy's husband. His friends have probably brought him home... drunk." Sarah glanced worriedly towards the hall. Even Conner was being still in his father's arms, his eyes focused on the ceiling as if trying to place the sudden flood of sounds.

Sarah reached for Conner as a barrage of cursing filled the house. "They might need you, Brennon."

Michaela was feeling a little anxious and also rose.

"You better stay here," Sarah admonished, trying to bounce Conner on her knee. He squirmed, his chubby little body, as if wanting to follow his dad. He was a beautiful child, but Michaela noticed that he seldom seemed to look directly at anyone, though he did seem to know his parents. She would have to do some research on autism.

The Temples' pleasant dining room and warm home atmosphere was now infiltrated by a drunken force. Michaela sat back down. The noise seemed to be descending.

"They're helping him to the basement. They have an apartment there."

"Tristan and her parents live in a basement apartment, here?"

"Yes," Sarah answered, struggling with Conner. She smoothed at the wispy blond hair on his head, before setting him back on the floor where his toys were. "Lucy and Tristan have lived here for about two years; Will for almost a year. They used to have a beautiful home just outside the military base, but... "

Michaela waited on Sarah's pause for a moment before finishing for her: "Will isn't well."

Sarah glanced towards the wide kitchen entrance where Hilda had apparently started washing up, judging from the sounds of running water and clattering dishes. Sarah placed her elbows on the table before speaking in a quiet voice.

"Will suffers from Post Traumatic Stress Disorder. He was almost killed in Afghanistan, but unfortunately, his best friend was. He recovered from his physical injuries, but not his mental ones." She ran her fingers over her eyes. "It's been very hard on the entire family. Lucy and Tristan moved back here while Will was in treatment."

Michaela reached down to pick up Conner who had crawled under the table. He was a heavy boy. He smelled like baby powder and apples and felt soft and warm. She squeezed him to herself, relishing the feel of him in her arms. He let her hold him for a moment, then seemed to look at her before struggling to get down again.

"He likes you," Sarah commented, smiling gently. She leaned back and sighed. "You know, I'm really glad you're here. I believe your coming is about more than your internship." She must have read the question in Michaela's eyes because she added, "I can't explain it. Let's just wait and see."

Chapter Five

Samuel felt an increasing stiffness in his knees as he struggled up from kneeling on the carpeted floor of his dimly-lit, upstairs den. He didn't always feel his age, but his son-in-law's afflictions certainly pushed him there. He loved Will, pitied him even, but he hated the toll on Lucy and Tristan. What could be done for a man who felt he was useless as a husband, father and human being? Will's demons had embedded this lie to the core and only the power of Christ could uproot it. That power would only come from time spent again and again on one's knees.

He squinted at the digital clock on his desk, before sitting in an armchair opposite the desk. He always woke extra early Sunday mornings to be in prayer. Four o'clock had been earlier than usual. He picked up his Bible from the side table, beside his chair, and reached for his reading glasses. He didn't put the glasses on but leaned back into the folds of the chair and breathed out loudly in the quietness of the house.

"Father, there's not more I can think of to say. He will destroy himself unless You deliver him from the destroyer."

Last night, Will had been escorted home by his drinking buddies who usually saw that he got home in one piece. At least one of them, designated to drive, was always sober. Sam wasn't sure if he should blame them for drinking with Will in the first place, or be grateful that they saw him home safely. He guessed the latter; Will would drink regardless of who he did or didn't do it with.

His son-in-law was a proud Air Force Captain who had taken his job seriously. He had also fallen in love with Lucy when she was just twenty. Even though Will had shown no real commitment to Christ, Lucy had insisted on marrying him. There had been no real conviction to dissuade her after her early pregnancy was revealed.

Will had provided well for his family, also providing for Lucy to finish university after Tristan was born. The family had moved frequently, for a time, as military life demanded; but Samuel and Hilda had always made it a point to stay very connected. The young family had seemed to thrive, even though Lucy's church life had diminished. Things changed after Will had experienced a suicide bombing accident that had nearly taken his life. That same accident, however, had succeeded in taking the life of Will's best friend.

Will was never the same again.

Samuel rubbed the bristles along the side of his face. He couldn't help but smile at his memory of the sight of Paul helping Brennon steady Will down to the basement apartment. God bless Paul, but he shouldered too many burdens. Last night, on the way down the basement stairs, Will had glanced at Paul through a drunken haze.

"Hey, Rev., I've b-been meaning t-to come see you. I r-really have." Will had nearly fallen after tripping at the base of the stairs. Both men had struggled under his weight; he was a large man. "S-schedule me up, will you?"

Paul had left Brennon and Lucy to assist Will to bed before sprawling, beside Samuel, on the McCrees' couch. "I'm failing him," he had declared to no one in particular.

Samuel had glanced across at him and had said emphatically, "Then I've also failed him. We've all failed him."

Paul had frowned at this, his eyes questioning.

Samuel had answered what was unspoken. "We can only do so much, Paul. Will has to be willing to do his part; the rest is up to God. We cannot do His part. We'll only get in the way."

Paul, with a grim set to his jaw line, had let his head fall back on the couch and had remained silent.

Samuel's reminiscing shifted to the new intern, Michaela. It had been interesting to see Paul's reaction to her. Hilda as much as had them married off—the child barely twenty-four hours in Milward.

"You should have seen the way he gawked at her, Sam," Hilda had rattled on, as he had finished helping her in the kitchen after everyone had left. "It was like the cat got his tongue."

Samuel had smiled indulgently at her, figuring this was better than her moaning about Will.

"Hilda, you women had better leave well enough alone. He was just shocked by her gender; he was expecting a young man. He's the minister and she's the intern. There can be none of that."

Hilda had swatted at him with her dish cloth. "Certainly not! I understand that. I'm thinking of the future. He's lived in the past way too long."

Samuel chuckled to himself in the dimness of his den. Judging by the events at the evening meal, he wasn't sure how Paul would handle this intern. She was definitely unlike any they'd had before, regardless of gender.

* * *

The following morning was like déjà vu to Michaela, as she descended the stairs to see a man standing at its base in the Temples' foyer. He was staring up at her with shell-shocked, very blue eyes, clearly wondering if he were seeing right. There was a wild look about him. His dark, almost black hair was dishevelled along with his shirt and pants. He was a big man, and she felt a little nervous until she realized who he was.

Michaela paused on the third step up. She was not a short woman, but he definitely had a body mass advantage. So, this was the culprit who had thrown the house into pandemonium last night.

"Good morning. You must be Tristan's dad," Michaela greeted as if all were well with the world.

He glared at her uncertainly, not answering.

"I'm Michaela. I just arrived yesterday at your in-laws' Church; I'm the new intern. There was some mix-up about where I should stay, so the Temples offered to put me up."

He cleared his throat with a grunt and mumbled, "Hi." He gazed at the floor, clearly ill at ease. He looked up at her again, and they took stock of each other in the quietness of the house.

Michaela felt the need to challenge growing in her; never mind that it often got her in trouble. This intense need came on a regular basis to *right the wrong*. "Do you do this sort of thing often?"

A puzzled look replaced his frown.

"What you did last night."

He looked at her like he couldn't believe she had just said that. He took a step back, as if he would escape.

She was down the remaining steps in a heartbeat. "No, don't go." He paused, his gaze wary. Michaela held a hand of truce up and smiled gently. "Are you getting help?"

Will shut his eyes tightly, then raked his big fingers through his hair. His breath came in gasps and his body shuddered as he seemed to try to control himself. Then he began weeping silently with his hands up over his face.

Michaela quietly moved towards him and touched one of his arms. She could feel the big muscles bulging there and smell the alcohol still on him. He could probably knock her flying across the foyer, yet she persisted.

"Hey," she said. "Hey!" she repeated more loudly, when he wouldn't look at her. That got his attention. "You've got to beat this. Do it for yourself. Do it for your wife and daughter."

He frowned down at her as if trying to absorb her words; then he jerked suddenly at the sound of footsteps on the stairs. It was Samuel. Michaela's hand was displaced, as he turned and quickly stumbled towards the front door. He opened it and stepped out, closing it firmly behind him. He had gone out with bare feet.

Michaela felt cool air from the door's motion penetrate the nylons below her navy blue skirt as she greeted Samuel. She was just getting to know this stout, white-haired man, but she believed he was full of kindness—he and his wife. As she watched him approach, still in his pyjamas under a light-weight bathrobe, she was filled with pity for him.

He gave her a big, albeit weary smile. "This is not a good start in our home for you. I apologize profoundly. It's not always like this."

Michaela smiled in turn. "It's okay. Believe me, this doesn't reflect on the wonderful hospitality you've extended to me. I finally got through to my parents this morning and they reminded me again of your close friendship in the past."

"Yes," Samuel acknowledged, breathing heavily. "It was so many years ago, but I just knew that having their daughter at Bethel Community would be very special."

"Sam?" They both looked up at the sound of Hilda's call from upstairs. Hilda poked her head around the bend in the stairs. "Why didn't you wake me up? I wanted to get a big breakfast for Michaela. For goodness sake, it's her special day!"

* * *

"No, Hilda, let her to stay where she is," Paul said for the third time. "It's her first day. Let's not make it any more stressful for her than it needs to be."

Hilda was the third person to ask if Michaela should join them for the usual leadership prayer in the Pastor's Office. Now, if people would just treat her like just any other intern, it would be less stressful... for him. Michaela would be just fine waiting in the Sanctuary with Sarah. He had already brought his other board members, Robert Dawson and Frank Harris, up to speed. They were Samuel's peers and seemed to support whatever Samuel approved.

"Are you sure, Paul?" Hilda questioned. She was dressed more spiffy than usual in a cream dress with her greying curls neatly arranged on her head. "Perhaps praying with her would help, if you think she's stressed."

"Hilda—"

"All right," she conceded, holding her hands up as she backed out of the Pastor's Office. "I'll round up the rest."

Paul shook his head. He checked his tie in the office mirror on the wall facing his desk. The Front Office seemed to have had people coming and going erratically all morning. You would think they'd never had an intern placement before. Granted, there was a lot of excitement now that word had gotten out about the mix-up. The irony was the error had nothing to do with the person; they had welcomed the person who had applied, but had expected her to be *him*.

He grabbed his dark grey suit jacket off a hook by the mirror and slid into it just as Brennon filed in with the rest of the praise and worship team, followed by the altar workers.

Brennon nodded towards the doorway. "Should I get Michaela?" he asked innocently.

* * *

After the announcements, prior to the morning service, Paul tried to keep his face expressionless as Michaela shared some personal details about herself with the BCC congregation. He was seated to her left, behind her, where he could see part of her profile and the back of her head. At this moment, the word he had in mind was no longer *inflexible*, but *engaging.* She knew how to work the crowd; the congregation's attention was fully hers. Yet, Paul couldn't discern anything but genuineness in her persona, as she spoke softly, yet firmly. She had a good speaking voice; deep enough to command attention, but soothing.

She was dressed modestly in a navy blue suit with the skirt just at her knees. Paul tried to keep his eyes trained above her shoulders, away from the appealing flow of her form and slender legs leading down to black high-heel shoes. He didn't need to give anyone the next dinner conversation topic about how the Pastor couldn't keep his eyes off the intern's legs. A male intern would have been less complicated.

He noticed she tended to be very expressive with her hands and had a commanding bearing that did nothing to dispel her femininity. It left him wanting to trust her and take care of her, simultaneously. Yet, trust was something built over time and a very independent spirit was evident in her.

"I hope to share more details about my parents' work in Haiti when I have opportunity to share my testimony with you... "

She was wrapping it up in five minutes just as he had asked, but Paul had a feeling the young men in the crowd—maybe some of the older ones too—would rather listen to her than him. She was a beautiful woman; nevertheless, she was his intern and that's where the line was drawn.

"... and one day, if Pastor Paul would allow," she was looking around at him, a slight smile in place, "perhaps we could talk about a trip to Haiti."

He smiled back—a pastorly smile—and nodded indulgently. What else was he to do, with everyone all but eating out of her hands? He glanced at the youth corner and saw Tristan whispering back and forth with the other youth, and then pausing regularly to hear Michaela. The excitement from that generation was evident.

He stood to his feet during the generous applause from the congregation. He received the cordless microphone from Michaela's outstretched hand, feeling slightly mesmerized by her grateful gaze and winsome smile.

"Thank you, Michaela," he said, switching the microphone off. He placed it on a shelf below the top of the pulpit before adjusting his mike headset. He faced his people. That was how he thought of them: his flock, his responsibility, and he took it very seriously. Now, she was part of that responsibility.

"Well, there you have it, folks. Michaela will be with us for the next five months and I want you to make her feel right at home. She'll be assisting me, but she'll also be working a great deal with Pastor Brennon and Pastor Sarah in Youth Ministries—" This brought a chorus of approval from the young people, except for Leroy who was sitting beside Blinder, slightly apart from the group.

Paul smiled and paused, before continuing: "—as well as some involvement with Children's Ministries." He glanced at the front row, to his right, where Karlene sat with a noticeably rigid posture. She was glancing over at Michaela who was in the middle row. "At this time, I believe Karlene has an announcement about the choir?"

Karlene switched her gaze to him, smiling sweetly. She uncrossed her long legs and strutted, in four-inch heels, to the platform. When she reached the pulpit, Paul stepped aside. However, she followed his movement and whispered conspiratorially, "I thought you'd forgotten me."

Paul stepped slightly ahead of her and reached for the cordless mike which he switched on and gave to her before stepping back. He hoped none of her words had registered in his headset.

Karlene smiled out at the congregation and, as was her usual way, spoke with great flare. "Well, yes, we are indeed glad to have our intern here and we certainly wish her well for her time with us." She paused significantly. "Now, let's turn our attention to the regular things of church life. We do have some choir practice details to attend to. Even though summer is approaching and the end of choir season is upon us, we still need to keep in mind the planned celebration for the opening of the Fellowship Hall... ."

Paul grimaced inwardly. He was fairly certain he was not the only one who had noticed Karlene's veiled slight at Michaela.

* * *

After the morning service, Paul, as was customary, spent time personally greeting the people as they filed out the front doors. The line was not its usual steady stream. There was another line deviating towards Michaela who was standing by the Front Office door. Things might have progressed faster if she had stood beside him. However, he wasn't comfortable with how that might look.

Robert Dawson and Frank Harris, the two board members who had just been introduced to Michaela that morning, joined him by the doorway. Robert Dawson was a thin, pale, scholarly-looking man with glasses and a quiet voice. Frank Harris was of medium build with mahogany skin: a very jovial, dependable man. Both men were widowers who had developed a steadfast friendship.

"She seems pretty good," Frank spoke in a deep baritone. "She really seems to have her priorities straight, isn't that right, Rob?"

"Most certainly she does," Robert agreed as he fiddled with his glasses. He squinted at Paul.

"We will do our utmost to make her feel at home."

"Thank you both, I'm sure she'll appreciate it," Paul told the men as they turned to leave.

"The youth seem quite taken with Michaela," Rashad Hakeem said as he approached Paul. Paul had noticed. Some of the parents were now warning that rides were leaving. Michaela seemed oblivious to it all as she seemed to give special attention to each youth.

"Yes," Paul agreed. "Well, she'll be spending a lot of time with them, so that's great." He faced Rashad. "How is your mother doing since your father's passing?"

Rashad hung his dark head slightly before looking up. There was sadness in his eyes.

"Not too badly. She visited India for a few weeks and she's been living with my sister for about a month now, in Brampton. It most likely will be permanent."

"And you?" Paul probed gently.

Rashad shrugged, then raised his arms with hands outstretched. "Every day, it seems, the Lord fills me up with what I need—no more, no less. I know you understand."

Paul smiled. Yes, he did understand. Rashad was a quiet man who grieved quietly for a father he had never really been close to. Paul had lost his wife and unborn child and he knew his biological father only from a distance. Yes, he could relate.

"Dennis Falconer had one of his sales guys out last Friday," Paul said, changing the subject.

Rashad looked at him with raised eyebrows. "He's still pushing for us to put his sales-pitch poster up?"

"You bet. Have you talked to the Mayor yet?"

"Yes, but I don't know what will come of it. It's pretty serious to make accusations about a building project having substandard work. They should never have allowed him to build on that part of the property. A lot of those basements are going to have water problems."

"But money talks," Paul said, reading Rashad's thoughts.

"It sure does," Rashad agreed, sighing deeply. "Somehow, I have the feeling that it's more than money with Falconer. It's power."

Paul nodded in agreement. He had the same suspicion as well. Both men were silent for a moment, while the youths' excited chatter prevailed.

"Did—umm—did Karlene leave yet?" Rashad asked quietly.

Paul smiled. "No, I think she's critiquing the Fellowship Hall." It was no secret that Rashad had a deep crush on the Latin beauty. Now, if she could take her eyes off him long enough, she would see the solid potential in Rashad. He was a nice-looking, shrewd and wealthy businessman who worked hard in his community and Church.

Rashad grinned sheepishly before saying good-bye, and then he walked in the direction of the Fellowship Hall.

"See you later, Pastor Paul," several youths chorused as they finally began to exit the Church Foyer. Tristan and her "special" friend Ian stopped by Paul.

"Pastor Paul, will Michaela be starting out with Youth or the kids?" Tristan asked with eager expectation in her eyes.

"What does it matter, Tristan?" Ian asked. He was a tall, lanky seventeen-year old with brown hair and braces. "We both work in Children's Church anyway. Either way, you get to work with her."

"It does matter, Ian." Tristan glared at him impatiently. "Pastor Paul?"

Paul decided to put her questioning to rest. "In one sense Ian is right, Tristan. Michaela will be doing a kind of potpourri—so she gets a taste of everything. She does, however, get to focus on one special project she'll complete before she's done."

"See, I told—" Ian didn't get to finish. Tristan's cherry blond hair lifted off her shoulders as she turned on him.

"Oh, Ian... " She rolled her eyes and shook her head. "I told you, I hate it when you do that. It's rude to say I told you so."

Ian dragged his big sneakered feet two steps back. "Well, it's just as bad to go around telling everyone how you were the first to meet her and all... " He paused. "Tristan?"

Paul had to stifle a chuckle as Tristan barrelled out the doors leaving Ian, with gaping mouth, staring after her. He looked, red faced, at Paul.

"Better go patch it up, bud," Paul advised. Ian didn't need to be told twice.

Paul heard Leroy chuckling before he saw him sauntering his way. The youth hadn't changed a thing about his attire for the Sunday service. The one thing he did to appease Paul was remaining hatless during the service in the Sanctuary.

"Something funny, Leroy?"

Leroy cocked his head to one side before slowly shaking it. "Wouldn't it just set her off if I told her I got the number one dibs on meeting Miss Michaela Laroche." He let a disdainful puff of air through his lips. "That scrawny, half-boyfriend of hers don't know how to handle her."

Paul leaned against the door jamb. Hilda and Samuel had left to prepare Sunday dinner.

Sarah and Michaela were further up the Foyer in deep conversation. He didn't know where Brennon and Conner were.

He focused on Leroy. "You want to come to the Temples' for dinner?"

Leroy raised his pierced eyebrow. He looked back at Michaela and Sarah. "Why? You afraid to be alone there with her?" he asked, grinning mischievously.

Paul frowned. It was uncanny how close the kid was to the truth. He leaned off the door jamb.

"Never mind. You probably want to go home to your family. You know, I haven't seen them in a while."

Leroy sighed and placed his hands with fingers interlocked on top of his cornrows. He had a sober look in his eyes. "Mom's busy, man. She's tired a lot. I'm trying to get my license so I can, you know, drive Lissa. It's not that far for me, but it might be for her to walk."

Paul looked beyond Leroy after a sudden burst of laughter from the women. "I told you I could get you a ride or come myself." He said, looking again at Leroy.

"Naw—I told you, my mother doesn't want to put anybody out. Since my dad died, she's become super-independent, man. I just don't want to ruffle her feathers. But, she thinks you're cool—nothing against you. She just don't trust church people all that much."

"I know—she's been burned once."

"Real bad."

Paul sighed. He had reached the son, somewhat. He wasn't sure how to reach the mother. She was a very private person, but at least he had some rapport with her. She figured his influence on Leroy was what kept Leroy from pitfalls, particularly fatal ones. "All right, Leroy. Don't forget we're doing basketball Tuesday."

Leroy edged away towards the doors. "Not on your life, man. I love showing you how it really goes down on the court."

Paul laughed and waved him off. He looked towards the women. Sarah was gone and Michaela was watching him. She smiled, then walked briskly towards him.

"Leroy actually came and gave me a hearty welcome. I was surprised. I noticed, during the service while I was talking, he seemed almost defiant." Her eyes were bright and she seemed full of energy.

"That's just Leroy's typical look. It's his wall against the world."

"I'd like to know more about him, sometime. He intrigues me." She had a perceptive look in her eyes. This woman was no loafer; she was definitely here for a challenge, and *she* intrigued him.

* * *

She watched them from the Sanctuary. Rashad had gone out to the rear parking lot after she had finally gotten rid of him. She had slipped through the side door of the Sanctuary to get her music. They hadn't even noticed her; so wrapped up they were in each other. She could see his face and her heart clenched at the focused attention she saw there—for *her*. Yet, wasn't he that way with everyone? No—not quite. This was different; she could tell. She was a woman and she could tell.

Chapter Six

"Hey, Conner-buddy," Paul called gently to the child crawling into the room. At two, Conner should have been toddling, but his autism delayed many things.

"Oh, sorry, guys," Sarah apologized to Paul and Brennon as she breezed into the living room to scoop up Conner. "He's so quick sometimes."

"Don't worry about it," Paul answered over Conner's loud voice of protest. He had a soft spot for Conner. He had a soft spot for all babies, considering he never had the privilege of seeing his.

"So, if she wants to do the mission trip, you should let her. That could be her special project." Brennon was continuing their vein of conversation before Conner's interruption. He was sitting across from Paul on his living room couch looking at a sheet of paper on the glass coffee table. He picked up a pen from the table and ticked a spot on the paper. He looked up at Paul's silence.

Paul leaned back in his seat and glanced around the Hursts' small, two-bedroom bungalow. The early afternoon sun shone through the wide window of the living room, brightening the place. "You know how long it takes to plan a mission trip, Brennon."

"Which is why plans would have to start now for late summer or early fall. Plus, her parents would be very accommodating because their daughter would be heading it. If that doesn't work out, maybe she can help me with the opening of the Fellowship Hall program." Brennon's sandy hair was rumpled and he looked quite relaxed in a T-shirt and track pants.

Paul knew it was Brennon's recoup day after the busyness of church life. It was his day off also, but he felt driven to lay out the agenda for Michaela's stay—today.

Yesterday, after the church service, he had dined at the Temples'. Neither Tristan, nor her family, nor the Hursts had been present. At first, he had felt awkward; but eventually, with the Temples' warm and familiar hospitality and Michaela's engaging personality, he had relaxed and quite enjoyed himself—maybe too much.

Paul sighed. "Okay, I'll talk to her tomorrow. She'll start with me on some visitations at the nursing homes and the hospital."

"Didn't Ethel take George to the hospital for abdominal pain, yesterday?"

"Yeah, he's been having a lot of nausea and vomiting too. He may have some sort of intestinal blockage. I think Ethel's quite anxious, but you know Ethel, she likes to appear all put together no matter what."

Brennon leaned back and put his feet up on the coffee table. "Are they still thinking of purchasing a house in the Seniors Community?"

"Yeah, I told them about Rashad's concerns, but Ethel has made up her mind; and where Ethel leads, George follows."

"It's not really like that, is it?"

Paul grinned. He lifted his legs to join Brennon's. "Naw, he lets her have her way most of the time, but I've seen him put his foot down a few times. Trust me though, if she were not a godly woman, I think he would have his work cut out for him. There would have been constant deadlock in that house, but she respects the biblical mandate of male leadership."

Brennon chuckled. "Sarah reminds me regularly that it's much easier for a wife to respect the husband-leader role, if she feels loved."

Paul was silent for a moment. Brennon's comment had stirred up buried memories. "Yeah, I remember that with Hannah." He gazed into Brennon's eyes, feeling surprisingly detached from his memories. "She actually taught me a lot about really caring for someone."

Brennon pulled his legs off the table and leaned forwards. "Sorry, man."

Paul shook his head. "No, Bren. You have a family; that's a fact. I love Sarah and Conner like my own. Never feel you can't talk about it. We go too far back for that."

"Okay," Brennon said, not looking fully convinced.

"I mean it," Paul emphasized. "Besides, it's been three years." He paused at the sound of Conner screaming. "Now—back to Michaela."

"Are you going to have her lead in worship at all?" Brennon asked. He seemed slightly distracted by Conner's screams.

"Probably, but I think we should keep her away from Karlene's choir."

That got Brennon's attention. He grinned. "You noticed too?" At Paul's nod, he continued. "Listen, what exactly are you going to do about Karlene? I mean, what's up with her? It's quite obvious to everyone she has her sights set on you."

Paul shrugged. "I think everyone's making more of it than they should."

"You do?" Brennon questioned in a tone of disbelief. "You're kidding, right? Come on, I think she sees Michaela as serious competition—"

"Now why would you say that?" Paul asked, cutting him off. He felt tension rising in his gut.

Brennon frowned, then leaned back and shoved his hands through his hair. "Why would I say what—that Michaela is serious competition?"

"Yeah," Paul challenged. He could tell Brennon felt put on the spot and was searching for the right words.

"Well—umm—I don't want to be out of line or anything, especially with her being an intern—but, man, look at her!"

Paul's feet quickly found the floor. He sat forwards with his elbows on his knees and his fingers interlocked. "Look, Bren, what are you doing? I'm not even going there. I don't care what she looks like. I need to be interested in her attributes as an intern, as a potential minister of the gospel. Beyond that... "

Brennon sat with his mouth opened and his face slightly reddened. He rubbed his upper lip intensely before pointing a finger at Paul. "I never mentioned you, Paul. I'm talking about what Karlene thinks."

Silence reigned.

"Paul."

"Look... " Paul started, but didn't know what to say. He could read the unasked questions in Brennon's eyes and tone. She'd only been in Milward for two days and already things were shifting. He watched Brennon nod slowly.

"Okay, I'm going to leave it where it is," Brennon spoke in a nonthreatening tone, "but if there's anything you want to tell me, I'm still your best friend."

Paul pushed himself up and looked down at Brennon. Part of him wanted to set his friend straight, part of him knew everything he would say in order to do that would be a lie. Plus, Brennon would see through it—they had been friends since Bible college. Better to leave it alone. "Bren, I gotta go. You're getting worked up about nothing. I'll see you tomorrow, man."

* * *

Michaela flopped down on the bed in her room at the Temples'. She had finally finished unpacking and felt tremendously relieved. She was not the most organized person but she didn't like to procrastinate when she had something that needed doing.

The Temples were out for the afternoon, and she knew that Tristan was at school and figured Lucy was at work. Will was supposedly out and about with Blinder who was, apparently, the only other person he hung with apart from his drinking buddies. Now what?

She sat up and looked out the doorway. It was so quiet. She was not used to so much quiet, after dorm life. She would welcome Tristan's bubbly company now.

However, Michaela's thoughts soon turned toward God and her heart began to commune with Him, then...

She felt His Presence.

"Oh, Father," she began praying immediately, "how awesome You are. How wonderful, my Light, my Life, my Everything." She slipped into the Haitian Creole she had learned as a child. It made her feel closer to her parents and their work among the Haitian earthquake orphans. She found herself on her knees; her lips and her heart still communing with her Maker, her Saviour.

After her time of prayer, Michaela felt renewed and more focused. "Lord, I don't know what I'd do without you. You're the only One who is with me in every situation, and You're available at any moment. Thank you, thank you so much."

She stood up, remembering the phone call she had received earlier. It had been the Assistant Pastor from another Church she had been interested in interning at. After learning about her present situation, the Pastor had asked her to consider a possible placement with them after her internship. She had been reluctant to make a commitment. What if BCC offered her a position? In fact, over breakfast, Hilda had suggested they would have welcomed another pastor if Paul had wanted.

"I think that young man buries himself in church work too much," Hilda had declared, after taking a sip of coffee. "If he had a family, he would have brought in another pastor by now."

Of course, Michaela didn't know if she would even accept if offered a position, and that was a big *if.* She couldn't help but notice that Paul seemed uncomfortable around her. Maybe it was her outspokenness. It was a hard trait to curb. Authority usually didn't like that; and, presently, he was her authority.

As for her own sense of him: she hadn't seriously thought about it. After all, she'd just met him and needed to get to know him. So what if she was initially attracted to him? Number one—that could change after knowing him better; two—he was a widower probably still not recovered; three—he was the Minister and she the Intern. Besides, he didn't exactly fit into her agenda of becoming a missionary. It was the mission field that had taken his wife. He most likely never wanted to see the backside of one again. There, that was settled!

Just as Michaela reached the doorway, feeling rather contented with the conclusion on her train of thought, she heard yelling from downstairs. Was she not alone in the house?

* * *

Paul's thoughts were focused on the last topic of his conversation with Brennon, as he drove from the south side of Milward away from the Hursts' place. Ten minutes later, he was close to the Temples' neighbourhood, not far from the Church and parsonage. He found himself turning onto their street, without really knowing why. The Temples' house had a standing-order, open-door policy for him, but he rarely visited on Mondays. Mondays he spent catching up on personal things or visiting his mother. Discussing Michaela's duties was church business and that's how it should have stayed.

Yet, here he was heading towards the Temples' house.

* * *

The noise was getting louder, and Michaela could tell the commotion was moving from the basement up to the main floor. She paused in the hall outside of her bedroom which was closest to the stairway. Her body tensed involuntarily when she heard a crash that literally shook the house. The last straw was the sound of a woman's cry.

Lucy!? Michaela took to the stairs.

"It has to stop, Will! I can't take anymore!"

Michaela reached the foyer just as Lucy let loose another torrent of words. Lucy was standing at the top of the basement stairs, five feet left of the front door.

"T-Tristan needs better than this—" Lucy stopped, jerking around at the sight of Michaela. She had her handbag in one hand and seemed dressed to go out, but her eyes were red and teary. Her other hand came up to her mouth. "Oh, Michaela, I-I didn't know you were here. I thought you had gone out with my parents."

Michaela stood were she was, feeling uncomfortable, but wanting to help. "Lucy, are you okay?" The question didn't get answered. A flood of cursing came up from the basement.

Lucy stifled a sob, then rushed past Michaela to the front door. She yanked the door opened, but then stopped to look at Michaela. She closed the door. "I-I can't leave you in here alone with him." She was shaking.

"It's never good enough anymore! Nothing's ever good—" Will froze at the top of the stairs after barrelling up unsteadily. He glared at Michaela, then at Lucy. For a moment, he seemed undecided. Suddenly, he veered right and headed for the kitchen. The backyard patio door slammed.

Michaela looked at Lucy.

"I'm so sorry," Lucy whispered. Her skin was flushed and sadness burdened her eyes.

"I'm so sorry," she repeated. "I thought you were out. I don't know what possessed my parents to bring you here. If I had known, I would have told them no, but I didn't."

"Don't worry about me, Lucy," Michaela said softly. She gently touched Lucy's arms. "Sarah explained about Will. Is he going to be okay?"

Lucy closed her eyes briefly. "I thought he was doing better. In fact, he just started acting up again just before you came. My parents don't even know everything that's going on. I keep a lot from them." She slipped away from Michaela's touch, moving towards the kitchen. Michaela followed her through the neatly organized kitchen to a small sunroom leading to the backyard. Her gaze searched the long, narrow yard with its white gazebo and few mature trees. There was no sign of Will.

"Where is he?" Michaela asked.

Lucy shrugged as she returned to the kitchen and lowered herself wearily on a white, wooden chair. She plopped her handbag on the kitchen table. "Sometimes he just disappears and nobody knows where he is. He usually comes back calmer, though." She raked her fingers through her hair. She was no longer shaking. "I'm just having a harder time with it today. I've had some very trying cases at work and I just feel overwhelmed with the unfairness of life." Suddenly, she looked at her watch. "Oh, gosh, I have to go."

Michaela trailed her out to the foyer. "Is there anything I can do?"

Lucy smiled, her eyes lighting up a little. She reached over and hugged Michaela. "Sometime, I'd like to sit and talk with you."

After Lucy left, Michaela wandered around the main floor for awhile, trying to process all she had witnessed. She knew enough about PTSD to realize the hardships it presented. Her heart went out to Lucy and her entire family. She paused in the sunroom to utter a prayer for the McCree and Temple families; praying for God's protection and mercy. She had just finished when she heard someone entering the front hall. They weren't being very quiet about it.

Michaela had just reached the hall from the kitchen when she saw Will heading for the basement. She quietly moved across the tiled floor towards the opened doorway and gasped at what she was hearing. He was grunting and cursing and banging around. Then she heard the most curious thing. He sounded like he was yelling at someone, desperately.

"Get down, Garret! Get down! This is no time for heroics!" Then he came running up the stairs, straight at Michaela. He suddenly stopped with four steps to go. He was staring at her, eyes wide and strange as if he wasn't seeing her, but something else.

Michaela felt her heart thudding as she gauged how much time she had to the front door, which had been left opened, before Will finished his ascent. This man did not look sane right now.

Even through the dimness of the basement stairway light, Will's eyes looked dangerously strange. Michaela felt, like an insect, pinned by his gaze to Bristol board.

"Jesus," she uttered the single word of prayer, as he took a step up. She read the determination in his eyes that she was the enemy to be exterminated! The fight-or-flight adrenaline coursed through her veins, and flight was the clear choice.

However, Will suddenly gasped loudly, his eyes bugging, then he stumbled backwards and fell down the stairs.

Michaela was stunned! She moved to peer down at the floor below where he lay still. *Dear God, what's happened!?* Her heart was still thudding in her ears as she tried to take stock. She wanted to go down and help him, but she wasn't sure if he would revive in the same state.

* * *

As Paul pulled into the Temples' driveway, he noticed the front door of the house standing wide opened. There were no cars in the driveway, but Michaela's was parked on the street. Once out of his car, he pocketed his keys and stood looking around. He didn't see anyone. The driveway was sloped upward; the houses on this side of the street were on higher ground. He started towards the front door, and almost turned back, remembering the list of Michaela's duties still on the passenger seat. He decided to see if anyone was home, first.

He jogged up the old concrete steps and grabbed hold of the door. He stuck his head inside and was about to announce his presence, but the words stuck in his throat. Michaela was standing just inside the doorway, looking as if she had just seen a ghost.

Paul entered the house and shut the door behind him. "Michaela?"

She laughed shakily, taking a deep breath. "Umm," she murmured, raising a hand towards the basement doorway before looking at him, "Will fell down the stairs. I think he's out cold. I was just about to call 911."

Paul rushed past her and looked down to see Will struggling to sit up. "He's getting up." Paul said over his shoulder as he quickly stomped down the stairs. "Will, are you okay?" Paul stooped down to give assistance. "Sit for a second, Will. Let's see if you're okay."

Will groaned. He put one hand up to the back of his head. "I think I hit my head," he said, wincing.

Paul braced against Will's back with one leg and gently felt through the mop of black hair.

There was a slight bump. "Yes, you did. What happened?" Will didn't seem drunk, and Paul couldn't smell any alcohol on him.

Paul felt Will's weight shift off his leg as Will started to answer him, but then he felt Will stiffen at the sight of Michaela coming slowly down the stairs.

"There were two guys with her!" Will said in a ragged, breathless voice. "T-there were two huge guys with her."

Paul frowned and looked at Michaela who had stopped on the stairway. "Did somebody shove him down, Michaela? What's he talking about?"

Half an hour later, Paul felt confident Will would be okay. He had left him lying on the basement living room couch and had come upstairs to find Michaela. He hadn't been able to make sense of Will's "vision" of the men. Michaela hadn't seen them. He needed to talk with Samuel and Lucy. It was obvious from Michaela's description of her episode with Will that Will was once again experiencing combat scenes that were very real to him.

Michaela was curled up on the Temples' living room couch. When she saw him, she sat up slowly, resting her feet on the carpeted floor. "I think he saw angels," she announced without any warning. Her gaze was intent on his.

A small, wooden coffee table separated them, as Paul stood looking down at her. Her hair was rolled in a fluffy bun on top of her head, accentuating her high cheek bones, and she was wearing a pale, loose-fitting, workout suit. Her caramel skin glowed with good health.

His earlier concern for her only made his attraction to her more difficult to ignore.

"He was delusional," Paul offered. He watched her eyes narrow slightly. She wasn't buying it. "I'm just glad you're okay. I need to talk to his family about this. It could have ended differently." He watched her run her hands up and down her arms. It was obvious she had been shaken.

"Thank you. I'm glad you came." She stood up to face him across the coffee table. "I was just wondering how I would have explained angels to paramedics."

Paul shook his head slowly, feeling the essence of her pulling at him. "You still haven't convinced me."

She smiled.

He smiled back. "But, as a minister, I guess I have to be more open to believe they could have been angels."

Chapter Seven

Leroy stayed hidden in the shadow of one of the portable toilets on the development site. A mature maple tree nearby helped his secrecy, but nothing could curb the rank smell stagnant in the air. It was like the construction crew had been doing their business behind the facilities instead of inside them.

He was watching Karlene Benedict. He knew she worked in the Milward Seniors Community Sales Centre and that she had a right to be on the property, but something wasn't sitting right with him. He had seen her there at odd hours when he knew the Centre was closed. In fact, Blinder had confirmed the same thing, and Blinder noticed a lot of things as he wandered around town. Plus, if that Rashad dude and Pastor Paul thought the contractor was a crook, why was Karlene working for him? Of course, a job was a job, and these days, with the high unemployment rates, people had to hang on to what they had.

He pulled his team-logo cap further down over his forehead as he watched Karlene flirting with one of the Centre's sales representatives, on the covered front porch of the newly built house used as a sales centre. He could hear her high-pitched voice float through the warm, summer air. He swatted at a mosquito just about to play vampire on his forearm, before slipping from his hiding place, and loping across the property to the roadway. Tomorrow was another day.

After making his way across the road, he passed Metro's Gas Bar. He was glad for the longer daylight, now that summer had started and school was almost out. He'd never admit it to anyone, but he loved going to the Youth Group at BCC. Now he loved it even more with Michaela Laroche assisting. There was just something about her. He didn't think he had a crush on her or anything—he better not! He could tell she was going to be Pastor Paul's girl. Maybe they didn't know it yet, but he could tell. No, she was more like a big sister. She was real classy and she made him feel good about himself—always complimenting him, always including him. Even the Youth Group kids who kind of avoided him were warming up to him because Michaela treated him—well—special.

He kept up his swagger along the side of the road, even when people stared suspiciously at him as they passed by in their vehicles. Let them stare. There were people in this town who knew him and didn't judge him by his appearance.

He turned off the main road to take a shortcut through a subdivision. His mother had warned him that the first thing people had to go by in knowing someone was their appearance. He didn't care! He liked his "bad-boy" look. The world needed to know he was tough and he could take care of his mother, his little sister and himself.

He kept his head high as a middle-aged woman, with a child on a tricycle, tried to subtly direct the child across to the other side of the street, when she saw him coming. Let people think what they wanted. Yet, inside, sometimes it hurt. However, his mind, from long practice, dismissed her as he kept moving on.

* * *

Michaela had just finished setting up for the Youth games night. She gently rolled her shoulders backwards to release a slight kink in her muscles. Her gaze wandered up to the row of windows looking down into the Gymnasium from the Fellowship Hall upstairs. She could only see parts of the ceiling of the Fellowship Hall, but knew someone was probably working there because all the lights were turned on.

Her gaze shifted when she noticed Tristan crossing the Gym floor towards her. She had been very quiet while helping Michaela set up, not her usual bubbly self. Michaela had wondered if she and Ian had had an argument. In the month since she had arrived, Michaela had noticed that Ian's early arrival to Youth Group usually coincided with Tristan's. He wasn't early today.

Tristan plopped down on the wooden chair Michaela had just finished positioning for a game. Her hair was pulled high in a ponytail and her slightly freckled complexion was free of makeup. She looked twelve instead of sixteen, but her eyes were troubled.

"Sometimes, I hate being a Christian!"

Michaela felt her breath catch slightly. Tristan's statement was said almost mournfully. In fact, her blue eyes were very moist. Michaela pulled another chair over and sat facing Tristan. "That's a pretty strong statement coming from someone who I know loves the Lord a great deal."

A tear ran down Tristan's left cheek. She looked at Michaela and sniffled. "I do love Jesus, but I can't stand the pressure sometimes, you know, to conform."

Michaela touched the sleeve of Tristan's light-weight hoodie. "You want to talk about it?" The Gym's yellow, block walls seemed to loom with just the two of them sitting in the centre of the room. Yet, Michaela wanted to take this opportunity while they were alone.

Tristan sighed. "Some of the girls at school, even the Christian ones, are putting me down because I refuse to see a vampire movie with them." She wiped her tear away. "I mean, I know it's supposedly the coolest thing out now; but, especially after Pastor Paul's sermons, I made a decision to stay away from that kind of stuff. They say it's just entertainment and that I'm taking it way too seriously."

"So, are you staying away from it because you think Pastor Paul wants you to or because you actually believe what he says is true?"

A slight frown wrinkled Tristan's forehead, but her gaze was certain. "Oh, I believe it all right. You wouldn't believe some of the stuff the kids at school get into. Anything to do with the supernatural... "

"Except for Christ," Michaela supplied.

"Yeah," Tristan agreed, no longer looking quite so mournful. "But, I think they're hungry for Him. They just don't know it."

Tristan's words brought joy to Michaela's heart. "You're so right, and we are the only Jesus some of these kids will ever see. We have to be His hands extended wherever He places us, even in school."

Tristan giggled, then gave Michaela an impulsive hug. "I wish I could be more like you."

Michaela smiled and shrugged. "Why do you say that?"

"I don't know. You just know what to do, what to say. You'd set those kids straight."

"But, it's not about setting them straight," Michaela said, gently squeezing Tristan's arm. "It's about loving them into the Kingdom. They may never set foot in a Church, but God the Holy Spirit is here in the world, tugging at their hearts. He also chooses to work through us to reach them. The real

Church isn't a building; it's the believers who, collectively, are called the Church. God's Spirit, or the Holy Spirit, is in us so we can be empowered to be effective."

Footsteps brought both their attentions to the opened doors of the Gym. It was Leroy. He paused uncertainly in the doorway.

"Hi, Leroy," Michaela greeted him cheerfully. She patted Tristan's shoulder as she rose.

"Sorry if I'm interrupting," Leroy said, hands thrust deep in his jeans pockets. His pants were so low, loose and baggy, it almost looked as if the weight of his hands could send them on a downward spiral. Michaela had faith that if that should happen, at least his black T-shirt was long enough. She smiled at the thought.

"No problem, Leroy. Tristan and I just finished having a little chit-chat. How are you doing? It's good to see you."

Leroy shrugged nonchalantly. "Doing all right?" He glanced at Tristan who had joined Michaela to stand in front of him.

"Hey, Leroy. I was just venting to Michaela about peer pressure and stuff."

Leroy smiled lopsidedly. "Yeah, there's lots of that all right. Anybody bugging you?"

Tristan pulled the sleeves of her hoodie over her hands. "Just some kids wanting me to watch stuff I don't want to—No big deal."

Leroy gazed at her intently, chewing gum slowly. "Well, they can chirp you all they want, but if you cave in for the small stuff, after a while... "

"It'll be the big stuff too," Tristan finished, without missing a beat. They smiled at each other.

"What's going on? What are you guys talking about?" Ian had walked in behind Leroy. He stepped around Leroy and stood between him and Tristan. He didn't seem too happy, but his expression cleared a little when he noticed Michaela. "Hi," he directed at her.

"How are you doing, Ian? I was expecting you here earlier with Tristan," Michaela said, smiling. She was trying to lighten the tension that had come with Ian.

"Yeah, I would have, but I just got a summer job, so I couldn't get away earlier. So what were you guys talking about?" He asked, looking first at Tristan, then at Leroy. Leroy hung his head, refusing to acknowledge Ian.

"Nothing, Ian—just peer pressure. In fact, you weren't very helpful today at school. I could have used your support."

Ian looked dumbfounded. He extended a hand, palm up, to Tristan. "Look, Tristan. I was meaning to talk about it later, but I had to go to work and you wouldn't talk on the phone."

"Ian, you made it perfectly clear you thought I should go see *Moon Blood* with the rest. You wanted to go yourself." Tristan's calm demeanour had disappeared.

"I-I didn't really want to go. I just didn't see what the big fuss was about."

"You should stand up for your friends, dude."

Michaela felt her eyes close briefly at Leroy's judgement. She had observed that, while Leroy and Tristan seemed to get along, he and Ian stayed out of each other's way. The "gangster" and the "prep" did not mesh. She watched Ian's face contort and knew this was not going to be good.

"Hey, who asked you?" Ian was clearly getting hot under the collar.

"Don't need to be asked. It's my opinion." Leroy seemed calm, but there was a vein throbbing at the side of his neck and his eyes had narrowed considerably.

Ian turned his back on the women to face Leroy. "So, now you're gonna tell us right from wrong, give me a break! I mean, look at you!"

"Okay, that's enough!" Michaela pronounced, standing between them. She had read the dangerous glint in Leroy's dark eyes and Ian didn't seem to realize he was in over his head where Leroy was concerned. The situation would only escalate.

"I'm not afraid of him, Michaela." Ian seemed bent on a destructive path. His mouth was set in a grim line and he was glaring at Leroy who stood his ground.

"Guys, you better listen to Michaela," Tristan warned, sounding worried.

"Is everything okay?" The sound of Paul's deep voice completely broke the spell. Ian stepped back as Paul walked into the Gym. He was dressed in a checkered shirt with the sleeves rolled up, black jeans and runners.

Both boys remained quiet. Michaela stepped from between them. While it was good that he had come, she wasn't so sure it stood well in her favour.

"Umm," Tristan began, but didn't finish.

"Michaela, could I see you for a moment?"

"Sure," she said, stepping away from the youth towards the doorway.

"Guys, keep it cool in here," Paul commanded as he followed Michaela out.

*   *   *

Okay, so he felt bad because of the worried look on her face, but what was she doing standing between two hot-headed, teenage boys? Granted, she was physically fit and only a few inches shorter than Leroy; and Ian, the taller boy, was a bean pole. However, the obvious tension between the boys had been like a ready-to-explode powder keg held back for too long.

They faced each other just outside of the Gym. "So, what happened?" He asked.

"I know what you're thinking," she began, "but I knew what I was doing."

"Just tell me what happened," Paul insisted. Working with her for over a month now had made him wise to her creative ability to gear a conversation in her own direction.

She took a deep breath, and then explained the situation.

"Brennon is just upstairs, you could have sent Tristan for him," Paul said, after she had finished.

"I didn't feel I needed to at the time," she responded adamantly. Her eyes held a determined look.

Paul didn't feel like arguing with her. In fact, he could hear the general commotion of kids coming down the stairs. He decided to wrap it up and get back to his work in the Fellowship Hall. "Just promise me you'll not try to handle something like that alone again. It would have been different if one of the other male youths had to been there to help out."

She was silent, her gaze directed somewhere over his right shoulder. He felt like shaking her.

"Michaela?"

She blinked rapidly. "I understand," she responded.

Paul almost hadn't heard her above the noise of the gathering masses. He let her go when they started calling out to her. He wasn't sure how he felt about the sensation in his chest at the sight of her being swallowed up by the crowd of youthful, enthusiastic energy.

Paul stood for a moment in the hall until he glimpsed Leroy poking his head around the gym doorway. He smiled at the youth, noticing his solemn demeanour. "So, you gonna stay with the rest or come upstairs and help me?"

Leroy grinned and moved towards him.

* * *

"So, why does she work for him?" Leroy asked almost an hour later.

Paul glanced over at Leroy who was assisting him with the painstaking job of applying drywall compound to the Fellowship Hall unfinished walls. Paul had been keeping a watchful eye on him, ensuring that the job was being done right. The kid was pretty good at it, considering it was the kind of work which required patience.

"Why does who work for whom?" Paul asked as he used his tool to remove some excess putty from the wall.

"Cat Woman—for Falconer?"

Paul sighed, but kept his nose facing the wall. "Leroy, if you're going to keep referring to people by those kinds of names, at least, do it outside the Church. One of these days someone's going to hear and be downright offended."

"I can't think of a better name for her," Leroy said, smirking.

Paul ignored the comment. "Karlene is just doing her job as a real estate agent—work she enjoys. It's her choice."

"Yeah—to work for the devil."

Paul turned to look at Leroy who had an intense expression on his face. His dark eyebrows almost connected as he frowned at Paul's silence.

"It's true. It's all around town. Falconer is a crook, paying big money to keep everything hush, hush. But, not everybody's buying into it. It's all gonna come down on him sooner or later."

Paul set his tool down on the edge of the pail between them. "You need to stay off that property, Leroy. No matter what you think, I want you to stay away from there."

"Ain't planning on getting caught."

"Leroy—"

"Well, well, well, look at our good Pastor getting his hands dirty, as usual." They both turned to see Karlene sail through the wide entrance of the Fellowship Hall. She wore her designer T-shirt and jeans like a second skin. Her dark, long hair was unbound, and floating from her was a hint of fragrance mixed with the scent of drywall putty. She was all smiles.

"Hello, Karlene," Paul acknowledged as he sent Leroy a warning look, before picking up his putty tool.

Karlene stood a few feet from Paul, hands on her hips, gazing around the nearly-finished Fellowship Hall. She glanced briefly at Leroy before fixing her amber gaze on Paul. "I saw Brennon working away in his Office. So, who's holding the fort tonight?"

Paul looked over at her briefly, but continued to work as he answered her question. "Michaela is on her own tonight. Conner is sick, so Sarah stayed home. Brennon's working on Sunday's sermon."

"So, no Youth for you tonight?" she directed at Leroy.

"Nope," Leroy responded shortly. He kept working at a steady pace.

"That's a shame. I'm sure they're having lots of fun." She seemed to wait for Leroy's response, but then focused on Paul when none was forthcoming. "I don't know why you insist on working in here so much when it's already under control—" She paused for a moment, then exclaimed sweetly, "Whoops!" the same moment Paul felt a glob of putty moisten his left cheek.

Karlene giggled girlishly. She reached up to gently wipe along his cheek with her fingers. "Can't have anything covering that gorgeous dimple."

Paul stepped back as she reached again with her other hand. "I got it, Karlene," he said. He wiped at his cheek. Next thing he knew, she was closer to him with tissue in hand. Her heady perfume filled his nostrils.

"Here, you're missing the spot, silly," she said, laughing lightly. She reached again and wiped more firmly with the tissue. "There," she pronounced as if she had just conquered the world. "You just needed a woman's touch."

Paul knew she was flirting with him; it was actually more that that—she was coming on to him. He picked up the pail of putty and moved so Leroy was between them.

"Paul."

All heads turned towards the doorway. Michaela was standing there.

"Could I see you for just a moment?"

"Keep it up, Leroy. I'll be right back." He grabbed a rag from the unfinished floor and wiped his hands, and then, without another word, headed in Michaela's direction. He was very aware of the fact that he was hoping she hadn't witnessed Karlene's unwanted attention to him. Somehow, it mattered a great deal that she not get the wrong idea about him and Karlene Benedict.

* * *

How easily he could turn away from her at just a whimper from the intern. Karlene stood where Paul had left her, suddenly oblivious to Leroy's presence, as she zeroed in on the two conversing quietly in the dim Foyer just outside of the Fellowship Hall doorway. She noticed how he leaned his tall frame down slightly to catch Michaela's every word. There was no need for him to stand so close to her, or for her to hold him with her dark gaze so securely. She grudgingly admitted they made a striking couple, but she and he would be much more striking. They were meant to be. She had waited long enough for his mourning to be completed; but, now, it looked as if this wolf in sheep's clothing was staking a claim on what was hers. Surely God knew how she had cultivated patience—one of the Fruit of the Spirit—in allowing Paul time and space to heal. Perhaps God had allowed Michaela's coming to show that Paul was ready to move on and she had been remiss to notice. The gloves would have to come off now. She would start to fight for what belonged to her.

* * *

Leroy couldn't believe his eyes. It was as if Karlene had forgotten he was in the room. He couldn't see her face, as her back was to him; but he could see the tension in her shoulders and the clenching and unclenching of her hands. He'd have to be a fool not to notice her strong opposition to Pastor Paul and Michaela being together. This would be one more thing he needed to keep an eye on. Pastor Paul had saved his life once, he wasn't about to see him get hurt by some conniving she-cat.

Chapter Eight

Michaela left the Conference Room where she had been working on a youth message and proceeded down the hall towards the Foyer. She paused uncertainly at the sight and sound that greeted her. Just outside the Front Office doorway, Paul was being hugged by a blonde woman, while an elderly lady in a wheelchair and another blonde woman looked on.

What was it about him that women couldn't keep their hands off him? Women hugging him, wiping his face... . She stopped when she realized where her thoughts were going. Good grief, was she jealous?

"Michaela." Hilda intercepted Michaela as she started pass the Sanctuary's side door. There was a wide smile on her face as she pulled Michaela aside. "Paul's mother and sisters are here. Come, I'll introduce you."

Michaela held back. "Hilda, I don't want to interrupt. I was actually just going out to lunch." For some reason, the homey scene she was witnessing filled her with a longing she couldn't quite interpret. Also, she had forgotten that Paul had been adopted into a White family and here she had been thinking badly about a sister's hug.

"But, honey, they want to meet you," Hilda insisted, pulling her along by the arm.

Michaela reluctantly allowed herself to be coerced, groaning inwardly. Paul and his family were all looking in their direction, as she and Hilda approached.

"Paul, I'll let you make the introductions," Hilda said, letting go of Michaela's arm. She seemed quite pleased with herself.

Paul stepped closer to his mother. "Mom, this is our intern, Michaela Laroche. Michaela, this is my mother, Eleanor Rayner; and my sisters Christy Bannon and Cassandra."

"That's Cassie," corrected the sister Paul had been hugging. The sisters were identical twins.

Michaela reached down to gently shake the hand of the white-haired lady in the wheelchair. "It's very nice to meet you, Mrs. Rayner." Eleanor's hand was small and unsteady.

"Hello, Michaela. We've heard so many good things about you."

Because of her noticeable frailness, the strength of Eleanor's voice surprised Michaela. There was nothing frail about that voice. Her pale blue eyes appeared clear and sharp as she intently studied Michaela. She smiled, as if please with what she saw. "It's very nice to finally meet you."

"Thank you," Michaela responded, smiling in turn. She greeted Cassie and Christy. Cassie had bright facial make-up, shoulder-length hair and was dressed in a colourful blouse with white capri pants and matching sandals. Christy was more casual in an aquamarine sundress and flip-flops. Her blonde hair was swept back in a ponytail. Both women seemed very friendly.

"Paul has been a little delinquent in visiting lately, so we decided to come see what was keeping him so bound to Milward," Christy remarked, smiling mischievously. Michaela felt even more uncomfortable. Did they think she was the cause?

"He does have a lot on his plate, Christy. We can't always expect him to drive an hour every week or two, as if we didn't have lives of our own," Eleanor chided gently. Everyone laughed, obviously not taking the comments as seriously as Michaela. Michaela felt herself relaxing.

"Well, I—for one—think this young man could do with some more time off," Hilda stated. "Eleanor, I've told you before, he thinks there are twenty-five hours in a day." She patted Eleanor's hand, and then asked Paul, "Shall I get some coffee, or will you all go to the parsonage?"

"Paul, why don't you finish up here and we'll meet you at the parsonage when you're through," Eleanor said, reaching a shaking hand out to grasp his. "We will manage until then, won't we, girls?"

"That sounds fine, Mom," Christy answered for herself and Cassie.

"Well, Michaela was just going out for lunch. Would you like to join them, Michaela?"

Michaela could have throttled Hilda. What was she doing? "Ah, well—"

"That's a great idea," Paul cut in. He was looking searchingly at Michaela. "That's if you don't have other plans."

Michaela felt cornered. "I don't want to impose... "

"It's no imposition," he assured her, smiling his dimpled smile. He addressed his family, "Right?"

Of course, everyone agreed.

* * *

After helping his sisters with assisting his mother into Christy's red minivan, Paul stood back to watch the rest board the vehicle. Even though his mother could walk, she experienced so much unsteadiness that it was easier for her to use a wheelchair. The Parkinson's was worsening. He felt guilt wash over him that he hadn't visited as frequently as usual. As if reading his mind, his mother smiled at him from the passenger seat.

"I can tell you're worrying about something, so stop. We'll see you soon," she said.

"Not worrying," he denied, laughing softly.

"Liar," his mother accused, still smiling.

Paul looked past his mother at Christy, "Help yourselves to whatever."

"Don't worry, we will." Cassie answered boldly from the middle seat. "Won't we, Michaela?" Paul didn't hear an answer from Michaela, just her resulting laughter.

As he watched the minivan drive the short distance to the parsonage, he couldn't help his feeling of contentment at his family's warmth toward Michaela. He glanced around, wishing he could stay out and enjoy the warm, sunny weather. It seemed a long time since he had felt that he could just relax and leisure a day away.

After a bone-cracking stretch, Paul stood observing the residential areas separated by the wide spread of fenced church property. The neatly divided plots of land with their mature trees and comfortable homes looked peaceful. After today, those yards would be busy with children on summer break from school.

What would it be like to once again have a home with the anticipation of a family? That anticipation had died with Hannah. Yet, things were changing. He could feel himself awakening to the possibility of life with someone again.

He decided to return to the Church and quickly wrap up some work so he could join his family, but he was distracted by a black sports car pulling up to stop a few feet from him under the canopy. He suddenly had a sense of forcboding.

Dennis Falconer hauled his large frame out of the car and stood examining Paul through dark sunglasses. He slowly pulled the glasses off with a large, beefy hand before speaking. "So, Stephen Rayner's adopted son refuses to advertise Milward Seniors Community in his Church." He attempted a crooked smile that didn't even come close to affecting the sinister look in his eyes. Letting one hand hang over the opened door of his car, he continued in a gravelly voice: "I've been asking myself, is it because Paul Stephen Rayner opposes my building development or is it because of his father?"

Paul took a deep breath, mentally sending up a quick prayer for wisdom. The deepest hatred he had ever felt, anytime in his life, had been toward this man. It was a hatred that he'd had to surrender to the Lord Almighty, not knowing what to do with it. This man who had been, at one time, a BCC member and who had given his father untold grief because of his schemes and lies, even in the house of God. If it hadn't been for the unfailing love of his parents for each other, his parents' ministry together could possibly have met an untimely end.

"Falconer, I wonder at the wisdom of you coming here. It's a big community with a lot of Churches, for one to be so important," Paul responded, both hands on his hips. He could feel the tension in his body as surely as he could feel the evil emanating from the man facing him.

Falconer smirked, causing the excess flesh of his face to bulge. His greying hair was slicked back from his receding hairline and the elaborate ring on his right hand sparkled in the sunlight. "Yes, but you underestimate the weight of your decision in the entire church community. Word has gotten around. So, I need to know what the holdup is."

"And the Churches have a lot of senior members," Paul added, meaningfully.

Falconer remained silent, but his steel grey eyes narrowed. "You shouldn't let your personal prejudices ruin opportunity for others, Paul."

"I've given those personal prejudices over to the Lord Jesus, Falconer. The present concerns I have are well founded. Until proven otherwise, I cannot in good conscience support your project in this Church body."

"It's a community project! It's not just mine!" Falconer's voice had risen, almost sounding like a growl. He seemed to realize it and went down a pitch. "People have wanted this for a long time. You know that."

Paul felt his patience running thin. He turned to go. "These people are mostly elderly. They want security and reliability in their homes." He started towards the church doors, but Falconer spoke forcefully.

"Are you the one who's been spreading lies to the Mayor?"

Paul stopped in his tracks, turning only his head towards his nemesis. "I wouldn't call them lies—but no, it wasn't me." Paul made to leave again, but another car joined them on the other side of the canopy. It was Samuel.

Falconer quickly returned to his car, but he sent parting words before slamming the door shut. "Paul Rayner, if you know what's good for you, you'll not let history repeat itself." The sports car revved and backed out with reckless speed from under the canopy, just as Samuel exited his vehicle.

"What the blazes was he doing here?" Samuel thundered, glaring at the disappearing car. He almost tripped over the curb bordering the canopied area, as he rushed over to Paul, huffing and puffing.

Paul shook his head slowly and sighed deeply. "That man's like hell; never satisfied until he's engulfed everything he touches. What do you think he wanted? He wants to force our support for the Seniors Community. And I can't believe it, Sam, but he threatened to repeat history!"

* * *

Michaela was pleasantly surprised at how easily she was working with Paul's family in the parsonage kitchen. They had all agreed to surprise him with an elaborate lunch. It wasn't hard. Obviously, someone was keeping his fridge and freezer fairly healthy. None of the women believed it was Paul.

Michaela discovered that Cassie was the mischievous one and Christy, married with three children, was the responsible one. Eleanor had insisted on being called by her first name, and Michaela found her very restful to be around. Eleanor sat at the kitchen island doing her share while quietly directing Michaela and her daughters. They ended up preparing tomato soup, garnished with shredded cheese and parsley; toasted bacon and tomato sandwiches; and a spinach garden salad. Cassie insisted on concocting her own lemonade.

The parsonage kitchen was easy to work in with its large, dark cupboards and pantry; wide work island; and grey, ceramic tiled floor. The appliances were surprisingly new and all in steel grey. Michaela had never been this far into the parsonage. She had only stopped in a couple of times, with Hilda, to make deliveries. She had gotten used to some of the church ladies dropping off meals and baked goods at the Church all hours of the day. No doubt about it, Paul was well taken care of.

As Paul's family shared about themselves and asked her about herself, Michaela could see how Paul would have grown up in this family feeling totally accepted. The women spoke so fondly and adoringly of him. She didn't doubt that they had also been very protective. His sisters were older than him by five years, and she could envision two little blonde five-year-olds completely doting over their new, little brown-skinned baby brother.

"At one point when Paul was about ten," Cassie reminisced, "he told me, in secret, that he wanted some Black friends so he could learn how to be Black. Of course, there weren't many Black people in Milward at the time, so it was pretty difficult for him. Our father used to take him on trips to Toronto regularly where, through contacts with some of my parents' friends, Paul actually connected with some Black families. When he was older, he moved to Toronto for university. He hardly came home. It just about broke Mom's heart, but she never pressured him. She always insisted he needed time and space. She was right. Eventually, he decided he actually hated living in such a big city."

"I thought Paul went to Bible college," Michaela commented.

"Oh, he did," Christy informed her. "That was after a year of psychology, after he decided to stop fighting God's call to enter the ministry."

"Remember when he had that crush on Lucy?" Cassie asked.

Michaela could feel her eyebrows rise.

"Oh, that was nothing but puppy love," Christy said, fluffing it off. "He was twelve and she was nineteen."

"And a year later she got married, unexpectedly, and broke his heart," Cassie said with an unladylike snort. She was setting the table in the big dining room off from the kitchen, but she seemed to be on a roll as she continued:

"And remember when he discovered that adoption laws had changed and he could actually find out about his biological parents?" Cassie paused to look at Michaela. "There was no rest for the weary that year. He found out his mother was Latino and African American but had died when he was a baby."

"Sadly, from a drug overdose," Christy added. "Paul wanted to go live in the Latino-American community, but our father drew the line at him leaving Canada. Paul couldn't do it without Dad's financial backing."

"I think he hated Dad that year," Cassie said, entering the kitchen.

"I don't think he hated your father. I think he was angry for a while." Eleanor had a faraway look in her eyes. "He eventually reconciled to the fact that he couldn't visit every country of his heritage after finding out his father was Black Jamaican-Canadian."

"But, he connected with his biological father, didn't he?" Michaela was sitting at the island beside Eleanor after she had finished making the sandwiches. They were heaped high on a platter in front of her. Cassie removed them to the dining room table, as Eleanor answered Michaela's question.

"Yes, they have what you would call a long-distance relationship. They've met maybe twice, but Paul calls him once in awhile."

The sound of a telephone ringing brought a halt to any further conversation. They all looked at the wall phone by the kitchen doorway.

"I guess I should answer it," Michaela said, uncertainly.

"It could be Paul," Eleanor said.

Michaela reached for the phone. "Hello, Bethel Community Church parsonage." There was silence on the other end. "Hello?" The dial tone greeted her. She looked at the phone, puzzled. "Maybe it was the wrong number."

Christy sat on the other side of her mother. "Maybe we should give Paul a call before everything gets cold." Everyone looked at Michaela expectantly. She had just hung up the phone.

Unexpectedly, the phone rang again, causing Michaela to startle and the other women to laugh. Michaela grinned, reaching for the phone again. It was Paul. She felt her heart thud at the sound of his voice. "Did you just call before now?" she asked him, willing herself to be at ease.

"No," he responded, drawing the "no" out. "Why?"

"We just had a call that was disconnected, so I wondered if it had been you trying to reach us."

"Oh. Well, I'll be there soon, but could you do me a favour?"

"Sure."

"Will you go into the office there—it's at the end of the hall—and let me know if there's a dark green folder on the desk? I don't want to search for it here if it's there."

"Sure," she was aware of the quietness of the others as they appeared to be listening. "I think everyone is wondering if you'll be here soon."

He laughed, causing warmth to flow through her. "Yeah, you can tell them five minutes, tops."

Michaela left the phone with Cassie, quickly explaining her mission on the way out of the kitchen. She found his office easily enough. There *was* a green folder lying on the centre of his desk. Her gaze rose from the folder, as if drawn by a magnetic force, to a silver-framed photo on the centre shelf of the bookcase behind the desk. Almost against her will, she found herself moving closer to the photo. So—this was Hannah.

* * *

Even though he felt as if he'd stepped outside his body, Paul knew what he was feeling was very real. He felt so relaxed, even after his encounter with Falconer earlier. Ten minutes ago, he had helped the women put his kitchen back in order after a delicious lunch; then he'd found himself here slouched in his living room armchair. His mother was reclining on his black, leather couch with her eyes closed and Christy and Cassie were squished in the matching loveseat with Michaela in between them, looking at his photo album. It had been a gift from his mother, after his graduation from college. There were a lot of baby pictures in there, and Michaela seemed to be enjoying his sisters' teasing commentaries of his growing up years.

The only thing that was disturbing his repose was the warning bells in the back of his mind accusing him of his increasing attraction toward Michaela. It was harder here, in his home and with the familiar company of his family, not to succumb to the pull of her. He admired the graceful movement of her hands, the flow of her neck and the inviting smile of her lips. Every time she looked across at him to gauge his reaction to their silly teasing and laughter, he felt mesmerized. When his relaxed state started becoming restless, he got up.

"Aww, Paul, did we hurt your feelings?" Cassie called out to him, laughing. Michaela was gazing up at him with her big, dark brown eyes.

"Not a chance," he joked lightly, not wanting to disturb his mother. "I just remembered something I have to do. I won't be long."

So, he escaped to his office, shutting the door firmly behind him. He stood with his hands planted on top of his desk and looked at Hannah. He didn't know what to say or what to think. He needed the sight of her to refocus him; to put things in perspective; but all he could do was feel, and everything he was feeling was not for her... it was for another woman.

Chapter Nine

"Come on, Sarah," Michaela called, laughing softly. She tugged at Sarah's arm so they could continue on to the grocery store instead of being stuck gazing through the window of Charlotte's Dresses.

"But it's such a gorgeous summer dress," Sarah explained, as she allowed herself to be redirected.

"You said yourself that you can't afford it," Michaela pointed out. "Besides, they're waiting for us at the Church. We're here for Styrofoam plates, remember?"

It was a beautiful, sunny afternoon; the type of day that was hard for people to give up to come finish the final sanding of the Fellowship Hall walls. After that, painting and carpeting would be the major things left for the Hall to be completed. The carpeting would be contracted out, as it would be such a big job. Michaela and Sarah had been designated to purchase some lunch supplies from a small plaza about five minutes from the Church.

Michaela frequently pondered about how much more grocery selection there was in North America than in a country like Haiti. So much was taken for granted; so much waste. Yet, there was a different kind of poverty in Canada. Generally speaking, people tended to be less aware of their community as a whole as each one bowed to the god of individualism. Me, myself and I was the new trinity; the unholy trinity that did its work through materialism, debt and information overload.

Inside Dega's Grocery was cool and moderately busy. The women bypassed the carts and headed for the dinnerware section. Sarah led the way as she was more familiar with the store. Suddenly, she increased her pace and waved a hand to motion Michaela along.

"Hello, you guys! How are you?" Sarah greeted a woman and a young girl. The woman straightened slowly from her bent-over position at a lower store shelf. She had a slight frown across her forehead, as if she were being disturbed unnecessarily. Her expression cleared when she recognized Sarah.

"Hello, Sarah. We're doing well. How are you?" She asked Sarah the question while her dark brown gaze observed Michaela. The girl who was about age eight or nine had a wide-eyed look. Suddenly, a generous smile lit up her little face.

"It's the intern, Mommy! It's the intern Leroy told us about!"

Sarah laughed before answering the woman's question. "Oh, I'm doing well." She bent down to the girl. "Yes, you're right, Lissa. This is Miss Michaela and she's been working at our Church for a little while now. Michaela, meet Leroy's mom, Carmel, and his little sister."

"Not so little anymore! I grew an inch this year. Ask Mom."

Michaela laughed along with Sarah and Carmel. She offered her hand to Carmel, then to Lissa. "It's so nice to finally meet you. Leroy has told me so much about you both... all good things, I assure you." This encouraged more laughter.

“So, are they treating you well there?” Carmel asked as she positioned her shopping cart in order not to block the aisle for other shoppers. She had smooth brown skin and her black hair was piled on top of her head. She was probably older than she appeared in a designer T-shirt and knee-length jeans shorts.

Michaela nodded. “Absolutely, they’ve been wonderful.” She smiled at Sarah. “Especially Sarah here.”

“Of course, you’d say that while I’m standing right here,” Sarah joked.

Michaela felt a pat on her arm. “I’ve been to your Church before,” Lissa informed her rather solemnly. “I’ve been with my mom and my brother, but I haven’t been in a long time.” She gazed up at her mother with continued solemnity. She was adorable with thick, shoulder-length braids, almond-shaped eyes and skin like her mother.

Carmel sighed audibly as she observed her daughter’s expression. She looked from Sarah to Michaela as if she wanted to respond but didn’t quite know what to say.

“We have a special celebration coming up in a few weeks. Would you like to visit us then?”

Carmel gazed thoughtfully at Michaela, then smiled. “I really haven’t been very good with the church scene lately and... ” she gazed fondly at Lissa. “I don’t really want Lissa missing out. I’ll see what I can do. Maybe one of you could give me a call.”

The women continued to chat a while longer, then Michaela reminded Sarah of their mission.

“Before you go,” Carmel began, delaying their departure, “I’ve been meaning to give Pastor Paul a call. I thought you should know: Will McCree has been hanging out with Blinder a lot more than usual. I don’t know what’s going on, but I don’t want to see Blinder hurt.”

“Has it been interfering with his work at the store?” Sarah asked in a concerned tone.

"No, he's been just great, as usual," Carmel responded. "I just thought someone should know."

A little later, in the parking lot, Michaela returned to the topic of Leroy's mom. "Carmel seems like a really nice woman," She said, as she and Sarah got into the Honda. "It has to be hard, though, raising two children on her own—especially one being a teenager."

Sarah pulled her seatbelt snug as Michaela started the car. "They moved here five years ago, after her husband was killed in Afghanistan."

Michaela paused with her hands on the steering wheel. "Yes, Paul told me that it had been his first trip there. That's so sad." She put the car in reverse before slowly directing it from its parking spot.

"You can speak to Paul about Will. I may forget after rescuing Tristan from Conner."

"Deal," Michaela agreed as she drove out of the plaza parking lot.

* * *

"Where are those two young women?" Ethel asked over the general din of workers in the Kitchen and Fellowship Hall, for the second time.

Hilda had to smile at Ethel's impatience. There was nothing like punctuality for Ethel. She had probably calculated in her mind how long it should take Michaela and Sarah to drive to Dega's Grocery, walk down the aisle, pick up the needed items and make their purchase, then return.

"I'm sure there'll be here soon," Hilda assured her, adding a gentle pat to Ethel's bony shoulder. Both women, along with some other elderly, church ladies, were in the Kitchen which was connected to the Fellowship Hall by a wide serving window. The well-equipped Kitchen had already been renovated two years prior, and now the Hall would soon measure up to the same standard. They were just about finished preparing the large lunch spread, but needed the disposable plates to serve the meal.

"Those young women need to know that hard-working men need to eat when the meal is well-heated and ready," Ethel continued. She seemed more irritable than usual. Perhaps she was worrying about George who had been re-admitted to the hospital after developing post-surgery complications.

Hilda paused from wiping the wide counter space by the serving window. "How is George today, Ethel? Any improvement?"

Ethel's tight expression loosened and she smiled. "Yes, I think so. He developed a fever that's cause for concern, but nothing as bad as before surgery. My word, all that nausea, vomiting and awful pain he complained about." She smoothed at the white smock she wore to protect her clothing. "I'll certainly be glad to have him home. One never seems to appreciate a person as much until they're gone."

"Well, I'm sure George will be tickled to get home and have you fuss over him. But, let him take his time. It's not that easy for a man his age to get over bowel surgery."

Ethel touched Hilda's busy hand still wiping the counter. "I know, dear." Her eyes were a little moist. "Thanks so much for your and Samuel's support and prayers. I really appreciate it."

Hilda gave her a gentle hug. Ethel dabbed at her eyes with a slightly shaky hand. "You know, it's good to know who your friends really are in times of crisis. Did you know I was accosted just outside of the hospital by a salesman from the development project?"

"What do you mean, Ethel?" Hilda asked. She noticed several of the other women had drawn closer at Ethel's statement.

Ethel's tears were forgotten, replaced by a fierce gleam in her eyes. "That young man must have assumed I was at the hospital to get a manicure done. He just pounced at me with all sorts of literature and pamphlets. I was very glad to tell him that I was already in the decision phase of purchasing a home at the site but would absolutely change my mind if he didn't go and bother someone else—preferably someone not at the hospital."

"Did he get the message?" a small, dark-haired woman asked.

"He surely did," Ethel remarked strongly. "He backed off like I was a rattler ready to strike!"

The women laughed. The dark-haired one spoke again: "You're not the only one, Ethel. I'm not sure what tactics they're trained to use, but I've never seen the likes."

"You've not seen the likes of what, Bernice?" All heads turned in the direction of the serving window where Paul was hunched over onto the counter. His brown hands were covered with grey dust.

"Paul Rayner, you get your hands off my clean counter this minute!" Hilda scolded, flicking at him with the dish cloth. He stepped back instantaneously, chuckling and raising his hands in surrender.

"All right, sorry, Hilda, but you shouldn't have opened up yet." He gestured towards the doors of the serving window. "I'm just here on behalf of the hard-working men," he glanced behind him, "and women who are salivating at the smell coming from in here," he edged cautiously closer to the serving window, "wondering when we'll be put out of our misery." He ended with a dimpled smile. He did not look very pastorly at the moment in his T-shirt and jeans, and Hilda could tell he was having the same effect on the other women. He was a darling boy.

"Can we not call the girls on Sarah's cell phone... ?"

"Pastor Paul, we'll just use a regular dish for you... "

"Why don't you slip around, Pastor, and we'll fix you up... "

* * *

Paul moved away from the kitchen, shaking his head in protest and laughing at the women's generous offers. There was no way he was going to eat before his fellow workers.

"Hey, they're here, ladies!" he shouted over the noise. He had spied Michaela and Sarah passing by the Fellowship Hall doorway, as someone else was coming in. He smiled at the cheers of the women as he escaped from the Hall. He dusted his hands on his jeans before securing the door behind him.

"Hey, girls, they're eager for the plates," he called to Michaela and Sarah.

Sarah smiled, and then took Michaela's package to add to her own before proceeding to the Kitchen door. Michaela held back, waiting for him. She was looking down at his feet, so he followed her gaze.

"What?"

She laughed softly. "You're tracking dust onto the carpet."

He looked back. A trial of footprints followed him. "Shoot," he said, looking at Michaela. "I hope the women don't come out here just now."

Michaela smiled. "I'm a woman."

For a moment Paul couldn't decipher the humour in her statement and his thoughts were verbalized before he could stop them. "There's no way I could mistake you for anything but... " He could tell the effect when her eyes widened and the caramel colour of her skin darkened slightly.

He placed his hands on his hips—examined the floor—then looked at her. There was a faint smile at the corners of her mouth.

"Sorry," he murmured quietly. Her gaze met his and he felt his chest tighten. This was not good.

"You're flirting with me, Pastor Paul?" she asked jokingly. Her arms were crossed tightly, belying her relaxed speech. "Don't worry. I won't tell anyone... yet." She smiled again, then turned and walked towards the Kitchen door. She didn't look back at him as she went through, but his eyes couldn't help but stay glued to her the whole way. This was *definitely* not good.

He took a cleansing breath, then decided to return to the Fellowship Hall. He turned and felt his heart thump at the sight of Karlene standing on the other side of the doorway, watching him.

For a moment, they simply stared at each other. He had no way of knowing how long she had been there. She smiled slowly as she approached him. Her long hair was swept back in a ponytail and she wore a floral sundress that reached just above her knees. There would be no renovating for this woman. She had already made it clear she was an organizer, not a manual labourer.

"Oh, look at you," she purred, brushing delicately at his shoulders. He stepped back from the warmth of her fingers. She frowned, but then quickly regained her smile, pulling at him with her amber gaze. "How are things going in there? Will it be finished, soon?"

He was relieved she didn't try and touch him again. Maybe Brennon was right about her seeing Michaela as a threat. Her behaviour toward him had definitely become more familiar since Michaela's arrival, and he was increasingly annoyed by her attentions to him; attentions definitely not solicited. However, he remained civil.

"It's all pretty much on schedule, Karlene. Actually, you're just in time for lunch." He pulled the door opened. "You may want to join the ladies in the Kitchen. It's pretty dusty in here."

Karlene slipped by him into the room. "I'm not afraid of a little dust," she flung at him, laughing flirtatiously.

* * *

Michaela was fairly certain that she was getting negative vibes from Karlene.

Sarah had taken Conner home and the other ladies had already left, but Michaela had volunteered to help Hilda finish up in the Kitchen. She also wanted to relay Carmel's concern, about Will, to Paul.

For some reason that seemed foreign to her character, Karlene had decided to also assist in this latter stage of clean-up duties. Her primary conversation with Michaela seemed to focus on Michaela's eventual release from her internship. Even Hilda was starting to send puzzled looks Karlene's way, but she seemed oblivious to it.

"You must be so tired of doing minor duties like this when your call is to the mission field," Karlene said over one shoulder as she replaced the paper towel on its holder. This was, perhaps, the fourth time she had mentioned "mission field."

Michaela made it a point to avoid Hilda's eye and gave her attention to Karlene. "Well, being in missions doesn't exempt one from dish washing. In fact, it could involve a lot more domestic jobs than you might think," she said while drying a casserole dish.

"What about the spiritual aspects: like winning souls, healing the sick, you know... ?" Karlene seemed a little dissatisfied with Michaela's response.

"Well, in any case, Karlene, I need to work through for my ordination after my internship, so I wouldn't be doing missions for a while."

Karlene leaned against the counter with her arms crossed and her back to the closed serving window. "Really? So, how long would that take?"

Michaela set the dried dish on the island counter. "Two to three years." She took the final serving dish from Hilda. Warm water trailed down her arm as she continued drying, but she was very aware of a slightly glazed look in Karlene's eyes. Was it her imagination? She looked at Hilda.

Hilda turned from the double sink. "Karlene, are you okay, dear?"

Karlene seemed to give herself a mental shake, then she smiled and smoothed at her dark hair. "Of course, I'm okay. There've just been some things on my mind lately."

"Anything we can help you with?" Hilda persisted. She leaned towards Karlene as if to emphasize the genuineness of her offer.

"Oh, no, Hilda," Karlene said, laughing as if the offer were absurd. Suddenly, she sobered.

"Actually, there was one little thing that just came to my mind you could perhaps help with."

She eyed Michaela as she spoke to Hilda. "Maybe you could help me give a little warning to Michaela... just a little caution. Someone told me they phoned the parsonage the other day and Michaela answered."

For a moment, Michaela was dumbfounded, but then the memory of the silent phone response during her visit with Paul's family surfaced. The sudden rush of heat in her face, cooled. She laughed in relief. "Oh, I wasn't there alone. That was the day Paul's mother and sisters were visiting, and I went to the parsonage with them for lunch. Do you remember, Hilda?"

"Yes, that's right," Hilda confirmed, frowning at Karlene. "Was someone concerned that anything improper was going on?"

Karlene clapped her hands delicately and laughed out loudly, almost forcefully. "You see, I told them not to be a busy-body. I knew there was an acceptable explanation why she would have been there."

"I hope no one is spreading rumours—"

"No, no, Hilda," Karlene assured her. She seemed slightly agitated, but kept a smile in place. "I shouldn't have even mentioned it, but I'll certainly set them straight." She looked at her watch before moving a few steps towards the Kitchen door. "I really should get going." She stopped in front of Michaela; their eyes level. "So, did you enjoy lunching with Paul... and his family?"

Michaela could feel the force of her penetrating gaze, and the heady scent of her perfume threatened to cloud her judgement. She answered cautiously. "Well, yes. Eleanor and her daughters were very nice, and I enjoyed getting to know them."

"Good—good. They are a lovely family and I treasure my relationship with them. I've known them for as long as Paul's been here." She smiled sweetly at Hilda. "Well... glad I could help out today. I'll see you both later."

The scent of Karlene's perfume trailed out of the Kitchen after her. Michaela could feel Hilda's gaze on her, as the sound of the Fellowship Hall clean-up penetrated what would have been a very silent Kitchen. Michaela shook her head in bewilderment.

Hilda shrugged. "I really don't know what that was all about, but I can hazard a guess. I know Karlene has her quirky ways, but this just takes the cake."

Michaela remained silent. She ran her hands up her cheeks and over her hair, stopping at the fluffy bun on top of her head. She looked at Hilda, then held her hands out. "Hilda, is there something else I need to know about her—something I'm missing?"

Hilda bowed her head; her hands clasped at her lips. She sighed deeply, turning a troubled gaze at Michaela. "I think Karlene has inner turmoil that is unresolved, even though she's received help in the past. I can't go into the details, but I think she sees herself as whole, but she is not."

Michaela didn't get a chance to respond because Samuel chose that moment to barge into the Kitchen.

"Are you two still in here?" He was partially cleaned up from the work. There was drywall dust along his hairline, but it was camouflaged throughout his grey hair. "Paul and Brennon went to the parsonage to get cleaned up. Will you be coming with us now, Michaela?"

Michaela shook her head. "Not yet, Sam. I need to prepare a craft for the children tomorrow, but I'll be there for supper."

Samuel's cheeks puffed up in a fatherly smile. "Okay, you do that and we'll see you later."

Michaela smiled in response. No one seemed to want to leave her alone at the house after what had transpired between her and Will, even though Will had been doing fairly well since then. Apparently, he was back in regular counselling and being diligent with his medications.

He had even consented to see Paul once or twice, but he seemed to go out of his way to avoid Michaela.

* * *

"So, Carmel is just concerned that they're spending too much time together, not about anything that has actually happened?"

"Yes," Michaela responded to Paul's question. Somehow, she didn't think he was taking her information very seriously. She had tracked him down in the Pastor's Office after he and Brennon had returned freshly showered. He smelled very nice... but she still had an issue to press. "She stressed that it was more than usual."

Paul looked at her, as if wondering what the concern was. They continued staring at each other. "Okay, I'll look into it," he finally said. He bent over to access his desk drawer, and then paused to look up at her still standing in the doorway.

"You don't think that it's cause for concern?" She couldn't help but feel slightly irritated with him.

He straightened. "Michaela, we have prayer tonight. I'll bring it up then. When I meet with Will, we'll talk about it."

"Okay," she responded, backing away slightly. She turned to leave, but then paused. She faced him. "Please forgive me if I'm stepping out of bounds, but don't you think it should be dealt with ASAP? I mean, Blinder is like a child and, even though Will has been doing better, we can't be sure how each day will be for him—"

"Michaela, I understand your concern, but you've got to trust that I've been dealing with Will for much longer than you've known him," he smiled, perhaps to soften his next words, "and if you do persist in questioning my judgement on this, you *will* be stepping out of bounds."

She could feel the tension rising in her and knew she needed to back down. Her parents always warned her not to let her "impulsive indignation" rule her—it was not glorifying to the Lord. She liked to remind them that the Bible allowed for anger without sin, but they always challenged that with the Scripture about being slow to anger. She started to count to ten as she continued on her way out of the room.

"Michaela."

She had made it to the Front Office doorway before she felt his hand at her elbow. She turned and felt greatly disturbed by his nearness. She impulsively stepped back, feeling even more anger by her flustered response to him. "You needn't explain any further. I do understand."

"What do you understand?" He challenged. "Your entire attitude is telling me you don't understand, or you don't want to understand."

She took a deep breath, reminding herself to be respectful and possibly... submissive. "Does being an intern mean I can't have my own opinions?"

He was silent, so she looked at him. He was assessing her carefully with his dark gaze. She felt her skin grow warmer.

"Is it just the sharing you wish to do, or does the implementation of those opinions come with the package?"

Her eyelids fluttered, betraying her tension. "I'm not sure I know what you mean?"

He crossed his arms. "Do you mean to have your say—and your way—at the same time?"

Michaela wasn't sure how to answer. He wasn't really asking her, he was making a judgement. However, she felt a conviction in her heart about this most difficult part of her that the Holy Spirit kept chipping away at. Sometimes she hated this process, but they were right—the Holy Spirit, and Paul.

"Hey."

She looked up at him and was glad to see the concern in his eyes. Of course, this was pride stepping in. *Well, I can't be perfect at every step, Lord.*

"Please trust me in this," he commanded gently. "I promise you, anything I need to learn from you, I'll try my best to be opened to."

She smiled warily, loving the dimples now appearing in his cheeks. The tension drained from her. She would be in prayer for Will tonight, but she would also need to be in much prayer and contemplation for the situation standing right in front of her. She wouldn't allow herself the luxury of denying that something was obviously happening between her, the intern, and him, the minister.

"Okay," she gave in. "Fair enough."

"Guys."

They tore their gazes from each other to give their attention to Brennon who was standing in the centre of the Foyer.

"Look at this," Brennon said, pointing at a large bulletin board on the wall across from the side sanctuary door.

Michaela felt the warmth of Paul's hand on her back, as he gently nudged her towards Brennon. She stood between the two men, looking up at the board.

"What the... " Paul's voice broke through the quietness.

The feeling of dread that threaded its way into Michaela couldn't really be explained. After all, it was only a poster, albeit an extremely large one. Someone had covered over a large section of other posters with one boldly broadcasting Milward Seniors Community.

Chapter Ten

"So, Blinder, why're you trailing Will so much, lately?" Leroy asked, eying the older man carefully.

It was Tuesday afternoon, and they were in the back room of the blinds and home decor store his mother owned, sorting through boxes of new merchandise. Leroy took his job with Blinder seriously. They did the he-man stuff for his mom; he liked to make things as easy as possible for her. He also preferred staying out of sight during the daytime when most people arrived in the store. His mother hadn't told him so, but he knew his "gangster" appearance made people—mostly women—uncomfortable. While he wasn't willing to compromise on his appearance, he didn't want to do anything to jeopardize the family business. His mother had worked too hard to build it; partially thanks to the insurance from his father's death.

Blinder paused without straightening up from the box he was unloading. His chestnut hair was a little wild today, but he had the same

"Blinder" innocence to his expression. "I-I have to keep him safe. I-I need to watch him."

"You're hanging with him more, on purpose? What for, man?"

Blinder's eyes were almost shut as he frowned in concentration. Leroy knew Blinder didn't really like to be interrupted as he worked. Blinder seemed to view his life as an opportunity from Heaven to serve and protect those he loved. He insisted he had been given a second chance at life for those reasons.

"I t-told you, Leroy. I'm keeping him safe." His eyes were tightly shut, but he opened them as the next words passed his lips. "The devil's after him and I'm keeping him safe." He resumed his worked before muttering almost fiercely. "Plus, I-I don't like what she's trying to do to him."

Leroy palmed away perspiration from his forehead as he perched on a wooden crate. Even though a side door had been left opened, it was warm and stuffy in the warehouse-type room. He gazed longingly at Blinder's closed bedroom door at one corner of the warehouse. The bedroom had air conditioning, and sometimes they would cool off in there. There was also an adjoining washroom they used during work, but it was mostly for Blinder's personal use. "What you talking about, Blinder? Who's she?"

"Karlene."

Leroy let that soak in for awhile, listening to Blinder's heavy breathing and the noises from his labour.

"Leroy, why are you sitting there while Blinder's doing all the work? Come on—off your butt—I need the specialty blinds in store before the day is out!"

Leroy swung his head around to grimace at his mother who was standing in the doorway leading into the store. He knew her bark was worse than her bite; but, as much as he didn't want to disappoint her, he sometimes wished he could work for someone other than his mother. "It's just about done, Ma. Quit checking."

She shook her head and gave him one last no-nonsense glare before she shut the door.

"She'll be coming," Blinder declared, after Carmel's disappearance. "I-I told her about the H-hall opening at the Church, and s-she said she would come."

"Ma?'

"Yes," Blinder confirmed, giving what was probably his first smile of the day.

* * *

"He's still chomping at the bit about the poster," Brennon announced to Michaela and Sarah, as he, with Conner in arms, appeared unexpectedly into the Church Conference Room. "Not that he's being verbal about it, but I can see the tension in his jaw line."

Michaela looked across the table at Sarah. They had been revamping the children's Sunday program, but Michaela welcomed the interruption. She would much rather wrestle with the midweek program with its outreach emphasis. Unfortunately, the midweek program didn't run during the summer months.

"Paul still doesn't know how it got up on the board?" Sarah asked as she accepted her reaching son. Once she had him in arms, Conner immediately grabbed his mother's shiny brown hair.

Brennon pulled out a chair and sat beside Michaela. He looked across at his wife. "The whole thing is still a mystery."

"I don't understand why there's so much controversy over that poster," Michaela directed to Brennon. "Paul even came by on Monday to talk to Samuel about it—alone."

"Michaela doesn't know the whole story, Bren," Sarah mumbled as Conner pulled at her bottom lip. She grabbed at his stubby hand, grimacing as he let out a piercing scream. He threw his little body backwards, but Sarah kept a firm hold on his back and his chubby legs which were bare beneath over-sized shorts.

"It's not my place to tell, hon, and it goes way back. Anyway, it really has nothing to do with this problem, Michaela." Brennon eyed his struggling family, before reaching across the table and firmly pushing on Conner's back. "All done, Conner, all done."

Conner's head movements paused in a flung-back position as if hearing his father's voice.

Sarah chuckled, then sighed. "I wish I could do that; it never works for me."

"All I'll tell you, Michaela, is that the man building Milward Seniors Community was the sworn enemy of Paul's father," Brennon continued.

* * *

Paul dribbled the basketball around the Gym in the church basement. He paused, looked up, then ran as he dribbled to do a perfect layup. The ball whooshed through the net and bounced onto the painted, concrete floor. He let it go. He had a counselling session in a couple of hours and didn't want to have to go shower at the parsonage. He shouldn't really be playing basketball in his dress shoes anyway. He stood with his hands on his hips, not really seeing the ball as its motion was stalled by the wall behind the net.

Lord, I really don't like what this is doing to me. It's like dredging up buried dross to steal the focus from worthy things. Please, Lord, I don't want to return to that place of bondage and hate. You showed me how to forgive and love through my parents' examples, and through Hannah's commitment to me, but a lot has changed since then. Help me do right.

"Paul?"

He turned to see Michaela enter the Gym. She had a stack of papers held before her and her eyes had a questioning look. She looked beautiful and fresh in a simple, short-sleeved summer dress, with her black hair fluffed out behind the broad band holding it back. Funny, he should ask the Lord for help, and she show up.

"We were supposed to make a quick visit to the hospital, to see George," she reminded him.

* * *

They did go to the hospital to see George... and Dahlia... and Francis... and people who weren't part of their Church. Paul noticed that Michaela had a knack for cheering people up, genuine compassion for their illness, and had no problems praying with them.

Once he would get past introducing her to someone, she would easily warm up to them which seemed to draw out the same response in them. She was definitely a people-person, but he noticed she didn't seem to tolerate the "complaining spirit" well, and seemed to go out of her way to bring optimism to each situation. The way she prayed for George, though, was what highlighted something really different about Michaela.

George had been lying with his bed head raised, propped up with pillows, looking quite content after conversing easily with Michaela. He had looked clean and his thin, white hair had been slicked back from the care he had received before their arrival. However, he had sometimes grimaced in pain that seemed to take his breath away.

Michaela had been seated on the right side of his bed, holding his gnarled hand. After asking George's permission to pray for him and receiving Paul's nod, she had gently and passionately thanked God for the medical care George was receiving. Then she had asked for his healing. After asking, she had paused quietly, as if listening; then, as if all in a day's work, had commanded healing upon George. Her words had been: "George Flint, be healed from this sickness in the name of Jesus." They had left George with tears in his old, grey eyes.

After reminding Michaela of his counselling appointment at the Church, Paul returned to his Beetle with her, pondering all that had happened. Once again, he wasn't exactly sure what to think of her.

"I still can't get over this car." Michaela laughed cheerfully as she buckled her belt. "I don't recall ever riding in a 'buggy' before. I've only done the 'punch-buggy-no-punch-backs' game as a child."

Paul smiled at her as he put the car in reverse, feeling anything but at ease with her sitting beside him, yet he liked being with her. "Well, it's not exactly the best car for the chauffeuring part of a pastor's job, but it was my father's... "

Michaela was silent for a moment, but then said, "You feel close to him when you drive it."

"Yes, sometimes. I'm sure I'll let go of it at some point."

"In Haiti, whatever could be driven was good. When I lived with my aunt here, she drove a minivan even though she had never married and had no children. I used to tease her about it. I wish she were still here to tease." She had a wistful tone to her voice.

Paul eased into traffic. "You miss your aunt?"

"Yes, sometimes," she said, looking at him. "She, and my friend Tilly, were my family away from my parents. She was very good to me."

He nodded understandingly.

"I'm sorry about your wife."

Paul's grip tightened on the steering wheel. *Where in the blazes had that come from?* All thoughts of healings and cars left his mind. He stared at the road ahead before glancing over at her. She was looking directly at him. He stared back at the road.

"Thank you," he managed. He didn't know what else to say. He hoped she wouldn't delve any further, but what she said next wasn't what he expected.

"Dennis Falconer is the man whose company is building the Seniors Community the poster at Church was advertising?"

His gaze was off the road to her again, but he didn't answer.

"You're frowning," she said with a little, nervous laugh.

"I'll tell you about it sometime," he said. He could feel her observing him and instinctively knew she was hoping for more. "Dennis Falconer was the man who nearly ruined my father's ministry and my parents' marriage." Then he repeated, "I'll tell you about it sometime."

Ten minutes later, as he drove up to the Church, Paul noticed Blinder waiting just outside the front doors. This wasn't unusual for Blinder, especially when he wanted to talk to Paul about something pressing. The late afternoon sky had darkened slightly and light rain had started, so he let Michaela off under the canopy.

"See what Blinder wants, will you?" he requested as she exited the car. He parked in the "Senior Pastor" spot, before joining Blinder and Michaela, who had remained outside the doors, talking.

"I-I think she's going to get him in trouble," Blinder was saying. He looked very distressed. Fine drops of rain covered his light, wind-breaker jacket, and Michaela was actually holding his hands.

"Why do you think so, Blinder? Will seems to be okay. Have you noticed something different that concerns you?" Michaela was focused on Blinder, her dark brown eyes wide and intent.

Paul decided to intervene. "Blinder, come in and we'll talk." He stepped closer to them, noticing Blinder didn't smell that good today, and there she was close to him holding his hands. Blinder looked over at him as if it were an effort to change focus, then he returned his gaze to Michaela.

"H-he goes t-to the same place she goes," Blinder responded in simple desperation. "A-ask Leroy; he knows."

"Where do they go, Blinder?" Michaela asked, as if they had all the time in the world. Paul felt irritation rising in him.

"Blinder—" Blinder looked at him. "Let's go inside." Blinder appeared to be struggling. Michaela let go of his hands and looked at Paul with a frown.

"Paul, could he not just finish his thought? He's really concerned."

"You go finish up with Sarah. I'll talk with Blinder."

"But—"

"Please, Michaela," he insisted, putting his hand on Blinder's shoulder to encourage him inside. Once Blinder was on his way in, Paul waited, holding the door opened for Michaela to follow. She stood gazing at him, still frowning.

He sighed. "I'd rather you not challenge me right now," he warned her. Her eyelids fluttered slightly, disbelief creeping into her gaze. So, let it be. He had let her have her way at the hospital with her super-faith prayers, but this was his turf. Here: there was order and decisions; problems and solutions; God and he working hand in hand. It gave his life vision and purpose, and in spite of their common church background, she was exhibiting ways unfamiliar to his scope of ministry. And... she was messing with emotions long held in check.

Michaela lowered her gaze and finally followed after Blinder.

* * *

"I-I like her," Blinder said as soon as they were alone in the Pastor's Office. "God likes her too."

Paul shifted uneasily on his seat. He had chosen to sit knee-to-knee, facing Blinder. Blinder always needed a more personal touch, but he also had a way of discerning people's intent as no one else Paul knew; as if his challenges, as a result of his brain injury, were compensated for by an uncanny insight into people's characters.

"Y-you like her too, b-but she makes you nervous."

Paul laughed lightly, running his fingers across the bridge of his nose. He looked directly at Blinder. "You don't know Michaela as well as I do, Blinder. Actually, she's easy to like. Everyone seems to like her. But why do you think she makes me nervous?" Blinder remained silent, avoiding Paul's gaze.

"You're not going to answer, are you?"

Blinder looked at him. "You like her a lot."

* * *

Michaela fumed in silent confusion in the Conference Room. She didn't understand Paul Rayner. Did he have control issues or was there something about her he didn't trust? She knew he had counselling as part of his credentials, and perhaps he felt she should leave that responsibility to him. After all, she was only a lowly intern. But she had only wanted to hear Blinder out, not counsel him.

She shuffled angrily at the papers Sarah had left on the table for her to critique. Sarah had left a note explaining that she had to leave and would give her a call later.

She sighed deeply, feeling suddenly alone, missing her parents. She allowed her gaze to stray around the spacious, well-lit Conference Room. Technically, she had the Children Pastor's Office at her disposal, since Sarah shared the Assistant Pastor's Office with Brennon. However, she preferred the Conference Room. It was closer to all the "comings" and "goings", compared to the other office down from the Fellowship Hall in the Children's Wing.

The Conference Room was rectangular with a wide window centred on the outer wall. Various framed pictures hung on the walls and a refreshment table graced one corner. The central piece to the room was a long table lined with five grey, fabric-stuffed chairs on either side and two at each end. Many events took place in this room: board meetings, planning committees, counselling sessions not done in the Pastor's Office, prayer sessions—the list went on.

How would she do in such a North-American-church setting, day in and day out? Is this what she would want? Didn't the *business* of Church sometimes get in the way of the *kingdom* of Church? It wasn't hard to do; even in missions it sometimes happened. The year after high school she spent working alongside her parents had shown her that. Her parents believed that "politics" was fair game for any organization—even the Church.

She turned her thoughts toward her Friend—her Comforter. "Help me in all of this, Lord, to truly know Your way for me," she whispered. "I admit, I've arrogantly assumed the mission field is my calling without really, really seeking You." Her forehead touched the table. "I mean, look at Blinder, Leroy and his family, Lucy, George, Karlene... ." The list probably went on more than she knew. Missions could be right here. She sighed deeply as another thought entered her mind. "Look at Will—"

It was truly uncanny that at the moment she whispered his name, the door of the Conference Room opened to slowly admit Will McCree.

Chapter Eleven

Will seemed frozen as he stood with his hand on the doorknob. His countenance carried surprise... and wariness. He was neatly dressed in a blue, short-sleeved shirt the colour of his eyes, and blue jeans. If it wasn't for the uncertainty registered in his eyes, Michaela would have pegged him as a confident man in the prime of life. But, she knew differently.

Michaela slowly shoved her chair back and stood up. "Hi, Will," she greeted gently, not sure what his reaction would be. Since the incident when he had fallen down the stairs, Will had basically stayed out of her way. She knew he was back in treatment for PTSD, and that he also met with Paul but she wasn't sure how often.

Will frowned as he seemed to mentally brace himself. "I-I'm sorry. Sam told me to wait here for the Reverend." He turned as if to retreat.

"No, please, Will, don't go," Michaela said quickly, hoping to stall him. Something had been left undone between her and Will, and she wanted to grab this opportunity to address it. He turned back to look at her with the door partially blocking his entrance like an armour.

"It's funny, we live in the same house and we don't see each other much," Michaela entreated, smiling. Will stared at her, then at the floor, then back at her.

"I'm very sorry about what happened that day. I-I don't really remember, but... " He seemed very uncomfortable.

"It's okay, Will. No harm done." Michaela could see progress when he let go of the doorknob and stepped further into the room, shoving his hands into his jeans pockets. "I need to apologize also," she admitted.

He squinted at her, seemingly confused.

"I've been warned about making snap judgements, but I seem to fall into that trap on a regular basis. I can't imagine what you've been going through, I'm sorry for being so hard on you."

Will crossed his arms, and the muscles in his jaw bulged under the skin. He was silent for a moment before speaking. "You were right, though." His eyes were sorrowful. He quickly rubbed his fingers across his nose, sighing deeply. "Lucy and Tristan deserve better. Sam and Hilda too... "

"It will happen, Will." Michaela kept her place across the table, fearing she might scare him off.

"I haven't gotten to know you the weeks you've been here," he chuckled softly, "but you definitely got to me."

Michaela remained silent. She was surprised by his admission.

"I do want to ask you something, though," he continued, taking a few steps closer to the table. He placed his hands flat on the table and looked directly at her. "That day, what I saw was unlike anything I had ever experienced. The Rev.—well, he said it was probably all part of the flashbacks—of war—I was experiencing that day. My shrink said the same thing. But, I want to know what you think."

He straightened up. "Those two men I saw with you that day... they were not wearing combat uniform and they were definitely not the Taliban."

* * *

Paul glanced at his watch as he watched Blinder limp towards Brennon's car. The rain was falling more heavily, so Brennon had offered Blinder a ride home. *He* should have been meeting with Will ten minutes ago.

He looked around the Church Foyer, finding it hard not to let his gaze roam over the bulletin boards. No unwanted posters today. Maybe it was just an isolated incident, but he still wanted to find out who was responsible.

For some reason, it seemed a little dismal in the building—dismal and empty. Hilda hadn't come in today; Sarah kept her own time based on Conner's schedule and now Brennon was out. He wondered where Michaela was.

Michaela. He wasn't sure how he was going to deal with three more months of her. Disturbingly enough, he wasn't sure he wanted to think about not having her to deal with. He felt like he was in a no-win situation with a woman six years his junior... and a strange woman, at that. Yet, the strangeness seemed to draw people to her, seemed to work for her. However, he was finding it very frustrating. What was he supposed to do with an intern with revolutionary views, mountain-moving faith and eyes that tugged at his soul every day?

Life had been good. His grief had been manageable and so was this Church; his domain. His sheep supported him well—a good legacy left by his father. He was even up for a fight with Falconer if it came to it. Above all, he loved and trusted the Lord; they had an understanding. But, Michaela? He had not been ready for Michaela.

"Son, you want to talk about it?"

Paul groaned inwardly, surprised by Samuel's sudden appearance in the Foyer. "What are you doing here?" Paul asked him.

"I dropped Will off—his truck's in the shop. He's in the Conference Room," Samuel answered, rubbing his hands across his portly belly. "Now, what's the problem—not Falconer again?"

Paul studied Samuel for a moment, noticing the genuine concern in his eyes, noticing how his seventy-odd years were telling on him more: this father-figure mentor of his. He didn't want to be dependent on Samuel for his sense of well being anymore than he wanted Samuel to fight his battles. He was guilty of keeping things from Samuel because he truly cared for the man and didn't want to worry him, but also because he believed Samuel was slow to see that he had come into his own—had become his own man—years ago.

"No, Sam—just wondering where Will is. Now I know."

"You sure?" Sam pressed. His deep voice cut through the quiet of the Foyer.

Paul stretched, flexing his arms above his head, trying to release the kinks in his shoulders in what he hoped Samuel would take as a relaxed stance. "I haven't seen or heard from Falconer since he dropped by here a couple of weeks ago." He placed a hand on Samuel's broad shoulder. Even though he was taller, Samuel surpassed him in girth. "Don't worry. I won't let him get to me." He looked at his watch. "Well, I better go see Will now, and I'll take him home."

Samuel's attention shifted to the topic of Will. "Yes, he's doing better, but he may yet have many years dealing with this." Samuel rubbed his broad hand across his eyes, then he looked at Paul. "I know he has problems dealing with what happened to him and his friend; that he has horrific flashbacks; but I also know he has deep spiritual issues." He stepped closer to Paul. "I've been concerned about some literature I've seen him with. He's looking in the wrong places for answers."

* * *

"The bottom line is, Will, I don't know exactly what you saw; but, as I've just relayed to you, some of my parents' experiences on the mission field included sightings of angels. Not because they'd seen angels, but because people who had meant them harm had testified about seeing others with them, protecting them, when my parents knew there had been no one."

Michaela held her hands tightly clasped on her lap beneath the table. She had been sharing with Will for the past ten or so minutes and didn't want to lose any moment of this opportunity to make an impact in his life. He was now seated directly across from her, elbows on the table, and seemed to be listening intently as she tried to answer his many questions.

"So, you really do believe in God—Jesus—and angels and the Kingdom of Heaven?" Will questioned as if longing for the truth—the proof. "How can you be so sure?" He pulled his elbows from the table and leaned back. "I've been to hell and back, yet hell stays with me. How do I find heaven, peace? How do... " He bowed his head and seemed to struggle for a moment. When he looked at her, his eyes were red. "How do I find the real meaning of life, of my being here?"

Michaela ached for him as her heart continually prayed for the Spirit's words in her mouth. There was no doubt this man was terribly bound by his illness and spiritual darkness, and that he wanted to be free from both. She felt overwhelmed by his needs, yet she wasn't relying on herself, but on the One who knew everything, saw all things and could do anything.

"Yes, I do believe in it all, in all that Pastor Paul shares with you, in all God's Word—the Bible—speaks of. God has a reason for each of us here, in this world—this existence. Jesus came to help us see that. He didn't have to, but yet He obeyed His Father's directive to pay the ultimate price to free us, to give us peace. The peace you crave, Will."

With his elbows back on the table, his broad knuckles prominent as he locked his fingers together, Will's blue eyes held a desperate look. "What about other roads—other religions? Don't they lead to Him—God? Don't they lead to peace?"

"If you choose to believe Jesus, He says He is the only way to the Father. He went further to say He is the truth and the life. He didn't say He was one way, or a truth or a type of life. If you choose Jesus, then you must believe all that He says."

"The Bible?"

"Yes."

Will sighed deeply and bowed his head.

Please, Lord, opened his eyes and understanding to You. Help him to see the truth of You. Touch his soul, oh, breathe on him breath of God.

"Will?" The door opened and Paul stepped into the room. "Oh—"His gaze scanned the room quickly. "You're still here, Michaela."

Michaela couldn't tell why she suddenly felt guilty, but she was dismayed that her moment with Will was officially over. She stood slowly, feeling like an errant student, yet defiantly so.

"I usually let you know when I'm leaving," she said, stating the obvious.

"Yes—yes you do," he agreed slowly. His shirt collar had been loosened and his sleeves rolled up, but he did not appear relaxed as his gaze continued to shift from Michaela to Will and back again.

"Hey, Rev.," Will spoke up as if coming out of a daze. He had shifted his body so he could see Paul, but remained in his chair. "Ready to join us? If you don't mind, I'd like to have Michaela hang out with us for this session."

If the floor would have opened up and swallowed her, Michaela would have welcomed it as she watched Paul's dark eyes narrow and his gaze rest in her direction. The traitorous floor remained solid under her feet.

* * *

"Are you sure, Ethel?" Samuel questioned for the second time. He and Hilda had welcomed Ethel into their living room just minutes ago. She and Hilda were sitting together on the couch while he sat in the armchair.

Ethel nodded vigorously as she gripped Hilda's hands. "Yes, Sam. Even the doctors are amazed at the change. I tell you George had a healing as sure as Jesus walked on water." She fixed her gaze on Hilda who smiled in encouragement. Ethel spoke to Samuel again. "George said when that slip of a girl prayed for him, he felt an incredible warmth flow through him, from his head through to his belly. As the warmth eased away, it took all the pain with it. His fever is gone, after just being up that morning."

"Yes, you said they were going to start him on some new antibiotics, but... "Hilda paused, smiling at Ethel.

"Now, they're going to wait and see. They can't understand why he suddenly has no tenderness at the surgery site," Ethel continued. "I was so worried about him. After his hernia was repaired, he seemed to be on the mend; but then he developed that terrible fever and the pain came back. Now, it's like he's a new man. He can't wait to come home."

"Oh, Ethel, that's so wonderful," Hilda cried, hugging Ethel's bony frame. "It's like, well—a miracle!"

"It is a miracle!" Ethel confirmed joyously. "And George wants so badly to talk to Michaela, but I haven't been able to get a hold of her."

"She's still at the Church, Ethel," Samuel said, pushing himself up from the armchair. He couldn't seem to stem the sense of excitement stirring in his inner being. "I'll go with you right now, if you want. You can talk to her face to face."

* * *

Paul kept his tone pleasant and comforting as he shared from the Bible in front of him. He was seated at the head of the table, with Michaela to his right, and Will still across from her. To her credit, she had tried excusing herself from the room, but Will had been insistent. Also, she allowed him to lead the session without any interruptions and only spoke when Will directly addressed her, which he did—frequently.

Paul struggled with his irritation, but couldn't quite label it as pride. He had worked with Will for months, until Will had chosen to break their scheduled sessions, seeming to disappear into a world of his own. Now Will seemed back on track with a therapist, Alcoholics Anonymous and the spiritual counselling sessions with him.

How was it that Will seemed to value Michaela's input as much as his own? Paul noticed how Will weighed her words and when she hesitated, he would push her for more. Paul could tell she was uneasy after what had happened with Blinder earlier. Every time she hesitated, she would glance at him before diving in with her opinions; her insights. And what she offered was good, even sound. So, why was he irritated?

"Do you believe in miracles?" Will directed this question to Michaela.

"Yes," Michaela answered softly, firmly.

Will glanced at Paul. "What about you, Rev.? Has there ever been one in this Church?"

Paul weighed his words carefully. "I do believe in miracles, Will. I think they happen every day; sometimes in ways we don't even recognize."

Will seemed to chew on that for a moment, then he said, "I mean an outright miracle: the kind you can't explain away or say is a coincidence. You know—the Bible kind."

"Yes, I do believe in those miracles," Paul offered, wondering where this was going.

He could almost feel the energy radiating from Michaela as she clasped and unclasped her fingers on the table before her. She wanted to speak and he was almost afraid of what she would say. He spoke before she could: "We may not see what you call 'outright' miracles much in our communities, but that doesn't mean they're not happening elsewhere."

"Like healings?" Will asked.

"Yeah, like healings," Paul assured him, feeling more confident.

"Why not?" Will persisted.

Paul was silent.

"We're not desperate enough... here." Michaela said, sounding all at once vulnerable, yet sure.

Will looked at her with intensity. "I'm desperate." His voice was raspy, filled with pleading.

Michaela returned Will's gaze with a different type of intensity. "Then, a miracle can be yours."

Silence reigned as Michaela and Will continued to hold each other's gazes. Paul could feel a charge in the air between them. Nothing in his training had prepared him for this. He needed to take control.

"Will, it will happen for you. Keep up with all your sessions and seeing your therapist, trying the best you know how, and—"

"Yes, I know, Rev.—give my life over to Christ," Will interrupted. He glanced from Paul to Michaela. Her lips spread in a sweet smile and she nodded gently.

"You need to accept His salvation, Will—His way. The Lord will bring miracles to whomever He chooses, but I'm sure it would help for you to surrender to Him," Michaela said.

Will seemed to weigh their words carefully. He sighed deeply, pursing his lips. "Thank you," he said as he shoved his chair back and stood up. "I really appreciate your time, both of you. I—ah, need to use the facilities, then... "

"Yes, I'll give you a ride," Paul added. He watched as Will smiled tentatively down at Michaela. Then Will turned and walked to the door, and let himself out.

The room was silent, but he could feel her gaze. He looked at her. They searched each other's gazes. He noticed he was no longer irritated with her; mystified maybe. He was in a weird place where she was concerned.

"You want to ask me, don't you?" he asked quietly.

She lowered her gaze and pulled her hands from the table to her lap. A smile tugged at her lips. Their fullness tempted him; it had been over three years since he had kissed a woman who was not his mother or sisters. He mentally reigned himself in, hoping his emotions would follow suit; that's not what he should be thinking about right now. He should be instructing her not to give Will false hope.

"Well, Paul Rayner, do you believe we could have 'outright' miracles here?" Michaela asked. She sat, half turned towards him, waiting for his answer.

Paul drank in the clear, warm, caramel colour of her skin. He wanted to touch her, not talk of supernatural things. The miracle transforming his heart, after three years of thinking he might never again feel for another woman what he had felt for his wife, was miracle enough. If he could, he would talk to her about miracles all right.

"Paul?"

He tore his gaze away and looked down at the Bible beneath his hands. "I do believe that God does the impossible, in His own way, His own timing."

"But, what about here—Bethel Community—the city of Milward?" Michaela persisted.

Paul looked at her, but then he was distracted by the door being pushed opened. He stood up. Samuel and Ethel entered, both beaming. Samuel stood slightly behind Ethel, both hands on her shoulders.

"Paul, Michaela, we have a miracle to report!" Samuel announced.

Chapter Twelve

Leroy was sitting on the top deck step listening to Tristan dramatize George Flint's so-called healing. He was a little sceptical about the whole thing, but he couldn't deny the story still held his attention.

"It's all true!" Tristan insisted. "Mr. Flint was totally healed. They're supposed to let him out today." Her words were laced with triumph.

Five other teenagers sat on lawn chairs on the Hursts' small backyard deck looking up at Tristan, wide-eyed. They had gathered, late afternoon, for a planning session with Brennon and Michaela for the opening of the Fellowship Hall. Leroy had been practically "force-invited" by Michaela who had insisted she wanted him to be part of the committee.

Apparently Michaela had been designated to help Pastor Brennon plan a ceremony for the opening of the Fellowship Hall. Even though Leroy wasn't one of the youth in leadership, she had drafted him. He had found it hard to say no and that kind of irritated him. He didn't feel like he belonged and he knew what she was trying to do. He had wanted to tell her he didn't need her charity, but she had seemed so genuine in her offer, so he had caved. Plus, Pastor Paul had thrown his weight behind her decision, and that had solidified it.

"He was probably getting better anyway," a kid with blue braces, a latecomer, spoke up. "How do you know he was really healed?"

Leroy had to listen to Tristan go over the whole "he felt warmth course through his body" rendition again. The kid's eyes widened as he leaned forwards to catch her every word.

Leroy flicked at an insect crawling up his calf-length, jeans shorts. It got lost in the baggy folds of the material, so he pulled the material straight to finish the job. Satisfied, he leaned his head against a wooden rail and sighed out loudly.

He was tired of all the drama. He didn't mind Tristan. Their moms were friends and Tristan was pretty nice to him—even went out of her way to be friendly. He could tell it irked Ian. Ian, he could do without, so he stayed out of his way. Pastor Brennon had already given them the needed lecture about their "immature behaviour," and he didn't feel like listening to another one.

For the most part, the kids at the Church had accepted him; some of them even thought he was cool. He had noticed some of the younger kids trying to dress like him. He didn't know if that was so good. Kids who dressed "gangster" didn't necessarily have a clue what the real deal was. He'd done the real deal in a Toronto ghetto most people didn't want to think about.

After his father's death, his mother had moved them in with family in a nice Toronto neighbourhood. Somehow, he had found himself more and more hanging with rough kids in areas where things went down—or had they found him? The death of his father had left an empty ache that had weighed him down. The guys in the gang had given him a sense of belonging; of purpose. He'd done the drugs—nothing too hard—he wasn't stupid; he had done the robberies, the staking out of the territories; the list went on... .

It wasn't long before his mother looked past her grief to see what was happening. With a quickness that had sent his world reeling, she'd packed them off to Milward—a place he'd never even heard of, but where his parents had lived at one time before his birth.

Taking the kid out of the ghetto didn't mean taking the ghetto out of the kid. He'd found like-minded company soon enough.

Leroy tuned out the group, hoping Michaela and Pastor Brennon would come out soon so they could get on with it. He leaned forwards with his elbows on his knees, appreciating the gentle, warm breeze on his skin. The scent of earth rose to his nostrils from the last two days of rain. He'd always liked that scent. Maybe one day he would have property to smell all the earth he wanted.

Yeah, that was possible. Pastor Paul had said anything was possible with God. God and Pastor Paul had saved his life. Even though he still didn't know what he really thought about God, he knew Pastor Paul, and he was a man of God.

If it hadn't been for Pastor Paul, he would have left the hospital stitched-up after a knife wound and would have returned to the same stupid life; a life where you couldn't trust your own friends and where you were always looking over your shoulder to see if someone would rat you out or put a knife in your back. He would have died. He didn't kid himself about that anymore—he'd seen it happen to others.

Yeah, he'd only considered God because of Pastor Paul.

"Hey, Leroy, come join us!"

Leroy swivelled on his backside to look up at Pastor Brennon and Michaela coming through the patio doors with loaded trays in their hands. His stomach rumbled. Maybe this meeting wasn't such a bad idea after all.

* * *

Paul slowed his pace as he jogged the last block back to the parsonage. He'd missed his morning run for the past two mornings because of rain. The heat of the afternoon wasn't the best time, but it still felt good to run. He did a lot of sitting and kneeling in his line of work, so basketball with Leroy—or anyone who was game enough—and jogging offset the sedentary part of his life.

His breath came sharply now, but he kept smiling and waving at the friendly Milward neighbours as he passed by. Early morning runs didn't require as much social niceties; it was usually just him and the birds.

He changed his jog to a walk, knowing he needed to warm down before reaching the parsonage. Slowing down his run didn't mean the thoughts that had been churning in his head took the same pattern. He hadn't seen much of Michaela in the past two days, as she was spending more time working with Brennon and the youth on plans for the Fellowship Hall opening ceremony.

He and Brennon had decided the project would be a good assignment for her. A mission trip would take too much time and planning for her to do while on internship. He wasn't sure how, but somehow she had still convinced them to have her lead a mission trip to her parents' place, in Haiti, at the end of summer just before school started. So, the plans for the trip were still being worked on while she assisted with the plans for the ceremony.

He smiled and waved at an elderly neighbour across the street who had called to him. All too soon his mind returned to its ramblings. All evidence had, indeed, pointed to George having been healed—miraculously. He had visited him, and George had been very emotional and steadfast in his belief of the occurrence. There had been no doubt in George's mind.

Paul ducked his head around the low-hanging branch of a maple tree. George and Ethel, of course, had spoken with Michaela. The whole Church would probably know about the *healing* before Sunday, in two days. What was his position? He had grappled with it; he had prayed about it. He hadn't liked the results. It was as if the Spirit were asking why he struggled with it so. It wasn't that he didn't believe in divine intervention. He had to face the obvious question. If a renowned evangelist had come and healing had followed, would he be wrestling with the results, or would he be pumped that God had truly visited them? Perhaps, it was the vessel through which it had come.

Michaela Laroche was supposed to be learning from him, yet he needed to be more opened to learning from her too.

As he turned onto the concrete walkway leading to the parsonage front steps, he pulled the neck of his sweaty T-shirt to wipe at the perspiration running down the sides of his face. Maybe the hour's trip to his mother's on Monday would do him good. Maybe, he would visit the cemetery there. Hannah had been such a good sounding board for him.

It was funny how he could think of Hannah so clearly without the weight of ache that had become his constant companion. Yes, he would visit the cemetery. He knew she wasn't there in spirit, but he still felt closer to her there. He needed to tell her about Michaela. He didn't know what he would say, but he needed to do it.

Paul's eyes quickly focused upwards. Even before he reached the last step up to the parsonage porch, he could smell her scent. Dressed in a black-and-white sundress, she rose up in one graceful sweep from the patio chair on the far right of the front door.

"I wondered why I couldn't get you at the Church, on your cell or here. Wow, look at you all sweaty." Karlene said the words as if his appearance repelled her, but her hand delicately stroking at his right bicep spoke a completely different language.

Paul waited until she removed her hand before he spoke. "Hi, Karlene. What's up?" There was a particularly vulnerable look in her eyes, and he instinctively knew he needed to keep things on a very casual level.

She nodded towards the front door. "I don't suppose you'll invite me in?"

He couldn't believe she would even ask him that. He didn't answer her question.

Karlene began to fidget with the handbag on her shoulder, but then raised her arms to smooth nervously at her dark hair. "I didn't think so," she said, answering her own question.

"Karlene, is something wrong?"

She turned her back to him and the thin heels of her black sandals tapped sharply on the concrete as she returned to the chair she had just vacated. She crossed one leg over the other in an agitated fashion, causing the skirt of her sundress to pull up mid-thigh. Paul averted his eyes.

"You mean besides you being so archaic?" She paused, then continued when he didn't answer. "Is it true that the intern will be directing the program for the opening ceremony?"

Paul frowned, wondering where this was going. "Michaela?"

"She's the only intern we have." Karlene's crossed arms and other body language spoke loudly and clearly. She was not pleased.

Paul's hands rested on his hips. He was sweaty and tired and he was in no mood for female hysterics. "Brennon is planning the ceremony, Karlene. Michaela is assisting him as part of her intern assignment. You, of course, will still be directing the choir. I've heard you guys practicing, and it sounds great."

"I assumed I would be planning the whole ceremony. I thought that had been discussed."

"By whom, Karlene?"

"I-I was sure it had been suggested that I look after it," Karlene stuttered slightly. She uncrossed her arms and legs and stood facing him. Her golden eyes were filled with emotions.

"I gave you free reign in preparing the choir, Karlene. The opening ceremony is not meant to be a one-person show. I'm not sure how you interpreted any discussions about the whole thing, but I'm sorry if someone gave you the wrong impression." Paul paused, feeling frustrated.

Karlene's eyes were blinking rapidly as if she were stemming tears. He touched her shoulder gently. "Look, I'm sorry—"

"Don't be," Karlene said forcefully, stepping away from his touch. "It's obvious I've made a mistake. It's fine." She walked quickly towards the steps before turning back to him. "Did you ever consider, Paul, why I'm here? Your biological mother, Isabella, was part Latino. We are not so different, you and I. Did you ever think about that?"

Paul felt totally stupefied. Karlene glared at him, then grabbed the rail as she took hasty steps down to the walkway, her black hair billowing out behind her. Paul ran his hands backwards over his head and down to grip the back of his neck, before flinging them down at his sides. What exactly had Karlene said? What had she meant? This was ridiculous! Something was very wrong with this picture.

* * *

"Okay, I think that's good," Michaela announced grandly. Working with the youth and Brennon had gone really well, even with little interruptions from Sarah and Conner. They had mapped out an amazing program she could present to Paul and the board. She was sure they would love it!

"I think it's great!" Tristan agreed, jumping up from her seat. "It's so awesome to work with you, Michaela."

Michaela looked up from the opened binder on the patio table, feeling a little uncomfortable.

"Well—umm—thanks, Tristan, but we all did it." She looked around at the group, smiling.

She loved working with these young people. They were so... themselves.

"What about me?" Brennon asked with mocked seriousness. He leaned back in his chair, grinning at the group.

Ian started laughing out loudly, and the group followed his lead.

"Aw, Pastor Brennon, we love you too," one of the girls said, giggling. Ian and the boy with blue braces took their cue from her and got up to hover over the back of Brennon's chair, aiming fake kisses at him.

"Oh, we love you, Pastor Brennon! We really do!" said the two boys in high-pitched voices.

"What's going on out here?" Sarah asked, as she stepped from the house unto the deck.

Michaela smiled and pointed at Brennon. "Apparently, he needs more encouragement and loving, Sarah. I think you have your job cut out for you."

The boys started hooting and hollering, while the three girls looked on with bemused expressions. Leroy sat between Michaela and Brennon, one side of his mouth raised in a half smile. Michaela gently elbowed him on his arm.

"Thanks for your great input. I'd really like for you to think about doing that rap. It'd be great in the program."

Leroy grimaced. He pulled at the skin on his neck. "Okay," he finally responded. "I'm only gonna think about it—not making any promises."

"I know," Michaela assured him, smiling. *He'll do it.*

"Okay, guys," Brennon said in a slightly raised voice, bringing order to the group. "Let's get things cleaned up; then you're free to go."

Michaela gathered her supplies, as Brennon tried to figure out who needed rides home. She noticed Sarah's nod towards the house, so she followed her into the living room.

"Conner is sleeping," Sarah said in a low voice. "I want to talk to you about something. Let's go downstairs before the rest come in."

Michaela followed Sarah down to the basement family room where a dehumidifier was running softly. It was a small area but adequate for a family of three. Conner's toys were strewn across the carpeted floor.

"How are things going with Conner?" Michaela asked, as they sat facing each other on the only couch in the room.

Sarah sighed, smiling. "It's difficult sometimes. He's almost three and he hasn't even shown any signs of pulling himself up, let alone walking. We were told to expect a delay in all of his functions, but he seems to respond very well to music."

"I've read that many people with autism are brilliant in some skills and learn to live independently, even hold jobs."

"Yes, there are different levels of autism and early detection and treatment are crucial to ensure the greatest level of development. Bren and I are very hopeful, and we trust the Lord for the outcome." Sarah's brown hair fell forwards as she leaned towards Michaela. "I'll let you in on a little secret. We hope to try for another child closer to the end of the year."

"Oh, Sarah... "

"Shush," Sarah extended her hand to cover Michaela's lips playfully. "It took us a while with Conner, so we'll have to see how it goes. Now, what I really want to do is warn you about something."

"Warn me, about what?"

Sarah pulled her hair behind one ear. She looked very serious. "Karlene does not like that you are helping with the ceremony. I overheard her complaining to Rashad about it. He tried to calm her down, but she insisted she was going to Paul to straighten it out. She feels she should be organizing the whole thing."

*   *   *

She hated that she was doing this, but she had no choice. She had been forced into it. It had been many years since she had left this path, many years since she had claimed Christianity as her new road, but her childhood exposure to the other world had always pulled at her. Lately, the pull had been stronger than ever and she had found herself flirting with the temptation to return to her roots.

As a result, many doubts had begun to assail her; unwelcomed thoughts had mingled with her despairing prayers to the Christian God, Jesus. Now, she was desperate.

Once again, she was yielding to the dark pull on her soul. She told herself it was familiar and she could renounce it at any time; yet, deep inside, she knew the lie, and... she was desperate.

"Have you made up your mind this time?" the deep voice asked her out of the dimness. Why he insisted on sitting in the dark, when she already knew who he was by daylight, was beyond her, but she dared not question.

"I have no choice." The words seemed to choke from her. She felt a dread she couldn't explain whispering at her essence. She was also experiencing an urgent prompting to flee, but the spirit of jealousy had overwhelmed her.

"You feel it is time, then?"

She tightened her grip on the arms of her chair. His desk loomed large and dark in front of her, the light from a small table lamp bathed only part of his face, the air felt heavy.

"Yes," she said, giving her permission for all she had vowed never to return to.

* * *

Beyond the sight of the physical world, yet existing along with it, two large columns of light glowed brightly just outside the perimeter of the Milward Seniors Community Sales Centre. Above the Centre were ominous clouds of darkness—a thick blackness—that billowed.

One of the light sources communed with the other. "She has made her choice." The other glowed in what seemed like fierce intensity.

"Yes, however, we are not to leave her."

* * *

Leroy paused on the sidewalk in front of Metro's Gas Bar. He looked across through the growing darkness at the Sales Centre. He watched Karlene grab the handrail as she seemed to almost stumble down the stairs from the Centre's front porch. She seemed to have difficulty getting into her car. He watched the car pull out of the driveway; then it made a right turn and headed down the street away from him.

He shook his head in disgust. "At least she didn't have Will with her this time," he spoke out loudly to himself. He put Karlene out of his mind and swaggered off down the lit sidewalk with good thoughts in his mind about his time at the Hursts' place.

Chapter Thirteen

Paul was lounging on the Hursts' living room couch, Saturday afternoon, holding Conner on his lap, waiting for Brennon to return from the kitchen. Sarah, Lucy and Carmel had been invited out to lunch by Michaela who seemed to have a natural talent for rounding people up.

Lucy and Carmel were already friends, especially because of their common experience as military wives. Also, Lucy had advised Carmel in the past during some difficult issues involving Leroy and the Children's Aid Society, but Paul knew it had been a while since the two women had connected.

Conner played contentedly with a brightly coloured toy with different dangly pieces, as Paul considered Brennon's earlier questions about George's healing. Brennon had been as excited as most people to hear about it and seemed to accept its authenticity.

Brennon walked in from the kitchen with two large glasses of soft drink. They had been discussing Paul's strange episode with Karlene.

"So what do you think she meant?" Brennon asked, as he placed the glasses on the coffee table.

"Well, it seemed kind of odd that she'd bring up the fact that I'm a quarter the same race as her. I mean, what does that have to do with anything? I was married to a Caucasian and she knows that."

"Maybe she was trying to slant things in her favour." Brennon slouched back in the loveseat on the other side of the coffee table. He ran his hands through his sandy hair. "Remember, we had this conversation right here not so long ago. You didn't think much of it though."

"What are you talking about? I didn't dismiss it." Paul bent over to retrieve Conner's toy from the floor. "I just didn't take it very seriously."

"Now you are?"

Paul pursed his lips and gave Brennon a direct gaze. "There's definitely something going on. It's beginning to look like—like... "

"Fatal attraction?" Brennon asked. He gestured at Conner who had started squealing loudly. "Do you want me to take him?"

"Naw," Paul said, smiling down at Conner as he repositioned him. Conner piped down, looked up at Paul, then seemed to look through him. "We're pals today, aren't we, little dude?" Paul returned his attention to Brennon. "Fatal attraction? I hope it's nothing that crazy; but, after what happened yesterday, I'm beginning to wonder."

"It wouldn't be the first time a pastor's had to deal with unwanted attention. What about Michaela?"

"What about her?" Paul asked. He could feel his tension level go up.

Brennon leaned forwards, giving him a direct gaze. "Sarah thinks Karlene may have it in for her. So does Rashad. Look, let's cut to the chase. I know you don't want to talk about it, but it's me, Paul. We go way back and you know anything you say will be safe with me."

Paul remained silent. He knew where Brennon was going with this. He took a deep breath, deciding to face the inevitable this time.

Brennon plunged in. "I just think Karlene was trying to slant the race thing in her favour because Michaela is Black and she wanted to even up the competition. Not to mention, Michaela is in the ministry, like you. You have to admit, Paul, Karlene might be a little off, but she's not stupid. She can see what Sarah sees, what Hilda sees and what I see. You like Michaela more than a little, and I'm putting that mildly."

Paul looked down at Conner, not really seeing him. It was somewhat of a relief, actually, to finally face this. "Nobody put in the manual what you do when you fall for the intern."

Brennon grinned and leaned back on the loveseat, hands behind his head. "That's because you don't do anything. You just wait it out until she's done her internship." He studied Paul for a moment. "Does admitting it feel any better?"

"Yes and no," Paul said. He groaned loudly, causing Conner to look directly at him. "You better be praying hard for me, 'cause I'll be needing it." Suddenly, he felt uncertain. "Besides, she may not... "

"Be interested?" Brennon finished for him. He winked conspiratorially. "Trust me, my wife picks up on more than you think. Not to mention Hilda. If all ends well, my friend, I'd say you have it in the bag." Brennon's gaze softened. "I think you're definitely ready to move on and I think Hannah would approve."

Paul gently lowered Conner, who had been squirming relentlessly, to the floor. He rotated his shoulders back, then clasped his hands above his knees. "Let's just say, I won't be counting my chickens before they hatch and I need to keep my primary responsibilities toward Michaela as my focus. Plus, we need to do something about Karlene, but I don't want to stir up too much before the Hall opens."

Brennon got up to remove their untouched drinks from Conner's reach. "You want to pray about it now?"

Paul got up and stretched. "No time like the present." He looked at his watch. "When will the girls be back?"

Brennon trailed Conner around the room, as the child crawled quickly from one attraction to the other. The room had been well baby-proofed. "Another hour, I think."

Paul noticed that Conner had found a new focus. "Okay, let's pray now while Conner-man's busy."

* * *

Michaela's heart was full as she watched the three women interact like old friends just out for lunch. These women, though, had unusual challenges to deal with from day to day.

Sarah, Lucy, Carmel and Michaela were in a little cafe not far from Carmel's blinds store. They had just finished lunch and were sipping cool drinks. The conversation had been pleasant and, for the most part, meaningful. She felt more hopeful for Lucy because Will seemed to be doing better in treatment and was meeting with Paul regularly.

"I'm so glad Tristan was able to hold the fort for you so you could join us, Carmel," Michaela remarked.

"Well, I lost my part-time summer help, so Lucy convinced me to give her a try. This is her third week. I'm sure she'll be okay for a couple of hours," Carmel responded. Her vest-like, linen blouse with a matching skirt gave her a casual-professional look. She had also taken great care with her make-up and hair which was pulled back to lay straight on her shoulders.

"I'm so glad she has this job, Carmel," Lucy said. "She's had such a trying year at school with peer pressure, and I believe working in your store has boosted her self-esteem. Plus, you're a good role model for a young girl."

Carmel gave Lucy a wry look. "I'm not a church-goer," she stated emphatically.

Lucy shook her head, causing her cherry blonde curls to sway around her shoulders.

"No matter, you love the Lord and He'll straighten you out."

Sarah seemed to be trying to stifle a giggle at Lucy's candour.

Lucy glanced at her, winked, then continued: "You're a strong, single mother who works hard to provide for her family and to raise them right."

Carmel looked down, fiddling with her glass on the table. "I didn't do so well with Leroy."

"But, you've done so much for him, Carmel. You've knocked on every door of opportunity for him to get help. He would have been worse off if you hadn't been pro-active," Lucy said.

"Leroy would probably be dead if it hadn't been for Pastor Paul." Carmel looked across the table at Michaela. "It's one of the reasons I still hold on to my faith, even if I don't seem to practice it well." She struggled with her emotions for a moment. "I turned my back on God when he took my husband. It was a while before I came out of grieving long enough to see that my son had morphed into a criminal."

"Yet, He had been there all the time," Michaela commented softly.

Carmel frowned as if not understanding Michaela, but then her face lightened. "Yes, I believe God was there. I also believe He'd been giving me many signals that I had missed. Yet, He persisted until He got my attention." She glanced around the table at them all. "It's not God, it's church people."

"Carmel had a bad episode at her last Church," Sarah explained. "They blamed Leroy for a fire in one of their Sunday school rooms. It was later found out to have been the Pastor's son fooling around with friends."

"Apparently, they decided Leroy fit the mould because of his gang affiliations and his appearance," Lucy further explained.

"That must have been so hard for both you and Leroy," Michaela said. She leaned forwards over the small table. "Have you forgiven them?"

Carmel lowered her gaze and sighed deeply. She was silent for a moment before redirecting her gaze to Michaela. "I'm working on it."

"I'm not judging you," Michaela assured her. She hadn't walked in Carmel's shoes, but she tried to imagine what it would have been like to have your child vilified, in spite of his innocence.

Carmel smiled slowly. "I know, but I do thank you for reminding me of the challenge." She placed both hands on the table, fingers clasped tightly. "I do need to forgive to be able to move on. It's healthier and better for Leroy too."

"Now, we can all get our hankies out," Sarah joked gently.

Quiet laughter mingled around the table, and Michaela felt as if a special bond had just formed between her and Carmel.

Twenty minutes later, Michaela walked with Carmel back to the blinds store after parting ways with Sarah and Lucy. It was comfortably warm and only slightly overcast as they kept up a steady pace to Carmel's store.

They were on a downtown sidewalk along one of Milward's main streets, which was fairly busy with traffic and pedestrians during the lunch-hour rush, but Michaela felt content in Carmel's company.

"So, do you miss your family? Do you talk with them much?" Carmel asked as they side-stepped around a young mom pulling a green wagon with two toddlers on board.

"Yes, to both. I don't always get them when I call. It depends on whether they're on the missionary compound or up in the hills."

"The hills?" Carmel asked, looking at her curiously.

"Yes. They go up to those who can't, or won't, come down. They minister to spiritual needs and often bring food and other supplies. There's a big gulf between the rich and poor in Haiti."

"Leroy told me that you hope to go with some of the youths at the end of summer."

"Well, I thought it would be a life-changing experience for them to see how much we take for granted here, when they see the lack there, and yet many people there are happier than many of us."

Carmel chuckled softly. "You're so right, girl. We definitely have issues with contentment in all of this affluence," she said, gesturing around. They strolled along. "One thing I'm very grateful for is the ability to support my family. I'm very thankful for that."

"I guess that's a challenge for most families here. We have such a high standard of living; it must be quite difficult for single moms. You can be proud."

"Thank you," Carmel said, pausing outside the front of her store. A huge, pink sign hung above the doorway—*Carmel's Blinds and Home Decor.*

"Speaking of being single," Carmel continued, "is there a special somebody pining for you somewhere?"

Michaela faced her, feeling slightly embarrassed. "Well, no. I'm pretty focused on my internship right now."

Carmel raised an eyebrow. "Oh, really—a pretty thing like you?" She laid a firm hand on Michaela's shoulder. "Well, take it from an older, if not necessarily wiser, sister. Don't have your nose so stuck to the grindstone that you let opportunity pass you by."

Michaela could feel her face grow warm. The topic of men and dating had never been her strong point. In Bible college, she had resolutely shrugged off the label "bridal college," determined that she would not be the expected casualty of an institution many thought habitually married off its female population before they graduated. Besides, she was fairly choosy about men; they had to live up to her father's image.

She could sense Carmel's curious gaze and she felt the warmth from her face spread to her chest and stomach, realizing that her thoughts had shifted from her father to the one man who was filling her thoughts more and more each day—Paul Rayner.

"Do you want to talk about it?" Carmel asked, a mischievous smile tipping her lips.

Michaela glanced briefly at her car which was parked on the street in front of Carmel's store. "Talk about what? There really is no one."

"Okay," Carmel said, as if she didn't believe her. She nodded towards the store. "You want to come in for a while before taking Tristan home?"

"Only, if you promise not to third degree me about my love life."

Carmel gave a hearty laugh. "What love life?"

* * *

Samuel repositioned his legs on the low stool in front of his den armchair. He had been sitting for the last fifteen minutes watching Paul slowly pace the room, as they talked about the upcoming celebrations and George's healing. Paul seemed more accepting that it had been divine intervention.

Over the years, Samuel had witnessed Paul grow from an unsure—albeit determined—youth, trying to find his way and identity, to a confident, well-admired, young man who took seriously the responsibilities of a wife and his call to the ministry. He had helped Paul's dear mother and sisters see him through the loss of his wife and unborn child.

Samuel didn't claim to understand all that came with being a minority by race or what being raised adopted entailed, but he loved Paul like the son he never had. He also felt a fierce loyalty toward him because of the close friendship he'd had with Stephen Rayner. It seemed that love and loyalty had been enough over the years, even when Paul, in his need for independence, had pulled away from him like a son distancing himself from a father to find his own path. Now, he believed they were at a good and steady place in their relationship.

At the moment, Samuel was fully aware that there was more on Paul's mind than ceremonies and miracles. He decided to get to the bottom of things. "Paul, son, what's really on your mind?"

Paul stopped abruptly and frowned. He looked down at Samuel, then started pacing again.

"Paul, please, stop the pacing and sit down, you're making my head swim."

Paul finally complied, lowering himself in the wooden rocker that Hilda used when she kept company with Samuel. Of course, the rocking of the chair replaced the pacing, and somehow when Hilda rocked, the squeaking emanating from it didn't sound quite so deliberate.

Samuel sighed, resolved to put up with the noise, but it stopped abruptly. Paul was leaning forwards, his long frame spilling out of the chair, looking at him.

"Sam, I need you and Hilda to do something for me." He sounded confident and determined, but Samuel perceived a hidden vulnerability.

"Anything," Samuel assured him.

Paul ran his hands forwards across his very dense, black curls and across his brows before resting them on his knees. "As you well know, there seems to be enough concern in the community regarding faulty building practices at the Seniors Community. I've decided to take the leadership in submitting this concern, officially, at the next ministerial meeting."

"I think that's good," Samuel said. "I figured it would come up soon enough. The Mayor seems to be grappling with the complaints without any real action. I think money is under the table—not with the Mayor—but at the inspection end of things."

"Possibly—at least Rashad thinks so. I don't want it to be about Falconer and me, because it's something that needs doing. So, I want you and Hilda to keep it in earnest prayer, perhaps even a fast."

"Absolutely. You know we'd do anything for you, son."

An easy smile softened the intensity of Paul's expression. "I know you would and I really appreciate it."

Samuel waited for a moment, watching Paul's fingers tap the tops of his knees before asking, "What else?"

A deep sigh preceded the answer. "I would also like to ask you both to take Karlene under your wings." He recounted the episode between him and Karlene.

Samuel sighed. He eased his large legs off the footstool, before smoothing at the creases of his trousers. "Yes, Hilda and I have been quite concerned about her. I know Rashad is, as well. I don't know exactly what's going on with her, but she's definitely set her cap for you. It's certainly become more evident since Michaela's arrival."

"I guess it took me longer to notice than most."

Samuel studied Paul silently.

The rocker squeaked as Paul leaned back in it. "Michaela doesn't need to get mixed-up in this. I feel very responsible for that." He shook his head slowly. "I couldn't have imagined in a million years that I'd be dealing with stuff like this."

Samuel remained silent, sensing that more would be forth coming if he didn't press the issue.

"I don't think Michaela is oblivious to it," Paul continued, "but I think she's probably chosen not to focus on it." He rubbed his hands over his face. "You know her—she's got a steadfast mind-set with a goal attached."

"Yes, she's one determined young woman. I admire her, but she could learn a lot from you."

Paul gave a short laugh. "I'm sure I could learn a lot from her too."

"I'm glad you're willing to admit that, but you also have the weight of maturity, experience and inner strength borne of tragedy, behind you. As much as she's had an unusual life and spiritual gifting, she will need someone with strength and backbone to lean on."

Paul's expression was one of surprise mixed with confusion.

Samuel smiled before clarifying the meaning of his last statement. "Hilda and I know, Paul. So, without you asking for it, I'll still advise you to remain steadfast in your responsibility toward her as an intern, but protect the blossoming of what is... until you're free to act on it. And just for your information, I think it's about time."

Chapter Fourteen

Paul looked over the congregation from his seat behind the pulpit, waiting for the offering collection to be completed. The melody of the piano offertory filled his soul, reinforcing all that had been taking place there.

In this earthly life, God's work in him would never be finished. There would always be another path, another journey, another lesson. Yet, he could be grateful that God would never allow him to walk the path alone, or without what he needed.

Samuel's insights had tipped things for him in acknowledging and dealing with the issues of his heart. He had spent a night of prayer, allowing the Spirit of God to speak to him and to challenge him. Afterwards, he had tugged at the wedding band on his finger until it came loose. He had sat for a good while just staring at the lighter brown strip on the skin of his finger where the ring had been.

He realized he had spent the last three years, after Hannah's death, in a cocoon of sorts. Not the kind that kept him from his responsibilities or hid him from the demands of life, but the kind that convinced him of the need to have control. No doubt, other parts of his life's history had also created the medium for its growth. Yet, he was not in control. He could only choose whether he would travel each path the best way or the worst way; in rebellion or denial; or in obedience to the One who held it all in His hands.

Yet, his heart was humbled that he didn't quite know how to give up his dependence on the structure he'd placed around his existence.

His glance rested on Michaela in the central front row. She had her head bowed over the Bible on her lap. He didn't know how to manage the feelings that were growing in him for her.

He shifted his gaze to Karlene. She was looking straight at him. He realized his need to hand her over to another's care, even though he was her pastor.

His gaze travelled over the congregation again, seeing Brennon, Sarah, the board members, and various other leaders. He was only one man; they all had a role to play in building the Kingdom of God.

He glanced at his Bible on the translucent pulpit. It was opened to *1 Corinthians 12*; a chapter which spoke of the Church as the body of Christ with many parts and giftings. Each part was necessary for the whole to function fully. The Church, of course, was the people who God expected to gift with different abilities.

Paul planned to tie that chapter in with the next one, chapter thirteen, which spoke about love being key in all of the gifts. Without love, in God's eyes, everything done would be empty. He planned to take the Church through it as a series.

The sermon he had intended for this morning still lay on his desk at the parsonage. This impulsive action with a sermon was a first for him.

He stood to his feet and approached the pulpit as the last strains of music died down. He took a deep breath. "Good morning, everyone!"

The congregation responded in kind, smiling at him.

"Before I begin, I'd like us to take a moment and verbally give glory and honour to the Lord Jesus! I'd like us to acknowledge Him and uphold Him in His rightful place!" Paul closed his eyes and began to lead in verbal accolades to the King of Kings and Lord of Lords; the Almighty Creator of all; Who was, is and is to come. His heart was encouraged greatly as the voices of the congregation began to swell around him.

* * *

Over two hours later, Michaela finally felt free to leave the Sanctuary. She returned to her seat to retrieve her belongings, but her eyes were drawn to the front of the room—to the Altar area.

Earlier, she had been asked to join with other leaders at the Altar to pray with those who had come for prayer. More people than usual had come forwards, and a wonderful, meaningful time of worship, prayer and fellowship had resulted. She was still experiencing the glow of God's Presence.

Following the time of prayer, Michaela had found herself caught up in the flurry of usual conversations and good-byes. Then she had spent time with Tristan and a few other girls, answering questions regarding some upcoming Youth activities, fundraising for the Haiti trip and the opening ceremony for the Fellowship Hall.

The greatest amount of her after-service time had been spent responding to people's constant interest in George's healing. News definitely travelled quickly in this Church. Yet, she couldn't fault them. It was the supernatural. Society was ripe for the supernatural.

She had found humour in what seemed like Tristan's steadfast mission to proclaim the "miracle" over and over.

"This is so much cooler than any fake vampire movie!" Tristan had said, looking at Michaela with what seemed like a mixture of pride and longing, showing a definite yearning for more of Christ!

After being released from the girls, Michaela had visited with George and Ethel who had been waiting patiently for her at the back of the Sanctuary. George had looked great and was almost back to his old self.

Michaela's heart, however, had remained significantly affected by Paul's sermon. He was, indeed, a brilliant speaker. He had already won her admiration when she had first heard him preach. Yet, there had been a difference about Paul and his preaching today. There had been a passionate freedom—an abandon—that she had not noticed before, and it had connected with her soul deeply.

Preaching was not her particular gifting, though she was good with words. She was more a one-to-one person. She definitely recognized the gift in Paul Rayner.

Now, Michaela briefly glanced through the rear sanctuary doors towards the front doors where Paul was, at his usual post, shaking hands. She gathered her belongings and prepared to exit the almost empty Sanctuary, but she was halted by two board members, Robert Dawson and Frank Harris.

The two men were all smiles as they shook her hands and offered words of encouragement and counsel.

"You've certainly been a real blessing to our congregation, my dear," Frank stated emphatically. His teeth contrasted whitely against his mahogany skin, as he grinned at her. Pride was written all over his countenance.

"Thank you so much, Mr. Harris," Michaela responded, smiling her appreciation.

"I think she'll be a real asset wherever she goes, don't you think, Rob?"

Robert nodded in agreement with his friend. "No doubt she will be." He adjusted his glasses over his prominent nose. His pale face was slightly flushed, probably from the effort of conversing with her. He was most likely more comfortable taking notes at board meetings than interacting with members of the Church.

"Do you know what your plans are after this, Michaela?" Frank questioned, his gaze fixed on her in fatherly appreciation.

Michaela repositioned the strap of her handbag on her shoulder as she hugged her Bible to her chest. "No, not quite yet. I've had one offer from a Church about an hour from here, in Georgeton. Have you heard of Hope Alive Church?"

"Ah—yes," Frank said, nodding slowly. "That's a wonderful Church. Well, never fear, the Lord has it in His hands. Even if you don't take on the responsibilities of a Church, yourself, I'm sure you would make an excellent pastor's wife, wouldn't she, Rob?"

Robert nodded in agreement, and Michaela cringed inwardly. A pastor's wife? Why did it always come back to that? No, she didn't want to be just a pastor's wife.

Michaela's conversation with the men soon finished and she strategically excused herself. They were good men, but their vision for her left her feeling boxed-in.

She attempted to exit the Sanctuary again, noticing that Paul was no longer at the front doors. She could see Brennon and Rashad conversing to the right side of the doors.

"How are you, Michaela?"

Michaela swung around to face Karlene who had approached her from behind. Karlene's beautiful, black hair was pulled high in an artistic coil and her makeup was flawless, emphasizing her eyes and full lips. Her white pants outfit, accented by a wide, black belt, fit her to perfection, and her feet were encased in black, sling-back, high heels.

"Oh, hello, Karlene," Michaela greeted her. She smoothed at her hair, suddenly feeling under-dressed in her simple, blue and white, short-sleeved dress. "I'm doing well—how about you?"

Karlene nodded slightly without answering. "Are things going well with plans for the ceremony?"

Michaela instinctively knew, even without Sarah's earlier warning, to tread carefully where Karlene was concerned. "Yes, thank you. Brennon is really good at this sort of thing. I'm learning a lot from him."

"I'm sure you have a lot of input as well."

"Well, he does give me opportunity. How is the choir doing?"

Karlene braced her hands on the top edge of the chair behind her, then leaned back against it. "The choir is fine as always. Will you be MC'ing?"

Michaela had the distinct impression that Karlene was fishing for information rather than just showing friendly interest. "Umm—I'm actually not sure about that." Michaela said, bracing herself for Karlene's next question. She noticed, however, that Karlene's focus was no longer on her.

Michaela looked behind and noticed that Paul had joined Brennon and Rashad in the Foyer.

"Excuse me," Karlene said, and without another word, she strutted towards the sanctuary doors, shoved through them, and made a bee-line for the men.

Michaela stared after her in disbelief. She took a deep breath, shaking her head, and decided to go through the side exit. Whatever Karlene was up to wasn't anything she wanted to be part of. She waved at the sole occupant left in the sound booth as she passed by. He gave her a thumbs-up, she smiled.

Without looking to see if anyone was on the other side, she pushed opened the side sanctuary door and walked out, nearly bumping into Paul.

He placed one hand on her left shoulder to keep her from colliding with him while reaching up to hold the door with the other. "Hey, there, watch out," he warned softly.

Michaela looked up into his eyes, suddenly feeling breathless. "Sorry," she managed as she stepped away from him. "I guess I should watch where I'm going."

"I guess you should," he agreed in easy humour. He let the door close and stood with his hands to his side, looking more casual without his jacket and tie, observing her.

Michaela glanced towards the front doors. Karlene was still there with Brennon and Rashad, looking her way. Michaela focused back on Paul, feeling awkward.

"Everything okay?" Paul asked. His dark eyes were intense. When she didn't respond, he lowered his head towards her. "Michaela?"

His cologne tickled her senses, and Michaela mentally shook herself, frustrated and piqued that he was making her feel vulnerable... and attracted to him. She took another step away from him. "Of course, I'm fine." She sought for an excuse. "I'm just a little tired, that's all."

"Was Karlene bugging you?" he persisted in asking.

Why was she feeling this way? Why didn't he just let her go? "Yes—I mean, no—I mean... It doesn't matter. I can handle Karlene."

Paul was frowning now. He looked away towards the others and whatever he saw caused him to take hold of her arm and pull her along with him. "Come here."

They walked past the Conference Room until they were just outside the Fellowship Hall. There, he let go of her arm. He pulled the doors opened and strolled to the windows on the far side, looking down into the Gym. He obviously expected her to follow him.

Michaela made it to the centre of the room. She stood watching him, clutching all the more tightly to her Bible. Paul, with his back to her, spread his hands along the window ledge to brace himself. It was then that she noticed something that clinched at her heart: his ring finger was bare!

Paul turned to face her. He walked slowly to about five feet from her, and then smiled, spreading his arms out. "Nice, isn't it?"

Michaela released the breath she'd been holding and glanced around the large room. From the pot-lit ceiling to the clay-coloured, wainscoted walls to the commercially carpeted floor; it was beautiful. It was a warm and inviting room and she could imagine it graced with round tables fit for a wedding feast. A slightly raised platform at the far end of the room was perfect for entertainment.

She focused on Paul. "It *is* very nice."

He lowered his arms, but continued to hold her gaze with his; his eyes communicating to her what she could hardly bear. Yet, she couldn't seem to look away. Whatever his eyes were telling her had also served to create a tangible, emotional charge that seemed to fill the space between them.

It seemed like forever before he let out a deep sigh, and then released her from his gaze. Michaela felt her eyes flutter shut, as if by their own accord. In a moment's whisper, her eyes re-opened to see his polished, black shoes take two steps towards her. She reluctantly re-connected with his gaze.

"Michaela, I want your internship to go well."

"I know," she responded tentatively.

"Promise me you'll let me know if you run into any problems—I mean anything."

"Okay, I will."

"Promise me."

"Okay, I promise," she said, laughing nervously. Suddenly, she remembered something.

"Actually, I have a lunch date, so I better get going." She was determined not to fall back under his spell.

"A lunch date?" Paul asked, his tone riddled with curiosity.

"Yes," Michaela confirmed, "with Carmel, Leroy and Lissa.'

He seemed to visibly relax. "Well, I won't keep you then. Have fun."

"Thanks," she said as she turned to go, feeling more herself. "I appreciate—you know—all of your concerns."

"Hey, it's nothing," he assured her, thrusting his hands into the pockets of his pants.

Michaela walked the length of the room towards the doorway, knowing he was watching her. Under the frame of the doorway, she turned to give him a little wave. She was right, he hadn't moved an inch. He smiled and waved back.

* * *

She felt her hands trembling on the steering wheel with the intensity of the emotions coursing through her. Her eyes burned with threatening tears, but she would not allow their release.

How dare he—how dare he dismiss her so easily for Michaela? Why could he not see that they were meant for each other; that they were perfect for each other? She could more than make up for the three years of emptiness left by his wife's death. She had studied him for the last two years. She knew the details of his life; his hopes and dreams; his wants and wishes.

Michaela did not know him like she did—only for three months.

Rashad—he meant well; but she didn't feel for him what she felt for Paul. The very sight of Paul Rayner filled her with intense longing that begged to be satisfied. Surely this was of God; surely He meant for them to be together. Surely, she had not bided her time these two years only to have a fresh-faced, doe-eyed, college graduate steal what belonged to her.

The Scriptures said that there was a time for peace and a time for war. This was war!

She guided her car round the circular driveway, grateful that the iron-wrought gate had been left opened. She parked in front of the cobblestoned walkway leading up to looming double doors. As she pushed the car door opened, she tried to still the trembling coursing through her body. She longed for the unsettled weight, sitting in the depth of her being, to go. It had been there since her first decision to seek the dark counsel, but she'd had no choice—just as she had no choice now.

When all was as it should be, she would shed the weight of her decision and truly walk the path of the straight and narrow. Yet, even as she tried to console herself with this intention, she realized the naivety of her plan. The dark forces didn't let you go that easily. Yet, she couldn't seem to help herself.

She couldn't imagine life without Paul Rayner. She would rather shrivel up and die. She would rather him remain alone for the rest of his life than to embrace an existence with that spell-binding she-wolf in sheep's clothing.

The door finally swung opened at the repeated peel of the doorbell. He stood before her, ominous and fierce, obviously not pleased to see her visit his home without an invitation. But, she didn't care. He owed her.

She shoved past him into the highly polished, vaulted foyer, allowing her tears to finally spill for effect. "It's not working! He only sees her!"

His beefy hand fell on her shoulder as the annoyance in his countenance changed to parental indulgence. "Then perhaps, my dear, we need to move on to the next level." He touched her cheek briefly, brushing away the tears. "But not here. Come see me tonight."

* * *

Two, tall, glowing columns of light remained outside the perimeter of the iron gates. Their intensity served to dispel some of the unnatural darkness around the mansion beyond the gates. Another bright form, larger than the first two, soon joined them. He communed with them:

"The enemies have become stronger around her, but the prayers stored up for her hold high rank that will not fail."

"What of the called and anointed ones?"

"The Enemy's power cannot penetrate their guard. The Spirit's work must continue through them. Their continued obedience has shut the door to the dark forces and the time for their great testing is not yet."

The Messenger hovered slightly above the other two. "Remain with her." The Messenger rose higher, then disappeared.

Chapter Fifteen

Paul traced the letters on the mid-sized headstone, spelling her name, *Hannah.* He hardly felt the intense heat of the mid-summer sun soaking through his T-shirt.

He removed his fingers and sat back on the still dewy grass, hugging his knees. He had met Hannah at Bible college and had dated her for two years before marrying her. They'd only been married for the same amount of time, when she died.

Because of the differences of their race, her parents had been hesitant about them marrying. Paul had, then, set out to prove to them that the colour of his skin was just that. He had persisted until they had gotten to know him; it had probably helped once they realized he had been adopted as an infant by a well-respected, White family.

Unfortunately, her death had alienated him from her family, even though they had assured him they didn't blame him. After all, he hadn't been driving when the car she was in had been broad-sided by a passenger van, and he had also tried to convince her to avoid the mission trip because of her pregnancy. Hannah had declared that being four months pregnant didn't make her an invalid. Hannah had been sweet and quiet by nature, but had also known how to dig her heels in for what really mattered.

Paul tried connecting with Hannah's parents once or twice a year, but it was always stilted and awkward. It was easier for him to phone his biological father, who didn't seem to be all that interested in fostering a relationship with him.

Paul phoned his biological father, John, a few times a year; more out of duty than anything else. Paul had visited him a couple of times and had already shared the gospel with him; hoping that, even in his senior years, he would accept Christ's salvation.

The cemetery brought thoughts of his adoptive father to mind. Stephen Rayner had truly been a minister of the gospel; the kind called from the womb, it seemed. His one obvious weakness had been his inability to stop and smell the roses; he had always been on the go, mostly doing the work of the Kingdom. Yet, he had been a thoughtful man to those in his care: his family, his friends, his flock—but he had taken little time for his own health, his own well-being.

Paul missed him. Even though his difficult teenage years had undoubtedly added some grey to his dad's head, Paul had loved and appreciated the man he was. Paul's eventual maturing had given them some good years of friendship that had deepened after Paul's decision to follow his dad's footsteps in the ministry.

After stretching his neck in gentle rotation, Paul squinted at the sun above. He slipped his sunglasses on, then shoved himself up from the ground, brushing at the seat of his shorts. With his hands on his hips, he stared down at the gravestone, then looked up to the heavens. His heart felt whole.

He turned to leave the cemetery, planning to visit his sister's country home ten minutes away, in Wardton. Also, he needed to get back to Milward in time to take Leroy out for a driving practice. He looked back at Hannah's grave one last time.

"I think you would have liked her, Hannah."

* * *

"So, you'll have to let us know when to come for the ceremony," Christy reminded Paul.

He was sitting at her kitchen table watching her load the dishwasher from the late lunch they had just finished.

"I'm pretty sure I told you the date already, Christy."

She straightened up from her task, sweeping her blonde hair behind one ear. "Don't be a smart aleck. You try managing three children, six-and-under, all day—day in and day out—and see how well you remember things."

As if right on cue, six-year-old Bessie came struggling into the kitchen with two-year-old Fred Junior in her arms, followed by four-year-old Amanda.

"Uncle Paul, can you help me with Freddie 'til Mommy is done with the dishes? He keeps trying to go to Grandma's room and she's resting. An' I can't get his baby gate up." Bessie practically dumped her brother onto Paul's lap.

Paul prevented the chubby, drooling tyke from falling off his lap. "Hey, buddy, you want to play with Uncle Paul?"

Fred Junior's blue eyes almost closed shut as his round face lit up in a grimace-like smile. "Unca, Unca, Unca," he chanted, shoving his feet into Paul's lap as he bounced.

"Me too, Uncle Paul. Play with me too!" Amanda chimed in. Her brown ponytail that had been secured by her older sister, stood up on top of her head at an odd angle.

Paul glanced at Christy. She was grinning from ear to ear. He sighed. "Okay, guys, I promise we'll go outside after I go see Grandma for a bit."

"Will you stay 'til Daddy comes home?" Bessie asked. She looked amazingly like her mother and her aunt Cassandra.

Paul got up from his seat and swung Fred Junior unto one hip. "You bet I will, then we can all play 'Pin the Tail on the Donkey', and Daddy can be the donkey!"

Paul grinned at Christy as he escaped from the room with the exuberant cheers of the children echoing in his ears. He paused at the entrance between the dining and living rooms to replace the baby gate, Bessie had mentioned, before moving through the living room to his mother's bedroom door.

Each time he visited, he was always grateful to Christy and her husband, Fred, for caring for his mother. Otherwise, she most likely would have been in a nursing home.

He tapped gently on the door before easing it opened. He closed the door behind him before moving slowly to his mother's bedside. She was lying semi-prone on her bed with a light throw over her legs to ward off the slight chill from the central air. She seemed small in the queen-sized bed. He noticed she was watching him.

"Is everything cleaned up from lunch?" she asked, holding a hand out to him.

Paul sat on one side of the bed and held her unsteady hand. Her skin felt cool and thin. "Yes, then Christy sat me down to third degree me about my love life."

A smile stretched her thin lips. "Hmm—I surmise it's not what you've told her, but what you won't tell that's got her antenna out. She's noticed the bareness of your finger."

"Christy is just being a busy body. I know she worries about me."

"Did you have a good visit with Hannah?"

Paul nodded slowly, and gently squeezed her hand. "I'm okay, Mom. I'm really okay."

She returned his squeeze. "I can tell, and I thank the Lord for answered prayers." She closed her eyes for a moment. "I do want to tell you something."

Paul leaned closer to her. "What?"

"Don't take Falconer for granted. I don't know why, but for some reason it's been on my heart to pray about him."

Paul frowned, sensing her anxiety. "I don't want you worrying about him, Mom. He can't hurt you anymore. It's ancient history." He decided to change the subject. "Christy said Cassie's been going back to Church."

Eleanor smiled widely; the beauty of long ago still evident in her face. "Yes, bless the Lord. I think she's coming around. She's realizing the pleasures offered by the world don't last." She suddenly gasped for breath, as a fit of coughing took over.

Paul reached behind her to help her sit up. Her coughing soon subsided, and she drank from the glass of water he offered from her bedside table.

"Thank you, sweetheart. Now, get that worried look off your face. It was just one of those dry coughs, caused by a tickle. And tickled I am about how that intern of yours has been emailing and—what do they call it?—messaging back and forth to Cassandra, on the computer, about spiritual things." His mother looked into his eyes searchingly as he continued to hold her upright. "What a wonderful, amazing young woman she is."

* * *

"No, Tilly. Things are going very well. I just needed to touch base, is all," Michaela assured her old roommate. "I mean, I feel very much at home here, but... "

"But you needed to hear an old, familiar voice," Matilda Klein cooed over the phone.

Michaela giggled as she repositioned herself along the length of her bed. She had been feeling slightly under the weather since her lunch with the Reynolds, the day before. It was her day off and she and Tristan were the only ones in the house, so she welcomed any distraction to keep her from analyzing whatever was sprouting between her and Paul.

"I guess you could say that," Michaela said.

"How are your parents?"

"Oh, they're fine. I do miss them, but I've been very busy here. Actually, I was talking with my mom just before you, but she had a sudden emergency. There's a guy, Maxime, who used to help them, but they let him go—he wasn't trustworthy. Apparently, he keeps coming back to the mission compound, begging them to take him back."

"Really?"

"I think it's making my parents anxious. He's been quite belligerent with them, at times." Michaela suddenly felt a cramping in her stomach. "Oh, *mwen anvi vonmi.*"

"What?" Tilly asked, sounding anxious.

"Sorry, Tilly. The Creole just pops up when I've been talking with my parents. I meant to say, *I feel nauseated.*"

"Oh, poor thing. Try some ginger ale."

Michaela continued to converse with Tilly for the next fifteen minutes, catching up on her life since Bible college. Tilly had already completed her internship, and was slated to assist a children's pastor in hopes of replacing that same pastor, who would be getting married and moving away in the next few months.

Michaela realized Tilly had no reason to visit BCC since her boyfriend's family had moved away, but she encouraged her to still come for a visit.

Right after she disconnected with Tilly, Michaela eased off the bed, thinking that a drink of ginger ale seemed like a very good idea. Whatever she had eaten at Carmel's didn't seem to agree with her, or maybe she was coming down with an illness. Thankfully, for the last three months in Milward, she had been in good health.

Her bare feet had just hit the cool floor in the front hall, when she heard footsteps bounding up from the basement apartment. Tristan appeared in the front foyer, breathing heavily. Her hair lay on her shoulders in disarray, her face was flushed and her eyes wide. She had, what looked like a bunch of pamphlets, clutched in her fingers. She held them out to Michaela the same time a tear slid down her cheek, leaving a wet trail.

"L-look," Tristan sobbed. "These are my dad's. Why would he have these? It's all occult stuff."

Michaela accepted the materials from Tristan's hands. She scanned a couple of them. They were invitations to psychic and séance-type activities. She noticed others with the headings: "Harness the God in You," "Be One with the Universe," and "The Dark Arts: Take Control of Your Destiny."

She searched Tristan's face, noticing the hurt there.

"He said he was seeking a new life in Christ," Tristan continued, her voice trembling slightly.

Michaela placed her pamphlet-laden hands on Tristan's upper arms. "Honey, you need to wait and ask your dad. He may have a good explanation. Where did you find them?"

"In storage," Tristan said, wiping her cheeks. "I was looking for stuff for the yard-sale fundraiser, and I found these in a small tote."

"Okay, so maybe he had them from before and has forgotten about them. Wait and... " Michaela stopped. There were sounds at the front door, which was being shoved opened, to admit Lucy, then Will. They both had excited expressions on their faces which instantly gave way to concern.

"Tristan—Michaela—what's wrong?" asked Lucy, rushing over to them.

* * *

Leroy flattened the last cardboard box, which had housed some small table lamps, and tossed it into the dumpster behind the store. He glanced over at Blinder who was working diligently, mowing the little fenced backyard adjacent to the gravelled space, where the dumpster sat. They lived above the store, and his mother prided herself in having a little yard for Lissa to play in. It had a picnic table and a swing set, and nice grass. It was all good, in his estimation, even if it was downtown and faced a bevy of other commercial yards with less desirable things.

One day, he would have property with a real yard; a big yard.

Leroy glanced at his watch. It was almost five; soon the store would close. Soon he'd be hitting the road for a driving practice with Pastor Paul. He felt ready for his driving license's test, but Pastor Paul felt he needed more practice before the big day. It was already scheduled. He couldn't wait! His mom would be so proud; and relieved too. At least, she hadn't needed to take on the responsibility of training him. Not to mention, Pastor Paul was a lot calmer than his mom.

Leroy made his way through the back door, through the warehouse, and into the store. It was cool in there and he could hear his mother talking to a customer. He decided to wait until she was finished. He preferred to be in the store after hours, when he could browse and dream of having a place with a lot of the same home decor stuff. He figured nobody, in a million years, would guess this little secret of his.

His mom had decorated their upstairs apartment nicely enough; but, one day, he wanted her to have a nice house with all the trimmings.

He listened more carefully. It sounded as if his mom were upset. Leroy edged his way to peek past the corner that separated the expanse of the store from his view. His mother was at the service counter with her hands braced on it. She was facing a man, whose profile was towards him. Leroy swore under his breath, hardly believing his eyes.

What in the world is that toad doing in my mother's store?

Leroy moved slowly and quietly behind a tall rack displaying living room drapes. Now, he was more behind Falconer. He moved along to where the rack ended, then moved forwards, closer to Falconer.

"Are you threatening me, Dennis?" Carmel asked calmly, though she seemed tense around her eyes and mouth. "I'm surprised you bothered to take the time instead of sending one of your cronies over to do your dirty work."

Falconer's broad head with slicked-back, greying hair moved from side to side. "I have no need to threaten you. Why would I do that?—A woman alone who has done well with her business and who has the responsibility of a family. I admire you. I came, myself, to avoid any misunderstandings." His arms crossed at his front, caused his white shirt to stretch across his broad back. The shirt bulged at his waist where excess flesh forced itself over the belted part of his pants.

"I'm just saying to keep reins on your employee or I'll have to take action." The tone of his gravelly voice was paternally condescending.

Carmel shifted impatiently. "Blinder is my employee, not my child. I have no control over his actions on his own time."

"Well, my people don't expect to see him at the site anymore. There's no need for him to be there snooping around. Talk to him."

Leroy could see his mother's ire was rising, so he stepped forwards.

Falconer turned suddenly at the sound. His steely grey eyes were piercing as he observed Leroy. A slow, deliberate smile touched his broad lips, but not his eyes. "Ahh—the ever protective son. Leroy, I believe?"

Leroy wasn't quite sure what he would have said given the chance, but it most likely would not have been good. At the moment he steeled himself to be a man for his mother, the front door of the store jingled opened.

Pastor Paul entered, his smile immediately dying as he looked at them. He paused in his trek and removed his sunglasses.

Leroy was relieved and very glad to see him.

"Well, well, well." Falconer chanted. "Not only the son, but the Minister also."

Paul glanced at Leroy briefly, then at Carmel. "Carmel, everything okay?"

"Why don't you tell him, Dennis?" Carmel asked, looking smug.

* * *

Even though Michaela still felt unwell in her stomach, she sat at the Temples' kitchen table with Tristan and her parents, trying to be as supportive as she could.

Will had seemed quite distressed trying to explain to Tristan that, while he had been curious about many spiritual avenues in the past, he had not committed to, or dabbled in any of them. From the puzzled, wary expression on Lucy's face, it seemed as if she could also benefit from his explanations.

"I want you to get well, Daddy," Tristan entreated, sounding like a young child. "This stuff would only set you back—make things worse." Indeed, she looked younger than her sixteen years as she sat at the table between her parents, looking quite vulnerable. "Tell him, Michaela."

Michaela observed the genuine concern in Will's eyes. Even if he were lying about how much his participation had been in the world of the occult, she believed he was no longer involved. "I believe your dad knows the pitfalls of dabbling with darkness, Tristan. I know, for a fact, that Pastor Paul has had extensive conversations with him about it."

Tristan frowned at her father. "Is that right, Dad?"

"What Michaela says is true," Will admitted. He took hold of Tristan's hand in both of his. "I've been trying very hard to grasp the salvation Christ has to offer. You must have noticed that I've been seeing the Pastor regularly. That's the only path I'm on, at present."

Lucy gently cupped her daughter's cheek. "I believe your father is telling the truth, Tristan. He's been back at the military base regularly, and today... " she paused to give Will a look, before continuing. "Today, we actually went house hunting."

"You did?" Tristan said, squealing.

"That's right," her mother confirmed. "We thought it was time to have our own place again."

"No more living in a basement! That's awesome! When do we move?"

Michaela had to chuckle at the enthusiasm of youth. It seemed the woes from the last fifteen minutes were already forgotten.

Will added a chuckle of his own. "Well, we're just looking right now."

"Okay," Tristan said, becoming subdued. She looked at her dad. "Dad, do you think we can take those pamphlets and burn them?"

"You bet," Will agreed with no hesitation. "But, let's use our kitchen sink. I don't think your grandma would want us doing it in hers."

After Will and Tristan had left, Lucy sighed loudly. "Wow," she said. "I'm so glad you were here when that happened."

"Me too. Tristan has a very sensitive spirit. She's told me before that she strongly believes in the Scripture that reminds us to stay away from what even appears to be evil."

Lucy regarded her wearily. "He's doing so much better, but I've been down this road before, and then there was a sudden hiccup that set us all reeling again." She placed her elbows on the table and clasped her fingers, resting her forehead on them.

Michaela reached up to stroke Lucy's shoulder gently. "Don't lose hope, Lucy. God doesn't ignore or forget our prayers. Through it all, He's with you. As much as we'd like Him to take us over or around things, He often brings us through them. He makes good out of bad and, if we allow, He takes us through to make us better than we were before—like gold having passed through an incredible process for its refining."

Lucy raised her head. "Yes, I do believe that. It does seem different this time with Will. He's finally acknowledged that he cannot do this on his own. It's a big thing for military pilots to admit dependency. Many of them think they've reached the optimum of success and there can be no going down from there."

"I agree, Will has definitely come to that realization."

"Michaela."

"Yes."

"Are you okay? You really don't seem well."

* * *

"Look, Falconer, I'll talk with Blinder. But, understand this, if anything happens to him, I'll know where to look."

Paul stood facing Falconer in front of the sales counter behind which Carmel had remained. Leroy had joined her there. Falconer's demeanour had changed from one of fatherly indulgence, albeit a condescending one, to open hostility.

"What do you take me for? Of course I wouldn't see him harmed. He's a mindless fool. I just don't want him thinking he can be wandering the streets of the community anytime he has a mind to, especially now that residents are moving in. I don't want him giving people the creeps."

"Blinder's no fool, Falconer, and he's got more decency in him than most people have in their little finger. And, as for giving people the creeps, most people around here know him and know he's harmless. You've been around long enough to know that." Paul braced a hand on the counter as he leaned into Falconer. "Besides, eventually you'll have your money and that community will be part of Milward. For all you know, some of Blinder's friends will be living there, welcoming him for visits."

Falconer shifted uneasily. He appeared to be having difficulty accepting the outcome of his visit. His fleshly face took on a determined look. "Not if you won't advertise in your Church. Most of Blinder's friends are in that Church, are they not? I also resent your unfair and unfounded defiance. I run things a certain way as you well know—as your father knew."

Paul felt the barb hit home. He glared at Falconer, then spoke as calmly as he could: "All too well, Falconer. He knew it all too well."

"Mommy, I'm finished vacuuming my room. Can I watch my show before... ?"

All eyes turned to Lissa who had just rushed through an opened doorway at the far end, left of the sales counter. Lissa's dark eyes were wide in her little face. Carmel quickly passed behind Leroy to go to her.

Falconer glanced at Leroy, smirked, then moved around Paul towards the front door. He paused between Paul and his destination. "Perhaps, we can have a different type of conversation over dinner, Paul. Personally, I have nothing against you. What happened between your father and me is now in the grave."

"Not quite. My mother is still living."

A surprisingly painful expression passed over Falconer's face, but then disappeared just as quickly as it had come. "Well, yes. Be as it may, my quarrel was not with her. She was young and easily misled. But, we need not venture down that road again, do we?" He continued towards the door.

"Falconer."

He turned around.

"I've asked you this before. Why is it so important to have a poster up in my Church? They're already all over town."

Falconer seemed to think for a moment. His eyes suddenly seemed cold and lifeless. "Perhaps, I'm trying to rectify what went wrong in the past, young Paul. Perhaps, I'm setting things right by specially singling out Bethel Community Church. You think about that?"

Paul watched him leave. There were contrary voices at war within him. What was he missing? He knew with discerning certainty that Falconer's words held their full weight of a hidden agenda. It left him feeling very unsettled.

Chapter Sixteen

The morning kept forging on while Paul and eleven other ministers, from other Milward Churches, seemed to be getting no further ahead. They were all seated in the BCC Conference Room, discussing their last agenda item: Milward Seniors Community.

Paul felt frustrated, yet hopeful. Most of his fellow ministers thought there were enough complaints among their congregations regarding homes already purchased in the Seniors Community, and about the aggressive marketing-style of Falconer's sales reps; however, none of the nine men and two women seemed to have a viable solution they all agreed on.

Since many of the homes seemed to be sound, they felt it unethical to boycott the project; especially since so many seniors had welcomed the project and were excited about it. Many people seemed to think only a few homes had problems.

"But it's not just a few homes," Paul insisted to the group. "The homes on the previous 'no-build zone' land all seem to have the same faults: water in the basements and structural problems."

"Wasn't that because of the spring thaw when the sump pumps were not yet functional?" asked a grey-haired man, who was considering purchasing a home himself.

"That's not what I heard," interjected Sandra Hawthorn, a middle-aged, female minister. "There is growing concern that the conditions of those homes are being covered up."

"Yes," another jumped in. "There is concrete evidence to back up the general consensus that no homes should have been built on that land."

"Yes," Paul agreed. "The twenty-year-old ban was lifted only recently."

"Exactly! How is it that a place pronounced unfit for building is suddenly fit, after all these years?"

"Better building techniques, perhaps?"

"No, I don't think so," Paul said. "I have an expert business man among my people—most of you know Rashad Hakeem. He says the land should have been excavated and replaced with suitable fill before being built on. It would have been extremely expensive."

They murmured in acknowledgement. For a moment, there was silence. Paul took a swallow from his glass of water. He didn't want to leave this meeting without some plan of action.

"Isn't the Mayor handling it? It is a municipal affair. Why do we have to be involved?"

Paul couldn't believe his ears, but he kept his mouth shut, waiting to see if anyone else would do the decent thing. He was not disappointed.

"For Pete's sake, Ron, we have a moral obligation," Sandra pointed out in a slightly disgusted tone. "Most of these people buying come to our Churches."

The skin of Ron's aged face infused with red. "Well, I just don't want this to be a private vendetta." He said, eying Paul meaningfully. "We all know Dennis Falconer committed a shameful act against your parents years ago, Paul. I want to make sure we're fighting for the people, not any grudges you might be holding on to."

The volley of protest that erupted astonished Paul.

"How could you think such a thing?"

"Ron, that's been dealt with years ago. You don't honestly think… "

And on it went.

Paul finally put his hand up, not wanting the issue to get lost in the show of support for him.

He was, however, deeply touched. "Okay, okay, everybody!" He waited for a moment. "I appreciate your support," he looked at Ron, "and your concern, Ron. In my heart I know this isn't personal. For me, it's a matter of right and wrong. I agree with Sandra and have put this on the table solely as a moral obligation."

Ron nodded briefly. "I apologize," he conceded quietly.

"No hard feelings, Ron." Paul looked around the table at them all staring at him. Finally someone spoke.

"I think we should collectively call a meeting of the Churches with the Mayor," an elderly minister suggested.

Paul smiled. He had been thinking this all along, but he was no fool. Not only was he in the minority by race, but he was one of the youngest ministers present. They needed to know it wasn't just his idea. Now they were talking!

After the meeting, Reverend Sandra Hawthorn approached him. "Paul, I've heard some very interesting news about one of your members—George Flint, I believe. Is it true that he experienced a supernatural healing?"

After Paul had spent some time in informal conversation with Sandra Hawthorn and some of the other clergy, he went to Carmel's to talk with

Blinder. He explained to Blinder that it was better for all concerned if he were to stay away from the Seniors Community site for a while.

"H-he's a crook, Pastor," Blinder responded tensely, as he stomped on some cardboard boxes behind Carmel's store. "F-Falconer is a crook. I t-told you, he laughs about people doing anything for money."

Blinder stopped his work to look Paul in the eye. His were sorrowful and angry looking.

"I heard him talking to his bad men. He b-bragged about paying the i-inspector people."

"You mean bribing the inspectors?" Paul asked.

"Yes!" Blinder said loudly. He looked around quickly, as if startled by his own voice. He focused on Paul again. "Pastor, he's the one K-Karlene meets. He's a devil man and she meets him."

"Karlene works for him, Blinder. You know that."

"No, I don't mean that. He teaches her devil stuff. He's evil!"

* * *

"Paul is here, love. Would you like him to come up and see you?"

Michaela heard Hilda's voice through a haze that suddenly cleared at the mention of Paul's name. "Paul?" The very thought of him visiting her in her weakened condition, left her feeling slightly panicked, yet strangely comforted.

"I'm only asking, honey. He does want to come see you—pray for you—but it's up to you." Hilda passed a cool hand across Michaela's forehead. "Are you sure you don't want to see a doctor?"

"I'm sure, Hilda. It's something I ate at Carmel's for lunch on Sunday. I've never tolerated seafood well, but I couldn't disappoint Carmel and Lissa after all the trouble they went through. I should have told them before."

"Poor love," Hilda sympathized. "Never mind, we'll nurse you back to health. Sam's making you some ginger tea."

"Uck! I hate ginger tea."

Hilda laughed softly. "Never mind, it'll do you good." She eased up from the chair by the bed and straightened the covers around Michaela's shoulders.

Michaela squinted up at Hilda, glad she hadn't drawn the trailing, blue curtains to let the sunlight in. The repeated retching and diarrhea were behind her, but a dull headache and generalized weakness had taken their place. "Thanks, Hilda. I'm sorry to put you out."

Hilda waved off her apology. "Put me out? Don't be silly. When I spoke with your mother on the phone, the other day, I assured her you were being well-taken care of. I mean to do that."

Michaela allowed a little chuckle to escape. "My parents are totally content, knowing I'm here with you and Sam. For that I'm grateful."

Hilda put her hands on her rounded hips. "So are we, child, so are we." She moved towards the door, then paused. "What about Paul, love? He's still waiting, I'm sure."

Michaela had been trying to think of an excuse all along, but couldn't find a believable one that would apply to a minister. One of their duties was to visit the sick. "Sure, Hilda, I'll see him."

Hilda's face crinkled into a big smile. "Okay, love. One minister coming right up."

The way she said it, you'd think it was my idea, Michaela thought. She gingerly pushed herself up to lean against the bed head. As she repositioned the hair band that held gathered the fluffy length of her hair, she felt grateful she had already had a chance to clean up.

Just as she finished fussing with her canary-yellow T-shirt, a gentle knock sounded at the partially-closed door.

Michaela took a deep breath. "Come in," she answered, wishing her voice didn't sound so pathetic. Well, it couldn't be helped after all that vomiting. Her throat still felt raw, but at least the bitter taste was gone from her mouth.

Paul pushed the door opened, filling the doorway with his height, and stood looking across at her. He hesitated as if unsure of her reaction.

"Hey, lazy bones, here we are still in bed at noon. How are you doing?" Paul asked as he left the door opened and finally approached her bed. He occupied the chair where Hilda had been sitting. He was dressed in a white shirt and tan slacks, looking long and wiry.

He could have been a basketball player, she thought, *creating havoc with the hearts of his female fans. Instead, it's with me and Karlene—and probably every other single woman in the Church. He should marry again and save himself some trouble.* The thought brought heat to her face.

Michaela tried clearing her throat, to no avail. "Much better than I was," she responded, with a gentle laugh. Her fingers played with the covers over her lap. "How are you?"

Paul leaned forwards, placing his arms across his thighs before clasping his fingers. He studied her for a moment, then smiled. "Oh, fine, fine—just came from a ministerial meeting. Hilda called you a poor little thing. I'm sorry you had such a rough go of it."

Michaela groaned, placing one hand across her eyes. "Oh, great, I can just imagine the details she gave you." She removed her hand to look at him. "I will never, ever have seafood again."

He laughed in an easy manner, his teeth white against his brown skin. "Never, ever is a long time."

"Trust me," she insisted, "never again." She rested her head on the wall behind her. "I'm sure I'll be able to return to the Church tomorrow."

Paul leaned back. "No—maybe the next day."

"But—"

"Don't argue." He warned, frowning. "Were you always this argumentative, or is it just with me?"

"Sorry," she apologized.

"Wow," he said, breathing a lone whistle through pursed lips. "You must not be feeling well."

Michaela allowed a tiny giggle to escape. "I'm not that bad."

Paul raised both eyebrows in mock astonishment and laughed. "Well, let's see, we have just under two months for the final conclusion on that." He seemed more relaxed. "By the way, thanks for talking to Cassie."

She threw him a puzzled look.

"My mother told me you've been talking online. Apparently, it's been making a difference in Cassie's life. She's even been attending Church with Christy and her family."

Michaela felt slightly embarrassed. "It's nothing really."

Paul shifted on his seat. "Uh-uh. That girl sailed through her teen years like an angel, only to completely walk off the path she was raised on in her late twenties. Her own twin couldn't reach her. We eventually just let her go, but kept praying for her like crazy." He paused and crossed his arms. "My father's death sobered her a bit, but you've obviously been a significant part of the answer to prayers for her. I really appreciate that you've been keeping in touch with her, after meeting her only once."

Michaela lowered her gaze from the tenderness she saw in his. "Well, you're welcome, but I really didn't—"

"Don't you even think of telling me it was nothing in a different way."

She looked at him, noticing his teasing smile. He held her gaze, and suddenly she couldn't think. "Umm, well," she tried. She realized she was thirsty and reached across to the bedside table, but Paul intercepted. He gently brushed her hand aside and aptly filled her glass from a small water pitcher. He got up to hand it to her.

She felt his fingers, lean and warm, as she accepted the glass. She took a gulp and started coughing.

"Hey, take it easy," Paul said, grabbing tissue from the bedside table. "You okay?" he asked, almost hovering over her. He took her glass.

Michaela dabbed at her mouth with the tissue. "Yes, sorry." She looked up at him, noticing the thickness of his eyebrows and lashes, the darkness along his jaw line and the strength of his forehead and nose. Was it appropriate to call a man beautiful? She looked away, feeling flustered.

Paul sat back down, and reached across to place his large hand over hers, where it lay on her lap folded over the tissue.

"Father, I thank you that Michaela is recovering from such a difficult ailment. I ask that Your hand be upon her for continued wellness, that she is strengthened and encouraged. I thank You that she's come to us and has been such a help and an inspiration. I pray that we, in turn, will be a real and lasting blessing to her. Guide her steps and her life, oh, Lord, I pray. In Jesus' name, amen."

He removed his hand from hers. She missed the warmth and suddenly felt like crying. It was a beautiful prayer, and he was such a wonderful person, even if he did have control issues.

"Michaela?"

She looked at him, feeling her eyes smart and a growing pressure in her chest.

"Hey, are you okay?" he asked, leaning forwards on the chair.

"Y-yes," she said, blinking rapidly. "Why do you ask?"

"Well—because... "

Michaela felt the tears relieved from her eyes, coursing down her face. She couldn't seem to stop them, and the pressure in her chest begged to be released. The sobs came from there, deep down. Through her periphery, she noticed Paul standing. He was silent and she seemed to be getting louder. He moved away from her.

"Hilda!" he yelled.

She shifted her body away from him, desperately trying to get a grip on herself, to no avail.

"Hilda!" Paul yelled again. He knelt by the bed and reached over to take her hand.

Michaela had one hand up over her mouth, trying to stifle her sobs, and the other trapped in Paul's grip; wishing he would do more than just hold her hand; yet knowing he couldn't—wouldn't—shouldn't; wishing she could bury her head in his chest and tell him she loved him knowing this went against everything she had planned for her future.

"Hilda!"

"What in the heavens... " Hilda stood in the doorway, staring.

Paul motioned her over. "I don't know—she just started crying."

Hilda rushed to the other side of the bed and sat on it. She gathered Michaela into her arms.

* * *

Hilda continued holding Michaela, allowing her to cry until the sobs quietened. Paul was sitting on the chair, his hands clasped tightly and a worried look in his dark eyes. Hilda had to smile. She had never seen him look so helpless. It always seemed to take a woman to do that to a man. There was no doubt in her mind that this man loved this woman—God help them.

The sobs had quietened. Now, if she could only figure out what had set Michaela off. She waved Paul out of the room. He left, it seemed, reluctantly, shutting the door after him.

"Now, love, if you ease up a bit, I'll get you some tissue."

Michaela leaned back, grabbing the cover to dab at her eyes before Hilda passed her the box of tissue. Hilda returned to her place on the side of the bed. She waited until Michaela seemed ready. Her dark eyes were moist and her nose slightly reddened. Hilda smoothed at the fluffy hair.

"All right, love, spit it out."

Michaela looked at her warily, sniffling. "I'm so sorry. Really—that was just stupid. I don't know what came over me."

"Was it something Paul said?"

"Oh, no, no," Michaela protested, looking alarmed. "Paul was very nice. It's—I don't know... ." She looked down. "I guess it's because I don't feel well," she finished lamely.

* * *

Paul hung around the base of the staircase, listening. Good, she didn't seem to be crying anymore. Of course, that knowledge didn't help him decipher what caused it in the first place. Sometimes it was hard to understand women. Thank God Hilda had been around. The effort it had taken for him to refrain from holding Michaela had left him feeling bereft.

Holding her would have been the most natural way to comfort her, because she had been crying—sounding almost like a child—and because she was sick. Yet, it wouldn't have been right; it would have been compromising and... it would have also been selfishly motivated. He had wanted to hold her as a man wanted to hold a woman. No, it wouldn't have been right.

He sighed deeply and moved away from the staircase.

"Everything okay, Paul?" Samuel asked, coming from the kitchen into the hall. He had a tray holding a small teapot and a cup.

"Umm, yes—I mean, I hope so. Hilda is with Michaela. She just started crying for no obvious reason that I could see. I—I felt it was better for Hilda to deal with it."

Samuel nodded understandingly. "Yes, that was wise." He studied Paul for a moment, smiling paternally. "It's hard, isn't it?"

"Yes," Paul agreed, "but it'll be okay. I'm sure she'll feel better in a couple of days and be back to her stubborn, opinionated, frustrating old self."

Samuel laughed, causing the tray to waver in his hands. "What self is she now?" he asked jovially.

Paul leaned against the wall and thought for a moment. "She's subdued, apologetic and weepy."

"What's wrong with that?"

"It's easier for me to deal with the former, under the circumstances."

"Ahh," Samuel said, nodding repeatedly. "Well, the Lord knows and He has a purpose in everything. I have no doubt this is all part of that purpose, or plan."

Paul shoved himself off the wall. "Well, I need to keep that on the back shelf of my mind for now. I do, however, want to discuss the meeting with you. Do you have time?"

"You bet. Just let me make this delivery and I'll meet you in the kitchen."

Chapter Seventeen

Michaela could hear the vibrant sound of the choir practicing in the Sanctuary as she made her way from the Conference Room, through the hall, and into the Foyer. It had been a couple of weeks since she had recovered from her illness and had returned to keeping regular hours at the Church.

This evening, she and Brennon were meeting with the youth for the final planning stages of the ceremony. Even though the Fellowship Hall had been completed for almost three weeks, the opening ceremony would take place the last week of August when most vacationers would have returned from their summer trips. That would be exactly a week after her internship at BCC was completed.

The most exciting thing for her, however, was the short-term mission trip to Haiti. She, Brennon and Sarah would lead a team of youths, who didn't seem to mind missing a week of school, to work with her parents. She couldn't wait, yet...

No, she wouldn't think about Paul. She was feeling very satisfied about being able to maintain a professional, albeit friendly, relationship between them. She still felt embarrassed about her melt-down two weeks ago and was grateful he hadn't brought it up. It would not happen again.

Afterwards, she would most likely accept the offer from Hope Alive Church to join their staff while in the process of receiving her minister's credentials. Yes, things were on track once more. That was her one fortifying and comforting thought to buffer against the increasing strength of her feelings for Paul. She viewed it as a sacrifice. It would prepare her for other sacrifices that were bound to come for her shaping and moulding into all she was predestined to be in Christ.

Why then did the *still small voice* seem to persist in bringing up her mother's consistent biblical reminder: "To obey is better than sacrifice"? Was this not obedience and sacrifice combined?

She had conceded to herself, and to the Lord, that she may have been hasty in deciding that her life's road was missions, and she had been in regular prayer, seeking His will.

And if My will is Paul?

Michaela stopped in midstride, as if the voice inside her were audible. Her heart hammered like a silent drum against the folders she held clutched to her chest, as the words echoed in her mind. She thought to herself, *Paul's ministry is not on the mission field, except through financial support.*

Wherever I place him is the mission field.

Michaela realized she was holding her breath as she waited. She slowly released it and continued to wait—nothing. Her gaze fell to the carpet under her feet as she sensed the Spirit's work in her and realized, once again, her need to submit to His way and not her own, regardless of where it led. This, indeed, was trust in the Almighty: an unseen Presence who was goodness, truth and love.

"Okay," she whispered hesitantly, "I will trust You." She felt a soothing release flow through her, causing her to sigh deeply. Suddenly she felt the urge to look up.

When had the banner been put up? Yet, there it hung, as bold as you please, high in the Church Foyer with the Milward Seniors Community logo spread across it. It had even been anchored with two elaborate hooks.

"Paul is going to be furious," she whispered to herself.

"What the... "

Michaela turned to see Brennon coming up from behind her. They looked at each other, then back at the banner—first a poster, now this banner.

Brennon looked around the Foyer with a perplexed expression on his face. "How in the world could that have gotten up there, and who put it up?"

"Paul has already expressed his wishes to everyone here. Who would do this?"

Brennon shook his head. "I don't know." He gaze shifted towards the Sanctuary. "But I have my wild guess."

Michaela followed his gaze. "Karlene? You don't mean Karlene, do you?"

"All I know is there's a major investigation going on because of the clergy's pressure on the Mayor. Falconer can't be happy and Karlene works for him. In fact, she seems to be flaunting it, of late—almost like a challenge, or revenge."

"Revenge?"

Brennon's brows were furrowed as he paced restlessly. "Yes—directed at Paul for—you know—resisting her."

"But Karlene wouldn't stoop so low."

Brennon threw her a challenging look. "Trust me, Michaela, there's a lot about Karlene you don't know."

Further conversation was delayed as they heard—then saw—Ian pushing his way through the front entrance, hauling a big gym bag with him. His brown hair, black shorts and white T-shirt looked sweaty.

"Hey, Pastor Brennon—Michaela! Is Tristan here yet?"

"Hi, Ian," Brennon responded. "No, but she should be here soon. Pastor Paul is picking her and Leroy up."

Ian was still in the doorway, pulling his muddy soccer cleats off, while listening to Brennon. He looked up. "Leroy?"

"Yes. Tristan was working at his mom's store today."

Ian mumbled something, looking disturbed. He held the cleats in one hand. "Okay, I'll wait here for her." He shoved his belongings into a corner by the doors and stepped back out into the Vestibule.

Brennon turned to Michaela. "Is it just me, or did you hear him swear?"

* * *

Paul's ears felt somewhat violated from the sound conglomeration of his Beetle's cranked air conditioner, Tristan and Leroy's loud conversing back and forth, and the noise coming from Leroy's friend's iPod.

The extreme August mugginess called for the air conditioner which meant that Tristan, who sat beside him in the front, was partly turned around almost yelling, over the sound of the air conditioner, at Leroy.

Paul looked through the rear-view mirror at Leroy's friend in the back seat. The kid desperately needed a haircut. How he could see through the mass of brown hair hanging over his eyes, was beyond Paul. His ears couldn't be in much better shape if he habitually turned his music up so loud that Paul could hear it fairly well, even though the iPod was connected to headphones.

Yet, Paul's heart went out to him. He had seen the look often enough, having worked a couple of summers in an inner-city mission, in Toronto.

Leroy used to have that look: the look where a kid couldn't meet your eyes for fear of the disgust he might see there. Away from judgemental adults, on their own turf with their gang buddies, the same kids strutted around like kings ruling their domain.

Leroy, who had dropped all of his past friends, had decided this one was worth wrestling over. There were some good things happening in Leroy, Paul realized. He was starting to see the fruit.

He turned onto the street leading to the Church. He felt as if he'd been chauffeuring people all day. This last trip consisted of delivering Blinder to have dinner with Will and Lucy, then taking the youth with him to Church for their meeting. He really should get a bigger car.

Somewhere along the line between Hannah's death and now, burying himself in the work of the Church had ceased to bring the same sense of satisfaction it once did. He wanted a life outside of work, but that seemed to contradict the excitement and joy that filled him lately when he got up in the mornings and briskly walked from the parsonage to the Church. But, he knew what the difference was. She would be there.

Even though Michaela was being the epitome of professional conduct, treating him with a slightly distant comradeship, she still enriched his life; his sense of well-being—even if she didn't know it. He knew, without a doubt, that she was not as immune to him as she tried to portray. Partly, he could tell by the way she seemed to have a hard time meeting his gaze, the way she seemed tense when alone with him, the way she watched him when she thought he didn't notice.

He also noticed that her personal bubble space was bigger for him than for anyone else. That was hard. She wouldn't even let him brush against her, while passing. Once they had decided to hold hands for a team prayer, and she had deliberately switched places so she wouldn't have to hold his hand.

After her internship was completed, he was having none of that. Things were going to have to change rapidly before she disappeared out of his life. It was a pity he wasn't the one going on the mission trip.

As soon as the thought entered his mind, he grimaced, feeling a surge of anxiety. He may have healed from life without Hannah, but he still had to come to terms with the fact that she had died on a short-term mission trip. He hadn't taken another trip since.

"Hey, Pastor Paul, isn't it true that we've raised enough money to cover the entire Haiti trip?" Tristan yelled across at him.

"Well, with the contribution from the church missionary funds, yes."

"See," she said to Leroy, "all you have to worry about is your passport."

After Paul parked his car, Tristan scrambled out and headed for the church doors. Leroy and his friend followed, moving more slowly. After getting some office supplies out of his car trunk, Paul followed them. He noticed that a significant number of people were gathered in the Foyer.

He saw Brennon turn from the group and start walking in his direction. Paul's entrance into the Foyer was delayed as Brennon pushed his way into the Vestibule the same time Paul noticed what was holding everyone's attention.

Brennon allowed the door to shut behind him. "Do you see it?"

Paul sighed, feeling his frustration level rise—more than that—anger was there competing for first place. "Yes, I see it," he declared bitterly.

"I have no idea how or when it even got there," Brennon said, shaking his head. "Michaela and I had just finished meeting with the worship leader when she went to get some photocopying done and she saw it. I think she was the first one to notice it."

Paul glanced around the Foyer. Most of the choir members and some youths were there. They were looking his way. "Where is Michaela?"

"She's with Karlene in the Conference Room."

"Karlene?"

Brennon ran his fingers across his mouth and seemed uncomfortable. "I—umm—I confronted Karlene and she became quite upset. Michaela went with her to calm her down."

Paul looked at him, puzzled.

Brennon answered his unspoken question. "I think she had something to do with it, Paul."

"I know, Brennon. We talked about the possibility, but I wish you had let me handle it. You didn't do it in front of everybody, did you?"

Brennon hung his head, then threw it back in frustration. He looked at Paul. "It just happened. The choir had finished practicing and was leaving the Sanctuary. I went in and she just ignored me, gathering her stuff with that smug look on her face. I asked her outright if she had anything to do with the banner. She basically told me that we should stop being childish and get over it. So, I shot back that she better watch it because her days in leadership were numbered."

Paul ran his hands over his face. "Okay," he said, placing a reassuring hand on Brennon's shoulder.

"Look, I'm sorry. I wasn't very pastor-like and probably made a mess of it, but she's been really ticking Sarah off lately; even making judgemental comments about how she should be handling Conner's autism."

"All right," Paul said, moving pass Brennon to open the door. "We'll talk later. I don't know that Michaela should be the one dealing with her." He paused as he noticed a figure walking from the parking lot towards them. "There's Rashad. Tell him to bring one of the women with him to the Conference Room."

* * *

Michaela stood close to the door of the lit Conference Room watching Karlene pace by the far side of the table. Even though Brennon had been fairly aggressive in his accusations toward Karlene, Michaela couldn't understand why she was taking it so hard. She was used to Karlene being self-assured and somewhat self-absorbed, but she wasn't sure what to think of this display of emotions from her.

Karlene was pacing and wiping at uncontrolled tears as she railed against Brennon and the leadership of the Church. She had ignored Michaela's offer of tissue and, instead, kept back-handing the tears from her face, causing her dark mascara to smear under her eyes.

"Look, Michaela, you think you want to be in the min-is-try," Karlene said, stressing the last word in a bitter fashion, "but you're fooling yourself. It's not about ministering or serving people; it's about the power."

Michaela started to speak, but Karlene cut her off.

"You have your eyes on him, don't you?" Karlene asked, pausing at the end of the table closest to Michaela. "You want him, don't you? You don't have to admit it, I know. But, let me tell you something, he wants a woman that is willing to stand up to him. A woman with power who will make his power even greater."

"Karlene, I don't understand—"

"Of course you don't and neither does he. He's mesmerized by you now; but, soon enough, he'll know who his true soul mate is." Karlene's eyes appeared wide and luminous from the tears that had now ceased. Her words were stilted, as if rehearsed for a play.

"Karlene, truly, I'm not in competition with you for Paul. I'm just here to do my job as an intern, which I hope will help me to serve."

"Reeeally?" Karlene stretched the word in a shrill voice. "I'm not blind. I see what's going on." She pointed a brightly painted finger at Michaela. "I know what's going on, but I believe in my destiny with Paul, and I will fight for it."

"That's enough, Karlene!"

Michaela jerked around. She hadn't even heard Paul enter the room behind her; not only he, but Rashad and a young Chinese woman.

Paul touched Michaela's arm lightly as he walked around to stand between her and Karlene. Karlene's olive skin was pale and she seemed frozen in place.

"I want to know the truth, Karlene. Did you put the Seniors Community banner up in the Foyer?"

Karlene seemed as if she wouldn't answer him; then she spoke very calmly and almost dully.

"Yes, Paul, I instructed two of the sales reps to hang it there. I opened the doors for them, I showed them the ladder, and I handed them the tools. Yes, I'm to blame."

Paul was quiet for a moment, then he spoke more gently. "Why, Karlene?—knowing my express wishes—why?"

Karlene's demeanour changed. Her face darkened and she put one hand on her hip. "Why? Why not? I, for one, don't understand why everyone is making such a fuss about a little community support. People want those new homes." She stepped towards Paul. "You need to let the past be the past, Paul Rayner!"

Paul's fingers clenched at his sides, then unclenched. The tenseness of his shoulders was evident under the light material of his short-sleeved shirt. He spoke firmly, "Regardless of your opinion, Karlene, you knew what my decision was. The board and I felt that we could not, in good conscience, advertise a project that was being investigated for possible fraud and mismanagement. As a person in leadership here, it's unseemly that you would purposefully counter our decision."

Karlene seemed to lose it. "Unseemly!?" She waved her hand at him and at Michaela. "W—what's unseemly is you and this, this—"

"That's enough, Karlene!" Paul said in a strong voice.

Karlene's body jerked and her eyes widened. She looked beyond Paul and Michaela to the other two. Her lips started to tremble as she focused back on Paul. "Why are you being so cruel? Why can't you understand that I'm trying to help you; make you stronger?" Again, she looked past Paul and Michaela. "Tell him, Rashad!"

Rashad remained quiet with sadness in his eyes. Paul turned around, went to Rashad, and spoke quietly to him and the Chinese woman, then beckoned to Michaela.

Michaela left the room, after Paul, with the sounds of Karlene's sobs following after them.

"Rashad, tell him! Tell him... "

Instinctively, she knew he would go to the Fellowship Hall.

This time he closed the door.

Again, she watched him walk to the windows over-looking the Gym. This time, she followed him all the way to there. They stood silently together, yet a part, watching the youth and Brennon gathered around a table at one end of the room.

"I should be down there with them," Michaela stated. A muddle of emotions churned in her.

Sadness was at the top of the list. She also felt dismay over Karlene's accusations. In spite of her feelings for Paul, she had prided herself in maintaining a proper relationship with him.

As if reading her mind, he said, "Karlene has nothing to back up her claims against you. Something isn't quite right with her." He continued looking straight ahead, his profile strong and noble. "Sam and Hilda have been trying to counsel her, but she refuses to meet with them. I just told Rashad to talk with her, pray with her—she trusts him."

"But, she wants you."

He looked at her, searching her eyes. "Yes," he agreed. His gaze strayed to her lips, then back to her eyes. "But I don't want her."

The fact that she couldn't look away from his eyes, and the betraying heat that was flooding her being, made her uneasy. He turned to her fully.

"No, it's not her I want," he whispered; a slight smile touched his lips.

He said it with such simplicity and honesty that it hurt. Michaela's breath caught in her throat and her eyes started to tear up like the day when she was sick, and he visited her. Except, this time she was well, with no excuse in sight. She forced her eyes to look at the beautifully carpeted floor, blinking rapidly. She moved a few feet back from the window.

"I wish you wouldn't... " she said.

Silence.

"Wouldn't what?" he asked, gently.

She hugged her body, keeping her eyes to the floor. "I think you're flirting with me again," she said in barely a whisper.

"Again?" he asked.

She dared a glance at him. He was smiling widely and the message in his eyes spoke volumes.

She took two steps back. He took two forwards. She took another two. He didn't move, allowing the increased distance between them. Yet, what she continued to witness in his eyes nullified any difference the distance would have made. Her heart started to thud, and she felt panicked.

"I have to go," she stated, her voice shaky. Without looking at him, she turned and fled from the room.

* * *

Paul watched Michaela walk rapidly towards the doors of the Fellowship Hall. She reached out to firmly shove the door opened. After she had disappeared, he smacked his forehead with the palm of his hand.

"You idiot!" he scolded himself quietly. Look how close he had come to behaving in the very way Karlene had accused them of. Worse of all, he had cause Michaela to flee from him like Joseph from Potipher's wife.

Honestly, he didn't know what he had planned to do. What if she hadn't backed away from him? What if she had allowed him to touch her? What kind of control would he have had?

Paul groaned out loudly. Enough had taken place this day. Then he felt the quiet whisper of the Spirit. He closed his eyes. Words formed in his thoughts, his mind: *Patience, my son, patience.*

Paul sighed deeply with his head bowed. Soon enough, he looked up and walked to the window. He looked down into the Gym and, almost at the same moment, she looked up.

Even from the distance, they locked gazes. He smiled; she just kept staring at him. He turned away, letting her go.

Chapter Eighteen

Leroy watched Lissa and one of her friends playing on the swings in the backyard. Lissa had been cooped up inside all day waiting for the muggy conditions to improve. Now, it was after five in the afternoon and the temperature seemed to be taking a dive in slow motion. While he watched the girls, he was listening to his mother admonish Blinder about roaming through the Seniors Community site.

"Blinder, you need to be careful about going there. Remember what Pastor Paul said," Carmel reminded Blinder gently, but firmly. They were standing about five feet away from Leroy by the dumpster behind the store. "Leroy said he's seen you there."

Leroy looked towards them at the mention of his name. He noticed Blinder looking over at him. His droopy facial expression made his prominent nose seem even larger.

"Blinder, are you hearing me?" Carmel asked.

Blinder looked at her. They were practically the same height, standing face-to-face. "I n-never promised. I j-just said I'd be careful."

Carmel sighed out loudly, raising her arms in frustration. She tried again: "Please, Blinder. I don't want anything bad to happen to you." She put one hand on Blinder's slouched shoulder. "You're like family. I would take it very, very personally."

Leroy moved over to them. His mom was right. Blinder was like family; they had known him ever since they moved to Milward. Even Leroy's cousins and their families admitted that having a single mother live in the same building with Blinder wasn't as risky as they had thought it might be.

"Hey, Blinder-man, you gotta listen to my mom. I wouldn't trust that Falconer dude for one sec."

Blinder smiled and nodded slowly. "Okay," he agreed softly. He started moving away. "I-I might visit Will. S-see you later."

They watched Blinder limp through the alley between the store and the building next door.

"I don't believe him for a minute," Carmel said in a frustrated tone. She ran her hands over her abdomen, smoothing the material of her dress. She reached up to squeeze Leroy's upper arm. "I'll go lock up. Watch out for him, will you? I think Pastor Paul needs to have another talk with him."

* * *

Hilda's desk in the Front Office finally seemed as neat as it had been when Hilda had departed earlier. Paul watched Michaela collect the last of the photocopied material that had been part of a significant pile on the desk. He had stayed in his office so she could work in peace, but he couldn't stay in there forever. She had her back to him and when she turned around and saw him, she dropped the pile.

He rushed over, feeling badly. He should have made enough noise over the drone of the photocopier so she would have known he was leaving his office.

He stooped down, and she kneeled. They picked up the sheets of paper in silence, and then stood up at the same time. She held her pile cradled in one arm while smoothing at her pale-yellow, capri-pants outfit with the other hand.

"Thanks," she said, sounding a little nervous.

"Sorry for startling you," he apologized. Her light fragrance touched his nostrils, causing him to forget whatever else he had to say.

She smoothed at her hair which was in a French braid and poufy on top. He liked that she hadn't straightened her hair. Maybe it was an enigma to him, because he had lived with straight-haired people all his life.

"No worries," she assured him, not really meeting his gaze. She looked meaningfully at the papers in his hands.

"Oh, here you go," he said, forcing himself back to earth.

She accepted his pile, which she added to her own. She turned and stuffed them into a pouch bag lying on one side of the desk.

"What are all those for?" he asked, partly out of curiosity, partly to delay her.

She pulled the bag from the desk and held it in front of her. "Oh, just some fact sheets on Haiti and missionary life for the youth."

He frowned. "Really? Exactly how many are going?"

She gave a slight laugh, shaking her head. "Only eight are going. These are for all of the youth; even the ones who aren't going."

"Ahh—I see," he said, leaning against the filing cabinets behind him. "Good thinking."

She smiled, and then began to turn away. "Well, I should be going. I've been invited to the Flints' for dinner."

"Another invitation? I mean—another one from the Flints?" To think he had turned down Hilda's invitation for dinner for Michaela's sake. He'd have to call and cancel his rain check.

"They're still very grateful," she admitted. "I keep telling them to just be grateful to the Lord, but I don't want to hurt their feelings, and plus... "

"Plus what?" he encouraged.

"Ethel is a really good cook."

"Better than Hilda?"

She giggled. "No, silly, not better. Hilda's cooking is good too—just different."

Silly? He was definitely not feeling silly where she was concerned, but her use of the adjective meant she was feeling more relaxed; that was good. "That's why I've noticed a distinct lapse in the number of my dinner invites. Before you came, I didn't share them with anyone. Now, it seems, I've been splitting them with you—unbeknownst to me!" That earned him a very wide, endearing smile.

"Well, my time's almost up, so you won't have to share for much longer." Suddenly her smile vanished, as if the real implications of her statement had just dawned on her. She looked towards the opened door.

Paul sensed her discomfort; her confusion. Certainly it was good for her to be finished her internship, but not if it meant she would walk out of his life. He had already determined he would do everything in his power for that not to happen, but he couldn't very well tell her that, now.

He would always have a special place in his heart for Hannah, but his waiting for her had been with less confidence. Maybe maturity and a settled life had a lot to do with his certainty about Michaela; as well as seeking the Lord's will. Regardless, he knew what he saw in her was what he wanted.

"So, are we all set for Saturday's celebration?" he asked, changing the subject. He was rewarded when her dark brown eyes lit up and the lost smile miraculously reappeared.

*　*　*

Dusk was settling as Leroy tried to be as inconspicuous as possible. He had been trailing Blinder because he had nothing better to do, and because Blinder needed tending to. He nearly swore when Blinder crossed the street towards the Seniors Community.

Leroy paused by Metro's Gas Bar for a moment, before he loped across the street after Blinder. He no longer felt inconspicuous. Many of the homes were already inhabited, as attested to by the glow of lights from their windows. They were really nice homes. He looked to the far right of the development site where the houses were dark. He knew there was a building freeze on those houses presently, and that Pastor Paul and other ministers were responsible for the freeze.

If he were a minister, would he stand up for something like that; something that had nothing to do with him? He guessed that's what ministers were supposed to do.

Man, things had improved a lot since he had last traipsed through the area. Most of the roads were paved. The houses were all bungalows of different styles with neat front yards and spacious backyards. His mom would love these, but she was far from being a senior.

Blinder had cut through one of the yards and Leroy knew where he was heading: the Sales Centre. Leroy suspected Blinder took the long, back way to get to the Centre because he didn't want to be seen. For a guy with a limp, Blinder walked pretty quickly. Leroy jogged a little to keep up. He tried not to dwell on what a bunch of old people might think if they spied a Black, gangster-looking teen, roaming their streets. It was hot, the mosquitoes were biting, and he was starting to get really ticked with Blinder.

Leroy decided he wasn't playing hide-and-seek anymore. He raced towards the Sales Centre where he noticed Blinder crouching along the back wall. Suddenly, Leroy braked to a stop at what was unexpectedly unfolding before his eyes.

Two hefty guys, one Black and one White, had come out of nowhere, it seemed, and had cornered Blinder. One took Blinder by the arms, and the other did the talking. Blinder started struggling, then he folded over after a blow to his midsection from the man who had been talking to him. His captor shoved him from behind to the ground, and then the other viciously kicked him in the head again and again.

"Hey! Hey!" Leroy shouted, his heart racing, as he started running again.

The men looked his way before rapidly marching around to the front of the house.

Seconds later, as Leroy's knees hit the lawn beside Blinder's still form, he heard a vehicle start, then screech away.

"Blinder—hey, Blinder-man!" he called, touching Blinder's shoulder, noticing his bloody forehead. Blinder didn't respond. Leroy looked around, breathing heavily. Not a soul in sight. He pulled out his cell phone.

* * *

Paul was just about to ring the Temples' doorbell when he heard a vehicle in the driveway. He smiled and stepped away from the door when he saw Will, in full uniform, exit his car.

"Well, well, well, Captain," Paul drawled slowly, as he walked towards Will. He saluted.

"Rev.," Will greeted as he returned the salute. They both shook hands firmly.

"You're looking great, Will. You were definitely made for uniform."

Will grinned, his eyes sparkling under the rim of his wedge cap. He seemed healthy and confident. "Try telling my wife that. She doesn't like me living at the base during the week."

"How's the house-hunting coming along?"

"Slow, but steady. We have a good list of possibilities. At least, we don't have to sell first."

Paul nodded in approval. "Well, as they say, slow and steady wins the race." He felt more confident about the changes he was seeing in Will. They met less often because of Will's work schedule, but Will had been digging into the Word, eating up the truths there. Paul believed Will was not long in coming into Christ's Kingdom; a Kingdom that was not of this world, but which co-existed with it.

Will, it seemed, was coming to terms with the truth that he alone wasn't enough to overcome his demons. That hadn't been easy for the military pilot, but it had been necessary to start the freeing, healing process.

Will was suddenly solemn. He stepped closer to Paul, head down. "Before we go in, I wanted to get something off my chest."

At that moment, Paul's cell phone shrilled. "Sorry, Will," he apologized as he pulled the phone from his pocket. He noticed it was Leroy and decided to call him back. He silenced the phone before giving Will his attention.

Will cleared his throat. "When I—ah—confessed to you that I had misled my family into believing that my interest in the occult had been years ago, there was something else I should have told you. It's been heavy on my heart, but Karlene had me promise not to say anything."

Paul waited for him to continue, knowing it wouldn't be good.

"Karlene has been meeting regularly with someone involved in witchcraft, and, if I'm not mistaken, she's still doing so."

Paul sighed, putting his hands deep into his pocket. "I'm glad you shared that, Will. A lot of things are starting to add up, including about Karlene." He gazed through the gathering darkness at the sky above.

Something suddenly dawned on him. "Tell me something, Will, does all of this have something to do with the Sales Centre at the site?"

Will nodded.

"That's why Blinder was adamant he had to watch you; why he kept going there so much. Are you trying to tell me that someone has occult meetings at the Sales Centre?"

"Not meetings... consultations."

Paul felt his cell phone vibrate. He pulled it from his pocket, impatiently. It was Michaela.

"One second, Will. It's Michaela." He put the phone to his ear. "Hi, Michaela."

"Paul, you've got to get to the Seniors Community Sales Centre! Leroy's been trying to get you. Something has happened to Blinder."

* * *

Five minutes later, Paul hurriedly parked his car behind a police cruiser in front of the Sales Centre. There was one other cruiser and a rescue vehicle. He slammed his door shut the same time Will shut the passenger door. They jogged towards a growing group of people that had gathered outside the Sales Centre. Whether by recognition, their purposeful stride, or the sight of Will's uniform, the crowd parted to let them through.

Two fire fighters were on their knees beside a prone figure. It was Blinder.

"Pastor Paul!"

Paul looked up and spotted Leroy by the side of the road behind the Centre. Leroy seemed okay, but it appeared that he was being interviewed by the police. "Be right over, Leroy," he said loudly. He recognized one of the fire fighters, as he stooped beside Blinder. "What happened, Dale?" he asked.

“Hey, Paul. According to the kid, two guys kicked his head in. His vitals are stable, but we’re getting no response.”

Paul noticed partially dried blood on Blinder’s forehead and hair. He looked towards Leroy and the officers as he heard sirens in the distance getting closer. “I’ll be with the police,” he said, standing up.

As he walked over to Leroy, the ambulance pulled onto the Seniors Community roadway.

“Reverend Rayner,” the older of the two police officers said, acknowledging Paul with familiarity. He nodded towards Leroy. “I believe you know Mr. Reynolds.”

“Yes, I do. What are you asking him?” Paul had noticed the belligerent look on Leroy’s face and he could just guess what the line of questioning had been.

“The usual—what was he doing on the scene; why had he been tailing the victim? Etc, etc, etc.” The officer tipped his hat back with his pen, as if looking for the expected opposition.

“Look, Sid, I was told that Leroy was the one who dialled 911 after trying to get hold of me?”

“Yes, and so?”

“Paul! Paul! What’s going on?” Samuel was making his way past the paramedics who had replaced the firemen.

“It looks to me like Leroy is a suspect.” Paul went over and placed a supportive hand on Leroy’s shoulder.

Samuel was breathing heavily from his hurrying, but that didn’t stop him from bellowing. “What? Are you crazy, Sid? Blinder lives with Leroy and his family, as you well know.”

Officer Sid’s angular face reddened. “Listen, I haven’t booked the kid. I’m simply looking at all the possibilities since the victim is out cold. If he doesn’t recover, we could have a murder investigation.”

"What?!" Leroy finally spoke, anger and fear laced his voice. "I didn't do anything! I didn't do anything, Pastor Paul!"

"Look," Paul said to Officer Sid, "do we have to go into all that? Innocent until proven guilty, remember?"

"Officer!"

Officer Sid looked to where Will was standing by the paramedics.

"The victim is conscious and would like to make a statement." Will spoke with authority; the kind earned as captain.

Officer Sid looked at Leroy grudgingly. "You, stay where you are." He backed up his command with a nod towards the other officer, before marching in Will's direction.

Paul looked at the other officer who smiled apologetically. The officer nodded towards the ambulance scene, and shrugged. Paul returned the nod, in understanding. He pulled Leroy along with him towards Blinder. Samuel followed them, the officer followed Samuel.

Blinder was strapped to a gurney, ready to be placed in the ambulance. His eyes were half-opened. He looked at Paul and Leroy, and smiled. His voice came out hoarsely. "L-Leroy's my friend. H-he helped me when the m-men attacked me."

* * *

Two hours later, at Milward Memorial Hospital, Paul sat in the half-filled ER waiting room, drinking his second cup of coffee. He had asked Samuel to take Leroy home and help explain things to Carmel. He could tell that Leroy had been really stressed out about being an assault suspect; which was much worse than being falsely accused of starting a fire in a Sunday school room. Will hadn't come to the hospital but had gone home to be with his family.

Paul took his empty Styrofoam cup to a garbage bin close by. Back at his seat, he bowed his head onto clasped fingers. He was grateful how everything had evolved. It could have been much worse. Blinder had needed a good number of stitches and there was still concern about his concussion. He would have to be observed for the next twenty-four to forty-eight hours. The police would also be questioning Falconer, since the incident was on his property.

He looked at his watch. It was after nine, and he was tired. He rotated his shoulders and twisted his torso from side to side. He yawned into his hand, then looked up when someone stood in front of him.

"Hi," Michaela greeted softly, looking down at him. He stood up, causing her to look up.

"What are you doing here?" he asked, feeling suddenly energetic; his tiredness forgotten. She was a sight for sore eyes, except hers wore a troubled look.

"Paul, I think you should sit back down."

He frowned, wanting to gather her in his arms because she looked so sweet and beautiful, and because he could do with some comforting. Instead, he shrugged and asked, "Why?"

With one hand clutching the strap of her bag to her shoulder, she placed the other on his chest and applied firm pressure.

Did she even know how the warmth of her fingers through his shirt was making his heart rate climb? He wanted to wrap his fingers around hers to keep it there. Instead, he lowered himself back onto his seat.

She sat beside him, turning slightly towards him. "Paul, I'm here with Sarah. We didn't want to bother you because of everything that has happened already, but Brennon is here."

"What do you mean?" he asked, trying to make sense of her words.

"You're not going to believe this, but Brennon has a broken leg. He fell off a ladder trying to repair some cracks left in the wall after the anchors for the Seniors Community banner were taken down."

Chapter Nineteen

Paul waited until the music from the youth band behind him died down, before speaking into the microphone.

"Okay. So, here we are... finally!"

The applause was deafening, especially in a room as jammed-packed as the Fellowship Hall. It wouldn't be as grand an affair as when they had dedicated the opening of the Sanctuary with all the dignitaries and such, but the turnout was awesome. It was just the people of BCC being proud of yet another accomplishment. He was feeling really good.

Instead of putting up tables, they had made a wise decision to line the room with brand new padded chairs to allow for as many as would come. There were long serving tables draped in white along the walls and filled with numerous assortment of dishes, with more being kept warm in the Kitchen. Some of the young mothers were having difficulty keeping their little ones from running over to peek at the tables.

Paul was on a slightly raised platform that jutted out from the back wall of the room. Michaela was just behind him, to his right.

His mother, Christy and her family, and Cassie were present. Will had joined Lucy and Tristan. Even Carmel had come with Lissa.

He shook his head at the sight of Brennon in a wheelchair, with his casted leg stuck out in front of him, beside Sarah and Conner. Brennon grinned and gave him a thumbs-up. Paul laughed. He held his hands up to quieten everyone.

"Before I give recognition to anyone—and believe me, there are a lot. I want to recognize the One who is truly worthy of it all!"

Another deafening applause! Paul grinned as he bowed his head in prayer.

* * *

Michaela had been feeling nervous. Since Brennon was somewhat out of commission, she felt the responsibility of the evening's event rested more heavily on her shoulders. However, after Paul started the ball rolling, she felt herself relaxing, realizing it truly was a party atmosphere; not pomp and circumstance. She also realized that Paul would be there to support her. So, when he handed the microphone to her, it felt very natural to step into her role as master of ceremonies.

After adding her own list of recognition, particularly of the youth, she decided to call upon Leroy to start them off with an original rap. He had begged to be first so he could be relieved from the misery of nerves, and she had given her promise.

Michaela handed the microphone to Leroy before returning to her MC's seat, off to the side. There was dead silence in the room, as if people were not sure what Leroy would do.

He had actually dressed up in a new pair of baggy jeans covered up with a long, white, button-up shirt; and his high-top sneakers were clean. His cornrows looked freshly done, his diamond ear stud was still in place, but the brow ring was missing.

Leroy pulled nervously at the long, silver chain with a large, dangling cross that lay against his white T-shirt, where his shirt opened. He looked across at Michaela.

Michaela gave him her widest smile, then nodded meaningfully at the youth responsible for the music. A few seconds later, the beat started. Another few seconds, Leroy started:

Used to be King Kong in a palace
Homies got money they all about it
Sit up in their rooms just count it
I'm in the fast lane making a lane change
I was dumb I didn't see what was important
Street smart savvy but was ignorant
Your life span on earth got a timeline
While I'm here may as well get mine
Eh man it's for Jesus I make rhymes...

He rapped, he moved, he grooved... Leroy told what nobody seemed to know. Leroy had made a change; he had met Christ!

As Michaela listened to the rest of the rap, she realized Leroy had made every effort to make sure the words could be heard and understood, yet kept the cool quality of the rap sound. He was doing a marvellous job. Even some of the older folks were moving to the beat of the music; a beat many of them didn't usually appreciate.

It was as if those present realized they were witnessing something of the heart: something real.

Michaela looked to her right at the front row where Paul was sitting. He seemed transfixed; intent on Leroy's words. Carmel seemed just as engrossed. If they didn't know, then who knew of Leroy's transformation? Michaela looked through the rocking crowd for Tristan. She was grinning from ear to ear, clapping her hands enthusiastically in tempo with the beat. Ian was seated beside her, looking somewhat sullen.

Big money cash money that's a big dream
It don't matter cuz it ain't nothing to me
Got more important things in life than jewellery
Happy life Jesus Christ is a good thing
Press the reset button got a new life
Chasin' God instead of girls with a flashlight
Block party for the King under street lights
Now I know what my purpose is...

The rap music faded as Leroy swaggered down the side to take his seat. The silence that followed was short-lived. The applause took much longer to die down. Leroy had set the stage for the party!

*   *   *

"We need to do something! They're there now celebrating, while I'm here with nothing! You said you would do something!" Karlene looked at Falconer as he sat sprawled across his foyer sofa. He had refused to let her any further into his dimly-lit house. She vaguely wondered why he insisted on living in such darkness. It wasn't as if he couldn't afford the bills.

He didn't seem to be taking her seriously, sitting with that stupid, impatient look on his big face.

"Perhaps if you calm down, we could have a purposeful conversation," Falconer grounded out, calmly. "I don't like hysterical females frequenting my home whenever they get the notion."

He stood up suddenly, his bearing rife with annoyance.

Karlene stepped back towards the doors, feeling suddenly afraid. Yet, she had always kept her end of the deal, doing whatever he asked her. So, where were the results? He owed her! Anger overruled her fear.

"I'm here because I'm beginning to wonder if you're a fraud!" As soon as she said it, she regretted it.

He faced her, looking fierce and powerful in his darkish domain. "You better watch your tongue before you lose it! This game's not over yet, and you better learn to play it well until it's done!"

She moved towards him, speaking in an entreating tone, "It's not a game to me, Dennis. It's my life—Paul is my life. Please."

He observed her for a long while. He smiled, yet his eyes remained untouched. "I do wonder just to what lengths you would go for that man. It's sickening, yet so... what shall we say... romantic?" He walked a few paces from her, laughing loudly.

She followed after him, her hands raised in supplication. "Please, Dennis. Because Brennon broke his leg, Paul's going on that dratted trip with her for ten days—ten days!"

He turned to her. "Why are you here anyway? Why are you not there celebrating with them?"

Karlene felt bitterness well up in her as she struggled to put her answer into words. "He sent Samuel to kick me out."

"Kick you out?" he asked incredulously.

"Well, not exactly kick me out, but they may as well have done that. They relieved me of my choir duties. I, who've been directing it for the last three years. H-how could they... ?" She couldn't finish. The dreaded burden in her stomach seemed to weigh her down, and she knew Falconer hated tears.

She looked up suddenly when she felt his hands on her shoulders. He smelled of expensive cigars and something else she couldn't identify. She found it hard to make eye contact with him.

"Look at me," he commanded, squeezing her shoulders with his big hands.

She looked as best as she could, but she hated what she saw there in the dark depths. It worried her that the more she came to him; the less she heard the *voice*. She was hardly hearing it anymore—the voice always insisting that she flee and surrender to Hilda and Samuel's care. What if the voice left and never came back? Why did she feel as if she were selling her soul? Why did she feel, in spite of Paul's apathy toward her and losing her position with the choir, she would be much better off in the Church; among the people there, than here in this palatial yet dark place? Falconer's voice cut through to her.

"You will get what you want, but there is a price to pay."

Karlene felt his gaze pulling at her, causing dizziness to come over her.

"Are you willing to pay the price?"

She felt nauseous. Her hand flew up to her mouth and she staggered back from him towards the door. "I-I don't feel well. I've got to go."

* * *

The rich voice of the choir filled the room with glorious energy as they belted out praises as one entity. The worship leader directing the group of twenty seemed very connected to the singers; probably because he had been one of them before taking Karlene's place as temporary director.

Paul rocked to the music, clapping his hands in sync with the beat. Even if some in the audience were clapping off beat, it didn't matter; they all seemed to be enjoying the evening.

Blinder was sitting beside him with his hands on his knees and his right foot tapping to the music. He seemed no worse from his injury, except for the long, dark stitch line that contrasted sharply against his pale skin.

The choir was the last item on the program's agenda. Before that, various groups and individuals had presented a rich potpourri of talents, including a humorous skit by the youth. Brennon, Michaela and the youth had done a great job organizing and planning the celebrations. He was thankful and proud of them, and proud to be part of such a thriving Church.

After the choir left the platform, Michaela stood up from her post and glanced over at him. He smiled at her before taking the choir's place.

"Wow, is it just me, or did it get really warm in here?"

They laughed.

"Let's give it up for the choir one more time!"

A wave of applause filled the room.

"Well, this has been a great evening!"

More applause followed his comment. He held his hand up. "Okay. Now, if you keep clapping after everything I say, we won't be getting to the food."

Laughter filled the Hall. Paul laughed along with them, and then he sobered. "As you all know, Michaela has been with us for the last five months, but her time with us officially ended last week."

"Awwww!" was the general consensus. Paul waited until the heartfelt protest died down.

"Yes, I know we don't want to talk about it, but I do want to acknowledge all that she's been to us—certainly more than just an intern."

* * *

For the next few minutes, Michaela listened as Paul held her in high esteem before the people of Bethel Community. Much of what he said reflected what any senior pastor might say about a successful intern, especially one who was beloved by the congregation. However, his tone suggested his heart was more committed to his words than would be expected.

Michaela was surprised when Samuel joined him and added his own accolades before asking her to join them. She stood to Paul's right, facing Samuel, feeling self-conscious and overwhelmed by their words of appreciation and the sense of that same appreciation from others in the room.

"Michaela, we want you to know you will always be welcomed here, so we don't really want to say good-bye," Samuel continued. His eyes were filled with a look of genuine fondness.

"She's still here for the mission trip!" someone yelled out; probably one of the youth.

"Michaela, I'll marry you if you stay!" a youthful male voice rang out.

After the laughter died down, Samuel held out an envelope and a rectangular package to her. "Pastor Paul, Pastor Brennon, Pastor Sarah, the board, and the people of Bethel Community would like to present these gifts as small tokens of our love, appreciation and support for you."

* * *

Paul knew it was difficult for Michaela as she stumbled through her words, trying to express her gratefulness toward everyone. Her hesitant speech of thankfulness was so unlike her usual straightforward confidence; it was obvious that her emotions were very much involved. This made her all the more endearing to everyone.

"And, as was mentioned before, I'm still here for the youth mission trip which will begin shortly. Thanks again, everyone!" She handed the microphone to Paul as the swell of applause and cheers rose around her.

"Now," Paul said, "I expect to hear that kind of cheering when I get up to preach tomorrow morning."

The room filled with laughter and more cheers.

"Now, let's bless the food!"

Half an hour later, people where eating and enjoying a time of fellowship with each other. Some had returned to their seats to hold their plates perched on knees, or laps, with cups in hand; while others roamed the room with their refreshments. A number of youths were sprawled on the floor by the platform almost in a semi-circle around a group of preschoolers. The youth stayed busy eating, chatting, and fielding their instruments from any toddler who decided to venture onto the platform.

Paul excused himself from his present company of three young women, all vying for his attention. He walked around the edge of the room, looking for Leroy.

Earlier, Christy and Fred Junior had left with his mother for the parsonage. The evening's events had taken a slight toll on Eleanor, but she had insisted that she wouldn't have missed it for the world and that she had thoroughly enjoyed herself.

He noticed Michaela conversing with Cassie and Christy's husband, Fred. He felt a tap on his shoulder, he turned around.

"Hey, Leroy, I was looking for you."

Leroy was grinning widely. "I figured you'd probably want to see me. Besides, I needed a break from the 'honeys.' Their mamas are all starting to look at me funny."

Paul laughed softly and draped his arm around Leroy's shoulder. "I know just what you mean, bro, I know just what you mean," he whispered, as he steered Leroy through the crowd and out of the Fellowship Hall. They paused just outside the doors.

Leroy faced him, rubbing his hands together nervously, but the grin was still in place. "It happened the day after Blinder was beat up," he said, diving right in.

Paul held his hands out in mock disgust. "What! And you didn't tell me?"

Leroy gave a short laugh, then he said, "Tristan helped me." He leaned against the wall, suddenly looking sober. "It was—you know—kinda hard what happened. I couldn't sleep and I just kept thinking how I begged God to make Blinder okay. I told him I'd do anything."

"Go on," Paul encouraged.

Leroy sighed deeply as he fiddled with the cross hanging from the chain around his neck. "After everything—I don't know—I just felt like the only thing he wanted was... me." He looked at Paul, then at the floor, then back at Paul. "It's like somethin' was happening to me—inside. I didn't feel confident enough to do what you told me to do—you know—about accepting Jesus, so I asked Tristan when she came to work the next day." He shrugged. "So now it's all good. The big 'J' and me are tight."

Paul struggled with his emotions as he felt his throat tighten up and his eyes burn. He didn't quite know how to express the flood of love he felt for the young man facing him. This boy; turning into a man, who had so many odds against him. This boy who he tried to be a living example for, knowing that preaching wasn't going to be enough.

Paul squeezed the bridge of his nose, and then did the only thing that would satisfy: he grabbed Leroy in a bear hug.

Leroy's tentative return of the hug reminded Paul that the boy was not big on showing affection, but still Paul held him. "Man... I'm so glad. I'm so glad, Leroy." Leroy remained quiet, and Paul realized something. The boy's shoulders were heaving. Leroy was crying.

* * *

Paul leaned against the kitchen counter, looking out through the serving window into the Fellowship Hall. The night was far spent and everyone was tired, especially those who had stayed for most of the clean-up, but now the Hall was empty except for two custodians.

Soft, worship music seemed to flow with the movements of the two custodians left to their duties. Paul looked at Rashad who had just swallowed a drink of bottled water.

"I know you're worried about her, Rashad, but I can't think of what else to do. You've seen how she's reacted to anyone who won't do what she wants, and she won't submit to any authority in this Church."

Rashad placed the bottled water on the island counter. Frustration was in his bearing. He ran a hand through is thick, dark hair. "I know, Paul. I'm not blaming you, but maybe we should have gone easier on her about the choir. It's the one thing she seemed to really enjoy."

"It wasn't an easy decision. You know that; you were part of it."

"What else was I supposed to do with everyone else bent on sentencing her?"

Paul didn't respond.

"I'm sorry," Rashad said. He rubbed his temple. "That was out of line."

The sound of the worship music disappeared under the hum of an industrial vacuum cleaner. Paul moved away from the serving window to face Rashad. "What do you want us to do, Rashad? I made it abundantly clear she was welcome to remain here with us, after asking her to step back for a sabbatical. We offered her counselling with Sam and Hilda—or with anyone else, for that matter. She wasn't willing to comply with anything. I'm sure you realize she seems a little... "

"I know—unbalanced."

"Yeah, and I'm not sure what that's all about, except that she's been dabbling in the occult."

Rashad looked defeated. "I know," he said. "I've tried talking to her, but she denies it. She just insists you need to come to your senses." He looked at Paul. "You know, if I didn't have the grace of God in my life, I might be blaming you for all of this. She's obsessed with you, yet she flirts with me to get what she wants; and I know she's using me, but… "

Paul noticed the pain in his expression. Unrequited love was not an easy thing. "Do you want to resign from the board?"

"Are you asking me to?"

"No," Paul assured him. "I just want to know that, in spite of your feelings for Karlene, you're committed to your office here."

"By God's grace, I am."

Paul studied him for a moment, seeing the genuineness in his response. "If it's any consolation, you must know that obsession is not love. Karlene doesn't love me; she just wants what she can't have. You know she was abused as a child and, for some reason, she's pinned all her hopes and dreams of happiness on me. Yet, she trusts you and is comfortable with you—she sees you as her friend. We need to keep praying that somehow she'll come to realize that neither one of us can ultimately satisfy her; only Christ can."

"After everything that's happened, I don't know if she sees me as a friend now."

* * *

Michaela watched the tail lights of Samuel and Hilda's car disappear down the church driveway. She had told them she would be along soon.

It was pleasantly warm; the high humidity having finally lifted. She listened for a moment to the chirps of crickets and the distant drone of vehicles, and she suddenly felt displaced.

She wasn't sure what she really wanted, but she felt she should at least thank Paul. She hadn't really had much interaction with him during the fellowship time, after the program. So many people had wanted her attention for best wishes and so forth. It had been a wonderful evening, and her tiredness felt good; the night had been worth it, but... .

She slammed her car trunk shut the same time she noticed Rashad leaving the Church. He paused under the canopy by her car. The lights above bathed his features. He seemed a little worn, and she could guess why.

"Hey, Michaela," he called to her. "You're still here?"

She laughed. "Yes—just some last minute stuff, but I can't wait to get out of these heels."

He pulled his car keys from his pocket. "Well, just remember you're done here now—and with a glowing report. You don't have to keep bowing to you-know-who anymore."

She laughed again, which brought a smile to Rashad's face.

"Well, good night," he said as he turned to go.

"Good night, Rashad, and God bless."

As he went to his car, Michaela moved towards the passenger side of hers. She looked towards the lit Foyer of the Church, and felt indecisive; but soon the decision was made for her. Paul appeared at the front doors. The lights went off, and he came out.

He stood on the walkway, looking at her, then looked across the parking lot. "You're the last one here," he stated the obvious.

She folded her arms and leaned against the car. "Well, I was the person in charge, so it only makes sense... ."

He smiled, then bowed his head slightly to her. "You did good," he stated simply.

She shifted, feeling uncomfortable with more praise. "No more, please," she protested jokingly. "I just wanted to say thank you so much, for everything. I—my time here has meant... " She paused as he stepped off the walkway unto the asphalt, three feet from her.

"Michaela, in a couple of days, I'll be with you, Sarah and a bunch of high-strung teenagers for ten days."

She looked at him, puzzled. She tried again. "I-I'm only thanking you, not saying good-bye."

He put his hands on his hips. "You and I have a lot to accomplish in those ten days. Remember, I wasn't even supposed to be on this trip. You can thank me all you want, afterwards."

Michaela had a distinct feeling that there was a dual meaning to his words. She couldn't think of what to say, and she nearly jumped when he lifted his hand and gently touched her cheek.

"Hey, I can see that mind of yours doing flip-flops. Don't think too hard on what I've said, just let it play out."

Her eyelids fluttered nervously, as he removed his hand. He had just further complicated matters with his last statement. Let what play out?

Paul walked around to the other side of the car and pulled the door opened. "Your chariot awaits, mademoiselle."

She hardly noticed the soreness in her feet as she made her way around the vehicle. She smiled her thanks while slipping into the car. After straightening her skirt around her knees, she looked up at him, waiting for the door to close.

"Sleep tight," he murmured.

"Thank you, I will," she responded. He held the door opened for a moment longer before shutting it firmly.

Michaela breathed a sigh of relief and disappointment as she drove away from the Church. She could see him in her rear view mirror still standing there under the lit canopy, and she asked herself how she would ever make it through ten days with him?

Chapter Twenty

After zipping his suitcase shut, Paul sat on the side of his bed. He had mixed feelings about this trip. Since Hannah's death, he hadn't been on another mission trip. Before that, he had been on a total of four trips, including the one which took Hannah's life.

Those trips had meant a lot to him and he had felt passionate about them. He had loved the work of Church planting and the experience of different cultures. Being adopted into a White family had taught him that one's culture had more to do with who a person was, than one's race.

His days of teenage rebellion, in trying to find his "Black" self, had led him on a search to discover that people were basically the same under the skin, once you looked past their worship, food, music and habitat. They loved or hated; they longed for peace or stirred up war; they yearned for their children to have a better life than they had. The list went on.

Missions had given him an appreciation for what God was willing to do everywhere and for all people; to satisfy their hungry bellies and their hungry souls; to shelter them from the elements and from the evil one; to cover their naked bodies with clothes and their sinful souls with His blood, washing them clean.

The Lord God chose to work through human hands; through the work of the Church—the Church being a living, breathing entity. Yet, at this moment, this was not foremost in his mind.

It was ironic that his first love had died on a mission trip, and, through a twist of circumstance, he found himself facing another trip... with Michaela. And love her, he did. There was no doubt in his mind, or in his heart.

In a way, he felt relieved. He knew the Lord would have him face this day sooner or later, but he had never anticipated that it would also involve a woman.

He stood up slowly at the peel of the doorbell, but then hurried down to answer it.

"Hello, Paul," Samuel greeted cheerfully as he stepped into the parsonage front hall, with a black umbrella trailing behind him. He paused to shake the umbrella outside, before allowing Paul to shut the door. "It's pouring out there!"

When Paul didn't answer, Samuel examined him, frowning. "What's up, son?"

Paul shook his head noncommittally. "Just busy packing, that's all."

Sam continued observing him, then put a hand on his shoulder. "Michaela is no novice in this, Paul. She's a missionary kid. It's in God's hand and there's no better place for it to be."

"Hannah died in His hands," Paul responded like a boomerang.

Samuel sighed heavily. He turned to lean the umbrella against the door, before nudging Paul's arm. "Fix me some coffee, will you? I haven't had breakfast yet."

* * *

Michaela had to smile at Tristan's enthusiasm, as the girl bounced out of the room. She didn't know how many times Tristan planned on racing up two flights of stairs to ask her yet one more detail about packing. She had given all the youth going on the trip an extensive list. Yet, she had to remember that, for her, packing for a trip to her parents' missionary compound in Haiti was like an everyday occurrence. This was new for Tristan and most of the group, except Paul. However, she knew the history of his wife's death. This was, perhaps, not easy for him.

No one else had been available to take Brennon's place at such short notice. She was a little suspicious of the Almighty. He would have known Brennon would break his leg. She couldn't help but wonder at His hand in the unexpected turn of events. Well, at least, He had provided Sarah's parents. Originally, Sarah's parents were supposed to take care of Conner in their home. Now the decision had been made for them to move into Brennon and Sarah's house to take care of both Brennon and Conner.

So, she was stuck with Paul.

She knew her parents would be thrilled to meet Paul, after hearing so much about the Church and its lead pastor. She didn't think they sensed anything beyond that. Although, one could never be too sure about her mother who had the gift of discerning. Her father, on the other hand, took people at face value, and then watched carefully to see if they proved true.

She gave the room a final perusal, and noticed the new Bible that had been in the package given to her by Samuel, the night of the Fellowship Hall ceremony. It was a beautiful Bible, and she didn't want to chance losing it on the trip. All of the leadership at BCC had signed it—she had been deeply touched after seeing the signatures and brief messages.

Michaela took the new Bible off the dresser and placed it in one of the top drawers, and then went to grab hold of a suitcase. She had two: one with her things and the other filled with gifts and supplies. It was just expected that any trip from Canada to Haiti meant bringing extras to share with others.

Michaela glanced at her watch as she headed out of the bedroom. She wanted to see if Tristan was ready; they needed to be at the Church before the other youth showed up. Hopefully, they would all be on time for the pre-flight procedures.

She turned backwards to pull the suitcase after her, feeling excited. She couldn't help it! She was going to Haiti to see her parents and the people there; it was her other world.

* * *

Paul unlocked the church front door. Thankfully, the earlier downpour had stopped as suddenly as it had started. He noticed that daylight was slower in coming now that summer seemed to be hastening to a close. Even so, he felt somewhat better in his spirit after Samuel's counsel and prayer. He had, once more, needed reminding that no one was an island, and that the slowly disintegrating cocoon he had spun had only been to protect him while he healed, not to keep the healthy support of others out.

He turned as he heard a vehicle and smiled at Tristan bursting out of Michaela's car. She was probably the only teen he knew who was a morning person.

"Yeahhh!—I'm the first one here! Hi, Pastor Paul!" Without waiting for his response, she moved quickly to the back of the car to attack the trunk.

"Morning, Tristan." He felt his smile grow wider as Michaela exited more slowly. "Good morning, Michaela." She stood beside the car, looking fresh and beautiful, causing a flood of warmth to flow in him.

"Hi, Paul, are you the first one here?"

"Were you expecting anyone else?"

She laughed and pointed a finger at him. "Coming from you, I'll take that as a yes."

He walked towards her as he spoke. "Carmel called to say Leroy would be a couple of minutes late. Ian's on his way. No one else has called, so I'm assuming they'll be on time."

"Okay," she said, shutting the car door. "I'll just pull my stuff out."

"Here, let me help you," he said, following her to the car trunk. Tristan had already wheeled her luggage onto the walkway in front of the church doors.

"Actually, I'll be fine. You go do what you have to do."

He didn't move, and she frowned at him before saying meaningfully, "I'm used to doing my own bags."

He stayed where he was with one hand on the opened trunk lid. He gave her what he hoped was a persuasive scowl. "Look, I'm not pretending to be macho and I hope you're not trying to be an overly-independent female, so let me help you."

She was quiet for a moment, and he could tell she was mulling his words over, so he took that moment to grab one suitcase and yank it out, before doing a repeat on the other. He took both suitcases and left her standing by the car. Sooner or later, she would have to figure out the rules had changed. He was banking on sooner.

He had just deposited Michaela's suitcases beside Tristan's, when Tristan started yelling.

"All right, Leroy is here!"

Leroy jumped out of his mother's car. He opened one of the back doors to pull his luggage out. His movements seemed a little tense.

"Hi, Tristan!" Lissa cried excitedly, as she struggled to get out on the opposite side of the car.

Tristan ran to give Lissa a hug. "I'm sooooo sorry you can't come this time, but before you know it, you'll be old enough."

Carmel said a few words to Michaela before marching right up to Paul. Something was wrong. "Hello, Pastor Paul. May I have a quick word with you?"

"Sure," Paul said, glancing in Leroy's direction. He was talking to Michaela. Paul directed Carmel into the Vestibule.

"I'm not sure what's gotten into Leroy, but he just up and told me this morning he's not going to college. We had agreed that he could work a little longer, then start in January. The boy has already been accepted and now he tells me it's not what he wants."

Paul could read every inch of frustration on Carmel's face; his heart went out to her. "Did he say what he wants to do?"

She shrugged and rolled her eyes. "He doesn't know, he says. He needs to think it over." She looked briefly over her shoulder. "First, he wanted to enter military service like his father. I didn't like it, but I supported him. When he changed his mind and decided to pursue business, I whooped for joy. Now... " She raised her hands in defeat.

Paul patted her shoulder gently. "I'm with him for ten days, I'll talk with him."

A grateful smile lit up her face. "I knew you would. I'd be very thankful if you could talk some sense into him." She shook her head slowly. "He's been so solid with you in his life. I don't want to see him slip back."

"Don't worry, Carmel, just pray. Can you do that?"

"I think I've worn out the rug by my bedside," she said, chuckling.

Paul smiled. "Keep doing that. Nothing's better." He looked away from her. "Wow, I guess everyone just decided to come all at once!"

* * *

With her head pressed back against the airplane seat and her eyes closed, Michaela breathed a deep sigh of relief. They were finally airborne. She tried to let the tension seep out of her body.

Organizing eight, starry-eyed teenagers to go overseas was not as simple as she had thought it would be, even with two other adults present. Also, they had been late because one of the girls had spent half an hour looking for her passport.

"I wish Brennon could have been here," Sarah said. She was in the aisle seat beside Michaela. "He said he'd be fine, but I feel sort of guilty leaving him with Conner and my parents."

Michaela smiled without opening her eyes. "Sarah, please, no guilt. You were supposed to leave that at the airport."

Sarah giggled, then squeezed Michaela's arm. "Easy for you to say. I've left my man and my child behind. You're going to your parents, and on board this very plane... is your man."

Michaela's eyes flew opened. She glanced to her left where Tristan was rapidly conversing with one of the other girls. Satisfied that the girls hadn't heard, she turned to Sarah.

The grin on Sarah's face would have been contagious had it not been for the subject at hand.

"Sarah, what are you talking about?"

The grin turned into a sweetish, sly smile. "Don't pretend you don't know."

Michaela continued to stare at her, then whispered fiercely, "Nothing has happened between Paul and me."

"Ahh, she says his name. You mean nothing physical has happened, but *stuff* has happened."

Michaela didn't want to be having this conversation. She couldn't believe Sarah had brought it up. She leaned back, deciding to ignore her.

Sarah whispered in her ear, "I'm going to love every minute seeing how you two handle a ten-day trip as co-team leaders. As far as I'm concerned, I'm the only legitimate chaperone on this trip."

Michaela stared straight ahead at the seat in front of her. "Sarah, I didn't know you could be so mean, but I'll prove you wrong."

Sarah squeezed Michaela's hand. "Don't worry; I'm on your side."

"Everyone here, okay?"

Michaela felt her breath catch in her throat, as she looked up at Paul standing in the aisle by their row.

Sarah answered, "We're just fine, Paul. How are the rest?"

Dimples appeared in his cheeks. "They're fine." He looked over at the two youth girls, before bending over to whisper: "I think Ian's a little put out about not sitting with Tristan. I gave him a strong reminder that there would be no fraternization on this trip."

Michaela felt her face grow warm, even though it was very cool in the plane.

Paul spoke again, "Sarah—umm—could I switch seats with you for a couple of minutes?"

"Sure," Sarah said cheerfully. "I need to use the facilities anyway."

After Sarah left, Paul slid his long form down into the seat. This got the two girls' attention. They asked Paul and Michaela a few questions before returning to their discussion.

"You okay?"

Michaela turned her head towards Paul, looking into his eyes briefly, then down at her hands. She nodded.

"Pretty quiet, aren't we."

She smiled. "Just tired, I think, but I'm really looking forward to seeing my parents." As his long fingers tapped the armrest between them, she noticed again the lack of a wedding band. "I'm sorry you have to make this trip. I-I know it can't be easy for you, even though it's not Jamaica."

"Michaela," he said her name softly, "I don't want you worrying about me. It's something I have to do anyway. It had to happen sooner or later."

She chanced a glance at him. His dark eyes had a gentle look which held her captive. She had never met a man who could speak so much with his eyes. It was unnerving. She looked away. "Still, I do appreciate it," she concluded.

"Don't sweat it. I do want to be here. It'll be nice to finally meet your parents—Samuel's old friends."

Michaela noticed Sarah returning.

Paul leaned towards her and whispered in her ear, "Ian's not the only one who's going to have a hard time." He got up and let Sarah take her place. "Thanks, Sarah," he said.

"Anytime, Paul," Sarah replied rather smugly.

Michaela smothered a groan. Surely, this was a conspiracy.

* * *

Karlene slowly opened the door of her townhouse condo. She had expected Rashad because he had phoned her and she had refused to talk to him. She hadn't wanted to see anyone. She was too depressed. She had not expected Falconer; he had never come to her door before.

She hugged herself, pulling her robe close, not caring what he thought. "What do you want? Don't you have enough to do fighting off city hall?" she asked rudely.

"Will you not let me in?" Falconer asked, smiling congenially.

"No. You told me they are too protected, so I don't see any further reason to continue, and I told you I was too sick to work today."

He shrugged, holding his hands palm up. "That's too bad, because I have the solution for you."

This piqued her interest, especially knowing Paul and Michaela were on a flight to Haiti this very moment. "What is it?" she asked noncommittally.

Falconer took a deep breath and, with a smirk, said, "I believe we need a more human element to have a break through."

She opened her door a little wider, noticing that the *voice* had been completely silent today. It made it easier for her to allow Falconer in.

As he stepped inside, he announced, "History, my dear, is about to repeat itself!"

* * *

Two columns of light had given way to the ominous cloud of darkness surrounding Dennis Falconer, as he stepped into Karlene Benedict's abode.

They seemed to hover uncertainly with gleaming, white-light swords drawn. A greater form of brilliant light joined them.

"Lower your swords! The time of her breaking has come! Yet, remain with her."

"What of the anointed ones?"

"The time of their great testing is even at the door! Yet, they have been provided a way of escape, according to the great mercy of the Risen One!"

Chapter Twenty-One

Haiti

The van ride out of Port au Prince, the capital of Haiti, had been erratic enough to take Paul's mind off the mixed emotions that had flooded his being, when he had first stepped off the plane.

No matter how much he had thought himself mentally prepared, he had not been ready for the sense of having been transported back to the Jamaica mission trip—the trip when he had lost Hannah.

It had been the same hot breeze and the same sight of mostly Black people with multiple shades of brown skin, teeming through the building. Granted, their speech had been different from the Jamaicans and the airport in obvious disrepair, but it had almost been like having a flashback. But, unlike Will, he had experienced it with his sanity intact.

Helping Michaela and Sarah with the hectic gathering of the youth and their belongings, and warding off overly ambitious porters, had forced him into motion and out of his surreal state of mind.

He had realized that this was what it felt like to get back on the horse after falling off. Unfortunately, it had been delayed for over three years.

Now, with the unpredictable drive through the chaotic streets of Port au Prince behind them, Paul realized his thoughts had become more focused on the results of the 2010 earthquake that had devastated parts of the country. He noticed, through the haze of the late afternoon sun, much of the debris and rubble from wrecked buildings still in evidence.

Yes, he had lost his wife and child, but some of these people had lost loved ones as well as their homes and livelihoods. The images of the relief camps were still in his mind.

"It's so sad," Tristan remarked wistfully from the seat in front of Paul, to no one in particular.

Along the sides of the road, the landscape was dotted with shanty towns, charcoal fires and people selling their wares. The smell of burning rubber from roadside tire repair shops added to the already strong vehicle fumes.

"Yet, they are a resilient people. No matter the natural disasters or political upheavals that have come their way, they somehow seem to rally back," Michaela commented. She, Tristan and one of the boys were behind the driver who her parents had sent into the city, days before, to pick them up. Her earlier, familiar interaction with the driver, alternating between Haitian Creole and English, had made her seem quite comfortable on this Haitian turf.

"That was a nasty earthquake, though," Ian said. He was shoved between Paul and one of the other boys "Maybe this one did them in."

"Well, we pray that it hasn't," Paul said, continuing to gaze out the window on their way north of Port au Prince. After the hustle and bustle out of the city, everyone seemed a little subdued.

Sarah spoke from the back where, with no seatbelt rules to abide by, she was squished in with the other three girls: "I think we take so much for granted in our society. Like Michaela has said before, everyone should have a taste of a third world country to realize how much we have and what we can give."

"My mother's struggled for everything she has," Leroy voiced from his privileged place in front with the driver.

Michaela looked at him soberly. "Yes, she has, Leroy. Yet, in Canada, we have social safety nets. Here, without the support and protection of their families, women are more easily victimized. They also don't have the same opportunities for jobs and income."

One of the boys piped up, "The fact sheet you gave us said one percent of the people own nearly half of Haiti's wealth."

"Sounds like corruption to me," Leroy grumbled.

They would continue to belabour the pros and cons of life in Haiti for much of the eight-hour drive.

One of their stops, along the way, was at a little house on a hill off the roadside. The house, made of cinder blocks, was a reddish brown colour; the same as most of the earth surrounding it.

After explaining that the inhabitants were childhood friends of hers, Michaela insisted they stopped for, what she called "piti piti" visit. When she translated, Paul laughed.

"What do you mean by *a little bit* of a visit? We're supposed to stop for bathroom and food—that's all. When women visit, that's not usually what happens." This insight created a humorous ruckus among the boys and protests from the girls.

"Ten minutes, tops," she promised, entreating him with her eyes. "I haven't seen Pierre and Joenne in years, but I did write to tell them we would try and stop by on our way."

So, Paul stood outside the van shaking his head as they all hustled out to follow Michaela up a meandering, well-worn, dirt path to the house.

The driver caught Paul's attention. "De women, eh? When you tink you rule dem… " he said in broken English.

"Yeah… they rule you," Paul finished, grinning. He turned to follow the others.

Once the young couple's surprise and excitement at the visit had died down, they and their two small children were the epitome of hospitality, even in their humble dwelling.

Fifteen minutes later, they were once more on their way.

"They were so kind, even though they don't have as much as we do," one of the girls commented in a small voice.

"Yes, Haiti is not just about poverty, violence and corruption. There is much friendliness toward foreigners and gratefulness for whatever help they bring; and there is also a spiritual element that is very challenging for missionaries," Michaela said. "If you've read your entire fact sheet, you'll notice that many here practice Vodou or Voodoo." She spelled the difference for them.

"Yes, but not the kind where people supposedly stick pins in dolls," Tristan said, as the van bumped along the uneven, rugged road.

"That's right," Michaela continued. "Vodou is a combination of West African, Arawakian and Catholic beliefs. When the Haitians embrace 'pure' Christianity, many missionaries try to help them shed the pagan practices, while still maintaining their cultural way of life."

"Not throwing the baby out with the bath water," Paul concluded for her.

Michaela smiled at him. "That's exactly right, Pastor Paul," she agreed teasingly.

* * *

It was pitch black when they finally arrived at the road, which was more path than road, to the missionary compound.

Paul manipulated his watch's light to check the time, before reaching over the seat to gently tap Michaela's head. "Hey, we're almost there, right?" He rested his hand on the back of the seat, after she had turned her head.

"Yes," she whispered in a tired voice. "Are they still asleep?"

"Looks that way," he said, peering through the dark around him, aided a little by the glow from the vehicle's dashboard. Steady breathing of different degrees could be heard competing with the sound of the van's rumble.

"This road is a bit long, so let's leave them for now."

"You okay?" he asked.

"Stiff, sore, hungry, but I'm okay. Next time, I'll fly in."

"You're definitely a trooper," he said, chuckling quietly. He raised his hand from off the seat and lightly caressed her temple with a curved finger. Her skin was soft and warm.

She was still for a moment, but then she pulled away slightly from his touch, before facing forwards.

He couldn't help it: he stroked the top of her head provokingly before settling back into his seat. He allowed the smile on his face to linger for awhile, remembering the bouncy texture of her hair under his fingers.

Almost five minutes later, the van entered a laneway that was slightly muddy from the rainy season. It led through a wide set of gates into a walled compound. There was light from only one building; but it was a cheerful, welcoming sight, after such a dark drive through the rural landscape of Haiti.

Paul breathed a quiet word of thankful prayer as they prepared to unload.

Fairly soon, the lifeless, yawning bodies of eight teenagers and three adults stirred to activity. They gave a healthy, albeit tired, applause for the driver in whose hands they had entrusted their lives. Then all eyes were directed at the commotion coming from what looked like the main compound building.

"Papa, Mama!" Michaela exclaimed, as she hurried over to a small group of people, who had lanterns lighting their way, accompanied by barking dogs. The man and woman who enveloped Michaela in an embrace were elderly. The man was tall and strong looking with dark brown skin; and the light brown-skinned woman was fine featured and of medium build.

By the light of lanterns, Paul finally met Michaela's parents, Reverend Michael and Dawn Laroche, who welcomed him heartily into Michaela's other world.

Pastor Laroche's wise gaze searched Paul's face by the lantern's glow. He nodded slowly, as if treasuring a secret only he knew. "It's our utmost pleasure to finally meet you Reverend Paul Rayner. *Bienvéni*. Welcome to Haiti."

Chapter Twenty-Two

Paul woke to the increasingly familiar sounds of crowing roosters and braying donkeys. This was their fourth day at the compound, and he relished the thought of stepping into the outdoors, with its lush, tropical vegetation dotting the landscape. Even the surrounding mountains made it easy to forget some of Michaela's accounts of what it cost the Laroches to forge such a path: sacrifices similar to those of many other missionaries.

His earlier apprehension about the mission trip had disappeared.

Yet, Paul realized that all was not as it seemed in paradise. Those very mountains had been scavenged of much of its wood for fuel and homes. As a result, mud slides were not uncommon during the rainy season, and the scarcity of mature trees had become a sobering problem.

He raised his head from his pillow. The guys, still out cold, were sprawled across two sets of bunk beds. The abundance of fresh air and hard work at the compound definitely thwarted any curfew conflicts. Getting them up in the mornings would have been a more difficult matter, had it not been for the mouth-watering aroma of a hearty Haitian breakfast floating into the men's dorm each morning.

Paul practiced personally thanking the local women, who came each morning to bless them with a breakfast feast which sometimes included: herring in sauce or boiled eggs, boiled or fried plantains, sliced avocado, Haitian bread, fresh juice and coffee. The women would tease him, vowing to fatten him up before his departure.

He was always amazed at how some missionary compounds were like little cities built of cinder blocks. Because supplies were so limited in Haiti, mission planes would routinely deliver cargos of supplies to be stored at the compound. Missionaries often had to do their own repairs of buildings and machinery. Hiring local people was necessary for the efficient flow of work on the compound. Volunteers and donations from abroad were always needed to offset expenses.

This compound was like a fifty-acre city with various buildings on site, including a clinic and an orphanage.

After their first full day of getting acquainted with the Laroches and the regular workers at the compound; touring the compound and the surrounding village; and being assigned their duties, the next three days had followed a set pattern.

The four girls mainly stayed at the compound with Mrs. Laroche, Michaela and Sarah, assisting the two nurses at the clinic and the workers at the orphanage on site. The household duties were also overseen by Mrs. Laroche, but mainly tended to by women workers from the village.

The four boys alternated between helping the regular men workers with repairs and yard work, and accompanying Paul and Pastor Laroche on rounds around the compound and the village. There was a school and several Churches outside the compound that Pastor Laroche routinely visited.

In spite of his age, he was still heavily involved in the teaching and training of Haitian pastors.

"I believe it's more effective for the Haitians to teach and disciple their own people," Pastor Laroche commented, four hours later, after a morning at one of the Churches where Paul had taken the opportunity to interact freely with the young men in training. The boys had remained at the compound doing some painting. "It's also one of Michaela's convictions. She believes the locals have more interest invested and would be more committed."

Paul chuckled. "Sounds like Michaela," he commented.

Pastor Laroche smiled broadly, lighting up his long face and causing the skin to crinkle around his eyes. "Yes, you have found her very opinionated, no doubt. That, she inherited from her mother who—by the way—is Haitian by birth. She only got her height from me."

"And your name, sir," Paul added.

"Yes—Michaela—that was also from me. My wife insisted she be named after me since there would be no sons. After Michaela's birth—a very difficult birth—it was determined we would have no more children."

Paul remained silent out of respect, as a far-away-look crept into the older man's eyes.

Pastor Laroche sighed. "Yet, He knows best. Our work here has been quite consuming, perhaps more children wouldn't have been wise."

Paul followed him to the pickup truck where a group of boys, probably in their early teens, waited.

One of them asked Pastor Laroche a question in Creole which caused Pastor Laroche to laugh loudly. When the answer was given, the boy grinned widely.

"He asked if you were a famous basketball player," Pastor Laroche told Paul. "I told him you were a pastor, but that you could play basketball."

Before Paul could comment, another boy spoke up. Pastor Laroche dialogued with him, which seemed to start all the boys talking and laughing at once. Pastor Laroche soon waved them away from the vehicle, and they scattered, sounding excited, stirring up dust with their bare feet.

On the bumpy ride back to the compound, Paul asked, "So what else did those boys say?"

"Oh, they just asked if you would play basketball with them, and I said you would be honoured to."

Paul found himself answering the older man's friendly smile, but he had a question of his own. "How did you know I played basketball?"

Pastor Laroche concentrated on a sharp turn before answering. "Well, I won't be stereotypical and say because you're a tall, Black man. We have gleaned much of our information about you from our daughter."

Paul relaxed against the seat, shaking his head mentally.

"I should be fair, Paul," Pastor Laroche continued. "Samuel was also instrumental in setting our minds at ease."

"Sir?"

Pastor Laroche chuckled softly. "Well, any young man who so captured our daughter's admiration would be able to stand up well to a little scrutiny."

Paul felt his mouth hanging opened; he shut it.

"My family will tell you, I'm one who takes time to form judgements about a person, but Samuel is a good judge of character. So, Paul Rayner, as you have opportunity for the next week with us to voice any—umm—wishes, please feel welcomed to do so."

Fifteen minutes later, Paul and his host were fairly close to the compound gate, when a bicycle and its occupant careened around the corner through the gateway. The young man on the bike was peddling madly as he glanced at the pickup, his eyes wide and his movements frantic.

Pastor Laroche braked suddenly, avoiding a collision that would most certainly have been to the detriment of the cyclist.

Paul stuck his head out the window to check the progress of the man. His movements had slowed down, but he kept glancing back at them. He soon turned a corner, disappearing from view.

"What was he doing here?" Pastor Laroche asked loudly, also looking behind him. He glanced at Paul before engaging the vehicle forwards. "That was a young man named Maxime. He worked for us at one time, but was let go. He has stolen from us on more than one occasion, but that was not our greatest concern. He came specifically to undermine our mission here—to win back the new converts who work for us."

"Really," Paul commented above the noise of barking dogs, as Pastor Laroche parked beside the depot building where yard and repair tools were housed.

"Yes, he is the grandson of a witch doctor—a woman named Lola." More questions from Paul were delayed as the barking grew closer.

"Come back here, Pedro!—August!" a voice called out.

Two dogs barrelled around the side of the depot, but then slowed up close to Pastor Laroche. Immediately their barking ceased. With wagging tails, the two medium-sized, tan dogs vied for Pastor Laroche's attention.

Shortly after, Leroy and Ian appeared, running. The boys stopped, breathing hard. Before catching their breath, they started talking at the same time.

"Whoa, whoa, now," Pastor Laroche said as he straightened up from the dogs. "One at a time, please."

Leroy looked at Ian and shrugged. Ian took the bait.

"The dogs were after that guy! Did you see him?"

"Yes, we saw him," Paul answered. Both boys seemed pumped with raw energy.

"He was here making trouble, and dumbo here decided to take matters in his own hands," Ian continued, gesturing at Leroy.

Without warning, Leroy sprang into action, shoving Ian on the chest causing him to stagger backwards.

"Who you calling dumbo, you coward?" Leroy growled.

"Young men!" Pastor Laroche called, as Ian righted himself and dove into Leroy's middle, knocking him to the ground. Ian landed on top of him. They grabbed at each other, twisting, turning, rolling, as they grappled for position on top. The dogs started barking and whining alternatively, as if unsure whether the boys were playing or fighting.

"Leroy, Ian!" Paul called sternly, trying to get their attention. The boys continued; each intent on gaining the upper hand.

Paul waited for an opportune moment before grabbing Leroy, who had straddled Ian, trying to get a punch in. Paul held him under the armpits and dragged him backwards, while Pastor Laroche held a cautionary hand in front of Ian, who was struggling to his feet.

Leroy shrugged off Paul's hold. "What was I supposed to do with that creep ogling Michaela and talking superstitious bull?"

Ian's face was beet red and he was breathing hard, but he didn't back down. "So you decided to play the hero? That's what set him off!"

"Okay—okay," Paul said, holding his hands up. "Are the women okay?"

"Yes," both boys answered simultaneously, still eying each other resentfully.

Soon enough Mrs. Laroche, Michaela, Sarah, and the other youth came into view, followed by some of the men workers. They slowed their hurried pace.

"Oh, good, you've got the dogs," Mrs. Laroche said, relief in her tone. "I thought those dogs would tear him to shreds. I've never seen them so agitated."

"My dear, what happened? We saw Maxime racing away like all hell was after him."

As Mrs. Laroche recalled the events, Paul watched Michaela's face carefully. She seemed okay, maybe a little tense. Sarah had her arms around the shoulders of two of the girls.

Maxime had, apparently, come to deliver a message with the knowledge that Michaela had returned from Canada. It was some hocus-pocus message that the ancestral spirits had declared her as the chosen one for him, and perhaps the next high priestess to succeed his grandmother. Leroy had taken exception to what he saw as a mixture between a bad pick-up line and threat to Michaela's safety.

Mrs. Laroche laughed at this part of her story. "Leroy ordered Maxime to leave before he kicked him out. Maxime got hot under the collar and started cursing at him. I'm sure we might have had a fight on our hands had the other men not been within earshot."

"Yes," Tristan broke in. "He said Leroy was a no-account trapped in a White man's world." She looked a little sheepish. "At least that's what one of the workers translated."

Michaela squeezed Tristan around the shoulders, affectionately. "That's exactly what he said, but it's over now. I think Maxime was speaking for his grandmother—just stirring up trouble. I think the part about me being chosen for him is another desperate attempt to pursue me."

"What?" Paul asked, frowning. This was news to him. He wondered how long this had been going on.

She looked at him and shrugged. "It's nothing to worry about."

"Maxime has been interested in Michaela since they were children," Pastor Laroche stated with a frustrated sigh. "I think he's now thinking to take a wife. However, he doesn't have our blessing now nor will he in the future."

Paul hated feeling out of the loop where Micheala was concerned. But, it was a reminder that he had only known her for over five months.

Pastor Laroche thanked the workers before excusing them. Except for Tristan, Leroy and Ian, the youth started wandering away, playing with the dogs. Paul decided to deal with the issue at hand.

"Do we need to be worried about this guy?"

Pastor Laroche glanced at his wife for a moment before answering. "If these incidents continue, we will consider posting a guard during the day-time. I think, by nature, Maxime is a coward. I don't think he anticipated this much opposition." He directed his smile at Leroy who seemed more relaxed.

"Okay," Paul said cautiously. "I'll take your word for it." He looked at Michaela and Sarah. "I think I'll have a word with Ian and Leroy."

He excused himself from Michaela's parents and headed for a mature grapefruit tree with the boys in tow. He faced them and noticed that Tristan had followed.

She stood with folded arms and a determined look on her face. "Did something happen between them? Because—if it did—I know why."

Paul decided to be straight with her. Like Tristan, he also had an inkling what the distrust was between the boys, and it needed to be resolved. "They had a fight," he told her.

"You guys are such idiots!" she directed at the boys. "Leroy's my friend and you don't like it, Ian. Ian's my boyfriend, but you don't like him, Leroy. You guys are supposed to be Christians, but you're acting like two losers instead of the winners you're supposed to be."

The boys stood gaping at her, then looked towards the ground. Leroy spoke first. "Yeah, she's right. But it's more like I don't get your attitude, man—always treating me like I don't belong."

Ian looked embarrassed. He glanced briefly at Paul, then focused on Leroy. "Okay, you're right. I haven't always treated you right and God's been dealing with me about it, but I've ignored Him." He took what seemed to be an agonizing breath. "So, sorry, man."

Both boys stood looking uncertainly at each other.

"A hand shake about now would be good, guys," Paul urged, feeling amazed and relieved at how God and a feisty teen girl could work miracles together.

The boys approached each other hesitantly, then clasped hands.

"Sorry I called you dumbo," Ian said.

"Sorry for ramming you," Leroy said. They stepped back from each other.

Ian spoke to Tristan. "Did you say I was your... "

"Yes, Ian—my boyfriend. I've told you before, I'm not allowed to date until I turn seventeen. I'll be seventeen in two weeks, so we can date then."

He looked puzzled. "But, I thought you were just putting me off."

Tristan shook her head in disgust. "Pastor Paul, when we get back, maybe you could tell Pastor Brennon we seriously need a class for the guys on how not to put words into a girl's mouth." With that, she turned and marched off.

"Wow," Ian breathed out, his eyes somewhat dazed.

Leroy grinned. "And you called me dumb."

* * *

Dusk had set in, and Paul was having a rare moment alone on the veranda of the main house, when Michaela joined him. This was the first time they were alone since their arrival at the mission, and he was very surprised when she eased into the bamboo chair next to his.

She wore a pale yellow, summer dress which contrasted beautifully with her caramel brown skin. Her black hair was pulled almost straight, into a thick bun, leaving some tight waves framing her face.

She must have noticed the surprise on his face because she said, "I thought maybe you'd want to talk to me."

"About what?" He shifted in his seat so he mostly faced her, praying that everyone else would stay away.

"About what happened today."

"Well, it's not every day women I know get proclamations from the grandson of a priestess."

Her laughter sounded warm and breezy like the air moving in cyclic motion along the veranda. "You've been on enough missionary trips to know that spiritism and sorcery are not covered up and re-packaged as harmless entertainment as in Western nations. It's out in the open as their way of life."

"Still, it's not the kind of thing to make a man sleep well at nights."

She was silent for a moment. "Well, in any case, thanks for being concerned."

"And you're not concerned?" he asked.

"Not really. As my father said, Maxime is harmless and I have a greater power that protects me against black, white, or any colour magic."

"As I recall, your father said he was a coward, not harmless. Sometimes cowards are the most dangerous."

She shook her head as if fluffing him off. "You're worrying over nothing."

Paul leaned towards her and captured her gaze. "I can't help but worry about you. You have a way of moving headlong into things."

"I'm old enough to know what I'm doing."

"I'm not debating that."

"Then what are we debating?"

Paul wasn't sure how to answer her, wasn't sure that he should. He took a cautious approach. "That you don't have to go it alone."

Her eyelids fluttered nervously as she looked away from him. "I'm not sure what you mean. I'm not alone. I have my family and my friends, and... I have the Lord."

His fingers gently redirected her face towards him. "That's not what I meant. I think you know what I mean." He removed his hand, no longer trusting himself to be satisfied with just touching her face. He leaned back in his seat and rested one ankle across his knee.

"I don't like to guess what people mean."

He ran a hand across his brow and looked out into the gloom. "So, you want me to spell it out?"

"I'm not sure I want you to do anything," she answered quickly, almost in a whisper. She pushed herself up from her seat.

Paul grabbed hold of her hand, preventing her from leaving. She froze, looking down at their joined hands, then at him. Her eyes widened.

"When we return home, I want you in my life. I want us to get to know each other better."

She remained still and silent, her chest rising and falling noticeably. He decided to press the point home.

"I want to be with you." He held tightly, as she tried to tug her hand away.

"Well, I should have something to say about it, shouldn't I?" she finally asked tersely.

He could tell she was trying to put up protective walls; that she was nervous, maybe feeling vulnerable. He wasn't about to let her off the train, though. Now that they had boarded, he was determined to keep her on until they reached the desired destination.

"Most definitely you get a say," he responded, smiling to hopefully ease some tension. As she averted her gaze, he noticed her lips turning up at the corners, slightly.

"Then... I say, let me go."

He slowly released her hand and stood up. She shifted backwards, nervously.

"I'm just following you in. It's not all I want, but I have to be—you know—a good example for the guys." He laughed softly, as she speared him with a sharp look before preceding him into the house.

Chapter Twenty-Three

Canada

Karlene allowed a lone tear to fall from her eye as she sat before the broad desk of the Church District Superintendent. It hadn't been hard to work up the tear. She had been emotionally charged all day, waiting for this moment to present her case as a follow up to the letter she had sent days before. Dennis had told her the story was believable, and that it was her only viable chance to make sure any romance between Paul and Michaela would never survive.

The distinguished looking man behind the desk glanced over at his assistant who was seated to Karlene's left. The assistant was present because of the nature of the complaint. She passed Karlene a box of tissue from the corner of the desk.

The Superintendent frowned down at the letter in his hand. He seemed very caring, but also seemed to be having difficulty with her story.

"Will you please explain to me, Ms. Benedict, why you insisted on bringing your complaint to us first rather than the church elders or board?"

Karlene allowed another tear to fall before she dabbed at her eyes and nose delicately. She felt a sickness inside, but it was too late to turn back now. She needed to follow it through. "I-I didn't think I could trust anyone there," she whispered, emphasizing her anguish by glancing helplessly in the direction of the assistant.

The assistant wore an empathetic expression that encouraged Karlene.

"They're all so close. The whole Church is like a family. None of them would believe me; least of all his board."

"I see," the Superintendent said. He laid the sheet of paper on his desk, then smoothed it with both hands. "This is a very grave complaint. We will use the utmost care in consideration of your sufferings, but you must understand that we need to proceed with a full and fair investigation of your allegations against Reverend Rayner."

"Thank you. Yes, I do understand. After all... " At this point, she choked up as if trying to stem more tears. "After all, it's only my word against his."

"Ms. Benedict, in God's kingdom, we weigh each person's value the same. We will be fair and in much prayer regarding such a sensitive matter."

Karlene stood up slowly as the Superintendent approached her.

"I personally will meet with Samuel Temple, then we'll go from there. Please be advised Ms. Benedict to keep these allegations to yourself, until we have had opportunity to hear Reverend Rayner's side, when he returns."

Minutes later, Karlene left the building feeling worse than ever. What had she done?

Haiti

The dust from the constant dribbling of the basketball rose higher as team Haiti and team Canada battled it out. True to his word, Pastor Laroche had invited some of the village boys to the compound for a game. About ten of them had shown up, eager and full of energy.

They were playing on a dirt court next door to the rectangular-shaped orphanage. Interestingly enough, both teams had a mix of Haitian and Canadian players. A good show of solidarity, Michaela had said.

Paul looked over at her now, as he and the boys took a water break. She, Sarah and some of the girls sat cheering with the orphans on the sidelines, while a few of the Canadian girls played with several younger children on a four-seat, wooden swing set about ten feet away. Some of the orphanage workers had also taken a break to watch the game.

Most of the twenty-five children, all under the age of twelve, were spread across the grass near Michaela and Sarah. The girls' bright hair ribbons made the occasion seem even more festive. Some of the boys kept darting in and out of the game, even though they had already played with Paul and the Canadian boys, earlier. It thrilled Paul's heart to see these kids so cheerful and enthusiastic, and they didn't have the latest electronic game or computer. Their lives seemed much simpler; less cluttered. Yet, there was much suffering.

Some of these little ones suffered from the same sickness as Will: PTSD. Many of them had lost their families and homes in the earthquake. For some of them, sudden noises could trigger a reminder of the earthquake all over again, causing irritability or panic.

The challenge wasn't just feeding and clothing the children, it was also the therapy and spiritual counsel for their minds and spirits.

"Leroy, Ian!" Paul called the boys over. "I think we need to get Michaela and Sarah a little dusty. I think we should challenge them to come join a team."

Looks of mischief spread across their faces, but then Ian balked.

"But, we can't even get the girls to play because of the dirt; the women won't wanna play."

Paul went over to talk to one of the boys who knew English. "Tell the others I'm going to bring the women into the game."

The boy looked surprised, but then a big grin covered his face. After his nod of agreement, Paul crossed the dirt court, followed by Ian and Leroy.

The children were suddenly quiet and wide-eyed, as Paul stood in front of them. He looked down at Michaela.

"We, the team, have decided that it would be an example of good sportsmanship to the girls here, for you women to join the team."

Michaela's eyes took on an incredulous look. She glanced over two little heads at Sarah.

"Oh, no, Paul," Sarah started protesting.

"Aw, come on," Ian begged. "Maybe Tristan and the others will play, if you do."

"But you're doing so well without us," Michaela commented, "and it's so—dusty." She wrinkled her nose.

"It would have been much worse without the rain. It's really not that bad," Paul threw in. He held out a hand to her. "Come on, set a good example."

Michaela's expression was pained.

"Oh, all right," Sarah said in disgust. "Brennon's never going to believe this." She separated herself from the children and stood up, straightening her knee-length shorts. She looked down at Michaela. "You may as well give in, Michaela. I don't think he's going away."

Michaela made a face, then spoke in Creole to the children. Afterwards, she took Paul's hand. He hauled her up.

"You'll enjoy it," he told her, holding tightly to her hand, not wanting to let go.

"I seriously doubt it and I know I'm going to regret it." She pulled her hand free and stepped away from him while tucking her sleeveless shirt into loose-fitting, knee-length shorts.

He smiled, loving her defiance, loving her. "Oh, ye of little faith," he told her, reclaiming her hand to pull her along with him.

"All right!" Leroy yelled as he raced ahead towards the court where the teen boys waited impatiently.

Fifteen minutes later, Tristan and another girl had also joined the game. Michaela and Sarah seemed to spend more time laughing at themselves and encouraging the boys, regardless of which team they were on, than playing. The dust was still flying, but fortunately the sky was slightly overcast and the wind dried much of their sweat.

At the moment, team Haiti was winning by four points and Paul wanted to even up the score. It was difficult with Leroy as team Haiti's point guard.

Paul looked ahead to the naked rim for an opening. He did a back pass to the boy on his right, who just as quickly passed it back over his opponent's head. Paul backhanded the sweat from his forehead. He dribbled around one of the younger boys, almost tripping in the process. He raised the ball above his head to pass to Ian who, he hoped, would use his height advantage for a slam dunk. Too late! Another tall boy had whipped out in front of Ian. Paul dribbled to the side.

He hadn't even seen her coming. Michaela seemed to come out of nowhere, charging at him. He could have passed the ball, but he took his chance, figuring she would balk at the last moment. When he realized she wasn't bluffing, he moved quickly to go around her while raising his arms to pass the ball. A split second before he hit her, he had known it would happen. He felt a jolt of pain in his right elbow.

Paul dropped the ball.

"Michaela!" he called as he rushed to stoop with one knee on the ground, beside her.

"Michaela—you okay?"

She was lying on her back with both knees up and both hands over her forehead. The game stopped and everyone started crowding around.

Paul gently pulled her hands away. Her eyes were closed, and she seemed to be in pain. A red mark was appearing on her left temple.

"I'll get ice," Sarah said before pushing her way through the children, who were starting to ask questions in Creole.

"I'm okay, Paul," Michaela finally said. "Just give me a minute." She put her hands back up over her face.

Paul glanced up at the sea of concerned and curious young faces. He spied the Haitian boy who spoke English and called to him.

The boy importantly pushed his way through the younger children.

"Tell the children that Miss Michaela is okay, but I'll be taking her to the house. Tell them she will visit them later."

The boy nodded. He turned to the others and started speaking in Creole, especially giving attention to the children of the orphanage.

Michaela slowly removed her hands from her face, and Paul took that moment to shove his arms under her to scoop her up.

She gasped loudly and instinctively threw her arms up around his neck. "Paul, what are you doing?"

"Taking you to the house," he answered, holding her securely as he walked away from the court.

"I can walk. Put me down."

"No."

"It's too far," she continued to protest.

"Well, here comes Sarah with that dilapidated golf cart." Paul stopped in his tracks to wait for Sarah as she drove an old golf cart in their direction.

"Okay, down, please," Michaela commanded, pushing one hand against his chest.

Paul smiled down at her, drinking in the sight of her face so close to his. "Why? You're no great weight." He noticed the rest of her skin was becoming as flushed as the injured area where a small lump was starting to form. "Sorry for knocking you down."

"Apology accepted. Now put me down."

He sighed loudly. He pulled his arm from under her knees, allowing her to stand. For a moment, she leaned against him.

"I thought you would want to take her back to the house," Sarah called as she scooted out of the cart. "Are you okay, Michaela? Wow, you're swelling already! Here's the icepack."

Michaela stepped away from Paul as she accepted the icepack from Sarah.

"Thanks," Paul told Sarah. "Why don't you take her to the house and I'll finish up with the kids?" It wasn't what he wanted to do, but it was what he should do.

Moments later, he watched the women drive away. Approximately ten feet away, Michaela, with the icepack pressed up against her temple, turned and looked at him. After he gave a little wave, she faced forwards.

Paul pressed his hands to the back of his head and flexed his shoulder muscles. Only three more days separated him from the freedom to let go of the restrictions he had placed on his and Michaela's relationship. He had waited for over five months. What was three days?

He looked towards the heavens. *How Jacob waited for seven years is beyond me.* Yet, the Spirit's admonition to be patient continued to echo in his soul.

Canada

Samuel witnessed the disbelief in all of their eyes: Brennon, Rashad, Ethel, Frank and Robert.

"There must be some mistake," Ethel said emphatically. She looked up at Hilda who was standing behind Samuel's chair in the Conference Room.

"It's no mistake, Ethel," Hilda informed her gently. "These were Karlene's accusations, in writing too."

Brennon was shaking his head from side to side. "I can't believe this—that she would stoop so low."

"It is an allegation, Brennon. It still has to be proven," Samuel said. He was feeling the heavy weight of all that had transpired during his recent meeting with the District Superintendent.

Brennon shifted his casted leg impatiently. "Yes, but this kind of allegation can wreck a man's life—his career—even if he's innocent."

"What's to be done?" Frank asked quietly, but in a shaky voice. He was clearly feeling disturbed. "Something has to be done."

Robert, who was sitting beside Frank, shook his head in agreement.

Samuel felt a groaning within his spirit. "Well, we must fast and pray. Nothing can be done until Paul returns, and we hear his side."

"I just spoke with him, yesterday," Brennon told them. "Everything seemed to be going very well, and he was looking forward to returning—said he missed everyone. My God, what's this going to do to him?"

"We must have faith, Brennon, and trust the Lord even in this. There has to be a purpose in this, greater than we know."

Rashad had been silent with his forehead cradled in his hands and his elbows on the table. He looked at the group with a pained expression. "Why did she go to them before coming to us? I don't understand."

"Because she knew we wouldn't believe her, probably," Hilda supplied. "I don't, for one minute, believe any of this. But as Sam says, there has to be a process."

"Is it possible there could be some truth to the young lady's accusations?" Robert asked nervously. He raked his glasses up the bridge of his nose.

Everyone stared at him. He shrugged, pursing his lips. "Well, the question has to be asked," he stated matter-of-factly.

"Of course, it has to be asked," Samuel agreed reluctantly. "In spite of our faith in Paul, we still have to ask the question and allow the process."

Chapter Twenty-Four

Haiti

Paul waited just outside the gate of a small Haitian property with its ivy and hibiscus-laden fencing. It was after three in the afternoon and Pastor Laroche was having a private word with a couple who had been receiving marital counselling from him.

Paul's French was very rusty: a pale high school version, at best. Even if he were fluent in French, he wouldn't understand the Haitian's broken French—Creole—which was spoken by the villagers. Yet, it was still interesting listening to their calls and conversations to each other across the road, over their fences, and in their yards. In spite of their many misfortunes, their communities seemed more connected and interdependent.

He had also found the earlier Sunday service very interesting. For some reason—maybe because of changes in himself—this service had struck him more than any other he had experienced on a mission trip. In spite of their difficulties, their poverty, and their country in turmoil, these people gave serious time to God. There was no sense of impatience, no looking at watches.

He had watched the faces of the men; and the women with their cloth head coverings, sitting separately from the men; and the children—they all seemed to expect to spend time.

Pastor Laroche had actually pointed out people who had been healed of sicknesses, even those who'd had demons cast out of them. He had also recounted that three weeks earlier, three young Haitian pastors had anointed a young boy with oil and had given up much prayer for him. The young boy with malformed feet had experienced a miraculous healing which, over a period of three days, left his feet in perfect form.

Paul tried to imagine all of that happening in his Church and he found it hard. Deep down in his soul, he knew there was more. More than the good works, the programs they funded, the counselling sessions... . Those were all crucial. Yet, something seemed to be missing.

There was something to be said about the supernatural touching the earth. Could it be why more and more North Americans were turning to Eastern religions and mysticism? Were they willing to look anywhere for fulfillment and answers that all the addictions of the world couldn't give? A world increasingly in turmoil because of wars, natural and economic disasters, sickness and diseases—the list went on. Christianity in its North American form didn't seem to have enough clout to draw the attention of the masses.

Yet, Jesus, while on earth, drew great crowds. Michaela had said it when they first met: they needed revival. He remembered his reaction and felt ashamed.

The more he knew about her, the more it was confirmed in his heart that she would complement him greatly. He would stabilize her, and she would inspire him.

Paul sighed deeply. Pastor Laroche joined him.

"I'm sure any moment you will share the meaning of that sigh with me."

Paul fell into step with Pastor Laroche on the dirt road leading away from the heart of the village, with its tin-roofed shops, and wooden and cinderblock buildings—most in various stages of disrepair.

"So, why do you think we don't see the manifestation of the supernatural—more of God's power—in our North American Churches, as much? What are we missing?" As they walked along the road, Paul found they were constantly greeting and nodding at others passing by.

Pastor Laroche strolled along looking very pastorly in his white short-sleeved shirt and tie, and dark pants; much the same way Paul had chosen to dress. He glanced over at Paul and smiled before asking, "Are you asking my personal opinion?"

"Yes," Paul answered.

Pastor Laroche stopped and faced him. "I think we are distracted in Western societies. Distracted with all that man has to offer, whether it be work, play, treatments for a host of physical and mental illnesses, addictions, families... the list goes on. There is nothing wrong with most of those things, but God often gets left out of the picture."

"But, how do we put him back in the picture? How do we, as leaders in our Churches, repackage God for people?" As soon as he asked the question, Paul knew he had used the wrong term.

Pastor Laroche shook his head, looking slightly fierce, and continued walking. "Paul, God cannot be repackaged. He will come only as He is. Many of us only give Him bits of our time and attention, until we want something from Him—then we want it immediately. Many have no concept of waiting on—or tarrying in the presence of God Almighty—yet expect Him to shower down material, physical and even spiritual gifts as if He were an instant-God machine."

Paul noticed they were closer to the house where Michaela was visiting with one of the church families. He stopped, which caused Pastor Laroche to halt. Pastor Laroche must have read the desperation in his eyes because his eyes gentled and he reached up to lay a hand on Paul's shoulder.

"You want to know how revival will happen? God will bring it. It is not only in these countries with its crippling poverty, crime and sickness where people are desperate. As the Bible speaks of the end of time, it refers to men's hearts failing them from fear. Look at your country and tell me fear and hopelessness is not abounding more and more. The desperation is there and, increasingly, the distractions will no longer be enough. If the world is not already ripe for revival, it soon will be."

Pastor Laroche searched Paul's face for a moment. "You referred to the Church as *your* Church."

"Well," Paul began, "I didn't mean—"

"Yes, I realize what you think you meant, but be careful. If you want God in the Church, then give it to Him. Let Him work among the believers who with millions of other believers form the universal Church, or Bride of Christ. For you to lead in that way, Paul, you must commit to a life-long journey of waiting upon Him, so He will work in you and through you for all He purposes to do."

Paul swallowed as the words sank into his heart. Suddenly, he felt very thirsty, but he wasn't able to linger on thoughts of his physical need for long. Pastor Laroche started walking at a rapid pace.

"Come, something is wrong."

Paul hurried after him, heading towards the high pitch screams of a woman. Moments later, they came upon the property where Michaela was supposed to be waiting for them.

The screams they had heard were actually shrieks, followed by guttural moans, coming from a broad-backed woman firmly planted on the dirt pathway leading up to the front of a thatched house.

Paul could see Michaela and her hostess with three young children, standing outside the front of the house. About half-way between them and the woman was a familiar-looking young man. The woman appeared to be shrieking at the two women.

As if sensing their presence, the shrieking woman whipped around as quickly as her ample girth would allow. She glared at them, breathing heavily.

Paul was shocked at her appearance. She looked like a tropical bag woman dressed in yards of cloth draped around her large frame. A bolt of white cloth was wrapped around her head above piercing dark eyes, a wide nose and intensely pursed lips. She was ill-kept and dirty with smears of yellow over her brown skin.

The woman backed up a few steps, then started laughing crazily, showing off dark gaps between her teeth. Paul was surprised when she spoke in English with a thick French accent.

"The man of God, come to interfere again!" She spat the words out. Her eyes were freakishly wide and a foul stench emanated from her. "Let us about our business."

"Not when it concerns my daughter, Lola." Pastor Laroche said in a strong voice. He stepped forwards and the woman recoiled. "Maxime, you need to remove your grandmother from this property."

The young man, who had been eying Paul suspiciously, held his hands out beseechingly as he spoke rapidly in Creole. He was a very handsome young man of solid build, dark-brown skin and loose black curls.

"Yes, I believe you've been trying, but you must do it now."

A loud shriek preceded Lola's next words. "Why do you speak as if I'm not here?"

Paul felt restless enough to start moving around the periphery of the insane scene, towards Michaela.

The woman reared her head, directing her piercing look in his direction. "You leave her be! She belongs to my grandson!"

The evil radiating from her was enough to cause Paul to stop in his tracks. Maxime spoke to her in a pleading voice. She fired back a response at him in Creole.

"He is not a coward, Lola. Your grandson knows what you are suggesting is wrong," countered Pastor Laroche. "You mustn't continue to manipulate him. Let him find his own path. Your path leads to destruction because it is dark. Light will always overtake darkness."

Paul continued to his destination. Lola started shrieking again, her body trembling and writhing, but Paul had had enough. He ignored her.

"Let her be! Let her be, you man of God!"

"Maxime!" Pastor Laroche called loudly.

When Paul reached the front of the house, he noticed the women weren't as shaken as he thought they would be. The children, two boys and a girl, were wide-eyed, but had remained very still, clinging to their young mother's skirt.

"Michaela?" He touched her shoulder as if to reassure her, but probably more to reassure himself that she was okay.

The smile she offered didn't hide the distress in her eyes. "Welcome to Haiti," she said, her voice raised above the continued shrieking. "We're okay." She proceeded to introduce Paul to the woman and the children. She spoke in Creole to them, probably explaining who he was.

The woman gave a tentative, shy smile as she nodded in his direction.

Paul noticed the sudden silence. Maxime's grandmother had slumped over unto the ground.

Maxime was supporting her under the armpits. Pastor Laroche seemed to be quietly praying over her.

"The spirits have left her, for now," Michaela said softly.

Paul felt way out of his element. This was not the grassroots psychiatry he was familiar with.

He wasn't naive enough to believe people weren't possessed by devils today, just as they were in Christ's day—he just hadn't experienced it firsthand. Or, if he had, he hadn't recognized it.

Maxime called loudly to someone outside the gate. A small group of people had gathered there and one big, burly man ventured in cautiously.

Maxime turned to look in the direction of Paul and the women. He seemed to have a resigned air about him. With the help of the big man, he finally hauled his grandmother away from the property. Michaela's father followed them.

Paul looked at Michaela. She had picked up one of the boys and seemed to be watching the scene intently. He rubbed her back gently in soothing, vertical motions. "Are you okay?" he asked.

"Yes," she assured him, but her eyes held a sober look.

He moved his hand around to her opposite shoulder. He squeezed her in a sideways hug, and then bent his head and kissed her right temple, noticing that the left one had a slight bruising from the day before.

"I think I prefer you to be in Canada," he said. He noticed the curious look of the child she was holding, realizing his speech would sound foreign to him. He gave him a gentle kiss on his forehead too. The boy smiled before turning his head to look at his mother.

The mother spoke laughingly, reaching for the boy. She said something to Michaela before gathering the children into the house.

"What did she say?" Paul asked curiously, hands thrust into his pockets.

"I don't think I should say," Michaela said, shaking her head.

Paul gave her his best frown.

She sighed and rolled her eyes dramatically. "She feels we need some time alone."

Paul threw back his head in laughter. "Wow! Man! How much more dramatic can this day get?" He pulled a hand from his pocket to tip her chin up so he could look directly into her eyes. "Don't worry. I plan on us having lots of alone time in the near future."

Her eyes widened and she pulled her chin away. "Seriously, Paul Rayner, you have too much of a one-track mind."

He stepped directly in front of her, facing the house. "I know what I want."

She put her hands on her hips and glared up at him. "I don't care if you know what you want. It may not be what I want. Not every woman needs a man in her life."

Man, how he wanted to kiss her. It was driving him crazy. Instead, he said, "I agree with you one hundred percent. Fortunately for me, you're not one of them."

She flung her arms down and took a step back. "I can't believe you. You're impossible!"

Paul swung around at the sound of chuckling behind him. It was Pastor Laroche, looking more relaxed, if a little battle worn.

"Do I need to resolve another conflict, today?" he asked, eying them both questioningly.

* * *

It was late evening, with all the chores completed, before Paul found opportunity to meet alone with Michaela's father. He had just finished talking with his mother and Brennon by phone. Everything had seemed fine with his mother. It was with Brennon that he had sensed something unexpected.

He could have sworn Brennon had been holding something back from him, even though he had assured Paul things were okay at the Church.

Then again, Brennon was probably missing Sarah, or he'd had enough of living with the in-laws, as well as in a cast.

However, the task he had before him needed his full concentration. This was something he had done before, but the circumstances had been different, as were the reasons for his nervousness.

He gently knocked on Pastor Laroche's office door before entering. The older man was seated relaxed in one of two well-worn armchairs, reading a book by lamplight. He placed his reading glasses on his desk and gave Paul his full attention.

"Have a seat, Paul," Pastor Laroche said.

He crossed the room and slowly lowered himself in the comfortable folds of the other armchair. There was no doubt about it, he was nervous.

"Paul?"

He decided to plunge in. "Sir, I'm sure you've heard the story of the mix-up when Michaela first came to us, at Bethel Community Church."

Pastor Laroche nodded, smiling. "Yes. What an extraordinary beginning for all of you. I remember when Michaela relayed the story. My wife and I had a good laugh."

"Well, sir, it wasn't funny for me." He took a deep breath. "You see, sir, the day I met your daughter turned out to be about more than a gender mix up. It was also the day I started falling in love with her."

* * *

Later that night, Paul escaped to the main house veranda for some time of reflecting and prayer. His mind shifted between thoughts of his talk with Michaela's father about her and all that had transpired in the village. Pastor Laroche's testimony of God's power among the Haitian people; his opinions regarding much of the apathy in Western Churches; and the crazy episode with Maxime and Lola were more than just fodder to chew on.

When he heard the front door of the house open, he thought it was Michaela coming to join him on the veranda again. It was Leroy.

The youth stood uncertainly by the doorway, partially bathed in moonlight. His clothing had been more conservative on this trip: basic T-shirts and long sports shorts. Paul hazarded a guess that Carmel had been very involved with the packing of Leroy's clothes.

As for getting any information out of Leroy about his changed mind about college: That was negative. Paul had tried quite a few times, but Leroy hadn't budged in the consistency of the reason for his decision. He just needed time to think. It had taken Leroy a while to finally explain what he meant by "think" was actually "think and pray." After Paul had learned that, he had left him alone.

During the daily devotional times, Paul had been deeply touched by Leroy's thirst for the Word. It was like he had become a sponge, soaking up whatever came his way. Leroy had always asked Paul questions about a life committed to Jesus Christ; but with more of a challenging attitude. Now, he asked with a thirst for knowledge—living knowledge.

"Hey, Leroy," Paul called to him. "You coming to join me?"

Leroy shut the door and shuffled towards him. He plopped down into the other bamboo chair, leaned forwards with his elbows on his knees, with his head turned in Paul's direction. "I—umm—need you to pray with me about something."

Somehow, Paul sensed that this was very important. "Okay," he responded encouragingly.

Leroy seemed to study the wooden floor of the veranda. "It's been easier for me to think and pray—here, without my mom breathing down my back." He looked at Paul. "This has been real good for me—you know what I mean?"

Paul smiled. "You don't expect me to let you off that easily. Tell me what you mean."

Leroy groaned a sigh. He slouched backwards in the chair. "I don't know—somethin's happened to me here. I mean, it's been happening for a while, but I notice it here more. I realize that people don't need a lot of stuff to be happy. The biggest thing God wants from me is my life. I think God wants me to be a minister—like you."

Paul was stunned. "Are you sure, Leroy?" It had never occurred to him that this would have been Leroy's struggle.

The youth laughed nervously. "That's why I need you to pray with me, but, yeah—I'm pretty sure."

Fifteen minutes later, after counselling and praying with Leroy, Paul stood looking at the door Leroy had just closed after going back into the house. He was still mystified at the change in Leroy's plans, but he shouldn't have been so surprised. All the signs had been there.

He turned away from the door, shaking his head. "God, You do it so much better."

He had decided to stay out a little longer in the warm, night air before retiring, when he heard the door open again. He turned, thinking Leroy had forgotten to say something.

Michaela stepped out, and Paul took a moment to catch his breath. She was holding a lantern, looking almost ethereal in its glow.

Her black hair, which earlier had been in a single, thick braid, was fluffed out shoulder length from underneath a white headband. She wore the same flowing, white sundress she had changed into for Sunday dinner.

"Did Leroy tell you the good news?" he asked, thinking it was why she was there.

"Paul, how could you?" she asked in an accusing tone.

He looked at her, puzzled. Obviously, she wasn't referring to Leroy's decision. He faced her fully. "How could I what?"

Michaela shut the door. She flounced past him to the far end of the veranda. "How could you have spoken to my father about—about us?"

Of course. He had momentarily forgotten because of his time with Leroy. He slowly walked over to her, noticing how upset she looked. He hadn't guessed her father would have spoken to her already. "It was the right thing to do," he explained to her.

"Before you've spoken to me?" she asked, sounding incredulous.

"We'll be gone in a couple of days. I needed to ask him while I could do it face to face. I'm not ready to ask *you*, yet."

She lowered the lantern, looking as if she would like to toss it at him instead. "I—you—a phone call would have been fine."

"Maybe. But it was important to me to do it face to face."

She remained silent for a moment, but her eyes and her heaving chest spoke loudly to him. "And, if I say no?" she asked defiantly.

"I haven't asked you, yet," he returned just as defiantly, then added gently, "So, you can't say no... yet."

"Do you want to bet?"

"It wouldn't be a legitimate answer because the question hasn't been asked... and I wouldn't accept it."

"It has been asked!" she whispered forcefully.

"Not to you."

"Oh, for Pete's sake," she said, sounding exasperated. She went to walk around him. "I'm not talking to you about this anymore."

Paul smiled, thinking she sounded like a miffed child. He grabbed her by the elbow, as she passed by him, causing her to freeze in her tracks. "We will talk about it again, but not until I know you'll say yes," he told her.

Michaela kept her back to him, so he pulled on her arm until she was facing him. He breathed in her fragrance, willing himself to concentrate on the words he needed to speak. "For now, all I'm asking you to do is openly and honestly ask the Lord where He is in all of this. Please don't deny us that, Michaela."

She lowered the lantern once again, holding her face away from him. "But, I don't want to do this now."

"It's not now," he reminded her.

"Well, if I were you, I wouldn't ask me for a long time... at least a year. There are things I need to do first—you're ruining my life!"

Paul thought she was being overly dramatic. He could understand her need to forge her own way. He believed she had strong feelings for him, which was probably why she was fighting so hard, but this was ridiculous.

"Michaela," he called sternly, still holding her arm. "It's enough."

She kept her head turned away from him. He let her go, and she stepped back. He moved towards her, but she turned and quickly walked to the door. There, she paused and looked his way.

"It's not that I don't have... feelings for you. It's just that once I commit to something, I have to do it well," she explained in a small voice. "This is not what I had planned."

He remained silent, but she stayed at the door, waiting.

"Are you asking me to let you off the hook?" he asked. Did she even know how frustrating this was for him? He was having a relationship with her, without really having a relationship with her. He felt handicapped.

"Yes and no," she said.

"Explain," he prompted.

So, she did, in a whisper: "I don't want off the hook, but I wish I hadn't been caught." She opened the door and stepped into the house.

The slam of the door echoed the pounding of Paul's heart. He felt like he could run a marathon! The woman he loved had just as much as admitted that she was in love with him.

Chapter Twenty-Five

Canada

Samuel sighed heavily, trying to read the same line multiple times, by lamp light. He just couldn't concentrate.

"I didn't think you were reading," Hilda said from the rocker in Samuel's den. She had been keeping him company for the last hour, gently rocking in her chair and knitting.

Samuel rested the open pages on his lap and looked at her. She appeared calm and unconcerned wrapped in a light housecoat, but he knew that she was just as worried as he.

"Hilda, this could just all blow over easily if the truth comes out soon; but, if not, it could drag on for months, taking his name through mud and mire." He removed his reading glasses and placed them on the lamp table. "The fact that I already walked this road once with Stephen is not even my greatest concern. Now, his son has to walk the same path. It's grieving my soul."

Hilda pushed herself up from the rocker and lay the knitting on its seat. She shuffled, with slippered feet, over to Samuel and bent to rest her hands on his shoulders.

"Sam, the Lord knows the past, the present and the future, and He has made provisions for them all. We are praying and we are trusting, and we will walk it with Him—that's all we can do."

At that moment, a knock sounded at the partially closed door. Hilda straightened, and Samuel called, "Come in." The door was fully opened, and Lucy came into the room followed by Will.

"Did you take Blinder home?" Hilda asked.

"Yes, we just came back from dropping him off," Lucy answered, walking over to her father's armchair. "I think he misses Leroy. Are you okay, Dad?"

"I'm fine, Lucy." He looked up at Will who had remained by the doorway. "Will, what do you think about Blinder's eavesdropping information?"

Will took a few steps in, dwarfing the little room. "Well, I believe he heard what he said. If there's anything I know about Blinder, his hearing compensates him for a lot."

Samuel nodded in agreement. "Even though the police can't prove it, Blinder's accusations would explain why Falconer's thugs beat him up."

"I don't understand how Falconer thinks he could get away with building on unsound land and paying for the hush-hush," Lucy declared. "I mean, didn't he think he had enough legitimate land to build on? Plus, these things have a way of coming out. What's he going to do when those houses start to show structural damages?"

"Greed can dull people's thinking, Lucy," Samuel said. "And those structural damages might not happen for years, until after the land is settled and the warranty period has run out."

"Surprisingly, some of it is happening already," Will informed them. "That's why it wasn't hard for the city to put a freeze on the project, after they had the other inspectors in to take a look."

"Yes," Hilda said, returning to the rocker. "And Dennis Falconer is spitting mad. I wouldn't be surprised if he had revenge on his mind."

"Revenge?" Lucy asked. She looked at her husband. "Will, remember how Blinder was concerned about you being misled by Karlene?"

Will shifted uneasily. "You mean trying to get me involved in the psychic fair?"

"Yes, but the fair had been rejected by the community, so Falconer accommodated it through the Sales Centre, at nights."

"Yes, but Falconer wasn't the one I met there. I only went twice, and there was a different instructor both times."

"Except, Karlene wasn't involved with the psychic fair, she was meeting directly with Falconer," Samuel concluded.

"Falconer is a psychic guru?" Lucy asked, incredulously.

"I don't know what he is, but it's something dark. Before Paul left, he said Blinder had used the word *evil*," Samuel said. "By the way, Hilda, has anyone been able to contact Karlene?"

Hilda shook her head sorrowfully. "No, dear. She's kept herself in hiding; not answering her door or phone. Rashad did get a peep out of her two days ago. He knew she was home because he could see her car through her garage window. He left a message on her machine, saying he was going to call the police and report her missing if she didn't call him."

"And did she?" Lucy asked.

"Yes, she basically told him to leave her alone before hanging up on him."

They were all silent for a moment, before Will spoke.

"What I'm wondering is, how possible is it that Falconer set Karlene up to take Paul out, as revenge? Revenge for the failed attempt with his father and because he had spear-headed the clergy to push for an investigation."

"Good Lord!" Samuel exclaimed, as if a revelation had just dawned on him. "Will, you might have a point. Why didn't I see it before? Karlene would have been the perfect person for him to manipulate because of her obsession with Paul."

"You're right, Sam," Hilda said, sitting forwards in the rocker. "I wish we could talk to Karlene and convince her to come clean, before Paul gets home."

Samuel held one hand up. "That's not likely. Paul called earlier to say they were expected back at the Church around nine, which was half an hour ago, and then they would be transporting most of the kids home with the church van. Plus, Karlene is talking to no one."

"So, I'm not saying anything to Tristan, right?" Lucy asked, settling on the carpeted floor in front of Samuel's desk.

"No," Samuel instructed. "The board and I agreed to keep it as quiet as possible until we've talked with Paul. He'll be tired, so I'm allowing him tonight to recuperate before I meet with him."

He closed the book that had still been on his lap. "There is one thing that I'm still wrestling with at the back of my mind. I agree with Will. If Falconer is involved in Karlene's accusations against Paul, his motive is most likely revenge. However, Paul is not Stephen's biological son. The seed of revenge would most likely be directed at Stephen's blood offspring. I think it's not so much any child of Stephen's, whether natural or adopted. I think it's more directed against all Stephen represented: the *Church* and all *she* stands for."

Samuel set his book on the lamp table beside his glasses. He slowly pushed himself up from the armchair. He was feeling new aches tonight, but he also felt a new determination.

"Dennis Falconer could never accept that Eleanor had chosen Stephen over him. He thought that with his wealth and influence, he could easily win her heart. She was the much needed trophy to complete his sphere of affluence. Instead, she chose the Minister and the work of the Church."

Samuel slowly knelt down, resting his arms on the seat of the armchair. "Let's gather to prayer. Prayer for the work of the Enemy to be bound and to fail, prayer for wisdom and strength for Paul and all of us, and prayer for Dennis Falconer's mission to come to an end."

*   *   *

"You have got to hold it together!" Falconer insisted impatiently. "If you fall apart now, you will lose everything. You will look like a fool and have nothing to show for it."

"I've probably lost everything anyway," Karlene told him, trying to keep calm even though she felt anything but. She felt as if she were losing her mind, but she had enough of it left not to want to reveal her fragility to the two thugs hovering in the background. "His reputation might be ruined, but he'll never want me now. He'll only blame me. I was a fool to listen to you!"

Karlene had come to the Sales Centre, under the cover of darkness, to meet Falconer. She rarely left her house in the daytime now. The stress of living was too much, at present. She felt as if her soul were barren; as if the life was being sucked out of her.

She hadn't felt like this since she had been rescued from the world of dark arts, where she had been told she had the *gift* and to use it. A world where her handlers had raked in loads of money paid by the foolish, the curious, and the desperate who had come looking for answers from a girl who apparently had the gift.

She had been raised to believe she could predict people's futures by a gypsy-like couple who had moved from place to place exploiting their niece. As she had matured, entering the teen years, increased attention from her aunt's husband had come at a more costly price. Even her concerned teachers hadn't been able to pull it out of her. How could she have ratted on the only family she knew, after being abandoned by a desperate teenage mother who hadn't wanted her baby?—a product of rape.

It was to the Pastor and his wife at the Church Mission, inner-city Toronto, that she had finally bared her soul. At sixteen years old, she had been rescued body and soul, or so she had thought.

Why was she here, yet again, being manipulated when all she wanted was to be loved, to belong?

But, Paul had rejected her.

"I told you, we should have discredited the intern... said that she was coming on to him. What good is it to me if he hates me for ruining his life?" she railed at Falconer in the living-room "office" of the Sales Centre.

"He would deny it, you little fool." Falconer told her. He was standing in front of a gas fireplace. His fleshly face was rigid with anger held in check.

Karlene felt she had nothing left to lose. "They would have thought he was trying to be noble."

Falconer shook his head in disgust. "Listen to me. You are confused and tired. When he loses everything, then you step in and become his comfort—and only friend."

Karlene took a step back, nonplussed. "I would be the last person he would want for comfort. He'd most likely run to *her* arms." Suddenly she felt something give in her. "You've probably pushed them more together than anything else!" she screamed.

"Karlene!"

She barely heard him. She just knew she needed to leave. *Run, run!* The words reverberated in her head. So, she ran.

* * *

Paul checked the time on the church van's dashboard as he pulled up beside Carmel's Blinds and Home Decor: his last stop before taking Michaela home. Both the store and upstairs lights were on, and he figured Carmel was waiting up for Leroy. He wondered if she would be as surprised as he had been about Leroy's change of career path. He hoped she would be pleased, even as he had no doubt she would be supportive. Carmel, above all, just wanted her boy to make it in the world.

He looked over to the passenger seat at Michaela, as he parked along the curb. She was looking out the side window.

Instead of the tiredness he would have normally felt after a trip like this, he felt invigorated. Her presence beside him was the sole contributor.

Leroy was already out of the vehicle, hauling his bags out. Paul exited the van and went around, joining Leroy on the sidewalk.

"It was a great trip, Michaela. Thanks a lot for giving me the opportunity," Leroy said, standing by her window.

Michaela smiled. A lovely tiredness etched her face. "You're very welcome, Leroy. I've just been so blessed by all of you on this trip. I'm especially pleased that you've decided to join our ranks, so to speak."

Leroy laughed softly. "Yeah, who woulda thought?"

"*He* would have thought, Leroy," Michaela said meaningfully.

Leroy seemed suddenly shy. "Yeah, I guess He would have."

"Here, let me give you a hand, Leroy," Paul said.

"Naw—I got it, Pastor Paul," he said. He hauled one bag over his shoulder and reached down to grab the smaller one. Before going, he eyed them both and grinned. "Well good night and... try getting her home at a decent hour, Pastor Paul." With that he staggered through the alley, heading for the back of the store.

* * *

Michaela felt her skin heat up at the implications behind Leroy's words. She watched Paul shake his head, as Leroy disappeared behind the building.

Paul turned slowly, casually, and placed his hands along her opened window. He leaned towards her.

"Are you ready to go home?" he asked. His lips held a gentle smile, causing his dimples to appear. But his eyes were solemn.

"Yes, please," she answered carefully. Since they had landed at Toronto Pearson Airport, she felt a certain restlessness; maybe nervousness. If she had to specifically define it, she would say it was a blind anticipation of the unknown, and the rejection of it and the desire for it all rolled up in one conflicting bundle.

Paul studied her for a brief moment. He pushed away from the window and walked around to the driver's side. He climbed in without a word, then started driving.

A cool breeze flowed into the van as they drove; much cooler than the breezy heat they had left behind in Haiti. Fall colours were already appearing on some of the trees, especially the maple trees.

The goodbyes to her family and friends had been emotional, yet joyful. Having everyone from the mission team returning with her had made the difference. She hadn't experienced the aloneness she often felt when returning to Canada.

For the next two days after Paul's talk with her father, she had stayed clear of Paul as much as possible. She had felt a distinct need to send him a clear message of her displeasure. Her mother, who, of course, knew everything, had tried to counsel her and that hadn't helped. It had just made her angrier that she had joined Paul and her father in ganging up on her.

Now, here she sat beside him... alone. She was no longer angry or frustrated. It was if she were outside of herself looking in, knowing there was no use fighting the inevitable; maybe just controlling it.

When Paul reached over, unexpectedly, to take her hand, she felt as if her heart would stop. He snaked his fingers between hers and curled them under.

Michaela looked down at their hands on her lap, feeling completely out of her element and totally unprepared for such intimacy.

"I promise I won't bite," Paul said, looking straight ahead, smiling. With no answer forthcoming, he glanced at her searchingly before paying attention to his driving. He squeezed her hand gently.

"I agree with Leroy. I thoroughly enjoyed the trip and I also found it very enriching. Your father—well, he is truly a man of God. He reminds me of my father. Even though they took different paths in the ministry, they shared the same passion. I hope to see him again."

"I appreciate that," Michaela managed. "I could tell he enjoyed having you—all of you."

They quietly talked about the trip for a while, until Michaela noticed something amiss.

"Paul, you missed the turn... ."

He kept driving with no reaction.

"Paul?"

"I know," he said, but made no move to correct the error. "I'm not taking you home, yet."

Michaela tried to suppress a slight feeling of panic. "But you said you were taking me home."

"I asked you if you were ready to go home, not that I would take you home. I will take you home... eventually."

The next thing she knew, he was driving up to a fast-food, drive-through place.

"I'm having coffee. What would you like?" he asked her, as if all were totally normal.

When a voice through the order speaker asked for their order, Paul pressed her. "Michaela?"

She sighed. "Coffee too, thanks."

His hand left hers as he fished for his wallet, and she realized she missed the pressure of it. She must be crazy. Here she was getting a little perturbed with him, yet wanted him to hold her hand. She also wanted to go to the Temples' and shower and have a goodnight's sleep before having to deal with any of this. He could have, at least, given her a goodnight's sleep. Yet, here they were as if the world would end tomorrow.

No wonder he had insisted Sarah take Tristan home. And Sarah, like a traitor, had immediately agreed.

Paul didn't take her hand again after he began driving. Soon, he turned down a quiet street, and she realized where he was taking her.

The van lights shone on rippling water as they drove into the community park towards a footbridge. He parked on the lawn by the bridge before turning the vehicle and lights off.

Michaela looked at Paul as he sat still, staring out the windshield. Suddenly, he picked up his coffee and took a sip. With coffee in hand, he opened his door and stepped out.

He pulled her door opened. "Will you go for a walk with me?" he asked quietly.

The lights from the surrounding homes and the buildings on the back side of the park were enough for Michaela to see sufficiently. His gaze bore into her and she found she couldn't resist.

"Please," he added gently. He held one hand out, palm up.

She tentatively placed her hand in his. "Okay, but just for a little while."

He grinned as she stepped down from the vehicle. "Don't forget your coffee," he reminded her.

They strolled across the bridge hand in hand. The quiet murmur of the water below and the sweet smell of nature were magical. Off the bridge, the grass was cushiony under their feet, and high above, the stars were bright in the sky.

Michaela felt herself relaxing with their fingers entwined, talking and sipping their coffee. They talked more about Haiti, coming home, the youth, and they talked about nothing. They just talked until their coffees were finished and the cups tossed into the park trash.

When they came to two big boulders by a small willow tree, Michaela tugged her hand away from Paul. She put a sneakered foot in the wedge between the two boulders and found leverage to shove herself up. She climbed up the larger rock and sat down with her jean-clad legs hanging down its front.

"One of my favourite games, growing up, was 'King of the Castle,'" she told Paul, as he moved towards her.

"Are you king, now?" he asked, placing both hands flat on the rock either side of her legs.

She looked down at him, having a slight height advantage. "No, I think I'm queen."

He chuckled, leaning slightly against her knees. "So, maybe, I could be king?"

Michaela smiled, thinking he looked every inch an aristocrat, even in jeans and a rumpled shirt. "Maybe," she answered.

"But every king needs a queen," he challenged her.

Michaela remained silent, almost holding her breath, wondering how their banter had managed to come full circle.

"This king needs a queen. Wants a queen," he continued.

Michaela closed her eyes as she felt the warmth of his hands on hers. "Please, don't ask me that, now."

"Ask you what?" Paul asked. He tugged at her hand until her eyes opened.

"What you asked my father."

"To marry you?"

"Yes."

He sighed. "I'm not asking you that, yet."

She shook her head adamantly, trying to resist him. "You are so, you liar. You're sneaking it in."

He released her hands, only to take hold of her arms. "I was only suggesting it, not asking." He half-lifted, half-slid her down from the boulder until her feet touched the ground. "I promised I would ask when I was sure of your answer."

Paul's hands cupped her cheeks and he tipped her head back. He searched her eyes; the windows to her soul. "It wouldn't be fair to ask you now," he whispered, his voice deep and incredibly soothing. "You're tired and jet-lagged."

He moved his hands to touch her head and smooth her hair. "But, I want to give you something to remember for when you're rested and recuperated." He gently touched his lips to her forehead, then each eye, then her lips.

His lips remained on hers for a moment, then his kiss deepened, and Michaela felt her world spinning out of control. Somehow, she had known it would be like this, but she couldn't have imagined it. It was what she had been afraid of; it was what she welcomed. It left her trembling in his arms.

Afterwards, Paul held her close, cradling her head against his shoulder, with the boulder supporting them from behind. Michaela breathed in the clean smell of him, loving the feel of his hand stroking her back, her arm; of being secure in his embrace.

"I love you," he murmured into her hair.

"I love you, too," she responded in a whisper, knowing she couldn't take the words back; knowing she had just committed to him by speaking them.

He pulled away from her slightly and looked into her eyes. "I've wanted to say it for a long time."

"I know," she acknowledged, feeling vulnerable for what he might ask next.

As if sensing her anxiety, he tapped the end of her nose gently and said, "That's all I need from you right now—just knowing you love me."

Chapter Twenty-Six

Hilda tried to concentrate on her desk work in the Front Office, but she was spending more time praying under her breath, fielding phone calls and taking occasional peeks through the Pastor's Office door.

Samuel and Paul had been closeted in there for about half an hour. Samuel had hoped to get Paul at the parsonage, but Paul had come into the Office earlier than they had expected, even for Paul. It pained her to know how difficult this was for Samuel, and for what Paul would have to endure.

Earlier that morning, when she and Samuel had arrived at the Church, Paul had seemed fresh and excited; eager, it had seemed, to see them. Now, Samuel's news would have killed all that. Yes, it pained her heart greatly.

A sudden movement from behind, startled her. She quickly swivelled her chair to see Paul emerging from his office. The mark of Karlene's accusations was already evident in the set of his head and shoulders, as if they bore an unbearable weight; a weight that was every pastor's worse nightmare. She stood up slowly as Samuel followed behind him.

"Oh, Paul," Hilda said, holding out her arms to him. "You must know we completely believe in your innocence."

Paul folded her in a gentle embrace. "Hilda, I know and I thank you." He let her go and turned to face them both. "But, just for the record, I've never touched Karlene." He held a hand up when Hilda started to protest. "I've already asked Sam this: Please, don't let my mother know anything; it would be too much for her. I'll let Christy know, if I have to. Sam and I are going to try and see Karlene, later."

"Is that wise?" Hilda asked.

Paul glanced at Samuel, and Samuel answered her question. "Paul would like to try and see her—reason with her—before the meeting with the District Superintendent, who will most likely advise him to avoid all contact with her."

"I would like to come," Hilda insisted. "It would be better to have another woman present."

"You're right, Hilda. But that's if she's willing to see us," Samuel said. "She may not want to see all three of us, but you definitely shouldn't go alone, Paul."

"No, but I do believe she'll want to see me regardless of who is with me. This whole thing has been about getting my attention—she'll definitely see me." Paul stepped closer to Hilda and placed his hands on her shoulders. "Hilda, something's happened between Michaela and me—Sam will fill you in. Will you do something for me?"

"Anything, love," Hilda assured him. She hated the look of the wounded already surfacing in his eyes, as if he had already calculated the price tag on his world being turned upside down.

"Please explain everything to Michaela. I want her to have time to process it all before I see her. Can you do that?"

She nodded, feeling her eyes tear up and her lips tremble. "Y-yes, I will."

Paul hugged her again. "Come on, Hilda—I need a stiff upper lip from you."

She nodded again, sniffling, but clamping down on her emotions. "Okay, love, stiff is what you'll get." She reached for Samuel's hand and his familiar strength. "That and lots of prayer."

Paul turned towards the door. "I'll need that for sure. I'll be at the parsonage for a bit, then I'll go see Brennon. Call my cell, if you need me, and please don't forget to see Michaela."

After Paul left, Hilda collapsed on her office chair. She looked up at Samuel. "Oh, Sam... "

"I know, dear." He patted her shoulder gently. "It's started, and we'll finish with him together."

Something suddenly dawned on Hilda. "Sam, what did he mean about Michaela?"

Sam laughed softly, rubbing his hands over his generous abdomen. "Well, my dear, there is one bright cloud among the stormy ones. Paul and Michaela have declared their love for each other."

* * *

"We've tried and tried—especially Rashad—to talk with her, Paul. She's consistently refused to see or talk with any of us."

"I know," Paul told Brennon. He could tell Brennon was having just as much difficulty as he did processing everything—asking the questions—wondering why.

"I mean, being a minister too, this hits close to home. Whatever it takes, Paul, I'm there with you."

"I know. Thanks, Bren." Paul stood up from the Hursts' living room couch, feeling restless. He hated what this was doing to everybody. What had Karlene been thinking? What had possessed her? They had reached out to her in every possible way and now, this.

"Here we go," Sarah said as she walked into the living room carrying a tray laden with three mugs. Conner toddled, then crawled in after her. To everyone's surprise, Conner had started walking while Sarah was away on the Haiti trip.

Paul stooped down close to Conner's level. "Hey, Conner-man. To think how much your poor mama must have been shocked to come back and see you walking."

Conner chortled as his chubby hands used Paul's knees as support. He looked up at Paul's face and grinned.

"You know what? I think he knows me," Paul said, surprised at the look of recognition in Conner's eyes. Conner had never really had good eye contact with anyone, even though he was almost three.

"Isn't it amazing?" Sarah asked. "To think, my parents and husband got to experience it all before me." She scooped Conner up with one hand and handed Paul a cup of coffee with the other. "But, I don't begrudge them that. I'm just happy for Conner."

"And he's happy to see you," Brennon told her from the loveseat. His casted leg was extended out to rest on the floor. "I swear, he crawled every corner of this place, looking for you. I think that's why he started walking. He needed to look in higher places."

They all laughed, then—except for Conner's murmurings—quietness filled the room. Paul sat back on the couch and sipped the coffee Sarah had given him.

"Paul, I'm so sorry," Sarah said softly. She sat on the couch beside him, after leaving Conner on the floor. "Is there anything we can do?"

Paul looked at his two friends, appreciating them more than ever. "Thanks, Sarah, for asking." He sighed deeply. "Your belief in me is strength for me. I just want your prayers. I'm hoping that Karlene will come clean without this thing dragging on."

"Have you tried contacting her, yet?" Sarah asked.

"Yeah. I was telling Brennon I left a message on her machine that I was coming by this afternoon. She doesn't know I'll be with Samuel and Hilda, so I'm hoping she'll see me."

"So what happens if she doesn't retract her story?"

"An investigation will be launched." Brennon answered.

Paul was quiet for a moment, then he said, "Even if she retracts her story, there will probably still be an investigation."

"Because of what she's accusing you of?"

"Right."

Sarah looked down, fiddling with the cup in her hands. She directed her next question at both men. "Will there be... charges?"

Paul laughed humourlessly. "Funny enough, she doesn't want to press charges."

Brennon snorted uncharitably.

"Sam was told at the meeting with David Black, the District Superintendent, that she was adamant about it." Paul continued.

"But why? It's a serious offence," Sarah insisted, playing devil's advocate.

"Sarah, honey, it's because he didn't do it. She knows he's innocent. She doesn't want the police involved," Brennon explained.

"Okay, okay," Sarah said, backing down. "Maybe, I could try talking with her."

Paul reached across the couch and patted her hand. "Thanks, Sarah," he said gently. "If it doesn't work out with me, I'll let you have a crack at her."

At that moment, Paul's cell alerted him. He reached into his pocket for it. "It's a text from Michaela. I need to go see her," he said, answering the text.

"Whatever happened last night after you and Michaela dropped everybody off?" Sarah asked curiously.

For the moment, all thoughts of Karlene and investigations were pushed aside. "It's none of your business, Sarah," Paul teased, stringing her along.

"W-what?" Sarah spluttered. She leaned towards him. "Paul Rayner, you better tell me, especially after being your cohort the whole trip."

"Hey, what are you guys talking about?"

They both ignored Brennon, as Paul left the couch, grinning. "I'm just teasing, Sarah. Let's just put it this way, Michaela and I have reached some kind of understanding. Now, I have to go. I'll talk to you guys about it, later."

After leaving Brennon and Sarah's, the drive to the Temples' allowed Paul time to regroup for this next meeting. Knowing Michaela, he believed she would have confidence in his claim of innocence, but he was not one hundred percent sure. After all, the others had known him for years. Michaela had known him for almost six months and their new relationship had officially begun last night.

It was no wonder he had felt such an urgency to initiate the romantic part of their relationship when he had. He couldn't have known what he would be facing today, but the Father had known.

Paul's fingers tightened on the steering wheel, feeling frustrated. His anger had abated while he was at the parsonage, after meeting with Samuel. There, he had spent time in prayer, realizing his dependency was on God for the outcome. He had chosen to believe that the Lord would work it out for good; His Word promised. It was for the in-between time that he would need wisdom and strength.

He drove into the Temples' driveway. He looked out at the house, suddenly feeling unprepared. He knew Hilda had already spoken to Michaela because Michaela's text had indicated that. He just wasn't sure what her reaction would be when he saw her.

Don't be a coward, he told himself as he braved his way out of the car. Maybe he should have gotten her something: a gift or flowers. It was too late, now. There was Hilda holding the front door opened.

"Are you okay, love?" Hilda asked, as Paul entered the house.

"I'm doing all right, Hilda," Paul told her as he returned her hug. Down the hall, Michaela appeared from out of the kitchen. Their gazes locked.

Hilda turned around and beckoned to Michaela. "Come, Michaela," she called. She whispered to Paul, "Just use Sam's den. Take all the time you need." She left them in the hall.

For a moment, they stood silently staring at each other. Paul tried to read her expression which wasn't hard because her big, dark brown eyes tended to give her away. He saw questions there, but he also saw enough to know she was not an accuser.

He reached out to take her hand. "Can we talk?" he asked quietly.

She nodded, folding her fingers around his. She followed him up the stairs.

In Samuel's office, Paul closed the door behind him. The afternoon sunlight brightened the room beautifully, but he wasn't interested in the room. He faced Michaela.

They searched each other's eyes again. She slowly moved towards him and into his embrace. Paul held her tightly, soaking in her warmth, drawing from her being. It was what he desperately needed for the moment.

After a long while, Michaela stepped back, still in the circle of Paul's arms. "Let me hear you say it," she whispered.

"Michaela, I never touched her. I never even—"

She pressed her fingers to his lips. "Shh, I know, I believe you."

Those simple words from her, more than from anyone else, were his undoing. The built up tension and pressure found a place of release through the tears and quiet sobs that escaped from him.

Eventually, Paul grabbed hold of his emotions, but when Michaela's arms snaked up around his neck, another kind of emotion took over. His lips moved from their buried place in the curve of her neck and shoulder, to find hers. He kissed her fiercely and passionately, and with intense longing.

It was Michaela who pushed them apart. When his lips reached for hers again, she kept her hands flat against his chest.

"No, Paul," she commanded gently.

"I love you," Paul whispered against her lips, still managing to steal a kiss.

"I know," she said, giggling, as he tried to kiss her again. She pushed herself away, putting some distance between them.

Paul let her go. She went and curled up in Samuel's armchair, leaving him to sit on the rocker.

"I wanted to talk about Hannah, but I think we should talk about Karlene, instead," she said quietly.

Paul rocked back in his chair and ran his hand down over his jaw line. He sighed. "We can talk about both, if you like."

"Okay," she agreed, putting him on the spot.

"One I could have hated, if not for the love of Christ, and the other I loved." He leaned forwards. "Michaela, you don't have to worry about living with a ghost. I loved Hannah very much. She will always have a special place in my memory. Part of who I am today is because of her. She was my first love. But, you... you fill my world now... my thoughts... "

Paul paused, searching for the right words to express what he didn't know how to say. He tried again: "Every part of me is aware of you, wants you—and if I could be sure of your answer, I could ultimately declare myself to you."

* * *

Michaela found herself smiling at Paul's obvious attempt to bring up marriage. Though, if he asked her right now, she couldn't have resisted. His pain was so much her pain; she couldn't have held back his joy. She knew she loved him and wanted to be with him, but she wasn't ready to face the finality of it, yet. Also, she needed to be in Georgeton by the end of the week to start assisting in the Youth department at Hope Alive Church.

"Nice try," she said, bringing humour to the situation.

He laughed and held his hands out. "I'm not trying. Just preparing you for what's to come."

She resisted his charm and asked the next question. "And, Karlene?"

This sobered him. He leaned back in his chair, once more. "Karlene, as you have witnessed already, has had an obsession with me from before you came. It just became more obvious once you arrived, because she saw you as a threat to her chance with me."

"I wouldn't have thought, though, that she would do something as drastic as... as this."

"No, you're right. Sam thinks Dennis Falconer could be behind it. He thinks Karlene was easy prey for Falconer because of her vulnerability. If I tell you something about Karlene and Falconer, you'll be able to see where we're coming from."

"Shoot," Michaela said.

Paul leaned forwards with his hands resting on his knees. "Karlene comes from an extremely abusive background where she was the victim; not only that, she was also the centre piece in a fraudulent occult ring."

Michaela listened as Paul relayed Karlene's history, and what she learned brought tears to her eyes.

"No wonder she picked you to pine after," she told Paul.

Paul looked grim, as if not appreciating her words. "And why is that?" he asked.

"She was rescued by a pastor and his wife. To her, they represented her salvation. She may have transferred those feelings to you, Paul."

The confused look he gave her was endearing. It was just like a man not to see the obvious when it came to his own life. "When did you become Karlene's pastor?"

"I've been her pastor for almost three years, not long after Hannah died."

"Who was her pastor before that?"

He frowned in concentration. "I think the Pastor who rescued her." Suddenly, understanding dawned in his eyes. "Sam told me that Pastor died shortly after Karlene came to Bethel Community, and she had come while an elderly, interim pastor was here."

"Then you came... "

Paul leaned back. "I see your point," he admitted, smiling. "You're pretty smart." He squinted as if observing her under a microscope. "In fact, you're just pretty all round. No—scrap that—you're just plain beautiful."

"Paul," she protested, laughing. "Tell me about Falconer."

He groaned. "Falconer is a thorn in the flesh—that's what he is. To make a long story short, Falconer lost my mother to my father. He was attending the Church my father was pastoring, at the time."

"No way! Falconer—a church-going man?"

"It just goes to show, you never know who's under the roof and not necessarily part of the body," Paul said, standing up. He began pacing as he spoke. "He stayed in the Church, even after my parents were married, but was planning his revenge all along. Everyone thought he had moved on, when he started dating other women. About a year later, he left the Church and the community without a word to anyone."

"I was about ten and Christy and Cassie were fifteen, when we moved to Milward. My father had been the Pastor at Bethel Community for about two years when Falconer moved into the community and started attending our Church." He went back to the rocker and sat down.

"My parents graciously welcomed him into the Church body, even though it must have been really hard for them. My mother was especially kind to him because she was sorry for him—I think."

"Falconer basically repaid my parents' kindness by spreading a rumour that almost destroyed my father's ministry. He claimed that he and my mother were having a secret affair, and that she really wanted to leave my father."

Michaela uncurled her legs, letting her feet touched the floor. "Oh, my goodness, Paul, that's awful."

"If it wasn't for my mother's savvy, I don't know what would have happened. She actually secretly taped them having a conversation where he threatened to destroy my father's ministry if she didn't divorce him."

"After all that time, he still wanted her for himself?" Michaela shuddered at the thought.

The rocker creaked as Paul came over to stoop in front of her. He took her hands in his. "Samuel thinks Falconer wasn't so much after my father, or me—if what we suspect in my case is true. He feels Falconer is basically thumbing his nose at the Church, the representative of Christ on earth, and ultimately at God."

After Paul was finished, Michaela put words to her thoughts: "And in a different perspective, Karlene sees the Minister or Pastor—you, in this case—as her salvation, instead of seeing Christ in that role." She leaned forwards and touched his forehead with her own. "What are we going do?"

* * *

The brightness of the gathering was fierce: a brightness no human eye could have endured. They were many, but seemed to be one force. And hardly distinguishable, in the consuming glow, were sword-like shapes held high.

The Messenger hovered close by.

"Prepare! The battle has begun for the wandering one to be reclaimed, and the ones being tested to overcome!"

"None will be lost, except the ones who persists on striving against the Risen One. Their time has run out!"

Chapter Twenty-Seven

"Well, if she won't talk to him, what's to be done, Sam?" Hilda asked for, it seemed, the third time that evening.

"Hilda, I don't know," Samuel said as he carefully stacked the dishes in the dishwasher. "You were there, yesterday, to see that her car was gone. She's disappeared."

Hilda wiped at the kitchen table vigorously as if transferring her upset feelings onto it. "Well, at least, it buys us some time, since it'll be harder for them to continue an investigation without her."

"Yes, but Paul had to admit that he had tried to contact her. David Black said it wasn't in his best interest to have gone to see her, because it makes it look like she ran because of him."

Hilda banged the cloth down on the table. "Oh, good grief!" she exclaimed. "Why does this have to happen, after all he's been through, losing his wife and child? Look at what he went through when his parents had the same hell poured out on them. I don't understand!"

Samuel went over to his wife and hugged her from behind. “Dear, it’ll be okay. Don’t stress yourself out so.”

“What’s wrong with Grandma?”

Samuel looked over Hilda’s head to see Tristan enter the kitchen. She pulled a pair of earbuds from her ears, letting them hang from white cords connected to a flat gadget in her hand.

Hilda sniffled softly. “Oh, honey, Grandma is doing fine. I’m just feeling a little under the weather, that’s all.”

“Oh,” Tristan said, looking uncertain. “I just came to show Grandpa my new iPod touch.”

“Is that what you call it?” Samuel said. He patted Hilda’s shoulder gently. He went over to his granddaughter. “Here, pet, let me have a look. Now tell me, what’s different about this one?” He peeked back at Hilda, satisfied that she had pulled herself together. Tristan was a curious one. No sense getting her radar going.

“Well, Grandpa, it’s an early birthday gift from Michaela since she’s leaving tomorrow. She got it on sale at a great price, but the coolest thing is it has video.”

“Really?” he asked, trying to show interest.

“Yes. Here, let me show you,” Tristan said as she held the iPod out to him. “It actually records picture and sound.”

* * *

Paul turned the pages of his Bible, looking for passages of Scripture he could glean some hope from. He had also spent the better part of the day in prayer and fasting.

Earlier, he had read about an evil king and a good king. The evil king had built pagan altars in God’s house and the good king had torn them down. Manasseh and Josiah had both become kings at early ages: twelve and eight. What determined why one was evil and the other good?

God had caused foreign armies to distress the people when they were in rebellion against Him under the wicked king, but blessed the people when they were in obedience under the upright king. Yet, it wasn't always that black and white. Job had been a righteous man when God allowed Satan to take all he had, but his life. Yet, through it all, Job was discovered to have a pride issue, and then God restored all he had lost, doubled. It seemed that the bottom line was: God could see things in people they couldn't see in themselves; His ways and understanding were so much greater.

So, exactly what was God refining in his life, and how long would it take?

He realized his meeting with District Superintendent David Black had gone better than it should have because of Samuel. Samuel had made sure to voice his concerns regarding Falconer's possible involvement. The position of District Superintendent had been held by a different man at the time when Falconer had brought havoc to Paul's parents' lives; but David Black had been a minister in the district and remembered it well. If it weren't for that, he might have been facing disciplinary measures for trying to contact Karlene. As it was, certain restrictions had already been placed on him.

As he sat sprawled on the wooden floor of his parsonage office, Reverend Michael Laroche's words came to mind: "Many have no concept of waiting on—or tarrying in the presence of God Almighty—yet, expect Him to shower down material, physical and even spiritual gifts as if He were an instant-God machine."

He let his head fall back against the wall behind him. Pastor Laroche had spoken truths to him in a place where the distractions had been limited. Here, the distractions were limited when tragedy fell. In crisis, people met God face-to-face for good or ill.

"Where will you allow this to take me, Lord?" he asked out loudly. "Did You give me the path of ministry, only to take it back?"

His head bowed, it seemed, of its own accord. "God, what do You want from me?" His shoulders, back and backside ached from his hours of vigil on the floor. Somehow, he sensed it was where he needed to be. He would make the time each day, for as long as he could, to wait upon Him.

Paul realized he must have dozed off when the chime of the doorbell woke him. He glanced at his watch.

"After eight," he mumbled, getting up from the floor. His Bible fell with a thud, scattering some loose notes on the floor. He hurriedly gathered the papers and his Bible and set them on his desk, before staggering to the door. When brief light-headedness washed over him, he realized he hadn't eaten all day.

He clicked on the hall light and straightened his clothes before opening the door.

"Hey, guys," he greeted Will and Rashad, as they shuffled around the door. "What are you doing here?"

"If you must know," Will began saying, "Lucy and Hilda insisted I come over and make sure you were okay. Hilda sent this over and said you should break your fast." He held up a small casserole dish.

Paul sighed, taking the dish reluctantly. He looked at Rashad.

Rashad cleared his throat. "We met with Brennon before coming here. We all agreed that Will and I should search for Karlene."

"You guys are kidding."

"No, we're not. It was Rashad and Sarah's idea," Will said. "We hate to see what's happening to you. It's just not right."

"And, I think I know where she might be," Rashad said.

Paul didn't get a chance to address the matter any further, the doorbell rang again. Rashad glanced at him, then reached back to open the door.

Leroy pushed his way in, followed by Michaela.

"Hey, how are you two doing?" Paul asked. He was beginning to feel like the pastor brigade was on duty.

"Leroy said he's been trying to get you all day," Michaela explained. "Hi, Rashad—Will," she added.

They responded to her greeting, and then Will looked at Paul, meaningfully. "We'll catch up with you later, Rev.," he said, as he and Rashad moved to go back out the door.

"You too, Michaela—Leroy," Rashad added, closing the door after them.

"What's up, Pastor Paul. Are you sick or something?"

Paul looked at Michaela. She responded by taking the casserole dish and heading towards the kitchen.

"Come on in, Leroy," Paul invited, leading Leroy to the living room. He was feeling very tired.

"You're not sick, are you?" Leroy persisted in asking. "I wanted to tell you how excited my mom is about me going to Bible college... ."

Half an hour later, Paul sat at the kitchen table with Michaela, while Leroy watched television in the living room. Michaela was watching him eat.

"You look so tired," she said, her eyes filled with compassion.

He didn't want her feeling sorry for him or worrying about him. She had to start a new position tomorrow which was enough for her right now. He took one last bite, not really tasting the food, before pushing the dish away.

"You're not finished," she told him.

"Can't eat anymore," he said, wiping his mouth with a paper napkin. "But, thank you for being here with me." They held hands on top of the table.

"Well, I'm leaving early, tomorrow."

"I want to see you off."

"No," she said quickly. "That's why I'm here tonight, but... "

"But," he prompted.

"I wish I weren't leaving you in all this mess. I—"

"Michaela, even though I want you with me, I have lots of support here," he interrupted, stroking her cheek with his fingers. "Just keep praying." Extra moisture seeped into her eyes.

Paul got up and pulled her into his arms, and somehow, he found the strength to pray, yet again.

* * *

Earlier Saturday morning, despite Michaela's words, Paul had gone to the Temples' to see her off. Now, driving back to the parsonage, Paul ached, knowing Michaela was gone. Maybe, he should have stayed for the breakfast Hilda had offered, but he had already committed to fasting and praying again.

It had been more difficult to say good-bye than he realized it would be. Aside from being crazy in-love with her, he had grown very attached to her. She was an easy person to like.

He got out of his car and walked up to the parsonage front porch. He decided to get the mail he had forgotten to pick up the day before.

He shut the mailbox and began thumbing through some envelopes. He stopped when he heard a vehicle pull into the driveway.

Ethel opened the door of her large Buick and came out, leaving George sitting in the driver's seat. Paul went halfway down to meet her.

When they met, Ethel placed a thin hand on his arm and the look in her eyes left his greeting stuck in his throat.

"Pastor Paul," she began with a tremor in her voice, "somehow, it's gotten out. We're just on our way to an appointment, but I had to stop by and let you know that I've been getting phone calls all morning from the church people. I-I don't know how it got out."

Paul felt sick in the pit of his stomach. He had hoped to avoid this. He had hoped to get a confession from Karlene before it came to this.

He patted Ethel's hand gently. "It was bound to happen, Ethel. What are people asking?"

"Well, they don't seem to know the particulars, but they know something has happened and want to know what."

After Ethel and George's departure, Paul let himself back into the parsonage. He left the unsorted mail on the hall table and went to the kitchen for a drink of water. Afterwards, he closeted himself in his office.

Almost an hour later, the phone rang, interrupting his prayers. He let it ring, but jumped up from the floor when he heard Christy's voice leaving a message. He picked up his desk phone.

"Paul, I'm glad you answered," Christy started right away. "Sarah told me what's going on. I can't believe you didn't call me. I'm very upset with you."

He sat on his office chair, not feeling up to a verbal thrashing from her. "Sorry, Christy, I had planned on calling."

"Paul, if this is Dennis Falconer up to his old tricks, I'm coming down there. For heaven's sakes, once was enough!"

"That's what Samuel thinks. We won't know for sure until we talk with Karlene. As much I appreciate you wanting to help, I don't want you coming down here causing a ruckus."

"Paul," she protested in a wounded voice.

"I didn't mean it like that, Christy, but I have lots of support here. If you get involved, Mom will want to know what's going on. You haven't told her, have you?"

"What do you take me for?"

"Sorry, I had to ask," he apologized in a gentler tone. "Will you just pray?"

"Wait a minute, Paul," Christy said. There was silence for a moment before she spoke again. "Mom's here, she says she needs to talk to you."

Paul felt his anxiety level go up. He hoped his mother hadn't heard Christy's exchange with him.

"Paul?" Eleanor's voice sounded strong.

"Hi, Mom, how are you?"

Soon after, Paul was relieved as his mother and he chatted easily, getting caught up. Obviously she was not aware of the recent events of his life.

"Before I hang up, Paul, there's a Scripture I want to leave with you. For some reason, it has plagued me all day, and I believe the Lord has put it on my heart for you."

As she shared the Bible verse, Paul felt an inexplicable peace spreading over him, saturating him.

"Again, Mom," he said; much like when she had finished reading his favourite stories when he was a small child.

Eleanor repeated the verse: " ' But may the God of all grace, who called us to His eternal glory by Christ Jesus, after you have suffered a while, perfect, establish, strengthen, and settle you.' "

For the remainder of the afternoon, Paul continued in prayer and fasting. He couldn't get away from the certainty in his spirit that he absolutely needed, more than anything else, to wait on the Lord. Pastor Laroche's words had remained embedded in his spirit.

* * *

Sunday morning, Paul sat in the front row, listening to Brennon bring the sermon. He had never felt more conspicuous in his life. This wasn't just one of his Sunday's off from speaking. He had been restricted from all of his pastoral duties except for administrative ones. At the end of the week there would be a formal hearing, with or without Karlene, to see what investigative measures would be taken. The Church would then be notified officially.

Unfortunately, for him, the Church seemed to already have tabs on the situation. He would have had to be in denial, or pathetically clueless, not to notice the avoidance and the whispers. The number of people who greeted him as usual were either still in the dark, or die-hard supporters in whose eyes he could see the questions, the discomfort.

His parents' story was probably being recycled by those who had witnessed it, but hopefully they would remember the lesson and withhold premature judgement.

When Leroy and Blinder came and sat on either side of him, Paul fought to hold his emotions in check. What would he say to them? How would he explain?

Brennon's sermon, Paul could tell, was heartfelt as he spoke about the body of Christ supporting and honouring each other. With his casted leg slightly out in front, he looked squarely at the congregation. "Some of you, no doubt, have been privy to some rumours flying around regarding Pastor Paul. If you are spreading or listening to this gossip, I would like you to stop and, instead, be in much prayer until we, working with the district, can give you more conclusive answers."

Brennon looked directly at Paul as he finished his sermon: "I would like to conclude this morning's message, by reading a verse from Matthew sixteen. The Lord Jesus knew the *Church* would go through hell on this earth; that the Devil wasn't going to just sit by twiddling his thumbs while *She* grew and abounded. But, Jesus also issued a promise that the Church would ultimately triumph. Here's what it says in verse eighteen: '... I will build my Church, and the gates of Hades shall not prevail against it.'"

After the service, Paul steeled himself as everyone filed out of the Church. He had remained by the sanctuary doors, shaking hands without his usual playful or admonishing words. Yet, he was greatly comforted by some people's show of support, just as he was wounded by the difficulty some found in meeting his gaze. He noticed that one of his board members fell into the latter category.

"Whatever it is, we believe in you, Pastor Paul," was the sentiment of many. Yet, Paul couldn't help but think how a week before Jesus' crucifixion, the same people who worshipped him, called for his death.

* * *

Paul lay his head on a cushion on his home office floor. Before meditating and praying, he allowed his thoughts to drift.

After the church service, he had felt badly about turning down another of Hilda's dinner invitations. She had looked almost ready to cry and had thumped Samuel on the arm in an unspoken message. Poor Samuel had tried to convince Paul to change his mind. Paul had eventually pulled Samuel and Brennon aside to explain what he felt he had to do.

He knew it was hard for the others also, but he needed to do what had been greatly impressed on him. He needed to continue waiting on the Lord. He knew the battle was spiritual—not really against Karlene or Falconer, or even his board member, Robert Dawson. It was an ancient battle from before time.

Chapter Twenty-Eight

"We need to do something to help Pastor Paul," Leroy told the others. He, Blinder, Tristan and Ian were behind his mother's store, after school.

"Duh, we know, Leroy. That's why we're here," Tristan stated matter-of-factly. The white earbud cords, hanging loosely around her neck, contrasted starkly against her long-sleeved purple top.

Leroy grimaced at her before getting down to business. "Well, I've got some ideas. Let's see what you guys have, and then we'll pick the best ones."

"Yeah, but how are we supposed to know how to help him when we don't even know what he—supposedly did?" Ian asked.

Leroy sighed, looking at each one in turn. "Okay, this is what I overheard, but it goes no further. Apparently, Karlene's accused him of something."

"Something?" Tristan asked, as if expecting more of an explanation.

"Yeah," Leroy said, sounding irritated. "But, Falconer is somehow involved."

"Well, that really helps," Tristan said in disgust.

"H-he raped her."

They all looked at Blinder. Leroy felt as shocked as the others looked.

"What?" Tristan whispered, her voiced filled with disbelief.

"How do you know that's what it is, Blinder?" Leroy asked.

Blinder looked down. He stuffed his hands into his pants pockets and shuffled the gravel with his boot. When he looked up at them, there was a determined expression on his face. "I know," he said, simply, but firmly. "I-I know too that Falconer bullied her."

"Karlene?" Leroy asked.

"Yes," Blinder confirmed. "He made her say that about Pastor Paul."

*   *   *

Paul shoved his sleeping bag out of his way with a socked foot, before easing into his home office chair. He opened up his laptop.

He was feeling really down, but not hopeless. He believed God's work was being done inside of him as well as outside of him. If anyone asked how he knew, he couldn't have given them anything concrete. He just knew.

He glanced at the framed pictures on his desk. He had placed his father's picture there since removing it and Hannah's from the bookcase. Stephen Rayner sat among his family as if he were still living. There was a family shot of himself, his mother, Cassie, Christy and her family, and a photo of his biological father John. Hannah's, he had put away.

Now that Michaela was away, he wished he had one of her.

When the screen of his laptop powered up, he clicked through to check his emails. Suddenly a chat window popped up. It was Michaela.

He began typing.

"hello!!!"

"how are you???"

"doing okay"

"now tell me the truth"

"miss you like crazy"

"i miss you too ☹, but what about the other matter?"

Paul paused for a moment, not wanting to burden her. He typed in,

"the Lord's working on it, keep praying☺ can i phone you?"

She took a moment to respond.

"not right now. pastor solomon is here on his day off,

pretending not to notice me messaging you☺"

Paul laughed out loudly. They continued communicating back and forth, until she had to go. He stood up, shaking his head. He was amazed at how little effort it took for Michaela to make him forget he was in the middle of the worst battle of his life.

He went into the hallway to head for the kitchen, but found himself moving towards the front door instead. His eyes were drawn to the pile of unsorted mail he had left there, two days ago.

He went over and picked up the pile and started riffling through it. Suddenly, he stopped. A plain, standard-sized envelope was staring up at him, with Karlene's return address on it. Paul placed the other mail back on the hall table.

He slowly sat down on the hall bench and, just as slowly, began tearing the envelope opened. He read the contents three times. Afterwards, he got up and went back into the office.

There, he sat in silence for a long time. A heavy burden was being placed in his spirit. When the weight of it became too much, he began to pray in earnest.

Paul poured out his heart to God, because the relief he should have felt wasn't there. Instead, he felt the burden of responsibility. He felt a new call of the Spirit upon his life in a way he had not experienced before.

The Presence that filled the room was familiar, but more consuming, and Paul fell on his face in anguish and humility, and with an awesome sense of responsibility. The cries that erupted from his soul were words he didn't know. Words, he didn't understand. Yet, they came nonetheless, until the anguish was gone and the brokenness complete. Until, the obedience was guaranteed.

Now, go to Dennis Falconer and tell him the words I've given you. Go.

*   *   *

"Hang on to your horses!" Samuel entreated as he hurried to get the door. He opened it, ready to blast whoever was being so impatient. It was Paul and he immediately shoved his way in. He held up a white envelope, excitedly.

"Sam, it's a letter from Karlene, confessing how Falconer put her up to the whole thing."

Samuel was stunned. "Oh, my good Lord." He took the envelope and pulled out the sheet of paper. He read it. "Oh, my gracious, Heavenly Father. Hilda!"

"I'm going to see Falconer."

Samuel snapped to attention. "You're going to what? No, Paul—"

"Sam, I gotta do it!"

"Okay, okay," Samuel said, reaching a hand towards Paul, as if to physically restrain him. "But, not alone. Hilda!"

Ten minutes later, Paul and Samuel were on their way to see Falconer. They left Hilda rounding up people, by phone, to pray.

*   *   *

The fiercely bright group surrounded the Beetle, as it sped down the street, so that it was hardly seen.

As the two occupants stepped out of the car and headed for the front door of the mansion, the brightness surrounding them chased much of the surrounding, billowing darkness to the sidelines.

Horrific screeches from malevolent forces, having their territory invaded by so many bright ones, erupted, but could not be heard by human ears. However, sudden disturbances in the wind, trees and animal behaviour could be seen.

* * *

Paul knew the peace and strength he felt, as he faced Dennis Falconer, were not his own. This was the first time he had stepped foot inside the man's impressive domain. He was certainly aware of the two, black-suited men watchfully waiting under an over-sized archway, about twelve feet behind Falconer.

"Well, well, well," Falconer began in an insufferable tone. "Samuel, Paul, to what do I owe the pleasure?" Before they could answer, he held up his beefy, ringed-fingered hand and directed his dark gaze at Paul. "Let me guess, you're not satisfied with interfering with my means of livelihood, but have come to do more damage."

Paul held Karlene's letter up. "Falconer, you preyed on a woman, who was already messed up, for your own selfish gain; just as you tried to do with my mother. You are the one who's not satisfied and bent on more damage!"

Falconer eyed the letter, suspiciously. "Karlene is a fool—a weak, snivelling fool. She deserves everything that's come to her."

"She didn't deserve to have her vulnerabilities used against her by a man whose main aim in life is to satisfy his greed."

Falconer laughed loudly, obscenely. He paced restlessly across the highly-polished, marble floor. "You don't know what you're talking about. I grew up in poverty and shame, and I vowed when I became a man, I would have the wealth and the power to control my own destiny. Your adoptive father took what belonged to me!"

"My mother chose! You were a poor loser."

"She chose?" Falconer asked with overwhelming incredulousness. "Why would any woman in her right mind choose the work of the Church, with its miserable, ungrateful people, over all that I offered?"

Paul folded Karlene's letter and put it in the front pocket of his shirt. He could feel Samuel's uneasiness beside him, but he stayed focused on Falconer. "My mother chose the man she loved, and the God she loves."

Falconer laughed again. He lowered his voice intimidatingly: "The god she loves. What god? This world is full of gods. She could have had her pick of any one of them and still have had me."

"She didn't want you, Falconer; just as I don't want Karlene. It's the god of this world who steals what doesn't belong to him, and you, Falconer, have that same spirit in you!"

If Paul hadn't been there to witness it, he wouldn't have believed someone's face could become so contorted with rage. Falconer's face had become swollen and infused with blood.

"I've just about had enough!" Falconer bellowed. The men behind him stood at attention and started moving closer. "Enough of your Church—your God—your Christianity! It's all a crutch; a lie to make us rely on fairytales instead of our own strength."

Paul suddenly felt power rise up in him. "Not so, Falconer! The very God who you call a lie has sent this message for you!"

Falconer stood, as if frozen. The men behind stood still.

As he spoke, Paul could hear his own voice strongly raised as if it weren't his own: "I have called out to you through many voices and in many ways, yet you've continued as stiff-necked as Pharaoh of Egypt. Now, hear my final words to you: 'For what profit is it to a man if he gains the whole world, and loses his own soul?' "

Falconer remained as if frozen, then he blinked twice. "Get out!" he bellowed, filled with rage. "Get out, now!"

* * *

Hours later, Paul finished up his last bite at Hilda's dining room table.

"Hurrah!" Hilda cheered dramatically. She was beaming as she cleared dishes from the spot in front of Paul.

"Hilda, it sure feels good to make you happy," Paul told her, rubbing his stomach.

She squeezed him from behind. "It's okay, love. I see now you had to do what you needed to do, and this old lady needs to learn to stay out of the Lord's way."

"That was quite the story, though," Sarah commented excitedly, as she helped Hilda clear the rest of the table.

"I wish I could have been there," Brennon echoed the sentiment. Conner was draped over his cast, trying to poke his fingers down the top opening just below Brennon's knee.

Samuel put his empty glass on the table. "Trust me Brennon, I was sweating in my pants. Just looking at Falconer and his two goons was enough to cause a hernia."

Everyone laughed.

"But, I'm telling you," Samuel continued, "Paul was none too tame. I've never seen the Spirit of God speak through anyone like that before. You could feel it, hear it, and almost taste it. It was incredible." He looked across the table at Paul. "Son, something's happened to you."

* * *

Paul watched the screen of his laptop light up. It was only after eight, but he was tired. He needed to spend some time in prayer before retiring, but he decided to check his emails first.

He had only heard from Will and Rashad once, and Will hadn't been telling Lucy everything. Granted, Will, with his military training, knew what he was doing, but Paul still wanted to know what was happening.

He smiled, as Michaela's chat window popped up as if she had been waiting for him.

"i haven't been able to get you on either phone."

Paul began typing.

"well, hello to you too☹"

"sorry, hello paul, come see me???"

"can i call you now?"

"hurry☺"

He relaxed in his office chair as he dialled. She answered immediately.

"Where were you? What's happening?"

Her voice sounded so sweet to his ears, but he still decided to tease her. "Boy, you don't learn, do you? Hi, Paul. How are you, Paul? I've missed you, Paul."

She was silent for a moment. "I thought we already went through all the preliminaries online," she said, sounding like a little girl.

He sighed.

"Okay. Hi and how are you?"

"Hi back. I'm good."

"I miss you."

"I miss you, more."

She laughed.

"That's more like it," Paul said. "How are things going there?"

"Oh, I love it. I mean, what I do is really no different from what I did at Bethel Community. I just love working with youth, except now, I'm also being paid for it. Also... I don't have you looking over my shoulder."

"I never looked over your shoulder," he protested. He pressed his feet against the floor, causing his chair to roll back against the bookcase behind. He settled his long legs on the desk.

"I'm not going to argue that. So, what's happening with you? I've been praying a lot."

"Can we talk about it when I come to see you?"

"Are you coming to see me?"

He gently banged the phone on the desk top before speaking into it, "I think we're having technical difficulties. My girlfriend isn't hearing me very well."

"Oh, Paul... "

"Of course, I'm coming to see you."

Half an hour later, Paul hung up the phone, only to have it ring again almost immediately.

"Hi, Rev. It's Will."

"I'm glad you've called, man. Where are you guys? What's going on?" Paul asked.

"We found Karlene. But it's not good. She's in bad shape."

Chapter Twenty-Nine

"I still don't see why Tristan has to be the one to go in," Ian complained quietly, at the side of the Sales Centre, crouched between Leroy and Blinder.

"I told you," Leroy whispered, "they've already seen me and Blinder, and you're too tall. You'd stand out like a sore thumb. A girl seems more harmless."

"What if she doesn't get to leave the iPod? What if they suspect—"

"Shut up, will you? You're starting to get on my nerves," Leroy whispered fiercely. "Now be quiet. Someone's at the door." He felt like socking Ian. He was nervous enough without all the whining. The last time he was here had been to help a badly injured Blinder.

If Blinder, who had come earlier to be their look-out, could return to the place where he'd been beaten up, then they could do their parts too. Plus, he wasn't letting Pastor Paul go down without a fight.

They remained quiet in the cool darkness, listening for Tristan's voice.

"Hi, I'm Tristan and I'm wondering if Ms. Benedict is here tonight?"

"Ms. Benedict?" It was a man's voice. "Oh, you mean Karlene. Naw, she doesn't work here anymore."

"Oh." Tristan sounded convincingly disappointed. "Well, she told me to come here for a—you know—psychic meeting."

"Listen, kid, I don't know what she told you, but we don't do that here."

"Oh, okay. Well, I walked here and I have a ways to go back, so can I use your washroom, please?"

Leroy had to give her credit. She was very convincing.

The guy sighed loudly. "Well, okay, but make it snappy."

The door slammed.

"I don't like this," Ian whispered.

"Just hang on, Ian," Leroy whispered back. "I don't like it either, but they've had too much attention lately. I don't think they're looking for any more. Plus, we gotta do this while Falconer's here."

It seemed like they had been waiting for ever. Even Blinder was getting restless, but Leroy's digital watch said it had only been a few minutes.

Finally, there were sounds from the porch, followed by footsteps.

"Thanks a lot," Tristan said, politely.

"Okay, but remember, we don't do any psychic things here."

"Gotcha. I guess I'll have to look somewhere else."

Leroy watched Tristan walk down the driveway, until the porch light no longer shone on her. He nudged the others. "Let's go."

He led them away behind the house. They would meet up with Tristan by Metro's Gas Bar.

* * *

Paul opened the church door to let Samuel in from the cool night. The older man looked tired and worn.

"How is she, Sam?"

"Let's go sit down, Paul."

Inside the Front Office, Paul handed Samuel a Styrofoam cup of coffee.

"Thanks, Paul," Samuel said, before taking a few big sips. He looked up at Paul. "Sit down, will you, son."

Paul pulled up a chair and sat facing Samuel.

"Lucy thinks Karlene's had a nervous breakdown. Will and Rashad found her, in Toronto, at the home of her previous pastor's widow. I guess that was the last safe place she knew." He took another sip of coffee.

"Rashad said, apparently, she tried to commit suicide just before they found her."

Paul was silent; his heart was heavy.

"When they found her, she kept saying she was sorry over and over. She thinks you hate her and that she deserves it."

Paul bowed his head.

"She needs to be hospitalized, we think. Rashad wants to hire someone to care for her in her home, but I don't know if that's possible. She needs to be evaluated."

Paul looked up. "I wish I could talk to her."

"You can't, Paul. The hearing is in two days. Don't mess it up."

"Maybe, I shouldn't leave—"

Samuel shook his head. "You need to go see Michaela. There's nothing you can do here now, and you'll have to deal with the temptation to try and fix things for Karlene. You shouldn't be the one to fix them. She needs to let go of you. Let Rashad be there for her."

Paul got the message loud and clear, but it didn't make him feel any better.

* * *

"Look, they're locking up now!" Tristan exclaimed excitedly.

Leroy looked through the windshield of his mother's car. They were parked inconspicuously between two other cars in Milward Seniors Community, not far from the Sales Centre. They had been waiting for a little over an hour. If it wasn't for the tenseness of the situation, Leroy would have died of boredom.

"W-we're going to wait, right, Leroy?" Blinder asked. He had been stuffing his face with popcorn the whole time and fiddling with the new cell phone Carmel had insisted he keep with him.

"Yeah," Leroy said, wondering how much popcorn he'd have to clean up. Leroy figured everyone had their own way of dealing with stress, but since getting his license, his mother let him use the car fairly regularly with the stipulation that he always brought it back the way he found it—cleanliness and gas, paramount.

Ian and Tristan had spent most of their time in the back seat holding hands, whispering and giggling.

"So, you guys can date now?" Leroy asked while keeping his gaze on the Sales Centre.

"Yes, Leroy," Tristan answered. "Public dating."

He looked around at them. "What's that?"

"Tristan's parents don't want her alone with me behind closed doors," Ian explained.

Leroy snorted loudly. He turned to continue his watchful vigilance.

"What's that supposed to mean?" Tristan asked, sounding a little offended.

Leroy grinned. "Hey, people can find ways to do it, even in public—just say'n."

"It? What exactly do you mean by it, Leroy?" Tristan asked, sounding even more offended.

"It. You know what I mean by—it." He wasn't about to elaborate on the birds and the bees to a girl, in a car full of guys.

"Well, I'm not people, Leroy, and I think you're disgusting."

Wisely, Ian said not a word. Glad for something else to do, Leroy started opening the car door.

"Okay, Blinder comes with me. You two, stay put."

Ian pushed himself forwards. "Why Blinder?"

Leroy groaned. "Because, he's the most watchful, and I don't want to be caught picking the lock. I do want them to let me into Bible college, you know."

"You're picking the lock? How'd you learn how to pick a lock?" Ian asked, sounding amazed.

Leroy slammed the door shut, ignoring him. He tapped on Tristan's window and waited for her to open it.

"Now that you two are breaking the rules by being behind closed doors alone," Leroy said smugly, "make sure it's your values and not just doors that's strong enough to keep you apart."

* * *

Paul slowed down, looking for Hope Alive Church. The hour-long, morning drive from Milward to Georgeton had afforded him much time to reflect and pray. Even though he knew Karlene's letter would most likely exonerate him, he still felt restless about the whole thing. Would people still wonder?

He was also concerned for Karlene's welfare. She was presently in the psychiatric ward of Milward Memorial Hospital. True to his word, Rashad had hired a companion for her so she wouldn't be alone when she came home.

Paul saw the church sign before he saw the medium-sized Church, and suddenly the problems of the day faded away.

Inside the church foyer, he paused to look around, but he didn't have to wait long before seeing her head poke out of a doorway in a long hallway to his right.

"Paul!" Michaela exclaimed. "Just one minute," she said, holding up a forefinger. Her head disappeared.

"May I help you?"

Paul looked to his left to see a big, middle-aged, Korean man walking towards him. Paul smiled and held out his hand in greeting. "Reverend Sung, Paul Rayner."

"Ah, yes, Reverend Rayner. It's good to finally meet you, but please call me Solomon."

"If you'll call me, Paul."

Solomon's kind eyes lit up as he smiled. "Agreed." He looked straight ahead. "Is the young lady keeping you waiting? Well, let's see what we can do about that."

Paul followed him towards the hallway.

Fifteen minutes later, after chatting with Solomon Sung, who gave him a tour of the Church, Paul was able to steal Michaela away.

She seemed excited and looked fresh and beautiful. She was wearing a long-sleeved, beige top and a loose, dark brown skirt. Her hair was pulled back in a cute, fluffy ponytail. Paul couldn't help but admire her as he closed the door on her side of the Beetle. He walked around and let himself in.

"I'm so glad to see you," Michaela said. "Did you find the Church okay?"

He didn't answer her. Instead, he leaned over and kissed her. When his hand held the back of her head, she pulled away, laughing.

"Paul, we're in a church parking lot."

"So, I practically grew up in one of those." He said, basking in the sound of her continued laughter.

They left the Church and went to a restaurant close by for take-out. Then Michaela directed him on a small tour of Georgeton. Afterwards, they drove to a wooded park and picnic area.

* * *

Michaela watched Paul float the picnic blanket into the air before allowing it to land perfectly on the grass, close to a large oak tree. It was a beautiful, slightly overcast day and fairly warm for early autumn.

They were on a bit of a slope that looked down into a wooded area, thick with alternating groups of needle and broadleaf trees. Yellow, orange, red and brown fall-leaf colours were starting to dot the landscape. A flock of geese trumpeted loudly as they passed overhead in perfect formation, heading south.

Michaela took a deep breath of the fresh air as she knelt on the blanket, trying to ignore the peculiar sense of anticipation that had been dogging her all morning, making her nervous.

"Isn't it beautiful?" she asked, preparing to sort their lunch, wondering if her mood had something to do with their time apart.

Paul seemed okay, but different. The charming good-looks were still there, with those adorable dimples, and he was as gentle and attentive as ever, but... "

She didn't want to make this day unpleasant for him, so she was determined that she would allow him to be the one to initiate conversation on the inevitable topic. He had already assured her, by phone, that Karlene had been found and that everything should work out okay.

Besides, he wasn't being very talkative, sitting across from her, watching her arrange the food packages.

Suddenly, he reached over and stilled her hand. "I almost get the feeling that you're lining those up between us, on purpose," he remarked casually.

She looked at him, noticing his challenging look. "Well, I know you've had a long drive and are probably hungry," she said, in her defence. "Aren't you?"

He smiled lazily, studying her for a moment. "Okay, have it your way for now," he said, releasing her hand.

So, they ate and talked of inconsequential things.

Their meal was finished when Paul asked, "So, you're living with a family?" He was lounging on his side, with one hand bracing his head up, and the other fiddling with a bent straw. His black shirt hung opened, showing a white T-shirt, and his legs were stretched out in black jeans.

"Yes—until I find a place of my own. Josiah and Elise Alexander live in a big, gorgeous house in the country. Josiah is a contractor and an architect. Elise teaches high-school French and History—but, not currently—they just had a baby girl a month ago. I love helping with her."

"The baby?"

"Yes, the baby. Actually, they're also funding a new community project, which I find very interesting."

"What's that?"

"A Christian drop-in centre for youth, and you know how I love working with youth."

"That is interesting," Paul agreed, sitting up. He stretched his arms above his head, then studied her. "Do you like it here?"

Michaela started closing up the boxes, even though they were mostly empty and would end up in the garbage. "I can be happy anywhere," she answered, without looking at him.

"Wow, that's extremely generous," he said.

She looked at him, puzzled. He was grinning, full dimples in place.

"I say that because I believe the Lord's calling me to a whole different life."

Michaela remained quiet for a moment, trying to read between the lines of his words. "What life?" she finally asked.

"I'm not completely sure, yet. It's being worked out in me." Paul informed her, somewhat soberly. Then he changed the subject.

"This is probably a good time to bring this up: Karlene wrote a letter of confession which also implicated Falconer. I confronted him."

"You did? What happened?"

Michaela listened carefully as Paul filled her in on the details of his meeting with Falconer. He also gave her a pretty good picture of other events since she had left, but she suspected he wasn't telling her everything.

"So, will Karlene be okay? Will she still be able to verbally retract her letter?"

Paul shook his head, slowly. "I don't know. We'll have to see how it plays out, trusting in the Lord."

Something was bothering her. She straightened her skirt around her knees as she sat sideways.

"So, how did you know to go and speak the things you did to Falconer?"

Paul was silent for a moment, looking down into the valley. When he spoke, a subdued passion emanated from him. "I was told to go and what to say." He looked at her, as if to measure her reaction. "The Lord spoke to me through my thoughts, but with distinct words."

Michaela's heartbeat sped up and, in spite of the warmth, she felt the hairs on her skin rise.

"I'll talk more about it another time, okay?"

She nodded, partially understanding.

Suddenly, Paul proceeded to move the food packages from between them. Afterwards, he repositioned himself closer to her and, with one leg folded flat and one knee up, he became almost like a wall halfway around her.

She hadn't seen it coming. She didn't know where he had pulled it from. But there it was in the ce ntre of his palm. Her gaze remained glued to the little black box.

"I said I would wait until I knew you would say yes." His voice was a low rumble, but the words were clear enough.

She looked at him, and his dark gaze held her captive.

"Michaela, I started loving you the first day I met you. Now I love you with every fibre of my being, and I can't imagine living without you to share my life, my path... my love."

Michaela felt the first tear fall, before she even realized it was there. She blinked rapidly, dislodging the other waiting drops. She didn't really want to cry.

"Michaela Jamie Laroche, will you marry me?"

"You know my middle name?" The question just slipped out as she wiped her tears with trembling hands.

Paul laughed softly. "Of course. I read your application, remember?"

"You didn't know I was a woman," she pressed.

"That was supposedly fax error, but I personally think God wiped that 'a' off the end of your name. He knew I wouldn't have accepted a woman."

Michaela laughed, wondering how long he would keep holding his hand up. She took a deep breath and exhaled her answer. "Yes!"

* * *

Paul nearly shouted his pleasure. He had thought she was stalling, so when she finally answered, he hadn't expected it. He pressed his forehead up against hers. A mixture of incredible joy and relief filled him.

Michaela's arms circled his neck. "I love you," she whispered.

The ring was forgotten as he pulled her close. He kissed the warm skin of her forehead. He kissed her cheeks and tasted the salt of her tears. When he finally claimed her lips, he felt like a thirsty man who had found his oasis.

Fifteen minutes later, found them lying on the blanket. Paul was on his back with Michaela curled up by his side nestled in the circle of his arm. Every now and then she held her left hand up to admire the diamond solitaire in a white gold setting.

Paul chuckled. "You know, Mick, I often wonder if women would say yes if a ring wasn't part of the deal."

She placed the same hand on his chest and partially shoved herself up to look at him. "Very funny," she said. "I'll have you know that I've never really been a ring person, but I'm not sure I'll take this one off. And, I'm not sure I like that nickname."

He laughed, feeling more contented than he had been in a long time. If only time stood still and he could lay here with her much longer, but she needed to return to work, and he had planned to drive into Toronto before returning to Milward, following a lead he felt God had given him.

That drive would take him about one and a half hours, but he needed to do it.

"My parents will be so excited. My mother, I think, has been a little afraid that I had been called to a life of singlehood."

"You mean spinsterhood?" he teased.

She sat up, looking down at him. "I don't like that word. It's negative, conjuring up images of the old school marm, while bachelorhood denotes a man who hasn't been caught, yet. I had many debates about this very thing in Bible college."

"I don't doubt it," Paul said, reaching up to caress her face. Her skin was soft and warm and beautiful, and the escaped strands of her hair had created a wispy, kinky cloud around her head. He pulled her down for a kiss.

"My parents will be so happy," she whispered against his lips. "They've been very concerned for you and have been praying a lot."

"I know," he responded, breathing in her scent, intoxicated by her nearness. "I called your father."

She pulled back. "You did? He didn't tell me."

"God has used him in my life greatly, Michaela. Haiti was necessary for me." Paul saw the emotions cross her face as she swallowed noticeably.

He reached for her again.

Chapter Thirty

"Hey, Paul, it's good to see you back." Brennon said, the next day, as Sarah preceded him into the Front Office. Brennon hobbled in on one crutch.

Paul stopped photocopying. "Well thanks, man, but I was only gone for one day." He had come into the Office early, hoping some practical work might help him focus before the meeting with the District Superintendent.

Brennon sat down on Hilda's chair. "You'll want to hear this," he told Paul before nodding at Sarah.

Sarah held her hand out. "Paul, this is amazing!"

Paul frowned, not understanding their enthusiasm. "Look, if you're both trying to relax me, or something, I don't think anything on that iPod is going to help." He turned back to his work. "But, I may as well tell you. I proposed to Michaela, yesterday, and she accepted."

They were silent for a moment, then Sarah squealed loudly.

"Oh, my goodness, Paul! Brennon, did you hear that?"

"I'm not deaf, Sarah. But after that scream, I might be," Brennon replied, pretending to clear his ears.

Sarah smacked him on the shoulder before going over to hug Paul. "Congratulations, Paul. I'm so happy for you!"

"That's great, Paul. I knew it would work out—congratulations," Brennon added, giving him a hearty handshake, followed by a hug and back pats.

"Thanks," Paul told them. "I must say, she seemed pretty happy too."

"Awww," Sarah cooed softly. "I'm so happy for you. I think Michaela is perfect for you—not that Hannah wasn't—" She suddenly put her hand up to her mouth.

"It's okay, Sarah," Paul said immediately, wanting to ease her obvious discomfort. "Focusing on just one woman is a full-time job."

Gradually, the humour of it seemed to penetrate Sarah's psyche and she started laughing.

"Oh, Paul, it's a good thing there's no marriage in heaven, or what would you do?"

Sarah and Brennon laughed heartily, while Paul smiled at them indulgently.

Suddenly, as if just remembering, Sarah grabbed Paul's hand and slapped the iPod onto his palm. "Paul, this is serious. The kids have Falconer recorded on this. You've got to listen before the meeting."

Paul looked at the flat, rectangular object in his hand. "Falconer? What kids?"

Five minutes later, Paul was flabbergasted. He couldn't believe Leroy, Tristan and Ian, along with Blinder, had accomplished what they had. Talk about spy savvy.

"I can't believe they actually broke into the house. I'm going to kill Leroy. And what was Blinder thinking going along with it?" He looked at Sarah and Brennon. They were holding hands and looking very relieved.

"That's solid evidence, Paul," Brennon said. "Not only did Falconer rail on about Karlene backing out of the plan to destroy your ministry, but he also implicated himself in fraudulent profiteering from the Seniors Community."

"It's like God was putting all the words into his mouth that night," Sarah said, then added, "Hallelujah!"

"Hallelujah," the men echoed.

Paul waved the iPod in front of them. "I don't think we can give this to the police, though."

"Why not?" Sarah asked.

"I'm not sure about the legality of the recording. I'll ask Will, but the guys need to know they can't give this to the police, and they better keep mum about Leroy breaking into the Sales Centre."

"I already told them that," Brennon assured him. "Just make sure you use it at the meeting. Saving your butt is number one priority in my book."

Paul shook his head again, still amazed. "Tell me something, what do you think Falconer was talking about when he yelled, 'Burn them out! Burn them all out!'?"

* * *

Paul was surprised when, after shaking David Black's hand, the older man reached out to hug him tightly.

"I knew what your parents went through, Paul. I have no difficulty saying I'm glad your record remains completely clean. Not only was there insufficient evidence for a hearing, but the allegations had been recalled by the complainant, and your church youth backed it up with solid evidence. I've never seen anything like this before. God's favour was upon you, greatly."

Not long after, Paul talked briefly with two other representatives from the district office, and then he was left alone with Samuel, Ethel and Frank, in the Conference Room.

Frank approached him at the door. "Pastor Paul, God was at work here today, and for that I am thankful." His eyes were moist with unshed tears. "And, I'm very sorry about Rob. I know he's broken."

Paul placed his hand on Frank's shoulder. "I know, Frank. I've told him I forgive him. I hold nothing against him. Thanks for your support and for believing in me."

After Frank left, Paul sat and talked with Ethel and Samuel for awhile. He felt as if he had been given a new lease on life. It had been news to him to learn that David Black had personally gone to see Karlene, before the meeting. Apparently, Karlene's demeanour and words had been enough to convince him that her retraction had been genuine. Paul was not sure that it alone would have been enough for everyone.

He walked out to the Foyer with Ethel and Samuel to see a small group of people waiting there. His gaze rested on Michaela. She had a wide smile on her face.

He stopped and waited for her with opened arms. She ran lightly towards him and, before the whole group, threw herself into his embrace.

Above the cheers, whistles and laughter from the group, he heard her say, "Oh, Paul, thank God, thank God!"

He kissed her right then, right there.

* * *

"Are you sure you want to do this?" Paul asked Michaela. They were alone in the Pastor's Office. He was in his chair with Michaela sitting on his lap.

"I came to support you and to be here for you," she said, resting her arms on his shoulders. "But, all the way down, I've felt strongly impressed to go to her."

He sighed. "Okay, but you know I can't go with you. Sam believes it's better if she heals without me, and I agree."

She touched her nose to his. "I know. Rashad's there for her and he loves her."

"In spite of everything."

"In spite of everything," she concurred.

"That's true love."

She laughed. "I hope you remember that when we've been married for ten years, and I've been nagging you for the last five."

"I think you'll be a cute nag," he said, flirting with her.

"I promise to try very hard not to be a nag, cute or otherwise." She shifted her weight to lay her head on his shoulder.

Paul tightened his hold on her. "Michaela?"

"Mmmm?"

"Here's what I promise. I promise what the Scripture says: 'Husbands love your wives, just as Christ also loved the Church and gave Himself for it... ' "

"That's what you promise?" she murmured.

"Till the day I die."

"I'll take it," she said.

* * *

After Michaela's time with Paul at Bethel Community, he left to go to the Temples,' while she left with Will to go see Karlene.

Karlene's appearance was so changed that, at first glance from the doorway, Michaela thought she was someone else. She was painfully thin and frail looking. Even her long, black hair seemed to have lost its vitality.

"It's Michaela, Karlene," Will said, as they entered Karlene's living room.

They had been let into the house by Karlene's companion, a shy, young Vietnamese woman named Doris.

Rashad couldn't be there, so Will had come with Michaela for moral support.

Michaela slowly followed Will and Doris into the living room. What she could see of the house, so far, certainly reflected Karlene's bold, sophisticated taste.

Yet the Karlene who looked up at her, from a black, leather couch, reflected none of that. Her golden eyes seemed enormous in the depleted contours of her face. She held a thin arm out to Michaela.

Michaela hurried over to her and took hold of her hand.

"Oh, Michaela, I'm so sorry. I've wronged you and I'm so sorry," she cried. Her voice sounded hoarse.

Michaela knelt before her, still holding her hand. "It's okay, Karlene. I forgive you. I've never held it against you. I just want you to get well."

She looked down at Michaela with tears streaming down her face. "But I almost ruined his life, and he didn't deserve any of it. I'm no good."

"Karlene, you are precious in God's sight. You have never stopped belonging to Him, and He has never failed to welcome one of his children back into the circle of His arms."

She started weeping with her head bowed low as if she couldn't bear to face Michaela. Michaela looked over at Doris who had been hovering by uncertainly. She held out a box of tissue and a glass of water to Michaela.

"Thanks, Doris," Michaela said, smiling her appreciation. She pulled her hands from Karlene and began to tend to her. When Karlene's sobbing finally ceased and her face was dabbed dry, she took a drink of water.

Afterwards, Michaela sat on the couch beside her, holding her hand, realizing that Karlene needed a tangible presence.

With Will and Doris patiently waiting, Michaela allowed Karlene to purge her heart by confessing her failed ambitions and sharing about her eventual flight.

"If it weren't for Rashad and Will, I would probably not be here today." Her eyes welled up with tears, once more. "And I've treated Rashad so badly, and he's still so good to me."

"He loves you, Karlene," Michaela told her gently.

"I know, but I loved Paul, and when he didn't return it, I felt I could make him love me. I'm so screwed up. I didn't know how to let him go."

"But you've let him go now."

"Yes, I have," she agreed, mournfully.

Michaela squeezed her hand. "And if Rashad could love you even when you didn't love him, how much more does God love you, even when you ran away from Him?"

She looked at Michaela. "He loves me very much."

"Yes," Michaela said, moving closer to her. "Karlene, I believe the Lord Jesus wants me to pray healing upon your mind. Will you let me do that?"

Her eyes widened, as hope dawned there. "Yes, please," she answered simply.

Michaela took Karlene's other hand. She closed her eyes and waited silently for a moment. When she started praying, she began by thanking God for Karlene's safe return and the care she had received. After a while, she felt the strong urging of the Holy Spirit, *in her*, to ask for Karlene's healing.

After the prayer, Karlene breathed out loudly before opening her eyes. "Thank you," she said. "I can feel Him and I can feel His peace."

"What else do you feel?"

"I feel hope," she said, smiling tentatively. She looked into Michaela's eyes. "I was told as a child that I had a gift. But the darkness that followed the first wave of euphoria from this so-called gift, nearly destroyed me. You have a true gift and it's full of light. Thank you."

"Is there anything else I can do for you, Karlene?"

She remained silent for a moment, before answering. "Yes, I need to see Paul. I need to tell him I'm sorry."

Chapter Thirty-One

"I'm sorry, Rev., the police can't use this and the kids could get in trouble for it," Will stated.

"That's what I figured," Paul responded. It was Saturday morning and Will had come by the parsonage with something obviously on his mind, but he seemed to be having difficulty spilling it, so Paul had used the opportunity to ask him about the iPod recording.

"If one of them had been part of the conversation, then it wouldn't have been illegal, but what they did is eavesdropping. They could be charged instead." Will continued.

"Not to mention, the police would want to know how they got into the house," Paul added.

"Right," Will agreed.

Paul picked up his mug from his kitchen table, then set it back down. "What is it, Will?" he finally asked.

Will smiled sheepishly. "Is it that obvious?" he asked, raking a hand through his dark hair.

"Yeah, man, it is."

Will exhaled forcefully. "It's been really hard for me, lately. I've finished treatment for the second time, and I've been keeping it together fairly well. I know I haven't been to see you as much because I'm traveling back and forth to work."

"I know, Will. It's a distance." Paul sat back in his chair. "Besides, counselling was one of my restrictions during this whole nightmare."

Will nodded. "Well, we did settle on a house, so we'll be closer to the military base now."

"Hey, that's awesome, man. Congratulations."

"Thanks," Will said. He turned his blue gaze on Paul. "Everything seems to be going well, but... " A red stain had crept up the side of his neck.

Paul leaned towards him. "What is it?" he asked again.

"I need something more. I know what I have, what I depend on won't be enough." He suddenly pushed his chair away from the table, as if needing more space. "I sat in that room with Karlene as Michaela let her pour her heart out. I watched Michaela show her unconditional love, and pray for her with a power I knew was real. Paul, I want that. I want what you have and I want what Michaela has. Heck, I want what Karlene has because it kept her from destroying herself when she was at her lowest."

Paul sensed the desperation and the power of Will's words, deeply. To his recollection, Will had never called him by his first name; always just "Rev." Something was happening here. It was like Will was allowing the barriers to come down.

"Do you want to commit your life to the Lord Jesus, Will?"

Will placed one arm on the kitchen table. His hand was closed into a tight fist. Slowly, the fist uncurled and his hand lay flat on the table. "I do," he said in a low, emotional voice.

Paul felt an awesome sense of responsibility, as the thrill of the moment filled him. “Let’s kneel, Will, as an act of surrender.”

They knelt at the seats of their chairs. “Talk to the Lord, Will. Tell Him your desire.”

The big man cleared his throat before praying. “God—Father, I’ve learned the hard way that I’m not enough for myself, my family and the communities I serve. I need You.” His voice broke, but he kept going.

“I’ve done my own thing and have ignored You and the gift of Your Son, who took my punishment on the cross. I don’t deserve Your salvation, but still Your love offers it to me.”

He fell back to sit on the kitchen floor with tears streaming down his upraised face. “God, I accept it. I accept You, Jesus, as my Saviour and... my Lord.”

Will’s simple prayer ended not long after, leaving him broken and weeping, yet the light of joy was on his face. Paul spent much time with him in prayer and deep conversation until he was satisfied it was enough.

Afterwards, Paul walked with Will to the front door. Out on the concrete porch, Will turned to look at him. His eyes were still red, but peace was written there on his face.

“Thanks a lot, Paul. I really appreciate you sticking with me, believing for me.”

“Just go with Him, Will. Cling to Him,” Paul encouraged him.

Before Will proceeded down the steps, he bent over to pick up a newspaper bundle.

Something must have caught his eye, because he had his head bowed over the bundle for awhile. Suddenly, he turned back to Paul and thrust the papers at him.

“Look at this.”

Paul accepted the papers, immediately noticing the bold headline: "Builder Caught Up in Money Laundering Charges." Paul continued reading. He noticed Will edging closer and started reading out loudly.

When Paul finished the article, he looked at Will. "I can't believe it. Falconer is not only implicated in bribery, but money laundering? Man, that's crazy!"

"I can believe it," Will said, taking the paper to have another look. "It looks like the investigations that you guys pushed for led to more doors than Falconer would have liked."

After Will left, Paul gave Brennon a call. "Bren, have you looked at your newspaper, yet?"

"No, why?" Brennon asked, sounding groggy. "I slept in. Conner had us up—he's got a cold."

"Anything serious?"

"Naw. He's just miserable when he's sick. I'm looking at the paper now."

Paul switched his cordless phone to speaker and set it down on the kitchen table. He sat down and started drumming his fingers on the table.

Brennon started speaking, "Hey, Paul, it sounds like you've got elephants stomping on your phone."

"Sorry," he said, stilling his fingers. Soon after, he heard Brennon's voice.

"Holy Moses, Paul! If you thought Falconer had it in for your family before, he's gotta be really ticked now."

After talking with Brennon, Paul spent some much needed time in prayer then, with his legs across his desk and a cup of coffee nearby, he poured over the Word. His hunger for God's Word had increased just as much as his desire to spend time waiting on Him. God was changing him day by day, and he knew this needed to happen for a lifetime.

Pastor Laroche had told him the journey for the true child of God should be one of constant change, morphing into the very likeness of

Christ. A Christian could experience moments of stagnation or find himself in a desert place, but not to remain so. It was essential to grow; to change—to be willing vessels in the Potter's hands.

Deep down, Paul realized the changes in him would affect his life choices. He knew Samuel and the others wouldn't like it, but it would also affect his time at BCC.

He realized, now that he had been clearly exonerated of any wrong doing, everyone expected him to step back into his role of beloved pastor, but he knew it was not to be. He hadn't shared this with anyone else, not even Michaela. Yet, God's voice was persistent and Paul had to obey.

After his Bible and prayer devotions, Paul completed some minor household chores, then took a quick shower. He had decided to run some errands in town, when the phone rang. When he read the caller ID on his bedroom phone, he smiled, feeling a rush of pleasure.

"Hey, Mick, what's up?" he asked, knowing what would come.

"Paul," she began, "it's your good fortune to have a name that can't be altered, I—on the other hand—had an abhorrent childhood with my name."

"Ahhh—Michaela, Michaela," he called, laughing while trying to placate her. "A rose by any other name... "

"Don't even start. I'm grumpy today."

He sat on his bed. "You get grumpy?"

She sighed. "Yes."

"I'm sorry I'm not there to make it better." He heard her faint laugh, and it felt good to hear it.

"Cassie called and she was being very mysterious. Apparently, she has to go to a formal dinner her work is hosting, and she really wants me to go with her when we go to visit your mom and Christy."

"And... "

"Well, I would rather spend the afternoon with you," she complained.

Her words filled him with warmth and he wished she were with him. "You're coming early, right? So, we'll have most of the day together."

"But I hardly see you all week, as it is," she whined, sighing. "Sorry, I'm being pathetic. Of course, I want to spend time with Cassie."

"It's okay, you're just feeling grumpy. Are they treating you okay?"

"No problems here. I just miss everyone."

"Everyone?" he asked playfully

"You, mostly," she said, giggling. "By the way, I have good news. My mother will come a month before the wedding—my father will come later."

"Hey, that's great!"

They talked about wedding plans for awhile, until Michaela said she had to going shopping with Elise and the baby.

"Are you guys shopping for yourselves, or the baby?"

She laughed. "Maybe both. Elise has great taste."

"Okay, enjoy—miss you."

"I miss you, too. You know, Paul, you should have hired me."

He laughed out loudly at the absurdity of her statement. "Are you kidding? You were hell bent on leaving to pave your own way. Plus, my darling, we would have had to marry right away. There's no way I'd have put myself through more months of torture trying to keep a proper relationship with you. No way, no take, no how!"

She was silent before saying in a quiet voice, "Well... So now that we're both grumpy... "

* * *

Later that evening, at the Temples' kitchen table, Paul watched Samuel shake his head over the newspaper.

"When I read this earlier, I said to myself this was bound to happen," Samuel said. "That man has built an empire on all the stuff it takes to make it come crashing down. People don't realize when the Devil gives you power and glory; it's only for a time. When you think you're in league with him, in the end, he's only bent on destroying you."

"A funny thing happened today—two, actually," Paul told him. "I had two reporters call me for my comment on the story."

"Really?" Samuel asked, shoving the paper aside. "What did you tell them?"

"I told them I had none."

* * *

Later that night, Paul awoke from a dream. He sat up in bed, feeling disoriented. He peered through the darkness at the illuminated numbers on his digital clock. It was only after three.

The dream had been so distinct: He had been trying to douse a raging fire by himself. Somehow, he had managed it, and when he looked down to see what had been burning, he saw a cross.

Paul pulled the rumpled sheets from around his legs and shoved himself out of bed. Then he remembered something else. As he was coming out of the dream, he had heard a voice saying over and over, "You saved the building for the Church... You saved the building for the Church... ."

He shook his head and had started towards the washroom when distinct words filled his thoughts.

Go to the Church, Paul!

For a moment, he was frozen. Then, when a sense of urgency filled him, he raced out to the hallway and across to the bedroom that looked out to the church parking lot.

"Oh, my God!" he exclaimed. He did a one-eighty and raced back into his bedroom. He quickly grabbed the phone and dialled 911.

When the dispatcher came through, he spoke quickly and clearly. "This is the Pastor of Bethel Community Church! The Church is on fire!"

* * *

Hours later, the fire team and three fire trucks were still in the church parking lot. As daylight broke through to a chilly day, the neighbourhood crowd that had gathered along the church premises became significantly depleted.

Paul was standing outside the canopy, in front of yellow police tape, talking with Samuel, Brennon, and a few other church members who lived close by.

He cast a wary eye at the one remaining TV van. Earlier, some local and big city reporters had accosted him, trying to get more out of the story than he could responsibly give. They had wanted to know if he thought Falconer had anything to do with the fire as revenge for Paul's influence in bringing about the Milward Seniors Community investigation. Paul had only talked about the fire and had refused to give them any fodder on Falconer. Needless to say, the persistence of the big-city reporters had left him really annoyed.

Paul watched the Fire Chief ease his way between two police cruisers as he headed towards Paul's little group.

"As I said before," the Fire Chief started saying, "it looks like arson. If you hadn't caught it when you did, this place would most likely have been gutted, leaving the bricks standing. As it is, the north interior of the Sanctuary suffered the most damage."

"Who would do such a thing to a church?" Samuel asked.

"Well, whoever did it, broke in through a back window, and it looks like they knew what they were doing," the Fire Chief stated.

Chapter Thirty-Two

Monday morning, Michaela's drive from Georgeton to Milward had given her a lot of time to ponder many things: including Paul's news about the recent church fire. As she neared the parsonage, curiosity got the better of her, so she directed her car onto the church parking lot rather than continue to the parsonage driveway.

She braked suddenly to avoid colliding with a black sports car that was partially blocking the entrance. The windows of the other car were darkly tinted, making it difficult to identify the driver.

Suddenly, the door of the sports car opened and a man stepped out. Michaela felt her breath catch in her throat. She had never personally met Dennis Falconer, but she had seen him before.

Michaela followed his movements, as he made his way with deliberate, almost intimidating steps, to her door. She quickly checked to make sure her doors were locked, forgetting they automatically locked when the car was engaged to drive.

He stood tall and glared down at her, studying her carefully for reasons unknown to her. Even through the thick glass of the car window, her sensitive spirit felt the darkness in him.

Suddenly, he lifted his gaze and started backing away. He walked with quick, militant strides back to his car. The vehicle reversed on squealing tires before speeding away.

Michaela turned to see Paul walking quickly towards her from the direction of the parsonage.

After making sure she was okay, he told her to meet him at the parsonage driveway.

At the driveway, Michaela watched Paul walk across the piece of lawn and over a small hedge that separated the driveway from the church premises.

"What a creepy man," she said as she proceeded to remove a small traveling bag from her car. "He just stood there staring at me."

"I'm surprised he showed up here with so many people wondering if he was responsible for the fire," Paul commented. He enveloped her in a big hug, then kissed her hungrily.

Michaela, momentarily, forgot everything else in Paul's embrace.

Minutes later, after Michaela had freshened up at the parsonage, they drove in Paul's Beetle to Karlene's town house, ten minutes away.

Rashad let them in.

"Hello, Paul. It's good to see you, Michaela," Rashad said, giving her a brief kiss on the cheek.

She hugged him lightly. "It's good to see you too, Rashad." She noticed he seemed happier; more at ease.

"Well," he said, waving a hand towards the interior of the house, "she's waiting for you."

In the living room, Michaela greeted Doris like an old friend before introducing her to Paul.

Michaela turned to see Karlene enter the living room from the hall beyond. The sight of Karlene's appearance filled her with joy.

"Hello, Michaela. Hello, Paul," Karlene greeted quietly.

"Oh, Karlene, you look wonderful!" Michaela exclaimed softly.

Karlene smiled shyly. Her black hair was pulled back in a sleek ponytail and, despite her extreme thinness, she seemed less fragile.

"Thank you, Michaela," she said, after they had embraced. She took Michaela's left hand in her own and looked down at it. "I'm sorry, I didn't notice the last time you were here. It's very beautiful. Congratulations."

"Thank you, Karlene," Michaela said, then hugged her again.

After the hug, Karlene looked across to Paul. Her mouth trembled slightly and her eyes took on a moist sheen.

"Paul, I'm so very sorry," she said, almost in a whisper.

* * *

The drive to Christy's house with Michaela started out very quietly. Paul's visit with Karlene had left him with much food for thought. Not to mention, Falconer's visit to the scene of the crime left him feeling very unsettled.

So far the police investigator had come up with no leads. Even if he hadn't told the reporters so, Paul was convinced that Falconer was behind the church fire. He hadn't forgotten the iPod recording. Too bad it couldn't be used as evidence.

Before starting out, he had phoned Brennon about seeing Falconer in the church driveway. Brennon had decided he would notify some of the church people who lived close by to keep an eye out for the Church.

When Paul felt Michaela reposition her hand in his, he looked over at her. She was regarding him with a soulful look in her eyes.

"You're far away," she said gently.

"I'm sorry, sweetheart. I don't mean to ignore you." He raised her hand to his lips and pressed a kiss to it.

"I do like *that* name," she said, smiling.

For awhile they did small talk, until Michaela asked him a very important question.

"Paul, will you remain at Bethel Community?"

At first, he thought she was asking where they would hold their services because of the Sanctuary repairs. She didn't know the decision had been made to have services in the Fellowship Hall. In fact, the fire had prevented him from giving his first sermon since his ministerial restrictions had been lifted. Then it dawned on him what she was asking, but he wanted to be sure.

"What do you mean?" he asked.

She shifted her body in his direction, causing her seatbelt to pull taut. "I mean, after everything that's happened, do you plan on staying indefinitely?"

Paul inhaled deeply, then his breath rush out. So, the moment of truth had finally come. It was one thing to plan changes, but when the plan was shared with someone else, it became reality.

"No," he responded. He looked over at her, noticing her raised eyebrows.

"And you were going to share this with me, when?"

He pursed his lips, knowing her reaction was justified. "I'm sorry. I just needed more time to be sure before breaking it to you." He kissed her hand again.

Now that she had brought up the topic, he decided to lay it out. "I feel the Lord has directed me to inner-city missions."

She was silent for awhile, then asked quietly, "Where?"

"Here—in Canada—Toronto—where Karlene needed it; where Leroy needed it; where scores of people need it, now."

Michaela was silent again, looking straight ahead.

"I went and checked out the Church where Karlene's old Pastor had ministered. Believe it or not, they're desperate for a pastor—preferably a young one. They have lots of youth."

He knew that would get her attention.

"Have you decided then?"

He shook his head. "No, I need to talk with you first. I know it's not Haiti or some other foreign mission, but the need is still great."

"I let go of that long ago."

"Really? And when did *you* plan on telling me that?"

She smiled. "Touché."

Their conversation continued along the same vein until Michaela's question, once again, surprised him.

"Paul, do you think we could visit Hannah's grave before we go to Christy's?"

He kept his eyes on the road, feeling thrown off balance.

"I mean, unless you would rather keep that private. We don't have—"

He quickly interrupted her, not wanting her to get the wrong idea. "No, it's perfectly fine. You just took me by surprise, that's all."

Less than an hour later, outside the small city of Wardton, Paul didn't try deceiving himself into thinking it didn't feel strange standing by Hannah's grave with Michaela. Yet, paradoxically, it also felt right.

Michaela pulled her dark brown blazer more tightly around her, possibly to ward off the autumn chill. She stooped down.

Paul stood by silently, realizing she was reading the epitaph on the tombstone. He also realized this was a very poignant moment for him. He hadn't expected her to want to do this.

"I wish I had some flowers," Michaela said, out of the blue.

She stood up slowly and went closer to him. He put his arms around her and rested the side of his face against her head.

"Are you okay?" she asked.

Paul moved his head to look into her eyes. "I'm more than okay. Thanks for doing this."

"Maybe we could come back another time... with some flowers?"

"I'd like that," he said. Suddenly, unexpected and deep emotions surfaced in him, and he held his face away.

"Paul?" She sounded a little panicked.

He turned back to her, fighting his tears. "I'm okay," he managed to say. He pulled her close, holding her tightly. "I-I never expected to have a second chance like this. You're more than I could have ever hoped for."

A little later, a chilly breeze stirred up as they walked down the cemetery laneway hand in hand. Paul let go of Michaela's hand and wrapped his arm around her.

"Are you cold?" he asked.

"I'm okay," she said, smiling up at him. "But, I'm curious about something."

"Go ahead," he said, hoping she didn't have any more surprises up her sleeve. He'd had his full share for one day.

"If you do commit to the inner-city Church, where would we live?"

As they approached the Beetle, he pulled the remote key from his pocket, stalling for time. "Well, I hadn't really thought of that. We wouldn't have to live there, necessarily, but we'd have to get a house fairly close."

"But could we afford it?"

Paul smiled, feeling more at ease. He opened her door. "Let's get in and I'll explain an important piece of detail I forgot to mention to you."

Once they were settled in the car, Paul faced Michaela. "There's something you need to know about my family. My mother is a woman of means."

"Eleanor? What do you mean?"

"She comes from old money. It's one of the reasons, I think, Falconer wanted so badly to marry her. The fact that she was also beautiful would have been just icing on the cake for him."

Paul found the look of disbelief on Michaela's face amusing. She was the one being surprised, for a change.

"Old money?"

"I'm telling the truth," he said, laughing. "She just chose to live a simple life with my father. They agreed she would keep most of her money in trust for us."

"But Christy told me when you wanted to go to the States to... find yourself, your father couldn't afford to help you."

Paul grinned. "That's what I was told, at the time. It was their way of controlling the situation. We kids didn't know until we were older that Mom had money. It paid for our tuitions and our houses. Except, after Hannah died, I sold mine, and then moved to the Bethel Community parsonage."

He leaned over to kiss her opened mouth closed.

"So you see, Mick, I can buy our new home with pure, unadulterated cash. The good thing is, at least I know you aren't marrying me... for my money."

*   *   *

By the time they arrived at Christy's country home, the chill in the air had been enhanced by a light drizzle of rain. However, Michaela found that the warm welcome and comfort at Christy's house more than made up for the chill. Christy had also made them a delicious, hot lunch.

Michaela enjoyed the time she spent with Eleanor and playing with Christy's two younger children. When six-year-old Bessie came in from the school bus, it took her awhile to calm down from seeing her Uncle Paul and soon-to-be Aunty Michaela—or Aunty Mick, as per Paul's introduction.

Of course, when Christy's husband Fred got home, the whole discussion about Karlene's accusation surfaced. Thankfully, especially for Eleanor's sake, they could also talk about the happy ending.

Before Michaela knew it, Cassie had arrived insisting they should get dressed at her place.

Michaela had left her change of clothes in Bessie's room, thinking she would be changing there. On her way up to get her bag, she heard someone behind her on the stairs.

"Are you sure you have everything from the car?" Paul asked, coming up behind her.

"Yes, I'm sure," she told him.

He followed her into Bessie's bedroom and closed the door. He hugged her from behind, before moving around to face her. "Thanks for going with Cassie, for making time for her."

"It's no problem. Will you meet us there, or should she bring me back here?"

He put his arms around her waist and pulled her close. "I'll come to you."

Michaela studied his face carefully, thinking he seemed a little mysterious.

"Okay," she said uncertainly. She tried pushing away from him, but he kept her close. "Cassie is waiting," she reminded him.

"I'm well aware," he said. He placed both hands on either side of her face and bent his head to kiss her.

When their lips met, Michaela moved her arms up around his neck the same time he returned his arms to her waist. When she buried her fingers in the tight curls at the nape of his neck, he suddenly pulled away.

"Okay," he said hoarsely, "you better go now."

* * *

About an hour and a half later, Michaela and Cassie stepped into an exquisite, dimly-lit restaurant. Michaela looked around the room, noticing its elegant decor and finely-dressed diners. As she and Cassie waited to be seated, Michaela felt relieved that her new friend Elise had helped her shop for her present attire.

"Do you see your group yet?" she asked Cassie, who was wearing a raspberry, spaghetti-strap dress with a short-opened, matching jacket. Her blonde hair hung loosely.

"No," Cassie said, sounding a little breathless. She looked at Michaela. "By the way, have I told you that you look stunning?"

"Yes, Cassie, but thanks again," Michaela responded. It had been a very long time since she had needed to dress so formally. Sequined, four-inched heels were not her idea of comfort or practicality, but Elise had insisted they were a perfect match for the sequined, black cocktail dress she was wearing. She adjusted the light, floaty material of her matching shawl, hoping that the rain hadn't started her hair frizzing out of its tight French twist.

Suddenly, Cassie grasped Michaela's arm as the maitre'd came towards them.

"Your group is waiting, madams," the maitre d' stated with a big smile.

Cassie slid her hand down to take Michaela's, as they were led to a private room at the back of the restaurant. Cassie kept a tight hold on her hand, even after the maitre d' had reached the doorway and stepped aside to gesture them in.

When the shout of "Surprise!" filled her ears, it finally dawned on Michaela why Cassie had kept such a tight grip on her hand.

She stood in the doorway, unable to move, thoroughly stunned at the sight that greeted her.

And Paul—he was walking towards her with the biggest grin on his face, looking extremely handsome in a black suit.

* * *

As he walked towards Michaela, Paul was totally captivated by her appearance. If he had thought her beautiful before; now she was breathtaking. Yet, it was more than that. It was the look that appeared in her eyes after her searching gaze finally found him. The look that said I've found the one I belong to.

Paul took over from Cassie by taking both of Michaela's hands and facing her. He leaned over. "Hey, you," he whispered in her ear. "You look absolutely gorgeous." He gently kissed the corner of her lips, feeling incredibly proud.

He was also grateful for his *God* and *Friend* who had orchestrated such an awesome plan of bringing him and Michaela together; grateful that *Jesus* that promised to always be with him whether in the valley or on the mountain.

"Paul, what is going on?" Michaela asked, gripping his hands tightly.

There was a sense of restrained silence in the room, as if everyone were waiting to hear their words.

"It's our engagement party," Paul said, "and we wanted to surprise you." He released her hands to place his on her lower back. He gently nudged her around until they were facing everyone.

Paul felt truly blessed, as he looked at his family and friends gathered around the beautifully dressed tables: Samuel and Hilda; Will, Lucy, Tristan and Ian; Brennon and Sarah; Leroy, Carmel and Lissa; his mother and Cassie; Christy and her family.

Indeed, he was blessed.

Chapter Thirty-Three

Paul sat up in bed to the crashing sound of thunder. A streak of light flashed into his room, followed by another roll of thunder—and another sound. It was the clattering of his vertical blinds. He turned his lamp on, then got up and went to the window. He pulled the blinds to one side so he could shut the window.

He went across the hall to the opposite bedroom and looked out that window. The rain was battering the glass. He shoved the window up so he could see across to the Church. The outside lights were on and everything looked okay.

"Not that anybody would be stupid enough to start a fire in this weather," he mumbled to himself.

Yet, he couldn't have helped but checked. He had just jumped out of a dream about another blaze of fire. It had been similar to the first dream, but this time he hadn't tried to put the fire out. This time something else had been burning, creating mountains of black smoke, but he had known it wasn't the cross. He didn't know what it was.

Interestingly enough, he hadn't felt panicked in this dream, as if the fire had a right to be burning.

After using the bathroom, Paul returned to bed. He sat, leaning back against the headboard.

It had been two weeks since the engagement party, and with a Valentine's Day wedding approaching, his life had taken on a different tone. Not only that, but he had recently notified the church board of his impending resignation. As he had expected, it had not gone over well, and he had not anticipated how difficult it would have been for him.

Except for the six years he had been away at university and Bible college, and a previous two-year assistant pastorate, Bethel Community Church had been his main place of worship since the age of ten. Anonymous donations from his mother had paid for a good part of the Sanctuary and Fellowship Hall renovations. His father had ministered there for many years.

Yet, the Lord had called him out, and the only person he needed on board with him was his future wife.

A week after the engagement party, Michaela had, of her own accord, asked him to take her to visit the Toronto Church.

When they had arrived at the Church, he had known she would see its solid structure rather than its bleary accommodations; she would see the potential instead of the obvious. And when she had looked at the wider community, he had known she would see the mission field, not the ghetto-like conditions.

He had known she would fall in love with the faithful ones who carried on, as visiting pastors came and went, hoping for one who would commit to the work. He had known she would walk by faith, not by sight.

When she had told him yes, he had not been surprised.

* * *

"Oh, good grief, Michaela," Sarah cried, laughing until tears filled her eyes. "I can't believe you're so naive."

Michaela sat with a bridal magazine opened across her lap, watching Sarah, Lucy and Carmel laugh at her. She sighed and leaned back against Sarah's living room couch. To think, she was using up her Saturday afternoon to subject herself to this.

"Okay, laugh all you want, ladies, but in case you've all forgotten, I'm the only one in this room who has never been married."

Carmel, who was sitting on her left, was the first to settle down. "She does have a point, girls," she said, delicately wiping under her eyes. "We're supposed to be helping her, not making her wish that Mrs. Laroche were here instead."

"Sorry, Michaela," Lucy said from the other side of Michaela. "I just have one thing to say. Honey, it won't matter what you wear on your wedding night. Trust me, he won't care."

Lucy's comment started them twittering again. Michaela felt the blood rush to her face. Her friends, along with Hilda, had committed to helping her with wedding plans, and she was grateful. However, they didn't seem to understand that she felt insecure because Paul had been married before.

"Okay, let's quit teasing Michaela," Sarah finally said, looking across at Michaela with sympathetic eyes. "I vote that we change the subject."

"Seconded," Carmel stated.

"Thirded," Lucy followed.

"Good," Sarah said, beaming. "Because I would like to share some good news."

They all looked at her.

Sarah cleared her throat dramatically. "The church board has decided to follow Paul's suggestion and retain Brennon as Bethel Community's Senior Pastor, when Paul leaves."

She held her hand up to dispel the excited chatter and applause that had followed her announcement. "I do have one more piece of news... I'm expecting!"

* * *

Paul groaned as Leroy snatched the basketball from him and drove a perfect layup into the net.

"You're getting slow, old man," Leroy taunted as he did a victory dance followed by a spectacular moonwalk across the floor of the Church Gym.

Paul pulled the neck of his T-shirt up to wipe the sweat from his face. He still couldn't get over the change in Leroy's appearance. When Leroy had shown up earlier at the parsonage, Paul had thought he was someone else.

Leroy's head had been shorn of its cornrows. Granted, Leroy had been minus his brow ring and heavy chains since the Haitian mission trip. Now, he really looked different; more clean-cut.

"I'll take my ear stud out when I go to Bible college in January," Leroy had told Paul. "But, I'll probably wear it on weekends."

"Why not just leave it out?" Paul had asked him.

Leroy had scowled at him. "What? I got a reputation to keep, man. I don't want my bloods thinkin' I'm going all pious."

When Paul had asked him what he meant, he had said, "I ain't coming back here every weekend. I plan on looking up some of the old gang and dragging their sorry butts to Harvest House."

Harvest House: the inner-city Church where Paul would be Pastor.

Paul and Leroy played one-on-one for another five minutes, before they were interrupted by Tristan and Ian.

"Hey, Leroy, I hope you save up some of that energy to help set up our moving yard sale, next week!" Tristan shouted from the gym doorway.

"Why? You got lover boy there to do that," Leroy retorted.

Ian grinned and loped past Tristan, catching Leroy's toss. He gave the ball a couple of bounces, then shot a three-pointer.

"Now, that's what I'm talking about!" Leroy cheered. He and Ian knocked knuckles.

Tristan's blonde ponytail switched from side to side as she shook her head at the display of male pride. She went over to Paul.

"Pastor Paul, my dad wanted me to remind you about the stuff the military base is donating to Harvest House. He says they'll have a truck loaded up by next Wednesday—he'll call to confirm with you."

"That's great, Tristan. Your dad sure moves fast."

She looked up at him with clear blue eyes, much like Will's. "Speaking of moves, I'm excited about this one, but I'll really miss everyone. I mean, Ian and I are probably going to have to split up—which is a drag—since we just started dating. Everyone's moving: Michaela moved; you're moving—course, she'll have to move again with you—we're moving; Leroy's moving." She paused to take a breath. "Seriously, what's with all the moving?"

Paul laughed, gently patting the top of her head. "Tristan, just think of us as chess pieces—except that we have free will—but God still puts us where He wants us. We have to trust Him with the big picture."

She sighed. "Yeah, you're right." She turned to look at the boys playing. "Well, I guess I better go over there and give them a little competition." She started to run off, but then glanced back at him. "Pastor Paul, I-I really wanted to thank you for helping my dad, and, of course, you know we'll be visiting Harvest House from time to time."

An hour later, after he had gone back to the parsonage for a shower and change of clothes, Paul picked Michaela up from Sarah's.

They were drinking coffee, after eating a late lunch at a small restaurant, and Paul noticed that Michaela seemed more subdued than usual. He slid closer to her in their cubicle seat and slipped an arm around her shoulder.

"All right, 'fess up. What's wrong?" he asked gently.

She leaned her head back against his arm. "What?"

"I can see it written all over you. Something's wrong," he persisted.

She frowned. "Nothing is wrong. I'm perfectly content."

"You're lying."

She turned her head to look at him. "It's kind of private," she whispered.

He looked around the almost empty restaurant. "Well, it's not like you need to broadcast it, and it better not be private from me."

Paul persisted until he finally dragged it out of her. What she told him just about broke his heart, yet made him want to laugh. He tightened his arm around her shoulder and laid his head against hers.

"Michaela," he began slowly and deliberately, "when the serpent tempted Eve, I'm sure he knew she could convince Adam to do what he couldn't; because Adam wouldn't have been able to resist her."

He looked directly into her eyes, giving her his full attention. "You are my Eve, and when the time comes for me to be complete with you, nothing else and no one else will fill my thoughts, but you."

* * *

The bright hosts waited outside the perimeter of the unnatural, billowing darkness over the Sales Centre. The darkness convulsed nervously as it swooped and contorted in useless intimidation.

The bright hosts watched as two men heaved containers of kerosene out of one vehicle to transfer them to another.

Within seconds, before the transfer could be made, the Messenger with sword held high separated from the hosts.

"Now! The Victory is now!"

The bright hosts separated into two starbursts; one larger than the other. The larger rushed in swiftly, causing the darkness to fan out. The smaller swirled towards the two men.

The men stumbled in confusion. The starburst danced a beautiful and terrible dance around and between them. The men began to move in sync with the starburst. They weaved with the brightness up the steps of the Sales Centre, carrying their load.

Seconds later, a dark sports car joined the other two cars. A lone man appeared from the sports car, and then entered the house. The door slammed shut!

* * *

That night, Paul's mind was filled with thoughts of Michaela, making it difficult to sleep. When he finally fell asleep, it didn't seem all that long before he was awakened by an urgent sense of danger. He couldn't explain it, but it filled him.

He noticed it was just after two and he wanted to go back to sleep.

Pray!

He got up and knelt by his bed and started praying. He didn't know what he was praying for; he just prayed whatever came to his mind, his heart.

At some point, Paul fell asleep still kneeling at his bedside. It was the cry of sirens that woke him.

Before he was even fully awake, he got up and, instinctively, stumbled to the bedroom across the hall to look out at the Church.

All seemed well at the Church, but the sirens continued to pierce through the night's quiet. Paul felt compelled to get dressed. He had just finished doing so when the phone rang.

"Pastor Paul, it's Carmel. I'm sorry to be calling so early, but Blinder is missing."

"Missing?" Paul asked. With everything that had already been happening, it didn't take much for Carmel's announcement to send his tension level up.

"Yes. The fire trucks woke me up. They're saying on the radio that the Sales Centre for the Seniors Community is on fire. I don't know why, but I thought to check on Blinder and he's not in his room. It doesn't look like he even slept in his bed, and he's not answering the cell I got him."

Paul was shocked. The Sales Centre? He remembered his dream. "Okay, Carmel. I'm going by there. Hopefully, Blinder will turn up soon."

He checked his digital clock while picking up the phone again. It was after four. He dialled.

"Sam, sorry to wake—"

"Never mind, Paul. Those god-forsaken sirens got to me before you. What's going on? It's like the whole army's out."

"Samuel, Blinder's not there, is he?"

"Blinder? Why would he be here at this time of morning?"

"Carmel says he's missing. She's worried." Paul waited. "Sam?"

"Er—sorry—Paul. I was just listening to the radio. The Sales Centre is on fire!"

"I know, Sam. That's why Carmel is worried."

* * *

Paul stood across the roadway, like so many others, looking at the dying embers still being battled by fire personnel. The continuing rise of grey smoke and the resulting smell were present reminders of the raging, hungry flames he had witnessed earlier. What was even more shocking was the possibility that there were casualties.

Apparently, three empty vehicles had been sitting on the Sales Centre driveway at the time of the fire. Fortunately, and surprisingly, the fire had been contained so no other homes had been affected.

"This is unreal," Hilda said, shaking her head sadly. She was wrapped in a long fall coat, nestled under Samuel's arm. She sighed heavily, then suddenly she perked up. "Look! There's Blinder."

Paul immediately separated himself from them and walked along the road to meet Blinder. Blinder was wearing an old fall coat and a knitted hat.

"Hey, Blinder, where've you been? We've been worried about you."

Blinder looked at Paul. He pulled a hand from his coat pocket and pointed across the street. "They d-did it to themselves—Falconer and the men who beat me up—they did it!"

Paul frowned, not understanding him.

Blinder tried again: "I saw them, Pastor. I thought they would go to the Church with the cans, but t-they went to the house, instead—Falconer too. They didn't come out, and then the fire started."

Paul was speechless.

"I didn't want to, but Carmel makes me have a phone now, so I called 911."

* * *

A week later, Paul left the Front Office and wandered absent-mindedly into the Sanctuary. He glanced around, noticing that the repair work was almost completed. He wasn't sure, but he suspected his mother had donated to the work, once again thwarting Falconer's plan.

He didn't stay there long, but went through the side door and into the Foyer. He went by the Assistant Pastor's Office and continued down the hall past the Conference Room to the double doors of the Fellowship Hall. He glanced towards his left past the Kitchen to the Children's wing.

He sighed. No doubt about it, he was going to miss it.

He pulled the Fellowship Hall doors opened and walked to the row of windows looking down into the Gym. He wasn't sure how long he had been standing there when he heard footsteps.

"Don't tell me they'll pay you, for the next month, to stand around doing nothing."

Paul smiled, feeling pleasure at the sound of her voice. He turned around.

Michaela stood looking at him, smiling broadly. She had her hair up in a fluffy bun, and she was wearing a short fall jacket, with her long legs encased in blue jeans.

Paul leaned back against the window ledge. "Naw, actually, they're paying me to keep up appearances by doing a sermon a week, while I run back and forth to Harvest House. When I'm not doing that, I spend the rest of my time pining... for you."

Her caramel brown skin darkened slightly. "Stop being such a flirt," she scolded, smiling.

He grinned. "Actually, things are getting pretty hot around here. Brennon might be starting another kind of fire, calling for three-day-fasts every month. He's set on revival."

"He's caught the vision?"

"God's given him the Vision." Paul responded.

"Wow, that's awesome!" Michaela exclaimed, clapping her hands. She crossed her arms.

"I heard about Falconer. I mean, he wasn't a nice man; but still, it was a terrible way to die."

Paul touched his palms to the back of his head and stretched his arms out. "I really don't get what went down with Falconer. They're saying it looks like he was trying to con his own men to implicate them in this money laundering thing, making him look innocent."

He walked towards her. "They're also saying the fire could be tied to the mob, who wanted to cut ties with Falconer, since he was going down." He put his arms around her. "Frankly, I don't think they really know what happened, and the only person who seems to know, nobody's asking."

"Blinder?"

"Yeah," he responded. He hugged her tightly and kissed her. Afterwards, he took her hand and started walking.

They stopped by the Pastor's Office to get Paul's fall jacket, then passed through the Vestibule into the parking lot.

"We'll take my new car," Paul told Michaela. They proceeded to walk, hand in hand, across to the parsonage. "You know, Blinder said the two guys at the Sales Centre looked like they were intoxicated, before the fire started. He also insists that God was protecting the Church."

Michaela suddenly stopped walking and faced him. "Intoxicated, or confused?"

Paul shrugged.

She raised her free hand to her chin, as if deep in thought. "You know, Paul, they could well have been confused by angels. I mean the Bible speaks of God confusing Israel's enemies so they actually turned on each other."

He looked at her.

"Don't frown at me," she said. "Maybe those cans of kerosene were meant to finish off the Church. Instead, God turned things around on them and the Sales Centre."

Paul felt his skin prickle. He looked back at the church steeple. The Cross on top sparkled in the sunlight. In his second dream something else had burned, not the cross.

He looked at Michaela and shook his head. "As I said before, you're pretty smart." He started walking again. "And you're probably right about Will seeing warrior angels, too."

She tugged at his hand. "Let's not go overboard with the compliments. Let's go help Will and his family with their yard sale."

"You bet, Mick," he teased.

Michaela glared at him before pulling her hand away. She started walking briskly, distancing herself from him.

"I hope, in the future, when we're making love and that name slips out, you don't take off like this," Paul called to her.

She whipped around, her eyes wide with astonishment. "Tell it to the whole neighbourhood, why don't you," she whispered loudly, fiercely.

He increased his pace, and she turned and started running. They had almost reached the parsonage lawn when he caught up to her and grabbed her from behind.

As Michaela screamed, Paul laughed and pulled her around into his arms. He held her tightly, until she ceased her struggles and rested in the circle of his embrace.

As they stood soaking in each other's warmth, a glimmer of light caught Paul's eye. His gaze was drawn to the Church building were, atop the steeple, the Cross sat gleaming.

Epilogue

Jamaica, W.I. Two years later

Michaela sat crossed-legged on a blanket, under a large beach umbrella. She adjusted her swim-wear wrap, before reaching down to scoop up the baby from beside her, and cradle him in her arms. He wriggled his brown, dimpled arms and legs vigorously, smiling drool at her. She smiled back, then brought his little round body, covered in a light tunic, up against her chest. She hugged his sweet cuddliness to herself, smelling his delicious baby smell.

"Oh, Mommy's precious dumpling, I wonder who that man is your father is talking to?" she asked, squinting to see Paul's tall form, in long trunks and a T-shirt, a little way down the moderately-crowded Jamaican beach. He was conversing intensely with a smaller man.

She continued to have a one-sided conversation with the baby: "Stephen Paul John Rayner, I hope your father remembers we are on vacation and that he's supposed to be resting."

The baby gurgled happily, as she laid him across her legs.

"Good, here he comes," Michaela told her son.

When Paul came back to them, he was smiling broadly. Michaela felt her heart swell with love for him.

"You won't believe who that was," he told her as he sat facing her on the blanket. He automatically reached for little Stephen.

"Try me," she responded, willingly handing the baby over.

"My old mission contact—poor guy. He was the one who had to tell me about Hannah's accident."

"Oh," Michaela said, suddenly feeling uncomfortable.

Paul cradled the baby in one arm while he reached over to touch her cheek with the other.

"Hey, wipe that look off your face," he said, smiling his gorgeous dimples into place. "You fill my heart and I'm content. He's thrilled about my new family and would like to meet you. How would you like to take a trip off the resort?"

Michaela reached to hold the hand he had removed from her face. "I'd love that. Besides, if I said no, you'd find a way to convince me. But, please, no more projects."

He laughed. He lifted her hand and pressed a kiss to it. "No, my Mick, my love. I think we're busy enough between Harvest House and Haiti, don't you?"

Also by Jennies M. Edwards

God in My House

A multiracial story that focuses not on race, but on the human condition in need of the divine. The ongoing battle between good and evil affects us all, regardless of race, age, gender or beliefs. One young woman, Elise Everson, searches for the ultimate truth to make sense of it all. Through the influence of a pastor, a friend, and a young architect who has her heart, Elise finds that truth in Christ. As her relationship with Christ blossoms, she is challenged by her growing love for Josiah Alexander. Both relationships are severely tested by a tragedy close to home and a sociopath's threat to her life. Through it all, Elise discovers the incredible assurance that "God in her" is enough for any circumstances.

ISBN: 978-1-926676-60-9
Word Alive Press